The Ba

》》》》》》》》》》 《《《《《《《《《《《

Miroslav Krleža

The Banquet in Blitva

TRANSLATED FROM THE CROATO–SERBIAN
BY EDWARD DENNIS GOY
AND JASNA LEVINGER–GOY

NORTHWESTERN UNIVERSITY PRESS
EVANSTON, ILLINOIS

》》》》》》》》》》 《《《《《《《《《《《

Northwestern University Press
Evanston, Illinois 60208-4210

Printed in the United States of America

10 9 8 7 6 5 4 3 2 1

ISBN 0-8101-1862-9

Library of Congress Cataloging-in-Publication Data

Krleža, Miroslav, 1893–
   [Banket u Blitvi. English]
   The banquet in Blitva / Miroslav Krleža ; translated from Croato-Serbian
by Edward Dennis Goy and Jasna Levinger-Goy.
       p. cm.
   ISBN 0-8101-1862-9
   I. Goy, E. D. (Edward Dennis), 1926– II. Levinger-Goy, Jasna. III. Title.
PG1618.K69 B3413 2002
891.8'235—dc21

                                                          2002012089

Blitva, my fatherland,
You're like a gangrenous disease.

A. Waldemaras

»»» CONTENTS «««

The Banquet in Blitva

A Form of Prologue or Sentimental Variations on the Blitvinian Question through the Ages

Thirty European nations slaughtered one another for four years, and out of this bloodletting emerged Blitva, like a child's tin rattle with the inscription *Blithuania Restituta*—for all those people whom Colonel Barutanski liked to label patriots. The free and independent Republic of Blitva was born out of the peace at Blato Blitvinsko in the year '17, when Colonel Barutanski's legionnaires loudly announced Blitva's independence, on the square dedicated to Andria Waldemaras, the Blitvinian romantic poet, chanting his legionary poem "March on, march on, oh you brigade of Blitva" for the first time as the Blitva national anthem. That very day, the old Blitva anthem "Men of Blitva, still within us dwell our fathers' voices clear" became the opposition anthem of all the Blitvinian malcontents, and due to these hymns much Blitvinian blood flowed, till the prime minister and ideologue of the Blitvinian Agrarian Party, Muzhikovski, thought to find a compromise and proclaim as the Blitvinian national anthem the old romantic reveille "Blitva shall not ever perish while we, her sons, are yet alive." The peace at Blato Blitvinsko created Blitva as an independent republic with 1.7 million Blitvinians, but it did not resolve the Blitvinian question; 1.3 million Blitvinians remained under the newly created Blatvia, and the high ambassadors at the green table in Versailles did not give free Blitva the right to liberate 800,000 Blitvinians from under the Hunnish yoke. This unresolved Blitvinian irredentism gave birth, on December 25, to the coup of Colonel Barutanski.

This so-called Christmas assault of Colonel Barutanski resulted in some 3,000 corpses. These 3,000 dead would bring about a countercoup against Colonel Barutanski, or else Colonel Barutanski would shoot another 3,000 rebels and declare war on Blatvia "to the last man" and so make Blatvia swim in blood, for Blatvia wished to devour Blitva, and so Blitva would go to war, since it had no other idea than the destruction of Blatvia. The Blitvinian capital city of Blitwanen, which under the Huns was known as Blitvas-Holm, would declare war on the Blatvian capital, Weider-Hunnen, and Weider-Hunnen together with Hunnia, Kobilia, and Ingermanlandia would set fire to and destroy Blitwanen, and so Blitwanen would give birth to a new struggle for the liberation of Blitva "from under a foreign yoke," and this new irredentism would set off a whole series of new European wars, and so these bloodstained plebeian fireworks would end in the surgery of some armistice in Blatvian Koprivnyak in the year 2048, and the Blitvinians would continue singing their rebellious hymn of liberation, "March on, march on, oh you brigade of Blitva," as the one token of their classical liberation in the twenty-first century. By the peace of 1917 the thousand-year-old pauper remained as truncated as it would be mutilated, in 130 years' time, in the eventual peace in Koprivnyak, and that shameful peace in the year 2048 would represent Blitva's national shame, as did the peace in Blato Blitvinsko in the year 1917, which the Blitvinians refer to sarcastically as the "Peace Mire," in their pathetic mourning for the "mortally wounded and humiliated people of Blitva." Should Colonel Barutanski succeed, together with Hunnia, Kobilia, and Ingermanlandia, in coming to such an arrangement with the international powers that the High Contracting Powers would take an interest in the liquidation of Blatvia, the newly reached ideal peace in Blitwanen would mean the resurrection of Blitvinian ideals and the definitive "humiliation and fall of the mortally wounded thousand-year-old pauper Blatvia."

That final defeat would evoke a national movement on the greatest scale by Blatvia, and national movements and wars of revival for the sake of "the honor and freedom of our national banners" would, quite naturally, be led by generals, and generals mean the taking of power and state coups. State coups give birth to bloodshed. Barutanski would shoot Kavalierski, or Kavalierski would shoot Barutanski. Bloodshed creates further human bloodshed, and so, in a logical circulation of wars and armistices and ever newer and newer wars and armistices, Blitva and Blatvia would perish, just as so many Blitvas and Blatvias perished before them in this same Karabaltic and Scythian mud, without it occurring to anyone to ask themselves and their countrymen, Blitvinians, Huns, Blatvians, and Kobilians, the same simple and natural question: "All right, brothers, are we really mad dogs, and how long are we going to go on tearing our own flesh and why?"

One of the first romantics who raised this question to himself and to his fellow citizens was Dr. Niels Nielsen, an independent publicist and the publisher of the *Tribune*. And what happened? They trampled on him like a mad dog and continued with their agenda, chanting their anthem: "March on, march on, oh you brigade of Blitva."

Already during the parliamentary rule of Dr. Muzhikovski, Dr. Nielsen had written an interesting and well-documented study, *The Law of Blitva—As an Essential Part of the Blitvinian Question.* Readers will forgive us if, in the framework of this informative introduction, we hold generally to Dr. Nielsen's ideas expressed in the abovementioned book. First, because we, looking at this unusually tangled complex of the Blitva-Blatvia-Hunnia question, from a dim and distant foreign country, lack the ability to create a clear picture for ourselves and, second, because the character of Dr. Nielsen will play a somewhat important role in our story. It seems to us that it may be no bad thing if we create for ourselves some sort of concept of this bold character who caused the death of almost all the main heroes of this sad history of Blitva.

The question of Blitva (according to Dr. Nielsen) had remained open since the second half of the eighteenth century, when the Blitva–Swedish line of the Hunnish throne died out, to be renewed after the revolutionary crises of '48 and '66 by the peace of Blato Blitvinsko in '17 and remained "open" through all the many changes to this very day, just as unresolved, just as fateful as it was from the beginning: too weak to solve itself, yet too strong to be solved by the forces that denied it.

The character of Flaming-Sandersen, in itself, represented nothing other than the politico-moral continuation, by inertia, of the revolutionary élan of '48, and Flaming-Sandersen's words concerning "the laws of Blitva" and of "Blitva's right to freedom" were no more than echoes of that freedom-loving, romantic, and hazy enthusiasm which dissolved so futilely beneath the walls of European feudalism. Yet as a distant reflection it still had the power to shine in the absolute darkness of the dark decades between the rule of absolutism and the world war, as a hope, a dream, an illusion, as a false and hypocritical phrase. This same poetic inspiration fluoresced with a magic glow, even at the time when, in Blitva, everything appeared to be on its deathbed. "The Blitvinian question," as a phrase, sounded like a fanfare signaling the denial of a whole list of violence and injustices, and yet the worn and tedious refrain regarding "Blitva's freedom" and "Blitva's right" was, chances are, conditioned by real and actual circumstances, for otherwise it would have been lost and vanished forever. All this vast and endless mass of deceit and injustice, of theft and robbery (which the socialists later defined, not very wittily, as "the infiltration of Hunnish and Ingermanlandish imperialism" and as "the creation of a market for the developed Karabaltic industries" in the poor and illiterate land of Blitva), all this inexhaustible mass of violence and varying forms of moral and material corruption over a period of more than thirty years was denied by the concept of "The Right of Blitva," that is, "The Right" of a poor, peasant, illiterate, and enslaved Blitvinian people not to be poor or illiterate or enslaved for the profit of others by other "more advanced" peoples, who were only "more advanced" because they had revolvers and could, in the interest of their state-supported plundering and murder, order the unarmed Blitvinian poor to put their hands up whenever it occurred to them in the name of high interest and the so-called creation of markets. The messieurs doctors of law and divinity (generally speaking humanistic gentlemen well read in literature) desired to define this basic "Blitvinian right" not to be enslaved, as was natural, in a bourgeois, petit bourgeois, and semifeudal manner, and so for the illiterate and poverty-stricken Blitvinian peasant masses they created a romantic Karabaltic legend concerning a rich thousand years of Blitva's past statehood, and thus began the fatal petit bourgeois diversion from the path of immediate reality into the illusion of "poor Blitva," of "the Blitvinian pagan traditions," of "the tragic character of the Blitvinian national hero Jarl Knutson," of "the Karabaltic mission," and so on and so forth. The millennium of the Hunnish kingdom gained its counterpart in the Blitvinian millennium. Paningermanlandia had to be overcome by Panblitvania. The Hunnish, Aragon, Swedish, and Blatvian kings lost battles in the sonnets written by patriotic Blitvinian poets, in which, by some superior logic, the heroic bearers of the Blitvinian crown conquered. For what sort of a royal Blitvinian tercet would it be if it lacked a victorious *Ausklang:* While we have sabers, Blitva will live?

As in the verses of Andria Waldemaras (the greatest romantic epigone of the new Blitvinian literature), the Blitvinian epic moved in the clouds of the Blitvinian Valhalla, and that romantic "historiographic" opera continues today in the "heroic" characters of the greatest and most famous, both in Europe and the two Americas, painter, sculptor, and political ideologue Roman Rayevski.

The main reason for this Pan-Blitvinian petit bourgeois diversion into romanticism was fear of destruction, horror at collapse and defeat, despair at the pending dangers that always threatened to swallow the existence and independence of the Blitvinian and Pan-Blitvinian national substance. In these endlessly tangled complexities, the Blitvinian question welled up like a spring. In this land it surged and flowed from all sides like an underground river, and there was nothing in Blitva around which and beneath which "the Blitvinian question" did not appear like a ghost: in politics; in literature; in the daily press; in church sermons; in street fights; in war; in peace; in foreign, Hunnish parliamentary discussions; in the independent Blitvinian Diet; in state coups; in blood, in the endless streams of Blitvinian blood that flowed and ran as from an open wound. All personal questions, all the circles of personal Blitvinian existence for the last hundred years, trembled, died, and rotted in the shadow of this question. Why should someone shoot themselves at a time when all the laws of a respectable career would imply that he had no good reason for doing so? Why did someone drink themselves to death? Why did somebody die as a wasted talent? Why was someone dismissed from the Hunnish or the Ingermanlandish state service for voting contra, and why did someone have to leave for Transilmengia to the Aragon Pantocrator in a humble deputation, so as to gain the concession for the first Blitvinian distillery, which the drunken Blitvinian peasants would burn down in a mindless political fury and then the imperial Hunnish army would intervene and forty-three men would be left lying in the mud, simply because some imperial drunk of an officer felt inclined to shoot? All the histories of the various outstanding Blitvinian personalities over the last hundred years tell us ever the same thing: that an individual may hang himself in the toilet by his own braces, out of shame at having sold himself as an informer to foreign powers, because, as the most popular tribune of the people, he had declaimed for years and from his own balcony the thousand-year cultural mission, when the citizens came under his windows, as to the Hunnish father of the nation and mayor of Blitvas-Holm. What this moral misery drove to such a revolting death was the specter of the Blitvinian question, which penetrated the dying Blitvinian patriots from head to toe, like an uneasy conscience, like the reflex of a suppressed and rejected feeling that was powerful enough to disturb people even on their deathbed. Why did Larsen hang himself? Because he realized that to make pictures in Blitva meant madness. The great men of Blitva who received the recognition of the Ingermanlandish, Aragon, or Hunnish powers because their patriotic greatness answered in every way the criteria laid down by foreign laws, were recognized by foreign powers and by high school textbooks as "Blitvinian giants" simply because they bore their political convictions within the framework of imposed loyalties, which, in truth, meant to be an informer, a perjurer, and a traitor to the true Blitvinian national feeling and civil dignity. To wear a decoration in Blitva was a national shame, while to end on the gallows was the poets' ideal. Who does not recall those Blitvinian renegades and corrupted cavaliers who played the role of provincial grand seigneurs, representing, in reality, the act of taking refuge from their own consciences in a semiliterate cynicism, in cards and alcohol. Under the pressure of centuries, the Blitvinian man was deformed. He moved about the world like a caricature of all human concepts. He had to choose between madness and drowning, whether to sell himself or take to drink and generally perish morally the moment he received a professorship or any other high Hunnish rank, as a sinecure, in return for the betrayal of Blitva's interests. The only music of Blitvinian civil careers was the whistles of the street accompanied by the stink of rotten eggs on ministers' top hats. Small, backward, uncultured towns and the narrow petit bourgeois conditions in these Blitvinian provincial backwaters gave birth to small people, and were any to outgrow these domestic, local Blitvinian standards, they would flee abroad or—surrendering to the force of circumstances—grow gray, be broken, and remain crushed at the mercy of everything. Except for quite weak and uninteresting lyricism and subjective resignation, everything else in Blitva was known as: my daily bread, my pension, my family. And for that bread, for that pension, and for that family the rebellious cosmic and social revolutionary poets, as, for example, Horetzki, wore the imperial tricorn hat of Aragon with its plumage and shamelessly wrote monographs for schools concerning the imperial Aragon Pantocrator, Menelaus the Last, dedicating their books to the national tyrants and Hunnish governors, while constantly voting in public elections for antinationalist candidates and saving themselves from reality in a wondrous dream of the Karabaltic mission of the Pan-Blitvinian movement, which at that time they were founding throughout the entire Karabaltic of the Ingermanlandish turnverein, forever singing the old Blitvinian hymn "Heh, Blitvinians!"

Regarding this politically and economically so often wrongly yet so often precisely formulated and wittily defined foreign political pressure, "the Blitvinian question" appeared as a chaotic and vague state of facts, ever changing their form and direction. Upon this dynamic Blitvinian question were born, nurtured, and arose: Flaming-Sandersen, the great ideologue of the second half of the nineteenth century; Muzhikovski, the leader and president of the last parliamentary government, who was physically liquidated by Colonel Kristian Barutanski in his Christmas coup of 1925; Bauer-Kmetynis, deputy chief of the Agrarians, now abroad; and finally, last but not least, Colonel Kristian Barutanski himself, who, with his legions,

created Blitva and who is on the shortest way, together with his
legions, to destroying it.

When (during the final prewar phase) Blitvinian politics were
under Muzhikovski, everything resembled a balalaika more than it
did politics. The "Blitvinian question" of that political period appeared in the flats of the petit bourgeoisie as the lithographed
princess Tugomila, a prisoner in the Weider-Hunnen fortress,
sending a dove from her cell to Blitva: "Oh, had I but the pinions of
a dove, I would fly away with you to Blitva." Now as a forbidden
banner in an obscure bookshop window, now as a broken window-
pane in the Hunnophile flats of a Blitvinian national renegade, now
as the corpse of a rebellious peasant who desired to remove the
Hunnish flag from the railway station roof, "the Blitvinian question" constantly appeared in the press as censored news, or before
the green cloth of justice as an offense in the sense of the Hunnish
imperial and royal laws. Or some apprentice was arrested for
spilling ink over a notice in a foreign language, or some high school
kid was expelled from all the Blitvinian high schools for splashing a
classmate for being a political rascal, or the police with their bare
sabers cut down schoolboys when they publicly set fire to foreign
banners on the square. Strikes, bloodshed at elections, bloodstained demonstrations, public unrest, constant murmuring in
Blitvinian jails when through those miserable apartments passed
processions of patriots, convinced that in this way they were promoting the Blitvinian cause from its state of torpor. In that tragically static moment in Blitvinian political awareness, at that politically crucial point when Blitva's power to resist was at its lowest,
people's brains in the kingdom of Blitva were overcome by apathy,
so that everything dissolved in a universal miasma of memory. The
Blitvinians forgot everything, even their own name! Processions
of emigrants crossed the seas and there, from another shore,
sprouted so-called freedom-loving Blitvinian newspapers, illiterate,

stammering, pathetic, but borne along by some definite ideal resistance, by a heroic denial of the injustice which, after centuries-long suffering, deserved to be dispensed with. In the body of the Aragon Empire, this "Blitvinian question" (a mere detail of all such similar questions in Yenisey, in the Caucasus, in the Karabaltic, and in Ister), in its struggle with the gendarmerie, with the Hunnish school, with imperial scholarships, with exceptionally tedious and practical-joking laws limiting the Blitvinian representative body, the zemstvo, vegetated in the form of a poverty-stricken and backward press, like an illiterate brochure, like a lost case concerning press laws, like an empty speech at an election meeting held in a smoky bar, when the elective consciousness of various Blitvinian fellow citizens was at such a low ebb that it could be purchased for a mug of beer and a stinking Hunnish *pörkölt*. At that time a single political vote could decide the fate of the imperial mandate and, for this reason, at elections to the Blitvinian zemstvo there was often shooting, in an attempt to kill those two or three patriotic electors whom the powers that were knew to be incorruptible and who would vote for "Blitvinian rights."

It presents a strange and fantastic question: What was the power of this worn, contemptible, obscure, and ridiculous "Blitvinian question," that it succeeded in not perishing and was able to maintain itself in conflict with immeasurably superior powers? In the shadow of this tricky question were innumerable lost battles. Many broken individuals surrendered unconditionally. Many a renegade concealed his so-called ideals and sold himself to "those in power" (as was said in the style of that time "for a mess of pottage"). The defeats of the Blitvinian movement were all the more seriously silhouetted against the horizon. In Europe everything grew ever darker. Coping with the Blitvinian muddles grew ever more intricate, and it is no wonder that individuals began to feel complete apathy, exactly similar to the despair of bankruptcy and of suicide:

everything ruined and everything sealed! Blitva, with its chances of liberation, could take its place in a respectable coffin at a second-class funeral, light two historical candles, cross its tired hands under Jarl's tower, where, for centuries, all Blitva's hopes and all its ideals slept their eternal sleep. Nobody in the whole of Blitva believed in the liberation and resurrection of the Blitvinian state, except for high school kids, and these loyal and hotheaded kids Barutanski recruited into his brigade, and when, by the concatenation of international events, one day in '17 he appeared in the Beauregard palace as the Lord Protector Republicae Blithuaniae, all the rubbish of the Blitvinian intelligentsia swam with him on the crest of a wave of Blitvinian megalomania, avengism, irredentism, great Blitvinian and Pan-Karabaltic programs, having before their eyes a single "ideal" which, at that time, took on a realistic, earthly form: the ideal of a profitable and distinguished ministerial wallet. Experience proved that the concept of Blitva meant, apart from "ideals," good and lucrative business according to all the laws of international roulette, which is known as the policy of the Great Powers.

The dramatic side of this patriotic wheeling and dealing may be seen in the first part of this medieval play, in which the main roles are played by two heroic characters, two childhood friends: Colonel Barutanski, the commandant of Blitva, and Dr. Nielsen, a neurotic, European-educated intellectual, of whom Kerinis, paid to dispatch him to another world, is known to have said, without a wink of an eye: "I'll kill this silly fool who doesn't know what he wants himself." Kerinis, in the third book of this Blitvinian poem, will travel to finish off this animal on the run, but will become the victim of his own noble and heroic act. This, how Dr. Nielsen changes from a sentimental bungler into a man who "knows what he wants" and how, on his path, like a burning fuse, he becomes the fatal destroyer of human lives, will be shown in this story, whose first chapter opens now, on the next page. *Incipit comoedia blithuanica!*

Book One

Dr. Nielsen's "Open Letter" to Colonel Barutanski

Colonel Kristian Barutanski, the Lord of Blitva, thought of himself and of his position in Blitvinian space and time roughly thus: "One day, sooner or later, they'll shoot me down like a dog, so it's logical that I hold to my line, and therefore the less I go in for psychologizing the better. World psychology agrees, with mathematical accuracy, with the conditions in which the world exists, and the world exists, without any doubt, in bloody, poverty-stricken, and backward conditions, so when it considers life, it does so in an equally bloody, poverty-stricken, and backward way. So why then do some fussers lately go in for psychologizing and airing their wisdom about me, one might say, moralizing?"

Always, without exception, it's the isolated individual who moralizes, the individual who has cut himself off, who imagines he has risen above reality. The average, the crowd, the mob, those who in the streets howl applause to the victors, what we call the masses, the bipedal herd, these don't moralize, these don't psychologize, these don't fuss, these exist, they live, they move, they drink beer, gnaw sausages, they bear a man in triumph, they're what we call the torch parade, the march-past, the army. They march with him; finally they're an end in themselves, and generally there is nothing superior to the logic of this pack of ours! What would happen if he, today, here, in Beauregard, when the whole of Blitva, the whole of Europe, had its eyes on him, if he, Barutanski, were to indulge in moralistic hairsplitting? He'd go to the devil in twenty-four hours, for sure, and he wouldn't succeed. Of course, he wouldn't rise above the situation. He'd collapse like a bad provincial actor, who stammers on the stage, in the footlights, having forgotten his lines and not knowing how to save himself from embarrassment.

Why all these hints of late that he should pay more attention to his immediate staff, to what the Blitvinian liberal press ironically referred to as "the Beauregard lot"? As though he didn't know that all those around him were more or less forgers, ungifted blabberers, flattering racketeers, third-rate scribblers, cheats, falsifiers of signatures, false witnesses, murderers, condemned criminals on bail, gamblers, defrauders, fugitives, snouts, detectives, and spies. And was it his fault personally that human society was made up of forgers, card cheats, and confidence men? From Shakespeare to today, no one had written a single play without such dubious characters, yet they expect in this solemn spectacle of Beauregard to have only saints and angelically pure souls. Ridiculous! The other evening one of those academically educated apes said that in the governing circles of the Philosophy Faculty it was considered the "minimal right of every citizen that the privacy of his correspondence be guaranteed." Well, well, there you are! These gentlemen had nothing else to do but get excited about the privacy of personal mail, as if he, Barutanski, were the head of the post office or a postman, and as if the privacy of the mail were his responsibility? Bloody nonsense! He, Barutanski, during his forty-nine years had written a fair number of letters, and all in invisible ink, because the privacy of his personal mail was never guaranteed by anyone, and now he was expected to get excited because the noble governors of the Philosophy Faculty had their private letters opened! Big deal! Beatings, prisons, distrainings, shootings, blood, drunkenness, fraud, banks, currency smuggling, wealth, luxury, cars, train crashes, carriages, women, villas, banners, battles, bloodstained elections, weeping and hunger everywhere over the whole world, and here, around him, some hypocrites squeal because of the "brutality" of his executives. As if one could restrain this flood of human stupidity and blind instinct with kid gloves and as though "brutality" were his invention? Wasn't the whole world a jungle? Didn't they teach you in divinity lessons that the world was created in God's image? Was the world created by this maker of worlds and times or was it perhaps by him, Barutanski? So why accuse him because the world was a jungle? Idiocy!

"The criminal methods of certain personal political systems," he'd read the other evening in the editorial of the liberal, Masonic organ *Blitwanen Tigdende,* and this referred exclusively to him personally and to his personal "criminal system," which was so "personal" and so "criminal" that it allowed Mr. Jensen, under his personal dictatorship, to harangue against him personally in such a criminal manner! And in any case, what was "good" and what was "evil"? What was crime and what was do-gooding? Without crime, there was no charity. If you wanted to make chicken soup for an invalid, then first of all, you had to kill a chicken. Be it a chicken or mankind was mere pedantry. Measured on a greater, let us say universal, scale, the two were absolutely the same. The rest was mere prejudice. To create Blitva, as a fait accompli, out of the chaos of war conditions, it was absolutely necessary to wring the necks of several thousand Blitvinian chickens. Now this Blitvinian soup was cooking, and whether this borscht of blood guaranteed the privacy of the private mail of the honorable governors of the Philosophy Faculty, and whether the moral test tube showed point zero, zero, zero of "brutality," this could be no problem for his personal plan, which, in the case of Blitva, was a locomotive of 80,000 HP, and in no way a decimal scale in the neurasthenic hand of some narrow-minded and quasi-religious waverer.

There existed on this earth a spinsterly species of masturbators, of moralistic semi-idiots, who usually occupied themselves with "humanistic" journalism and who would do better to have remained as clerics or idlers without any definite occupation, who lamented and moaned from their provincial pulpits about the question of murder. How could an average Blitvinian petit bourgeois possibly grasp the problem of murder? According to such people's understanding, murder was a constituent part of the criminal law and that was that! But what if murder were no more than a tiny constituent detail in the essence of the dynamics of life, and if, without murder, life were inconceivable? Was everyone a criminal for wanting to live, to kill, to move, to rule?

"He slaughtered," they say of Barutanski and that's what they wrote about him in the European press, "Blitvinian peasants in their masses." And why should I not have slaughtered peasants in their masses, when that Blitvinian peasant in his masses had done nothing else for centuries but be slaughtered in his masses and grunt in his masses, in his immobility and massive criminal stupidity? Barutanski's operation, when he created Blitva in '17 and then in the coup eight years later, both, for God's sake, were surgical acts. There was no birth without blood! That was the law of nature. Every surgical operation, unfortunately, involved blood.

"If only he hadn't killed Kavalierski"—this (among other things) was what was whispered in all probability in the governing body of the Divinity Faculty. Indeed! Muzhikovski's and Sandersen's deaths, that was civil war. Civil war possessed an element of fair, chivalrous, gladiatorial struggle. It was like a poker game when you couldn't tell who'd get the bank. In civil war the risk was always on the side of the one who, by his own initiative, put himself outside the framework of positive civil law. If I hadn't taken Blitwanen by direct assault, if I hadn't lost 1,700 men of my own in the attack on the Beauregard palace, Messieurs Muzhikovski and Sandersen would have shot me down like a dog. According to the civil law! That the gentlemen from the governing body of the Divinity Faculty fully understood—that was to say, when the shooting's done according to the positive laws, and the "positive" laws, for them, meant only those which "positively" guaranteed their "university" autonomy! The gentlemen were formalists. For those formalistic gentlemen from the Divinity Faculty my toreador's pass was not a hundred percent appealing, but more or less humanly understandable. According to their opportunism, the main thing was to preserve formalities. But, leaving this aside, these highly educated gentlemen, these cardinals, prelates, and bishops, were always glad of an iron glove that could give a bloody nose to the godless, illiterate, lazy mob. So as far as the late Muzhikovski was concerned (may he rest in peace), he was just a most ordinary demagogue and vulgar anticleric, while I got his lordship Bishop Armstrong the first Blitvinian cardinal's hat, and under my rule were being built twenty-seven new Blitvinian churches, and all those devout constructions subsidized out of the state budget.

But Kavalierski "wasn't liquidated according to the formal process of civil law." I had Kavalierski "shot in the fortress prison." Kavalierski was killed "without formal process." Kavalierski, "a blot on my knightly escutcheon." This was "an error." Kavalierski's death was "merely a case of malicious, cowardly murder." Tra-ta-ta!

When the old and demented gentlemen of the university whispered their irresponsible senile stupidities, that was what the other side complacently and pathetically called "public opinion." Public opinion, then, thinks I'm a murderer, because I "murdered" Kavalierski. And who was Kavalierski? Wasn't Kavalierski at least as much a murderer as Barutanski? Why and for what reason did everybody sympathize with Kavalierski? Just because he was dead? As if I didn't personally see Kavalierski shoot a high school kid who was a legionnaire, because he'd stolen a slab of chocolate from the legionnaires' supply room at Plavystok? Why did that swine have to shoot a pale-faced anemic kid like that? It was because he was born a nasty criminal type. He felt the organic need to murder. He shot Zhenya Visotzka as she fled by car to Ankersgarden, when Mackensen stood before Blitvinska. And then Dr. Jakobsen shot at Kavalierski and later it was proved in the brigade legion inquiry that this was not insubordination but simply revenge for Visotzka's death, but he still had Jakobsen shot, cold-bloodedly, like a hound. He commanded the firing squad himself and lit a cigarette over Jakobsen's dead body and spat the butt into his face, as though Jakobsen's cheek were a spittoon. Kavalierski murdered at least several thousand people, and then began to moralize with the gentlemen of the Divinity Faculty about how I'd killed Muzhikovski. A typical criminal in a hair shirt, Kavalierski was ever on the hunt, believing, even in his last days, that he couldn't count his beads without spilling someone's blood. Kavalierski killed wild boar and deer, pheasants, hares, partridges, dogs, and cats in inconceivable numbers. Kavalierski shot his three dogs and Nastasya, the only daughter of his gamekeeper, while I? I shot Kavalierski. And now what? Olaf Knutson, that pathetic hanger-on of Rayevski's, that stupid bungler of a man, that idiotic nerve case, who was good for nothing but painting three peaches on a napkin or two sardines and an empty beer bottle, that shadow of a half man, who the other day, when, as Rayevski's assistant, he was modeling my hand for my own statue, had the gall to say that, in his incompetent opinion, it would have been in the interest of the "cause" if I'd liquidated Kavalierski "by due legal process." In what "interest" and what "cause," and when in history has "due legal process" been less an evil than such surgical faits accomplis? Plotters, conspirators, pub crawlers, underground agitators, café slanderers, blabberers, all that scum had to be registered, and then, from time to time, *circumdederunt,* amen, thunder, lightning, it's over, *pour toujours*! To liquidate murderers and criminal types who plotted against other people's lives, who corresponded with bandits abroad, who held secret meetings with commanders of divisional units, such dangerous individuals as the late Kavalierski deal with them by the formal "process of law"? This might be logical only to such a neurasthenic, *l'art pour l'artistically* inclined dauber as Olaf Knutson, but in fact, this was unintelligent—more than that, naive, just bloody silly! Politics in the court—a ridiculous phrase, even for a revolver journalist! Politics had dwelled in theaters and churches for centuries, but in the court—why, no one knows—it was forbidden! Was there ever in history a court in which politics played no role? So why fool with lies, as if one were at a masked ball given for shop assistants or dental technicians who affected the guitar? That we all wear masks we know, and why should I do something openly when I can do it covertly and more effectively at that? Let the court carry out its feebleminded civil functions dealing with private disputes, wills, and semidetached property! Better strike from the dark—that was the way to use the mask. It certainly had a healthy effect on the nerves of cowards and moreover excluded the need for the comedy with the executioner and the old-fashioned ritual of reading a death sentence. Spare me the court, spare me the letter of the law! There, toothless old men munched pretzels and argued the toss like a lot of garrulous old maids at the post office, convinced that not a single letter should be delivered except by official regulations. One undercover Georgis is worth more to me than the entire legal profession of the much respected Blitvinian Republic. A communiqué from the Ministry of the Interior in black letters, outlined in black like an obituary—that the said criminal was shot while trying to escape—two or three stupid articles abroad, in the socialist press which had no possible influence, a couple of mentions on the radio news, and the whole matter was definitely forgotten. It wouldn't give us a headache for the next hundred years. And fear in the citizens' bones was the best cure. It was a miraculous remedy that made even the arthritic get up and jump. The only way to do this was with gunpowder. And damn what anybody thought, gunpowder had its own profound and mighty useful logic. I've seen quite a few shitty pants due to gunpowder fever. Gunpowder clears the bowels better than the finest glycerine or castor oil. These were pills that cured the worst of bellyaches. People were creatures of prey and, as such, fell into the category of the most dangerous of carnivores. So they needed keeping in well-locked cages, and training by means of the pistol and the stinking carrion of a so-called civil career. He who wanted to be the perfect tamer in this modern madhouse, as our modern comedy in Beauregard appeared, needed to be a generous miser, a sentimental sadist, and a merciful, even angelically compassionate tyrant in one person. Ever ready to swear to three constitutions, strictly democratically formalistic in the election of a new president of the Republic (just as I appeared aloofly selfless when I proposed Roman Rayevski as a candidate for that most prestigious post), a perjurer who, between one game of tennis and another, cut off people's heads, but one who took a gentlemanly care not to break trifling, everyday promises, especially if they were given in public. Face-to-face one could break any promise one liked, but for the vulgar public, for the gossiping crowd, there one had to appear a model of honor. He was a good actor who could make the public think he was sincere. How one managed that, by tears, anger, or gentleness, by charming them with what they call good manners, that didn't matter a damn. Pure sincerity, not even acted sincerity, had never led to success. False tears, shed from the stage, had always worked better than genuine tears. Even in poetry, real tears were a bore and that was why I never read poetry. That's the world of my dear Ingrid, who has systematically and stupidly bored me stiff with infants and white swans for years. (Or whatever else of her bloody lyricism!)

Lately one heard more and more that Beauregard was sinking in luxury. I've just read in the confidential report of Witusz Kantorowicz that they're saying in the cafés that, as head of Blitva, I sign foreign deals and that my private fortune is estimated by the Parisian stock market at 800 million francs, that all this lot, whom the Blitvinian muck refers to sarcastically as the "Beauregardists," all these "Beauregardists" of mine, so to speak, have built themselves palaces, summer residences, eight-storied houses, that they all have villas in Lausanne, they all cruise the southern seas in their own yachts, and that Beauregard is nothing but a center for the export of wheat, alcohol, game, cloth, and sugar beets! Cafés, bars, patisseries, the streets—they're all spreading libelous rumors that Blitva has no constitution, no mandate, no elections, no judges, no justice, and no legal security, that crime is growing, that court procedure is invalid, that laws don't apply, that money's worthless and without backing, that signatures on state documents aren't worth a penny, that neither trade nor legal guarantees exist, that there's no credit, no confidence in the administration, that bribery's the sole means of government, that state decrees can be bought, that there's no political cohesion, no foreign policy, that remand prisons are torture chambers, that the guilty are shot while escaping, that there's no security of the individual, that Blitva drinks, that Blitva gets drunk, that Blitva's going to the dogs, at an ever more reckless speed, that there's no justice, no prosperity, no bread, and all that's built is mere sand in the eyes of the people, mere empty and above all expensive decoration. So all the palaces and public buildings on Waldemaras Square were just decoration? Ankersgarden port, with its thirty thousand inhabitants, seventeen elevators, with its three docks and six new breakwaters, was also decoration? The Blitvinian fleet was decoration? Seventeen new Blitvinian enterprises and this too was mere decor with nothing behind it but blood, hunger, deceit, and slaughter? People killed one another, hatred had crept into the idyll of quiet family life. All citizens were disturbed, were losing their nerve in an ever increasing anxiety. Everyone spied on everyone. It was all a tangle of informers. Every other man was a hired agent. Everything was turning into an agitated Blitvinian anthill, in which the alarmed populace ran hither and thither in all directions, in mindless panic, without order, without sense, sick to their souls, without honor. Everything had become a completely senseless seething of the mass, a vast conglomeration of human stupidity, turned to vampires by their own terror, a demonic mindlessness, a saturnalian cannibalization of its own flesh, a hellish Blitvinian nocturne, in fact, an accursed Walpurgis night in which Barutanski raged like a madman, killing right, left, and center. There was slaughter all around us. Around us everything was ablaze; fire, chaos, and destruction on every side; banditry, robbery, a pitiful surge of criminality. The peasants slaughtered each other like wild beasts, devoured one another, tore their own throats, waylaid, killed, swilled vodka, bit their own noses off, poisoned the wells, broke the legs of their cattle, got drunk on poisonous methyl alcohol, destroyed the bridges, like arsonists, set fire to each other's roofs, murdered one another politically, shot at the police, a true Blitvinian jacquerie at its height, a state of emergency, in which nothing was heard but the hooves of heavy cavalry and the tramp of Barutanski's executioners: gallows, courts-martial, misery, drunkenness, the crying of widows, fog, the dense Blitvinian fog, and death everywhere. And Olaf Knutson who, amidst all this, could do nothing but paint three sardines or three pears on a plate, that silky gentleman, that thin-skinned lyricist, modestly remarked that he was "neither a courtier nor a flatterer," and that he "will not play the role of Rosencrantz and Guildenstern," and so thought it necessary for me to be told that they were saying in Blitwanen that "there's too much luxury in Beauregard"! Again that famous luxury? What luxury? Where was it?

And Roman Rayevski, whom I paid 3.5 million lei for my own equestrian statue (that the city of Blitwanen was raising on its own initiative) and to whom I allocated an appanage of 2 million as the future president of the Republic, that hypocritical ape also thought "thrift is the only solid basis for any economy" and that His Excellency, "He," as the newly elected president of the Republic, would begin his presidential career "by a general and compulsory economy."

Phrases and neurasthenia! I see no reason for furioso in what goes on around me. It's all pretty boring, bureaucratically gray and monotonous. That so-called Beauregard luxury, those thirty lackeys and those braided generals and doormen, is that luxury? Every better hotel in Paris has more luxury than I have. And lastly: Here, in this place, in this backward and mud-filled Blitva, which never had anything, the fact that I, Colonel Barutanski, live in the palace of the Aragon and Hunnish governors, is that "luxury"? And after all, what was this hysterical, affected blather that "Blitva is poverty stricken"? As though Blitva would be less so because I organized the first Blitvinian philharmonic orchestra that performs Strauss's *Till Eulenspiegel* to perfection? Because I built churches with Cardinal Armstrong? That I raised monuments? Nonsense! And that's reasoning? Blitva, as it is, whether those pygmies sitting in cafés like it or not, is my own personal creation, whether these neurasthenic blatherers want it or not, "I," compared with these bedbugs and this dwarfish rabble, am forever at least a Francesco Sforza, compared with these stuttering, hunchbacked pastry cooks and stupid petty traders. For if "I" had not appeared in the general chaos and disintegration of '17 with "My" sword, if "I" had not stood up in the name of this, our Blitvinian slime, before the high council of Parisian advocates, if "I" had not created Blitva as it is today—an independent, sovereign European state—if it had not been for "Me" and what they so kindly term the "satrap," my humble self, some Hunnish, Blatvian, or Aragon imperial prince would have sat here today in this very Beauregard, and the defeatist café blabberers wouldn't be able to slander "Me" as a usurper, self-appointed, just because I built Blitva, raised towns, and armed the Blitvinian forces. It wouldn't be the dictatorship of a Barutanski, but the centuries-long slavery under a foreign yoke. If it hadn't been for "Me," Blitva would still be an exotic prejudice, and the brilliant painter and sculptor Mr. Rayevski would not have had a royal reception in America when, last year, he arrived in New York to explain to a load of American ignoramuses that Blitva did not produce only Sforzas but Donatellos and Verrocchios. Our Quattrocento has come five hundred years late, but it has come! In Paris Rayevski exhibited Blitva in a golden helmet and holding a lance like a coquettish Pallas Athene, and to see in this development only that the Blitvinian peasants slaughtered one another and drank themselves stupid and that the land was just mud and fog—this was to be simply maliciously moronic. I created Blitva entirely on my own, as a usurper, without anybody's help, and while the Blitvinians increased around this full dish, much water would flow through the Blatva and the Ister. Cretins needed training like dogs till they turned into politically mature people. How to make a man out of a dog was a basic question of political training, and that that could not be achieved by the writing of obscure, humanistic, and querulous articles was beyond doubt! In Blitva there was no state tradition; it had no precedents. Blitva was the dream of pimply-faced schoolboys at all-night parties. It was the nebulous illusion of hungry primary school teachers about the ancient and historic Blitvinian glories (which, if the truth be told, never existed). Blitva meant a provincial sinking into narcosis, and today's leap into a sovereign etatistic freedom was too great for the Blitvinian peasant to be able in any way to grasp its meaning, and why Colonel Barutanski, by his own will and at his own risk, should have, so to speak, forged it in his own smithy, as an armor for all Blitvinians and that that silver and costly armor "of Blitvinian freedom," once delivered over to Dr. Muzhikovski as a token of that "Blitvinian freedom," the honorable Dr. Muzhikovski, as a truly primitive provincial lawyer, politician, and demagogue, thought that those silver and precious symbols of "national sovereignty" existed solely to be used like some peasant piss pot, and when that yokel defiled everything in Blitva that should have remained pure, when he brought the sovereign and noble concept of Blitvinian state-hood down to vulgar popular, so-called parliamentary wheeling and dealing, then Colonel Barutanski once more took on himself the selfless, self-sacrificing, and sublime mission of freeing Blitva from that quasi-democratic pestilence and, having dispersed this peasant scum, cleansed this backward Blitvinian cattle market of ours and, today, when he desired to march with the times, today they called it his personal satrapy. And now the hungry, toothless bohemians and ungifted poets sneered at him for raising a monu-ment to himself, during his lifetime, in the park in front of Jarl Knutson's tower, and he might as well have written to his protégé, Cardinal Armstrong, demanding that the church proclaim him a saint. If the phenomenon of Jarl Knutson in Blitvinian history was really so important that the children of Blitva still dreamt of it, nine hundred years later, with pathos, then he, Barutanski, with a clear conscience might accept the gift of an equestrian statue, which, as an acceptable and decorative ornament, would excel-lently fill that empty space between Beauregard and Knutson's fortress. If for no other reason than simply as urban improvement, such a gesture was fully justified. The neurasthenics were upset at his personality being used as aggressive, tasteless, and utterly su-perfluous propaganda, that "in fact" it had no purpose, for what "in fact" was the use of this American popularization of his per-sonality? This was no longer just the cult of a historical person, but pure fetishism. To tell the truth, it was neither a cult, nor popularization, nor fetishism, but a common trick of small traders who hawked the cheapest goods with his picture, so as to sell as much of this rubbish as possible. And if Colonel Barutanski appeared on the stamps used on printed matter, or on some gilded mug with its four-colored medallion, immortalized on his white horse Atlanta at that moment when, as Lord Protector of Blitva, he rode into the green waves of the sea at Plavystok, what universal honors, what transcendental fetishism that he had lived to appear on the gilded mug of an illiterate office worker which, with a subject's humblest gratitude, he dirtied every morning with his wet mustaches, soaked in coffee with cream, in which the land of Blitva was spongily swollen like a dead frog. How could human nature be so selfish and petty that even a gilded proletarian mug with a medallion could become the object of malicious envy? They were building him a monument while he was still alive, but after all, what was the point of false modesty? "He" had well and truly earned it, "while he was still alive."

It was easy to take the way others had trod, to shine, 300 years after Cromwell, at international meetings, when you were sitting on the 207 percent interest of an East Indian Company all paid off 250 years before and every pound sterling representing a valuable imperial capital on all exchanges. You were approached by advocates in unpressed trousers, fiddling with their safe keys in their ridiculously wide pockets, smoking cigars as thick as your thumb, occupying Morocco by telephone, who preached to the Blitvinians about the "parliamentary and democratic" establishment of their Mediterranean, arranged as a national park, in which its citizens sipped champagne and sucked oysters and nibbled hors d'oeuvres. Above all, this perfumed and aperitifed Mediterranean of theirs wasn't so perfectly organized as those arrogant gentlemen thought, so what was the point—I beg you—150 years after the fall of the

Bastille of declaiming about the perfection of their Mediterranean parliamentary regime, as though such a regime were unattainable by the barbarians. To dance the old parliamentary polka *à la Tardieu*, 250 years after the glorious thunder of Louis XIV's *pavane royale*—that was not clever, especially when, to support your much respected excuse of *raison d'état*, you had at your disposal the just as traditional and respected Deuxième Bureau, which was not under the control of the seven cafés of the Blitvinian capital of the Republic, as it was with us, where a whole so-called public opinion of fools, Masons, and priests conducted an entire double-entry bookkeeping at every most innocent police arrest. You, my dear Western European statesmen, try dancing your mazurka between Ankersgarden and Plavystok, please do! Between the Blitvinian small traders and poultry farmers. Go ahead and dance your impeccable Western democratic quadrille, if you can, my dear honorable statesmen, where there's no rhythm, nor rules, where there's nothing laid down anywhere, no protocol, no Deuxième Bureau, no tradition, no ceremonial, no common law, since there was no custom for having laws, and no dancing schools in the vicinity in which one might learn to dance our Blitvinian carmagnole, our lively czardas, which, naked, barefoot, and contemptible, we dance in front of you and you watch us from your expensive gilded theater boxes. You call yourself Europe and so we have to pay for everything at 143 percent interest, if not more, because you're Europe, because you sit in the gilded box of Louis XIV and announce yourselves as Jacobins, while we daren't have even a monument, for monuments, of course, are the privileged right of your famous so-called Jacobin managers whom, God knows why, you call statesmen. In fact, the only person who truly had the right to call himself a statesman was the politician who had created the state, which I took the liberty of doing myself, personally, on my own, and so your Barber of Seville need have nothing to say to me, because the decision to raise a statue will be mine, personally and alone, and I will not be influenced by your journalist scum, but I'll invite to its unveiling your esteemed and valued ambassadors and envoys, according to Jacobin protocol, in their gold-braided dress suits and in three-cornered hats with abbreviated ostrich feathers and rosettes, looking ridiculously like undertakers' men from one of our provincial towns. And, added to that, I'll hang a Blithuania Restituta around the neck of every one of those envoys, like a dog collar, voilà! And the fact that the clerics, chaplains, and the deacons of the Philosophy Faculty protest about this stupid statue, that's completely natural and normal. They trade in knowledge, just as the small merchants trade in feathers and fat. These stinking pedants, these narrow-minded specialists and mediocrities of so-called free and academic persuasion, where would they find the heart and guts and brain of a pioneer, bold enough to dare on his own to root out the stupidity and darkness of the Blitvinian centuries? And while Barutanski, completely alone at the head of a national procession, broke through the fog with his lamp, like a true leader, these petty Blitvinian souls hid their heads under their duvets, quietly farting and sniffing their own academic aroma under their quilts, nodding their heads at the wind that roared so as to shake the glass in the windows of Blitvinian cottages, as if Blitva were a stagecoach rolling in a mad gallop through the mud and the ditches, whither no one knows. The fact that "We," here in Beauregard, against our better judgment, took on the duty of being legislators, this we did with such Taylorized and American speed, simply because generally, through the centuries, no one ever ruled Blitva according to her own laws and therefore there was a need for haste if she were to catch up with other "Western civilizations"!

They say bureaucracy has pupped. The bureaucracy, they say, is skinning the peasants. And before all this, when there wasn't any Blitva, did the bureaucrats not skin them? Bollocks! Mere arrogance!

The peasants are skinned, that's true, but they're skinned by Blitvinian bureaucrats who talk to the Blitvinian peasant as though he is a
Blitvinian, and here and there will build him the odd hygienic
Blitvinian toilet! Bottom line: the Blitvinian peasant probably
doesn't lose out. No way! When it came to getting rid of that whore-
house around Muzhikovski, then that pleased the various urban and
petit bourgeois interests. Then they approved of me, as
if I were some particularly favorite coloratura soprano! And now
they're grumbling, so they are! They don't like my Beauregard music! As if we're bandmasters and as if we seized power in order to
play to the hairy ears of Blitvinian petit bourgeois idiots. The
tempo's getting faster for the citizens; they're fat and short of breath.
They haven't the puff. Running doesn't suit them at all, especially
not running after civilization! The citizen prefers to look on. He's of
a contemplative nature and because of this passivity of his, it happens that the slaves have raised their heads. That was it! His, Barutanski's, Beauregard team that ran with him was pathetic. They were
just a lot of softies, lazy cowards, debauchees, sybarites who had but
a single idea: to drive a Horch, to buy themselves a villa in Meudon-
Val-Fleury, to go abroad out of this mud. For those gentlemen
Blitva stank and, surrounded by such faithful followers, Colonel
Barutanski lived in this menagerie entirely on his own. Alone, like
the Caucasus, above those gray, muddy, Blitvinian plowlands.

Thinking of himself, Barutanski felt as if he really was looking
at the gray, granite, Promethean panorama of high snowy peaks,
around which the icy wind whistled with a razor-sharp hiss, like a
guillotine, and there below, far beneath his feet, the white, sunlit
cloud masses snowballed one another. There, far below, one heard
the hoarse bass of the thunder. There, rain fell; there, smoke bil-
lowed vertically. There, normal daily human life went on. The
tinkling of flocks, the murmur of streams, the smoke of hearths,

morning glories climbing up human homes, somewhere a child crying behind a rock. But here there was a solemn emptiness, in the absolute azure of an apotheosis. An eagle-eyed view, like the landscape on a thousand-lei note.

With all his native intelligence, bewildered by contrasts, at that moment Barutanski had no further control over the picture that arose in his brain, and he failed to notice, at that moment, that he was truly ridiculous. Reality had ceased to harmonize with his conception of it, for this was pure fantasy bordering on operatic kitsch, which had horrified him for years. "Please, not the Caucasus on the opera stage! Not the theatrical thunder with which the thunder gods descend from their shimmering peaks onto the stage of provincial theaters, where the actors sneeze in a cloud of dust. Not Promethean cliffs made of paper!" All this lasted only a moment.

He was sitting there in Beauregard, in his study, leafing through the guest list for the great, solemn banquet which he, Colonel Barutanski, was to give in honor of the newly elected president of the Republic, the honorary president of the Blitvinian Academy of Arts and Sciences, the member of forty-seven most distinguished European and American cultural societies, the Blitvinian delegate at the Peace Conference in Paris, and the Blitvinian signatory of the peace in Blato Blitvinsko in the year 1917 and in Versailles in the year 1919, the academic sculptor, Roman Rayevski. The honorable Roman Rayevski would take over the representation of the Republic's sovereignty for diplomatic and other less important international reasons, while Barutanski would remain in Beauregard as a kind of Lord Protector of Blitva, in the role of chief inspector of the fleet, but in fact everything would continue in the same way as hitherto, until, in two or three years' time, "possibly" the normal preconditions for the possible maneuver might arise by which the Blitvinian ship might return to parliamentarianism. Under Rayevski, he would rule just as he always had: by shootings and banquets. The citizens of Blitva were cattle. And cattle were to be ruled according to the old and well-tried principles of cattle breeding. Cattle were made for the yoke, and, once harnessed, then, logically, they pulled. The means to make cattle put their shoulder to the yoke were endless. The best way was to give them a few banquets every year, for the citizens were as mad for solemn banquets as cows were for salt. You'd never believe how many cigarettes and sweets and candied fruit were stolen at these solemn Blitvinian banquets. And those exalted individuals who considered it beneath them to be welcomed at the white tablecloths of Beauregard, those moralistic gentlemen who spread malevolent and damaging stories, that the tablecloths at Barutanski's banquets were spattered with human blood, those humanist pedants meant nothing even in the days of the democratic parliamentary government of Muzhikovski, because they were the same *quantité négligeable* then as they were now. Those gentlemen could not manage. Those gentlemen overestimated the significance of their subjective squealing and would be crushed as a meaningless and worthless lump of nothingness, crushed, alas, and justly at that. For it was not the intellectual hyper wheelers and dealers who ruled affairs, but people who had formed their own correct opinion of affairs, an opinion in whose framework the view of affairs, more or less, agreed with experience. Softies complained about the state of affairs, but a real man overcame them and, beating them, created new and ever newer preconditions for the development of newer and newer affairs. Yes, you had to have luck, that was true! But luck came through autosuggestion. One had to prepare for one's vocation! One had to believe in the attainment of one's goals and be able to desire the right things at the right time! One had to shoot according to the laws of ballistics. One had to ride soberly, swim with the wind, and never overestimate oneself, and never believe the hairsplitters, the pedants, the waverers, the naggers, the yes-men. Not believe the egoists and the cunning that they were not pedants, yes-

men, and cunning, and not be deceived into thinking that a sly coward would serve at the time and place where only a brave and naive
fool could win. If anyone were so unintelligent as to engage in
preparing an army, if anyone decided to engage in military affairs,
then let him work according to Frederick the Great's advice: "only
with naive and brave fools." An army was a machine, like any other
machine: a steam engine, a steam saw, a steam plow, or a steam ship.
One controlled an army as one controlled a car. On the left, one
moved with the defense of international legal guarantees as long as
one could, and on the right, one had full magazines of machine guns
against one's own citizens. The clash of swords was to be recom-
mended. From time to time it always worked, but the performance
should never slacken. At the first signs of boredom, then, a new program! New programs were necessary for the press, for the photo-
journalists, for Fox Movietone, for advertisements, for the sake of
public opinion, for the sake of a lucrative loan abroad, for the sake of
raising one's own political credibility. All this one had to bear in
mind, and, like the score of a musical work written for a monster orchestra, conduct it from memory by one's own instinct, so that it
seemed as if a stormy sea beat in waves beneath our own baton, and
if things went on stirring and beating on their own, even without
our direction, only unknown to the broad masses, that was something only skeptics understood! There was wisdom in the statement
that man moved with the current. Let the dogs bark as much as they
liked, the main thing was that they were there, when we whistled
them to a banquet. They were all there, wagging their tails, all happily rolling on their backs: the civil-service poodles and the generals' Great Danes and two or three pinschers from the Philosophy
Faculty. They were all taken up with a fire that was lit in the rubbish
within their doggy brains, with the stinking vodka in their hearts,
with their blue-blooded, noble ladies who'd spent three days nervously pacing about their three-room flats, with their canaries and

rubber plants, worrying how they'd get on at the banquet and whether they'd manage to pinch enough cigarettes and praline and candied fruit for their breed that waited for public chocolate and wagged its tail to the third generation. Bow-wow-wow, my dear doggies! There, you've come, answered my call, faithful doggies, wagging your stinking tails, crawling on all fours, licking the legs, boots, spurs, heels, palms, and fingers; there, there, there, not so hard. I know you're faithful civil servants. You want to express your unconditional loyalty and devotion to His Excellency. There, there, well done, hop, hop, *garde à vous,* careful, watch it, here you are, a fistful of Blithuaniae Restitutae. Ask nicely; whoever fetches it can have it. Psst, who wants to prolong their overdraft, or a golden minister's collar? Here you are, hop, careful, and not so much barking. Here you are, seventy silver dishes of praline and cigarettes, a rain of cigarettes from Beauregard, the ringing of bells, the unveiling of monuments, triumphal arches, cannonades, the victorious howling of the masses—and in all this, in between this canine barking and victorious shouting, a man was still utterly alone.

To have behind you the so-called masses of your supporters, crowds of political followers, of so-called like-minded people (who merely pretended that they thought the same as we, while their only aim was to row across in somebody else's boat when faced with shipwreck), to look around one at one's so-called faithful friends who, like Kavalierski, plotted against one's life, to sleep with a Browning under one's pillow and move about, apparently, calmly superior, through the ranks of bowed heads, constantly looking at bald skulls, whole heaps of de-top-hatted pumpkins, to bow to obscure and unknown faces and oneself with a frowning face made of rubber, which was drawn out into the recognized Hollywood smile in front of the lens, to look at people humbly bowing, ever to be reading the same boring hymns of praise, paid by the line, to march at the head of a chosen people, at the head of history, of tradition, of Blitva, of the Karabaltic, to stand here in this Scythian mud as the standard-bearer between Blatvia and Hunnia, to be the weathervane for the Mongol, Aragon, and Asiatic storms that roared on the far horizon, and be utterly alone, trusting nobody and waiting for the bullet to come, for everything to vanish in a parabola, in a single second: and the ringing of bells, the exploding of mortars, and the waving of banners, and the joyful cries of the masses who waved to us with flowers and white handkerchiefs to the left and right of the carriage, who pronounced the handkerchiefs to be little banners, and they were the symbol of a triumph and a festival. He had muck like this around him in their thousands. For instance, to this banquet alone, more than 360 people were invited, and where, among these 360, was there a single one on whom he could rely at a given moment, should it come to that final battle, that he'd not be shot in the back on the run, but that he'd fall like a hero, face-to-face before those who were only waiting for the chance to break in to Beauregard? Where was that one person, to hell with him, that hundred-percent-loyal person from all those hundreds and hundreds of thousands who howled around him on the streets, waving pocket handkerchiefs as though it were a case of runny noses, of influenza! Where was he among these 360 privileged representatives of that Blitvinian elite, that muck of all muck, in that select cream of dignitaries? Swensen? What, that member of the Blitvinian Academy of Arts and Sciences? The academic Swensen, the great Blitvinian poet, who'd written a book of sonnets about Blitvinian kings and who, the year before, in honor of Barutanski's forty-ninth birthday had published his sonnet "The Lord Protector Blithuaniae" in the *Turulun Gazette*? Swensen was a professor of the first Blitvinian university named after its founder, Colonel Barutanski (Barutanski was its first honorary doctor). Swensen was the bearer of the order Blithuaniae Restitutae, Second Class, which he, Barutanski, had founded, established, and awarded. Swensen had received the Chair of the History of Blitvinian Art in that first Blitvinian university. Swensen had voted for him in the Senate. Swensen had lectured about him. Swensen had dedicated his sonnet to his forty-ninth birthday in the *Turulun Gazette.* Swensen wore his order. He was his favorite guest. Of all the Beauregard court chatterers, Swensen was the most educated. Swensen was the most witty. But despite all this, he, Barutanski, personally had no faith in a single word of his and would not have risked sending this loyal Mr. Swensen on a single dangerous, confidential, or risky mission. Swensen owned a house on Jarl Knutson Boulevard. Swensen owned a five-story building with an adjoining shopping area, and all this provided a fair income and from all this Swensen lived comfortably and independently. All these Swensens that surrounded him were house owners, damn them! Seventy-five percent of that lot, who were invited to Beauregard by his Civil Office, in his name, in honor of Roman Rayevski, all of them were house owners. All these Swensens could go on being house owners, without interference, while, at a given moment, in that possible critical given moment, for him, Colonel Barutanski, there would be no roof under which to hide! Outside, storms were raging and no one could foretell from where the wind would come, but these Swensens could cover their heads with their duvets in their burrows and go on snoring, for their house-owning existence was well insured, while he, Barutanski, had no duvet to hide under, for he stood there alone in front of Knutson's tower like a bronze horseman on a rearing horse and was unable to move away. He was chained to his Beauregard plinth, while a Swensen could withdraw his sonnet on the Lord Protector Blithuaniae and publish an announcement in the newspapers that, from the very beginning, he'd considered Barutanski to be a criminal type, that he'd collected signatures against the irresponsible method of secret political killings, while he, Barutanski, could publish no announcement, could not flee to a single one of those streets of that Hunnish military nest, which he had turned from a small and obscure area into a thoroughly respectable place with fifteen monumental houses and twenty-three factory chimneys.

He had a confidential report from Witusz Kantorowicz that there had been talk about him in the Chamber of Commerce: that he was overstrained and that, recently, he was showing signs of exaggerated irritability.

Without a salute, at the door on the left, in a recess beneath bookshelves, appeared Reserve Major Georgis. In front of Barutanski's Renaissance desk stood an upholstered Lutheran chair, and Major Georgis, appearing noiselessly on his rubber soles from out of the semidarkness of the vast room, dropped into it without a single word. The only lighting in the room was a dark, yellow-shaded lamp on Barutanski's desk, while through the open windows in their deep wooden frames, through their light greenish squares, came the distant noise from the Blitvinian *corso*. One could hear the trams as they slid over the bridges under the fortress, the sharp staccato of distant car horns, from the end of Jarl Knutson Boulevard, and distant bells borne on the breeze of the mild September evening.

Barutanski interrupted his reading of the guest list for the banquet in honor of Roman Rayevski and, with his left hand, extracting a Maryland-Jaune cigarette from the packet in front of him on the desk, with the forefinger of the same hand slid the packet toward Major Georgis, somewhat sternly, with the sort of gesture one uses to kill an irritating fly. The packet of Maryland-Jaunes flew over the smooth surface of the oak table in a straight line and the major, for fear it might fall on the floor, covered the bright yellow missile with a loud slap of his hand, and the blow on the tabletop echoed with such a threateningly dull sound that this sudden gaffe on the part of Major Georgis appeared all too contradictory: on the one side almost servile and on the other clumsy. He threw himself on that yellow packet of cigarettes like a bird dog when recovering game, and yet in that blow there was something of a sense of dignified equality. The major's left hand hung from his shoulder like a dead object. Somewhere on the Hunnish battlefield, somebody had hacked his left arm at the shoulder so thoroughly that they'd sewn it back on to his body like a torn sleeve and so it had remained. A completely superfluous requisite. The cigarettes glowed. With his right hand (somewhat clumsily), Georgis drew from his pocket a quarto-size booklet and, placing it on the table edge, flicked it toward Barutanski. The action seemed like a small revenge for the delivery of the Maryland-Jaunes.

"Well, what's that?"

"What is it? Very simple! If we'd stuck to my first plan and confiscated them all at the printing house, there and then, it would have been much simpler. This way seventy thousand copies have been printed and delivered God knows where. The whole issue, to the last copy. There isn't a man in the town this evening who hasn't had it in his hand. So it turns out that my diagnosis of the situation was immeasurably nearer the reality than your exalted, half-metaphysical quibbling. I say, and I stand by it, that all we need is just one fuse not extinguished in time. We're living on a powder keg, man!"

"Yes! And what do you think we ought to have done?"

"We should have confiscated everything, at the source!"

"Nonsense! He'd just have printed it somewhere else. I think this way is the best."

Letting go an exceptionally deep puff of smoke which, when drawn in, had, for the experienced ear, almost the hint of a sigh, Colonel Barutanski threw his Maryland-Jaune into a huge, silver-mounted ashtray, took the carefully presented booklet, and, leafing through this sheaf of yet half-dried paper so that certain letters stuck to his sweating fingertips, yellowed by nicotine, began to read.

The text, printed in small type, so close that it was scarcely legible, read as follows: *An "Open Letter" to Kristian Barutanski from Niels Nielsen. Your name, Kristian Barutanski, was famous in this country ten years ago, when together with apprentices and high school boys and under the protection of Ingermanlandish bayonets, you created your fait accompli, which today they call Blitva. That you had, in all probability, a clearer picture than the rest of Blitvinian citizens of the fact that small political groups, without any particular program, are capable of saving a country from universal chaos, that there are certain conditions in which only a naked gun barrel acts as a proof, that is beyond doubt, just as experience taught us that, faced with shipwreck, the revolver means more than a quotation from the wisest of open letters. To accuse you today of those several thousand dead from the year 1917 would be hypocritical, for your name appeared at that moment when you took command during a shipwreck, foreseeing that there was no other way out than that we save ourselves as best we could! The hungry Blitvinian flesh, for centuries the fodder of foreign cannon, successfully swam out on the further shore, on the shore of our present, modern Blitvinian reality, in blood, in hunger, in fear before the horror, without any civic consciousness of their own and without any feeling of their own self-respect.*

Regardless of the circumstances that have led to it, Blitva today is ruled according to your laws. For the last three years sentences are pronounced in Blitvinian courts in your name, without, to this very day, anybody asking the one simple question: In whose name do you, Kristian Barutanski, demand that we should subject ourselves to your verdicts and sentences? What sort of a self-appointed legislator are you, when nobody stands behind you?

What phrases, what everyday banal phrases, Barutanski thought, lighting a fresh cigarette.

Throughout the centuries of its dark past Blitva has never been free, not for one moment, and today, under your personal command, Blitva is just a bloody chaos in a series of criminal acts of violence. You person-

ally are cutting Blitva, today less free than it ever was in the worst days of foreign enslavement, with your spurs, while assuring us that you are the sole guarantor of our civil liberty. A gambler by nature, you find it easy to gamble with the people's fate, but in this present game of ours which is being played at undoubted loss, it is no longer a question of your own personal risk, but of us all and hence our anxiety which drives us to address a few sincere words to you. Addressing you as an individual, I do not use this royal plural "We" out of some pretended presumption, but simply out of the conviction that I speak in the name of the vast majority of Blitvinian citizens, who have shrouded themselves in an ill-fated silence simply because they tremble before the most everyday Blitvinian phenomenon, lest they find themselves an unknown headless corpse on some foggy Blitvinian railway line. I write to you as to a man who knows me and who knows that I have proved in my life my lack of various qualities, but among my weaknesses a lack of courage may not be included. We two, you, Colonel Kristian Barutanski, and I, a humble Blitvinian legionnaire without rank, we two together have looked death in the eye several times and for that very reason I am aware that you know I am no coward when faced with death. For that very reason the last spark of hope has not extinguished in me that these my words will find a path to a man who is able to judge the meaning of: to look death in the eye and to speak the truth.

"Poor bugger! He's shitting his pants with fear!"

Judging by your actions, it would appear that you have decided, in this chaos of ours, to put certain things right. This clearing out of our rubbish, this cleaning of our Blitvinian room, this you emotionally refer to in your proclamations to the people as your "historic mission." For sorting out the most everyday trifles—that the streets should be swept or that there should be spittoons in railway station waiting rooms—such trifles do not require saber rattling. In order to build two or three hygienic toilets in this mud of ours, a man does not have to call himself colonel, nor wear an operatic helmet with a swan's feather, nor threaten his neighbors—without the slightest reason—with cannon. There is no one around you who dares to tell you the truth to your face, that your Blatvian irredentism is the most obvious nonsense! Your cabinet, with your ministers, today resembles a circus cage in which you, dressed in the laughable gala uniform of a head tamer, fire your blank pistol, and your ministerial monkeys sit grinning on their gold chairs with one single thought in their miserable heads, how to get themselves out of this act in good time and alive, preferably with a solid income and a three-story house somewhere abroad. You will never gain anything from these your hurdy-gurdy monkeys!

"No, I've had enough. This is pure cretinism! Apart from anything else, it's boring. In any case, I love it when somebody decides on their own initiative to raise the curtain in front of my eyes and tell me the truth! Oh God, give me strength! That Nielsen! What's the matter with him? Does he think I'm an idiot? He used to have a lively, racy style, that chap, and now he's writing like a stuffed shirt with a pretentious, puritanical pathos. It's as if he's talking from behind a high starched collar. To me it has the smell of a moth-balled provincial prewar schoolmaster's dress coat. No, thanks very much, it doesn't interest me!"

Barutanski tossed Nielsen's booklet aside with such vehemence that the eight pages bound into a brochure fell apart over the table. Then he got up, lit another cigarette, went to the window, and came back to Georgis.

"Niels Nielsen! He's a doctor of law! Would you believe it, he's my childhood friend! We were at high school together!"

"Read on!"

"And I knew his mother. She was a nice lady! When I escaped from the Ankersgarden guardhouse in 'thirteen, Nielsen's mother hid me in her house and there I slept for more than three weeks in her bed! Her flat smelled of vanilla, and for days on end I ate rose hip jam!"

"Read on, for God's sake!"

"Why should I? I know that idiot by heart! He's being insolent just to prove his civil courage! He wants to wash off the stain of his soiled civil dignity! There's a type of muddled fool who spends their whole life doing nothing else but sniffing around to find some imagined moral smear on their friends. They're forever feeling the need to wash them free of stains! In their own name and in that of those around them. Why don't they open a type of moral dry cleaner's? Why go in for politics?"

"That one's not washing any dignity, my friend, he's demanding the gallows for us, my dear colonel! Here, I beg you, read on! Very simple: What this moralist needs is speedy liquidation!"

As though against his will, Barutanski retrieved Nielsen's booklet and threw it onto the table as though disgusted at touching such filth. "Where do I read? What should I read?"

"Here you are. Read from '*Blitva is falling apart*,' and on from there!"

"Ah, so: '*The truth is that Blitva is falling apart. In stating this generally well-known fact, any, even the slightest, hint that might lead me to accuse you personally for that falling apart is far from my intention, and I consider it superfluous to repeat this on this occasion.*'

"So what's this? Am I guilty or am I not guilty that Blitva's falling apart? This affectation, this tone from the House of Lords, that's the type of 'parliamentarianism' which Dr. Nielsen offers as the only cure for our situation."

And despite all this, it is still true that Blitva is falling apart! It's true that the Blitvinian peasant's rags expose his naked flesh and, I tell you, our Blitvinian peasant has to pay more than seven times for a box of matches than what he gets for a single hen's egg. I think I have repeated an elementary truth which is known to everybody and for which you bear the responsibility neither before God nor before the Blitvinians, but which, nonetheless, loses none of its evidential significance. I am aware that you cannot be held responsible for the fact that Blitvinian hens do not lay eggs that would gain a better price on the foreign market, but if a man has taken political power into his hands, in order eventually to raise the price of his nation's eggs, still he has no need to slaughter all those fellow citizens who are convinced that this rise in the price of Blitvinian domestic eggs could be attained probably by other means than those of you and your hirelings, your burglars, your cheats and common thieves! Murderers!

Having taken power into your own hands, you have driven off our illiterate Blitvinian poulterers, who have clucked and crowed on the dung heap of our "Blitvinian parliamentarianism," and if you ever used the right word in the right place, it was when, in your first tyrannical announcement, you called that leaderless assembly of our peasants "a brothel."

Indeed! That which in recent Blitvinian political history is known as "the parliamentarian and constitutional regime of Prime Minister Dr. Muzhikovski" was the rule of illiterate charlatans, chosen and selected under the most unhappy of circumstances. Under the rule of Prime Minister Muzhikovski, for a thousand Blitvinian lei a man could obtain any type of document from the administrative powers. For five thousand Blitvinian lei he could get a license to work as a dentist or qualification for a head of department, and for ten to twenty-five thousand, any profitable state employment, a doctor's diploma, and even the rank of major in the republican army. Under the rule of Prime Minister Muzhikovski the value of the individual Blitvinian citizen was reduced to a single measure, that of the gold piece in the citizen's pocket, as in the true, peasant, provincial petty affairs, under Muzhikovski's parliamentarianism, the citizen could purchase anything for two or three gold coins, whatever he needed for his existence in our world of mud and slime, be it a passport or export certificate, should he desire to go abroad or export goods for sale to foreign countries.

"In this cattle market of our conscience" you appeared one day as the self-appointed "judge who judged in the name of civil law"! You shone

like "a brilliant meteor above our eternal Blitvinian darkness" (if I may use a term from your semiofficial Blitvinian Gazette, *emotionally describing your coup of the twenty-second of December 1925), when partly with the aid of machine guns and partly with ordinary infantry weapons and artillery, you killed more than three thousand Blitvinian citizens and set yourself on the throne of Beauregard, in agreement with your historical mission—to liberate the Blitva which you had created and to heal it from its worst affliction, from its new so-called parliamentarianism.*

And what happened? While under the rule of Prime Minister Muzhikovski, for a thousand Blitvinian lei the citizen could obtain administrative documents and for ten to fifteen thousand any more valuable decree or diploma, today the price of an egg is just as low as it was before your coup, only the charge for official documents has risen. For twenty thousand Blitvinian lei your minions are prepared to sell their conscience, if not their wives, and these gentlemen ministers of yours, their secretaries and oversecretaries, their chancellors and heads of departments, and your majors (Georgis), your bishops (Armstrong), your journalists (Wernis), and academicians (Roman Rayevski)—in a word, all that devilish company of yours does nothing else but trade under the Blitvinian banner, as though Blitvinian sovereignty is no more than a trading public company, and you the only authorized shareholders of that enterprise. And while under Muzhikovski's government people merely stole, under your tyranny they both steal and kill. You appeared in Blitva as a surgeon, and your surgeon's knife turned into a burglar's jimmy. Instead of a doctor, you became a disguised burglar who massacres his opponents where he finds them. Headless corpses on railway lines, faked suicides in prison, political refugees lying shot in ditches by the roadside, sudden attacks by unknown assailants on night walkers—this is how you deal with your political opponents to the honor and glory of our Blitvinian freedom, which you, as our "Lord Protector," have given us (quotation from the sonnet by the academician Swensen). This that is taking place today in the quiet corners of

Blitvinian pubs, this outcry and gnashing of teeth in our misery, this twisted mob of slaves who serve you for a miserable bureaucrat's wage, this downtrodden mass of beggars which is known as the population of this country, all these are silent, patiently waiting, with the silence of cattle, for Blitva has, for centuries, swallowed its spittle beneath a foreign yoke, living a life worse than that of its own cows, and I, addressing these lines to you, know very well that should my head roll one day, not a single Blitvinian rooster will crow for it. You have torn up the constitution. You killed the legal president of the Republic, Professor Sandersen, while in internment. You had Muzhikovski shot while a refugee abroad. You dissolved Parliament. You have ridden roughshod over all Blitva's laws, destroyed every form of legal security. At the elections for Senate and those for the presidency of the Republic you failed, and thus, driven into the dark cul-de-sac of your own shortsightedness, today you are killing your own subjects, assured that the way to salvation leads over the rotting corpses of your opponents. After the vile and cowardly killing of Colonel Kavalierski (whom you murdered out of your own pride and vengeance), today when you have taken power in the struggle against the illiterate tyranny of Muzhikovski, offering no program except that of your personal domination, when you have shot chief editor Jensen for the sole reason that he dared inquire who was that mysterious lady, that young girl from California, that "wonderful and unknown Dolores" (whom we have the honor to know as the plaster cast Blitva in public institutions, as the goddess Justice in the vestibule of the new Ministry of Justice, as the patroness of Blitvinian agriculture on the new thousand-lei notes), to demand, today, from you, Kristian Barutanski, as an exposed murderer, any form of satisfaction would be both naive and ridiculous. The only true solution would be that the court should deliver you and your entire Beauregard band to the executioner and the fact that such an inglorious end sooner or later awaits you is a possibility to which I must draw your attention, sure that viewing affairs from the perspective of Beauregard, you no longer discern the movement of what, at first glance, are insignificant details, which for you, in your imagined exaltation, have no particular meaning, but which to me appear so significant that they have led me to address these lines to you with the best of intentions and with all due respect to a giant to whom his own people, even during his physical life, are raising a monument. This my letter might well be called a letter concerning your monument.

"OK! What does this nitpicker want from me?"

"He wants to hang you, my friend! Simply and concisely: to deliver you to the executioner and hang you!"

Since you have raped Blitva and stained it in blood as no Tartar ever did in its shameful past, you have got the urge in your vain megalomania to tower in the form of a bronze horseman over this our mire as a warning to the generations that never yet was there a criminal who sat on a better-sculptured stallion than that wild, Blitvinian, rearing horse with its flying mane, the work of the academic and future president of the Republic, Roman Rayevski, who could find no more worthy motif for his gifted hand that this equestrian statue that portrays to us a cunning burglar as our Lord Protector of Blitva, clad in knightly armor. Roman Rayevski thinks you will appear for future generations as a general who, with his legions, created Blitva, who, like Columbus, led us to the farther shore and gave us all the elements of our real, modern Blitvinian life: alcohol, hops, hens, and sugar beet! It's time you thought what it means when a living man considers it normal that his contemporaries should raise him to the stature of a demigod and what it means when someone has turned themselves into a mysterious concept concealed behind a curtain before which the common folk kneel and pray. Your favorites, those who use you, your flatterers, your arse lickers, your suckers, your honorable crawlers, your court jesters, your hirelings, your bribed scribblers, your academicians, your cardinals, all that motley band of parrots and apes, all of these kneel before your monument, but I tell you that there will be no justice in this unhappy land of Blitva until you either dangle from a rope or your head is placed upon the executioner's block.

A pause. A cigarette. Smoke.

"OK. So what? Is that it?"

"Yes, that's it!"

"So what now?"

"Nothing! It's been printed in seventy thousand copies and it's being read in a geometric progression. In twenty-four hours' time there won't be a man in Blitva who hasn't read this *cochonnerie.*"

"OK. So what?"

"So what? I'm not Copernicus! I don't consider street pamphlets that call on our citizens to lynch us in the same way as one might the eternity of stars! Seventy thousand!"

"You're always thinking of statistics. The thing is written so badly, palely, wordily. The man couldn't find a single direct, human word. It's all a bunch of boring clichés. And in any case, how can one deny the facts in such a stupid way? What does he mean by saying I'm a gambler by nature and that I'm gambling with the nation's fate? Headless corpses on misty railway lines! What sort of a pistol-packing journalistic tone is that? It all suggests rather a separate edition than a confession. Muzhikovski, Sandersen, Kavalierski, Jensen, little Dolores on the banknotes, Dolores as a goddess of Justice and gallows! It's not bad! You might say it's even pretty good! So it would seem, Dr. Nielsen, 'the humble nameless legionnaire without rank,' is against my having a statue! Favorites, crawlers, court jesters! How pathetic! No, writing that nonsense, the man hadn't a single idea in his head! Senile dementia! The first signs of senility! Yet Nielsen's the same age as I am."

"I don't think we're here to waste our time criticizing style. The question is what are we to do?"

Silence. Barutanski got up and rang the bell by the library door. In the deep, heavily timbered framework appeared a cavalry captain in red uniform trousers and dark brown blouse. He clicked his spurs smartly.

"Good evening, Flaming! Is Dupont there?"

"No, sir! Mr. Dupont is at the opera this evening. He left the message for Your Excellency that, after the opera, he'll be at the Café Valencia. We can reach him there by telephone."

"Thank you!"

A click of spurs and the red-trousered captain vanished.

"And what do you want Dupont for? I'd bet my life he's working for some foreign service!"

"You're a fool! Dupont's the one man who is beginning to understand what's going on. He spent the whole of last evening with Nielsen and didn't say a word to me about the pamphlet! It's impossible that it hadn't been written by last night! In any case, what of it? What's your opinion about it all?"

Georgis rose and stood to attention in front of his commandant at the regulation distance of three paces. (It was his habit to behave with such pathetic ceremony whenever it was a matter of making a decision.)

"So, sir, I would suggest the following: I'll visit this gentleman and demand that within the next forty-eight hours, on his own initiative, he publish a statement by which he regrets et cetera, et cetera. The statement to be published in all the Blitwanen dailies at his expense."

"He won't agree to that!"

"That's up to him! I hope I'll manage to explain to him that it'll certainly be far less an evil for him to have it published than to have a different statement published which might result et cetera, et cetera."

"He was married once. What happened to his wife?"

"She's living somewhere abroad. In Berlin, I think."

"On what?"

"I think she runs a photography studio."

"Apart from that? Who's he friendly with?"

"He moved in a circle of people around Rayevski. But lately he hasn't been seen there. He meets some young folk in cafés. Oh yes, and Olaf Knutson."

"What does he do for women?"

"I don't know. There was talk that he was engaged to Karin Michelson."

"To what Michelson?"

"To Karin Michelson! General Michelson's widow!"

"What, to our Michelson?"

"Yes. The Karin Michelson who works in the correspondence department of your Civil Office."

"Oh, that business is still going on, is it?"

"I suppose it is!"

"That's rather inconvenient."

"That lady needs to take the consequences! That's up to her. But we're not talking about her, but about him. What am I to do with him? Am I to take him an 'open' reply to his 'open' letter?"

"Do what you like."

"*Pleins pouvoirs?*"

Barutanski waved a hand and Georgis withdrew. Silently.

CHAPTER 2

Colonel Barutanski's Reply

Major Georgis appeared the next evening at Dr. Nielsen's, just as the first darkness was beginning to settle in the corners of the room. At dusk Major Georgis made his appearance in Nielsen's courtyard-facing flat, but did not arrive unannounced. Exactly at midday he had inquired by telephone whether the doctor would find it convenient to receive him on a private matter. On a private matter but, more or less, one of principle, and, although it affected no one but him, Major Georgis, personally, on the other hand it was not so unintriguing as not to interest a man who, like Dr. Nielsen, above all, dealt with public matters and social problems which, after all, touched upon our Blitvinian community as such, did they not, ha, ha!

When the telephone rang and Dr. Nielsen heard Georgis's nervous laughter, it became immediately obvious to him that matters were taking a serious turn. It was everything he might have expected from Barutanski. Nielsen had known Georgis personally from his Legion days. He knew that Georgis, sometime between 1917 and '18, had been condemned to death either by the Hunnish or Ingermanlandish military authorities and that he'd managed to escape in unusually dramatic circumstances from a Blitvinian prison on the eve of his execution, and later, during the peasant *Schweinerei* of Muzhikovski's parliamentary government, he'd taken a shot at a senator and was condemned to several years' imprisonment, but had escaped abroad where, in America, he'd survived by selling various wares, including even ice cream, and then, after Barutanski's coup, had returned to Blitva and now hung around Beauregard as the executioner and fulfiller of the tyrant's will. All those corpses on fogbound Blitvinian railway lines, the fateful deaths of unknown and nameless people without identity, suicides in detention, that mysterious Blitvinian performance which was known to be under Georgis's direction and a part of his dramatic repertoire—all this was the realization of the personal schemes of this major, whom a French journalist once honored with the adjective *néfaste*! At one time there were rumors in the cafés that Georgis was destined for a higher post, but nothing came of them. He gained his majority, was put on the retired list, and, after the killing of Kavalierski, went abroad only, suddenly, to return and now gambled, drank, and was well supplied with money, and, according to the ladies of the nightclubs, was generous, since, apparently, he had a cut in the state-supported Beetex.

It was dusk. Dr. Nielsen was sitting by the open window of a downstairs room in his flat, listening to the startled chirruping of the sparrows in the top of an old lime tree. There were such frightened chirpings from this tiny sparrow synagogue, as though in this nervous ornithological gathering some unusual event were taking place. Fear at the thought of autumn winds, or perhaps at the appearance of a sparrow hawk above the roofs.

The misgivings of birds are multifarious and highly sophisticated, Nielsen mused. There are cats, hawks, children, winds, rain, all sorts of climatic problems. What must a swallow feel when it's over the open, rough, gray, and foggy sea on its way from Blitva to Egypt, and does it, one might ask, suffer from pneumonia? Do swallows ever die of pneumonia?

A knock.

Silently as a cat, Georgis appeared at Nielsen's door. The entrance to Nielsen's flat was through a long corridor which was not locked. At the end of it a dental technician of doubtful qualifications had his surgery. Georgis went up to Nielsen with a show of amicability, clicking his heels with exact military etiquette and shaking hands with him as with an old acquaintance and legionnaire comrade. His bow was unusually respectful. He bowed almost horizontally at the waist, and this was perhaps his only sign of nerves. His bow was rather too deep. Overdone. Like a puppet! Like a clockwork puppet!

This one bows like a real diplomat, Dr. Nielsen thought, stretching his hand to this alien with the light green eyes, so light green that they seemed phosphorescent. He goes silently on rubber soles, but his eyes gleam like those of a lynx. He's a dangerous animal!

"Please, sit down, Major. What can I do for you? Glad to see you! A cigarette, perhaps?"

Georgis clicked his heels once more, bowed, but the speed of his bow was the same (just as hasty, just as mechanical), only its depth was rather less, perhaps slightly less nervous. He lit a cigarette, sat down, and, still without saying a word, examining the furniture in Nielsen's room with the greatest of interest, exhaled intermittently.

"You've a lot of pictures, Doctor! They're Knutson's, aren't they? I've no understanding for paintings! But I do know Knutson personally. An interesting and extremely educated man! A man of parts! Not the sort of person you meet every day. A while ago when, as the academic Rayevski's assistant, he was modeling the Commandant I had the opportunity, at Beauregard, of hearing him explain various questions in an unusual and original manner. He's certainly intellectually more interesting than the maestro Rayevski. Rayevski has too little to say. I think Knutson's influence on Rayevski should not be underestimated as is the case *en général*. Of course, you understand these things better than I do! I'm a pure layman in these matters! Are those fish Knutson's too?"

"No, they're by Jensen."

"Jensen? I've never heard of him."

"Never heard of him? He's the son of Jensen the editor."

"Of what Jensen?"

"Jensen the editor, who 'died in prison.'"

"Oh, him? So his son is a painter? That's interesting. Very interesting. It's strange what happened to his father. The man got periostitis overnight. They sent for a dentist to extract a tooth, and, bloody bad luck, he got sepsis and died of a normal inflammation of the periosteum."

"Yes, only Jensen got his periostitis in detention, but he 'died' in the nick."

"Yes, but you think, Doctor, that people don't get a toothache in detention? Just because a man's under arrest doesn't give him immunity against periostitis. So his son's a painter, is he? Well, that I didn't know! That's interesting. And where's this son of Jensen living?"

"In Paris."

"In Paris! Of course, naturally, one can see it in his pictures. The Parisian school. Even I can see that: pure Paris! Vlaminck, pure Vlaminck! Those dark, stormy clouds in the background, that's Vlaminck. But, unless I'm mistaken, there is a general alert out for that young Jensen. He was involved in an attempted assassination at the Boule Blanche in the rue de Vaugirard, when that Armenian took a shot at the Commandant. That Jensen from the Boule Blanche is a subtle, dangerous, and cunning customer! 'Painter!' 'A good painter!' All honor to talent! I had no clue that in the case of Jensen's son we were dealing with an artistic talent! A criminal type, however you look at it!"

"I don't know. General alerts aren't my métier, Major. Pictures are pictures, politics are politics!"

As if he hadn't heard Nielsen's last remark, Major Georgis continued to admire the taste of Nielsen's *intérieur,* of his pictures and sculptures, the entire valuable collection that so well represented the high European standard of modern Blitvinian artistic culture!

"By the way, I don't know if you remember, you've probably forgotten it, but this isn't the first time I've been in your home! It must be three or four years ago that one morning we dropped in on you for coffee! It was a mad carnival night! Your wife was dressed as a Carmelite nun, and I was as pissed as a newt. I have a strange, unusual characteristic. When I'm drunk, I get an uncanny, peculiar ability: an utterly clear, perceptive, indeed lucid memory! I could quote you now every single word, as if it were on a phonograph! You were talking about how in today's peripheral civilizations, as, for instance, our small, provincial Blitvinian civilization, everything is imitated. They imitate machines, umbrellas, prayer books, sonnets, gadgets, institutions, sabers, guns—everything's imitated, that's what you said then, very wittily and, I must admit, extremely logically, that it was quite right and proper that things should be imitated. And after all, there's nothing in the world that can't be imitated, adapted, and learned by heart in its best version: postage stamps, highway codes, pathological anatomy, various ideologies, sonnets, or umbrellas. What of it! But this apish imitation—you actually deigned to use such a coarse expression—such an apish imitation, which in the mouths of common people is expressed as 'our original Blitvinian, autochthonic culture,' or 'the level of our Western culture,' all this proves only one thing, that even the European models on which our Blitvinian ersatz is based have little meaning, and, taking it all together, it's just a common sale of flea-market rejects, a fraud, in other words, making a quid or two and trading in toilet bowls wholesale and retail for the blacks and Blitvinian natives. You spoke generally about the internal value of various civilizations and portrayed the whole of Europe as a building of clay, of canvas and boards, like some pavilion erected ad hoc for some exhibition, which, with its pseudomonumentalism, represents in fact a clumsy cultural scandal that has no other purpose than to serve as a roof for some industrial fair under which are exhibited various examples of rejects for the use of native, black, Hunnish, Blitvinian civilizations! You even talked about wars between these pseudocivilizations, based as they are on interest alone, and which are constructed entirely for the purpose of falling victim to profitable destruction! Today I couldn't really say what was the real sense of what you said, nor could I tell you now which of your arguments were so convincing that everything that exists 'as imitation is unworthy to exist as imitation,' since 'the imitation of a model that is, in itself, no more that just another example of a reject for third-class Blitvinian and Hunnish so-called civilizations . . .' and I don't know what it was you said that evening that so struck me, but I do remember that long after that carnival night, all I could see everywhere were just reject buildings and reject goods. All our monumental buildings looked like imitations, simple imitations made of clay and wattles, wretched imitations of true buildings which in themselves are nothing but bluff, cheat, and rejects, and all our gadgets, our Blitvinian umbrellas and our Blitvinian prayer books, had no sense, since they were simply copies of copies, and so on and so forth, and that was the point of it, that your vague conclusion that made such an impact on me, so wrapped me in its coils, like an anaconda, so crushed me that all I could see in everything was falsehood, forgeries, and surrogates. . . . Yes, that night you so fascinated me with your negative views that I was really gripped by the serpentine, carnival coilings of what we might call your pessimism! You really do possess an extraordinarily subtle gift, and that is the unusual, the quite exceptional, conviction of your eloquence and its ability to act with such power! You write a quite ordinary, banal, everyday word in one of your articles, for instance: 'gallows.' And those gallows of yours have such a supernatural effect on me that I can see myself hanging there on your gallows like a dead object. The wind's playing with my honorable self and I dangle thirty centimeters above the ground, according to the strict rule of the Blitvinian criminal code, thirty centimeters exactly, and one can hear a shepherd's pipe from the nearby woods. A Blitvinian pastoral, an idyll."

After some moments' silence, Georgis took on a more serious expression, frowned, and it looked as though, without further conventional politeness, he was prepared to come to the point, but instead he appeared to change his mind, got up, walked down the room, stopped in front of Jensen's fish, lit a cigarette, and then suddenly asked for a glass of water.

Nielsen lived alone, without servants. While he was in the kitchen, on the other side of the long corridor, pouring a glass of water, Major Georgis concluded that this was the best moment for what had to happen, to take place, immediately, as soon as Nielsen's figure, with the glass of water on a silver tray, appeared in the doorway.

The dental technician has locked his surgery, Georgis observed to himself; the house is completely empty, but the window's open. That's no good—the shot'll echo in the yard. I'd better shut the window.

At once, following the irresistible logic of his carnivorous instinct, Georgis went up to the window to close it, when from down in the graying dusk came the voice of somebody from under the window asking whether Dr. Nielsen was at home.

"What do you want?"

"I am from the police!"

"What's the matter?"

"Nothing! A summons regarding sending printed matter abroad!"

"Doctor! The police want you!" Major Georgis called to Nielsen in the kitchen, closing the window as had been his original plan. But at that very moment, a better idea occurred to him: Better to leave it, this evening! That copper's seen him anyway, and some of

59

the old women will have noticed him, because he spends whole nights writing by his window. And after all, it might be better to have a few more words with the man! The thing needs discussing. Perhaps we might find a way out?

Nielsen returned, bearing the summons and a glass of water, surprised that Georgis had closed the window.

"Ah, you shut the window?"

"Yes, Doctor, I took the liberty! These evening chills play hell with us old sufferers from rheumatism. Forgive me! As soon as the sun sets you can feel the temperature fall as much as seven or eight degrees. Later on you don't notice it so much."

"By all means! But I had the impression you were closing the window to muffle the sound."

"What sound?"

"The sound of the shot, Major! Your revolver shot! What's the point of these stupid games, Georgis? You're here to get a statement from me regarding my 'Open Letter' to Barutanski—in other words, to put it succinctly, to liquidate me."

"Oh no, Doctor. I just came to have a few words with you. And to tell you the truth, I find it most convenient that you've raised the subject of your letter to the Commandant." (It was the third time that evening that he'd referred to Barutanski theatrically as the Commandant. That term created a sort of intimate, mystical link between comrades, for whom the Commandant was a mutual memory of the war and a symbol of Blitva.)

As an old fencer, Georgis preferred to speak openly, eye to eye. Man to man, like a soldier. Come what may. Georgis had only one thing to say to Nielsen, that he considered him one hundred percent a man, a person who had found himself, and that, among the half persons of Blitva, was extremely hard to find. In Blitva we simply lacked real men. People were not whole! And where could whole persons develop in such conditions? One might think of

Nielsen as one wished, but one thing had to be admitted, without any trace of flattery: Nielsen was no coward! For when anyone was as isolated as he, as helpless, when a man was as sober, logical, as clear-sightedly aware of his isolation, when he so resignedly and calmly proclaimed his political views, so resignedly conscious of the dangerous consequences of such an adventure, then he, Major Georgis, an old soldier and campaigner, a man who had some personal experience of what it meant to look death in the eye, he, a soldier, a major, had to admit without reservation that he was impressed! Out of solidarity, such as only gamblers can feel, he, Georgis, felt a need to show his respect, to click his heels, and, without further words, to express all honor to him! And, to begin with, he felt the need to say a few words about himself, about his failed and totally wasted life, his experiences, his feelings, for with whom could a man discuss such matters other than with a man who was a hundred percent a man? Complete, of one piece—a real man!

"Always, from my earliest childhood, I've hated everything that was boring, gray. The empty, senseless boozing of young men (with a Virginia cigarette hanging from their mouths, just to show the local bourgeoisie how sophisticated we were), and all you'd hear in our company were tales of unsuccessful adventures with other men's wives. You wouldn't believe me, Doctor, but I swear to you on my mother's grave that I hadn't slept with a woman until I was twenty-seven. By nature I'm a Puritan! The gossip, the lies that such-and-such was sleeping with two women, that another lived with boys, and that another was an informant for the Hunnish police—all this seemed to me a lot of malicious imaginings. It was only in the Legion that I began to grasp what it meant when someone called someone else a cad! Believe you me, I was born naive, and I don't know whether you'll believe me, but I killed poor Violetta, that famous singer Hellmuth-Endres, simply because I discovered that she was the paid agent of the Aragon governor. You must remember that particular scandal? When I barricaded myself in her flat and the shooting went on all night? But I held out against a whole unit of the Imperial Gendarmerie entirely on my own and then slid to the ground via the lightning rod of the neighboring house and into a conservatory. Do you remember the uproar there was about that whore? The whole of Blitva raised hell because I'd cut the throat of the 'Blitvinian Nightingale,' the famous Violetta Endres, but what were the facts? That cow was an informant. I'm telling you, in general, our Blitvinian intelligentsia is such a load of rubbish that it isn't worth risking anything for the sake of such human material! It's trash, as you very well know, stinking street trash! Anyone who has ever truly mixed with our girls (whose only sensation is another's legal separation), any who has slept his fill with our stinking, filthy ladies, who has dribbled, drinking *Bruderschaft* with our academically educated lot, all he's learned from these obedient civil-servant dogs is that an average Blitvinian quasi intellectual can deceive our uneducated and illiterate public with his academic rank, but beside all the obtrusive blathering and prattle and self-satisfied exaggeration of the importance of some tiny and absolutely unimportant details regarding the significance of his totally trivial self (for example, what do X and Y think of him?) is in general just an obedient dog and, in return for a monthly salary of two and a half thousand Blitvinian lei, is ready to be silent to the grave with his tail between his legs. To look among these low-class windbags, these guitarists, these wankers, madmen, scribblers, and informants, in this mud of ours, for the type of 'A Man,' a man in the noble sense of the word, 'a man' as a concept to be written with a capital letter, this is a false assumption, my dear doctor! This our Blitvinian rubbish doesn't know itself what it wants. It has no idea of any essential truths. It's a pathetic lousy mob! And the apes deceive themselves with some mysterious half-magical lies about so-called freedom, about which they have no clue and in which, as a realizable program, nobody believes and, in general, in this our tangle of malice, muddle, and petty jealousies, there's no sense wasting one's time, and anyone who hasn't learned to despise it, spit on it, is not an intelligent man. And that's why you surprise me, my dear Nielsen."

"I don't understand a word of what you're saying. Why should you be surprised at me and why show such hypersensitive concern for my person? And why, in any case, this cascade of verbiage?"

"Of course you don't understand me! You take everything too simplistically! For you I'm just a bandit, a paid assassin from an Italian opera, a criminal! Barutanski's the same: a criminal, a mega-lomaniac. You're wrong on both counts, and even if you weren't, you're forgetting that the truth does not consist solely of two con-cepts: yes and no. It involves an entire scale of nuances. Small yeses and small noes. It's a piano that may be well played by him who has an ear for such nuances, if you understand my meaning, Doctor. You need to take us at our word, that all our sympathies are on your side. For instance, Barutanski, talking about you only today, his voice trembled with sentimentality, warmth, and human feel-ing! I came to prove to you that we're human beings! That we un-derstand everything that's human!"

"You're neither people, nor nonpeople, nor half people, nor su-perpeople, but just ordinary fools without imagination! That's what you are!"

"Is that so? Well, you should know that we 'fools without imagi-nation' possess, in this country of one million seven hundred thou-sand citizens, more than four hundred thousand registered mem-bers of the Legion and, in Blitwanen alone, seven thousand paid informants, one of whom is Mrs. Michelson, General Michelson's widow."

Nielsen lit a cigarette and laughed sarcastically. "Don't be funny, Georgis! This evening's not the first time I've had a conversation

with a police agent! If you'd used that trick in some provincial dancing school like a drawing-room intriguer in a provincial comedy . . ."

"Here you are, then!" Georgis threw a manuscript onto the table
in front of Nielsen. It was a draft written in Mrs. Michelson's
handwriting and rather nervously crossed out in many places.

It was Nielsen's first draft for his "Open Letter" to Barutanski
which he'd written in the Hotel Meduza in Koromandia two or
three weeks before, during a trip with Mrs. Michelson. There
could be no doubt: it was Nielsen's draft of the "Open Letter"
which Mrs. Michelson had copied out in her own hand. It was her
handwriting and her violet ink. It all had the weight of a trump
card in the game.

"Don't be ridiculous! All this doesn't mean that it has to be Mrs.
Michelson!" Nielsen repeated the phrase like a gramophone record.
"This still is no proof of the guilt of the lady under discussion."

Georgis laughed aloud. Sincerely. Then he got up and, with an
expression of friendly concern, almost amicably tapped Nielsen on
the shoulder. "Oh, my dear doctor! You really are a naive and innocent child! I was as silly as you are today at the age of twenty-
seven! And today, looking back, I see myself as I was then, as an
immature young fool! In Blitva, my dear fellow, which is ruled by
'a Tartar upstart,' 'a vampire-tyrant armed with knout and revolver' such as Barutanski, here a true rebel who is not 'a fool
without imagination' shouldn't have a lady friend who is in the
confidential service of that same vampire! It's pathetic and childish. Dim-witted. That's no way of pursuing successful politics!
And I can tell you that this so-called Open Letter of yours would
never have been printed had not Barutanski wished it. I don't
know why he's so sentimental about you. Such childish weaknesses always lead to trouble. An eye for an eye, that is the only
true politics, and not an album of childish memories of Mama and
jam."

"Yes, indeed, an eye for an eye, headless bodies on railway tracks, dead men without identity—is that what politics is for you? Is politics in Blitva to consist of placing microphones in every lovers' bed?"

"Are we then to allow ourselves to be sent to the gallows, in the sense of your naive 'Open Letter'? For God's sake! And if it's a matter of one of us falling, then I guarantee you that you'll finish with a bullet hole in your coat before I will, do you understand me?"

"To me, that's a matter of sheer indifference, as you've had a chance of seeing!" Nielsen replied. "I stand for a principle, and not myself and my personal interests. I too, had I wished, could have acted to promote my personal interests. I think you have no doubts about that, do you? But in this matter I pay no regard to myself! It is not 'I' who figure in this matter, but the more powerful truths than those concerning our subjective will. It was high time that someone spoke out in the name of Blitva's trampled human dignity!"

"What 'trampled Blitva dignity'? Come off it! That's a petit bourgeois prejudice. Man as such in nature, in the animal world, doesn't exist. There are different attitudes between individuals: One lot wants to send the other lot to the gallows. Beneath the gallows on which one's enemy swings one gets an excellent appetite. Nowhere does one enjoy such a good meal washed down with a good burgundy as when sitting on an enemy's grave. And to have such a repast over Barutanski's grave, that's your ideal! And, in any case, why these humanistic phrases? You'll allow me to shoot you before you cut my throat, and that's what you've decided; if you haven't, then why this comedy with the 'Open Letter,' where you demand that Blitva hand us over to the executioner. I like those sorts of defenders of humanism, whose only logic is the gallows. Or even 'the butcher's block'! The place for rogues, they say, is under the axe! But you, you see, are no rogue, but just a fool! You've climbed onto the highest tower of your private, subjective megalomania and there you want to organize a mass jumping from the tower, out of human-istic solidarity with a liquidated adventurer as was Kavalierski. The only Blitvinian who so far has understood you in your noble, ethical enthusiasm is Mrs. Karin Michelson. And as soon as she'd copied that stupid *J'accuse* . . . of yours, there was a copy of it on my desk that same evening. And I tell you, if Barutanski hadn't opposed it so energetically, you'd long ago have appeared in the *Blitwanen Tig-dende* in the guise of domestic news about a funeral. You're getting excited about Kavalierski? You call his death 'a base murder'? But I tell you: Kavalierski was a criminal and deserved no better fate. And I'll tell you this too, that I'm not worried about Barutanski! I don't give a damn for anyone! Not for you, not for me, not for anyone! And be so kind as to take note of this: What is demanded of you in this matter is a withdrawal! How you'll get yourself out of this mess is your problem! You've got just one chance. Barutanski has a weak-ness for you! He's never forgotten your mother's jam! No definite decision has been reached. So be so kind as to understand: Either an announcement in the newspapers that the 'Open Letter' has been forged without your knowledge, or, if you will, a short trip abroad, or, if you're against going abroad, then the third, for you certainly the most unpleasant, solution, and that is that we shall, by a bizarre set of circumstances (regardless of whether your window is open or not), be forced to place the whole 'open question' of your 'Open Letter' in the hands of your legal heirs," Georgis finished.

"I have no legal heirs."

"There's not a man alive in Blitva who has no legal heirs and, after you, there'll always be someone who'll be delighted to cash in your insurance. If you aren't insured, you'd be doing your legal heirs a considerable service to insure yourself. And if possible, to-morrow! That would be an excellent move! Good night!"

CHAPTER 3

Panic

This afternoon, in the large hall of the Blitvinian Academy of Arts and Sciences, you, Roman Rayevski, will be proclaimed by the highest representatives of Blitvinian society the official candidate for the position of president of the Republic of Blitva. Since there is no doubt that you agreed to this nomination as a pawn in the hands of Kristian Barutanski, the real despot of Blitva, and since it is known to us all that this man, by his coup of December 25, took power into his own hands, having killed the president of the Republic, Professor Sandersen, and the president of the democratic parliamentary government, Muzhikovski, your decision (to accept this, the highest honor in Blitva, from the hands of a murderer) absolves me from even the slightest consideration that I might have felt for your talent and for your name. I feel the necessity to state to your face certain frank and sincere words . . .

For the thirty-third time, Nielsen began to draft this, his proclamation, his "Open Letter" to Roman Rayevski, feeling he lacked the strength to gather his thoughts, feeling that every word was in the wrong place, that it sounded wrong, unconvincing, empty, silly, indeed purely idiotic!

For the thirty-third time, he sat at his desk to write, to announce, to tell the people around him that he had been banned, blackmailed, condemned to death, that he would be shot like a mad dog. His intention was to tell his fellow citizens how Georgis had visited him at his home and threatened his liquidation. But when he tried to define, formulate, portray, announce it, it all seemed empty and every word rang like the commonest, most everyday cliché.

These are mere phrases! Am I going to fight against these black-guards with mere clichés? Nielsen asked himself. But on the other hand, if I let them shoot me without any protest, that too would be stupid! "This afternoon, in the large hall of the Blitvinian Academy of Arts and Sciences, you, Roman Rayevski, will be proclaimed by the highest representatives of Blitvinian society—since there is no doubt—and since it is known to all of us—and since—having killed the president and the president—this et cetera, et cetera . . ." No! No way! The false pathos of a badly written business letter, "since, since, since, having," it all sounds too legal—it has no strength, no vitality, no truth—it's mere phrases, and in the first person at that. I, I, and again I think, I consider, I'm shitting my pants. And what about "we"? We all? Who are this "we all"? And why "we"?

For the thirty-third time, Nielsen got up from his desk and paced the room from wall to wall, from window to door, lit a cigarette, stubbed it out, lit another, returned to the window, opened it and stood there in the square of light, listening to the rain echoing down the gutters, and there, somewhere high above the roofs, came the crying calls of cranes. It was the dense, glycerine, foggy Blitvinian night that was crying in the darkness, and that song of the cranes in the heights far above all that was crushed and petty, confused, wounded, trampled, and human, the strange vertical of those bird voices out of the dark, their immense height, comforted Nielsen, and the damp night fog came to him like a strange and calming remedy, that the bird voices had carried the dark space of his depression away on their wings, as if something had opened up, freeing him from pressure, that life was not the Blitvinian criminality, but the song of the migrating birds, above all state frontiers, out of reach of any Barutanski, a song that told how life did not have to be a stupid and limited phrase!

The phrase had dominated all written documents of human civilization for centuries! The phrase was not even a forged banality. The phrase was not even distorted reality. The phrase was not a wrong expression in the wrong place. The phrase was the schematized murder of every noble human impulse. The phrase was lethal, a stupid liquidation of human intelligence! The phrase was death! "We," "I," "if," "how," "since"—all mere words! But here it wasn't a matter of words, but of to be or not to be! Of revolvers! Of life or death!

Carried away in his thoughts by his convincing concept of the meaninglessness of phrases in that given moment, Nielsen gave a start instinctively, like an animal, feeling that, framed as he was in the lighted window, somebody was watching him out of the darkness. Nielsen's large, long shadow, which to the height of a man's waist fell across the wall of a locked warehouse on the other side of the courtyard, swayed over the lighted window like a dark giant, and, as he jumped hysterically out of the sheaf of light from the window, a cat, hypnotized by the reflection from the lamp, froze for a second and then, with a panic-stricken leap, vanished into the darkness.

So that's it! I've come down to being scared of cats! Nielsen thought. And that should be told to future generations: that there was a time when mankind was taken over by gorillas and such panic-stricken fear was driven into the bones of everyone to the extent that even the boldest spirits dared write nothing except ordinary, everyday phrases, and their hearts throbbed in their throats and their fingers sweated cold with fear at the look of a cat. Shame on the human race!

From fear, nerves, disgust, or God knows what, Dr. Niels Nielsen was falling apart more and more with each day, and all he felt was that he was disintegrating, spilling out, pouring on all sides like a torn sack, that he was losing control over himself, that he no longer possessed the strength to restrain himself but was running astray, rolling like a cart down a steep hill without horse or brake, and it seemed pretty certain that this hectic career would end somewhere in a ditch. The final chapter was approaching with mathematical precision: a bullet in the head, a grave, the end.

Nielsen sat in a café, surrounded by newspapers. There was the official *Blitvinian Gazette*, the *Letter*, the *Blitva Herald*, *Blitwanen Tigdende*. He had the whole Blitvinian press in front of him, and each and every paper carried what was, at first glance, an unimportant, everyday piece of news, clearly edited for all the press in the form of a semiofficial announcement.

Mysterious death. On the night of Friday/Saturday on the road leading from Turul Park under the old mills, a twenty-nine-year-old senior law student, F. Kulinis, presently employed by the Blitvinian civil airport, was found dead. He was holding an empty automatic, and examination revealed that all six bullets had been fired. Kulinis was killed by a bullet in the back of the head and therefore any thought of suicide is eliminated. In the grass beside the body was found a silver case with a manicure set. The case was lined with dark blue velvet, and on its lid was a crest with a monogram M. S. The police have carried out a strict inquiry in order to trace the cause of this crime. Several arrests have been made, but for the time being, in the interests of the inquiry, no names will be published.

In less than three or four weeks, in these same newspapers, in that repulsive *Tigdende*, in that Masonic *Herald*, in that hateful *Gazette*, in that stinking and corrupt *Lampe de fort*, there would be a similar item of local news concerning the suicide of the well-known publicist Nielsen.

In the reeds of Ankersgarden the body of Dr. Nielsen, editor and publisher of the political and cultural review the Tribune, *has been found. It would appear he sought refuge in death during a moment of mental disturbance, since definite signs of imbalance have lately been noted in his behavior.*

Or perhaps like this:

It is reported from the Blatvian frontier that in Halompestis, in the Hotel Hunnia, the Blitvinian publicist Nielsen has committed suicide. He had gone to Halompestis . . .

No! That doesn't make sense. How could they know about my journey to Halompestis? Better this way:

Returning home to his flat on February 11th Street, Dr. Nielsen was attacked by two unknown pedestrians with iron bars and . . . And so on and so forth. *The police have managed to trace his attackers.*

No! Most likely would be this way:

Yesterday, in his home, Dr. Nielsen was murdered . . .

Who would kill Dr. Nielsen? An unknown pedestrian?

An unknown man knocked on the door of Dr. Nielsen's flat. Neighbors had noticed, during the last few days, that Dr. Nielsen's flat . . . No! That's too much a cliché. Better this way:

Suicide in detention. Dr. Nielsen, whom the state prosecutor had committed to detention on the basis of paragraphs this and that, was found hanging . . .

or:

Dr. Nielsen threw himself from the third story of the court building.

or:

Body on railway line! His identity? A foggy morning. Photographers. Photograph in the *Blitva Herald* on the third page with a sentimental obituary: *The author of a book on Blitvinian law, a witty conversationalist and publicist of European reputation, Dr. Nielsen threw himself under the engine of the express train Ankersgarden-Berolinen . . .*

And what is most amusing is that the average Blitvinian, that is the 1.7 million Baltrushaitises, Vasilinises, Swensens, Nielsens, Kristiansens, Agnises, Buryansens, Armstrongs, any of these, God's ruminants, who believe that the hand of the Lord has endowed our Blitva with hops, wheat, and sugar beet, honey and fish oil simply in order that these Swensens and Baltrushaitises may play bridge and buy expensive foreign cars abroad, will read this local news concerning the suicide of Dr. Nielsen with perfect equanimity. The mechanism of so-called civil public opinion will buzz in their brains like a chocolate vending machine at a station and their bourgeois awareness will receive the following impressions: Thank God, the fate of our homeland, Blitva, is in safe hands and we, as loyal citizens, should preserve complete calm, no matter what happens!

This unhappy, eternal, and truly tragic "no matter what" has dominated Blitva for the last thousand years, and the fate of our homeland has been in "safe" and "iron" hands more than a thousand years, but someone whose head is at risk and therefore is unable to preserve his absolute calm, since this "no matter what" for him means certain death, such an individual is "a foreign agent," in other words, a blind, destructive, and mercenary weapon in the hands of the enemy, and should be crushed. These stupid slogans concerning "destructive, mercenary, and foreign" agents have been employed in Blitva for several decades!

That conversation with the head of department and member of the Academy, the historiographer, the pride of Blitvinian historians, the author of a monograph on Barutanski and on the Blitvinian kings of the early Middle Ages, Dr. Fernandis, regarding what should be the task of the modern Blitvinian historiographer:

"You, Doctor, have written about your Blitvinian kings so tendentiously that one might think they were organized members of Barutanski's political party."

"And you, my dear fellow, consider Blitvinian affairs as though you were a paid foreign agent. Everything that is 'ours' for you isn't worth spitting on! Such views are, more or less, a Hunnish-Blatvian import! What we need today is not criticism but justification."

"Where justifications are concerned, you're a specialist! Who wrote an apology for the Hunnish Empire? I or you?"

"Money will do anything in Blitva, my dear fellow! Convictions change like the fashions in women's hats! I'm not a follower of fashion myself! I stick to my own conviction: the justification of our country. And you are a traitor!"

What did it mean to be born in Blitva and live only so as to become the subject of a dry announcement to the Blitvinian public, an item of local news in the *Blitwanen Tigdende,* which on page one carried an interview with the newly appointed minister of the interior, His Excellency Mr. Rekyavinis, who stated to our correspondent: *Only a few days ago I took over the portfolio of the Ministry of the Interior and have not yet had time to review the state of affairs in that ministry. My policy, in two or three words, is the setting up of legal authority, order, work, and law, internal peace, public security, good and speedy and reliable government, the maintenance of peace and order, respect for authority, order, work, and the law, etc.*

Like an old domino, the worn rectangles of political phrases clicked on the green cloth of the Blitvinian casino and, in this stinking gambling house, Niels Nielsen was fated to kick the bucket with a hole in his skull under the protection of the "legal power" of Mr. Rekyavinis, the European guarantor of Blitvinian internal peace, of Blitvinian public security, and of speedy and reliable government.

Under Nielsen there vibrated the mysterious magnetic pole of death, and the fairly tangled and confused quantity of Blitvinian reality began to waver with ever more agitated wavering: every tiniest particle, all the components of the whole, all phenomena, all this both excited and scared him and, in the frightening chaos of things and concepts, Nielsen began to feel a loss of equilibrium. He felt himself sinking. Around him there crawled a mass of political lizards, an obstetrician founding the old Blitvinian church against the Vatican's will, Blitvinian mustard sold abroad, a fool purchasing on the international intellectual market of fleas and umbrellas, for two or three coins, some Western European intelligence and passed this small and worn coinage on the Blitvinian stock exchange to the point of triumphant uproar. The national spirit moved through Blitva like a gingerbread cake decorated with ribbons, mirrors, and tin rosemary leaves, and, in all this hubbub, in the old theater on the Petris Promenade they were presenting Sidney Jones's *Geisha:* "Trata-rata, trata-rata, tsin, tsin, tsin." The theater was sold out, and none of the public realized that Nielsen was condemned to death by a lot of the most ordinary burglars, and what was most interesting, nobody would come to his aid, even if during the intermission between the second and the third acts of *The Geisha* it was publicly announced. Major Georgis was lying in wait for him and would shoot him like a dog! What of it? People would go on gnawing their praline and listening to Sidney Jones's *Geisha:* "Trata-rata, tsin, tsin, tsin!" What could Dr. Fernandis say or do about it all? Thank God! We've got rid of a foreign agent! One less destructive element in Blitva—good!

On the Blitvinian crest, a panther rampant holding in its right paw a double Levantine cross and a golden rose. At the bottom of this label for very sweet Blitvinian beer, dressed in purple and ermine, Barutanski slaughtered his opponents. One of these bleeding heads was that of Niels Nielsen, a nervous moron who tilted at windmills, and the ghostly Blitvinian windmills had caught him in their sails and were whirling him around and around and it would all end as a joke rather than as a tragedy. His end would be futile and, what was sadder, stupid! All was in the hands of Barutanski!

Barutanski and Nielsen sat together in class 7B of the Blitvinian-Hunnish high school in the old fortress, in the left-hand row in the next-to-last bench by the window. When one stood up, one could see through the window the yellow, muddy Blitva River meandering among the willow trees, and the steam from a locomotive vanishing into the fog on the Ankersgarden line, crossing the Blitwanen bridge in the distance. Barutanski had appeared one day at the Blitvinian school in 7B at the beginning of the second semester, having been thrown out of the Ankersgarden high school and expelled from all other Hunnish secondary schools because of a very complex and obscure incident: an offense against discipline, based on the findings of a police search. In 7B a growing unrest was felt: it was the time of great and bloody battles, the whole of the Karabaltic was shaking to its foundations. In 7B the first cigarettes and the first sexual illnesses had long ceased to be a mysterious question, as two or three years ago, when they read Ovid, and the most popular writer in the class was Petronius, who were certainly not read for scholarly reasons as, indeed, was Horace, the most tedious poet on God's earth. Someone in the secondhand bookshop on Jesuit Street, near the old cathedral, had found a seventeenth-centry Venetian edition of Petronius's *Satires* with illustrations, and that book then circulated through the class as though it were a prayer book and a final hope that life, nonetheless, would not be as boring as Horace or Greek irregular verbs, when such witty civilizations had existed, when a clay phallus served as an oil lamp at the front door of reputable Roman houses. At that time, ghosts began to circle around 7B, two dangerous panthers lurking about the cackling intellectual boyish henhouse: Stirner and Marx. From the street penetrated the roar of a mortally wounded monster: the captivated and despised Blitvinian people.

There had been expulsions from the class for theft, for free-thinking; in other words, for publicly declared atheistic convictions, and boys two or three years older were already serving in the imperial Aragon cavalry as uhlan cadets. They drank beer publicly in the beer halls, sat provocatively at the windows of the larger cafés, drinking double jugs of beer and puffing smoke from thick cigars under the noses of their ex-professors, banging their heavy, flat cavalry sabers on the floor, like real cavalry men. And the clerics from the Catholic seminaries, the peers of these Blitvinian six-formers, also had their dramas: there were rumors that the cleric Andersen had slashed his wrists because of an unhappy love affair. Some second-rowers from 7B were known to be contributors to the liberal *Tigdende,* and, during break, the discussion was about Zola and Strindberg. Into these boyish debates someone introduced a new and unknown word: *automobile.* This object possessed, as a technical concept, the extraordinary property of traveling at the terrifying speed of 33 kilometers per hour, all on its own. With the automobile appeared yet another mysterious word: *decadence*! No one was quite clear as to what it actually meant, but it sounded lyrically obscure, and for this very reason attractive. Like a warm cat purring on a man's lap. Or like a silken veil through which could be made out the form of a young, tubercular girl, with a waist as thin as one's finger and a richly folded skirt like a gray lily that fell about her as a drape. Secession.

The case of Kristian Barutanski had a somewhat disturbing effect. Kristian Barutanski appeared in 7B at the beginning of the second semester, with a strange aureole as appears around the heads of the more exalted and select spirits. In Ankersgarden was organized the ceremonial launching of the heavy imperial battleship *Panther,* equipped in the imperial Ankersgarden arsenal, and the Grand Palatine the Imperial Prince Rainer Maria was to be present to christen this victorious triumph of the imperial Karabaltic maritime industry. An unusually widespread plot against the physical integrity of the Imperial Prince had been discovered and several hundred people in Ankersgarden had been arrested. Among that mass of innocent Blitvinian citizens was the schoolboy from the seventh grade, Kristian Barutanski. The real reason for his arrest was not known in the Blitwanen high school, but there was talk of explosives, of huge quantities of explosives, and all this took on the form of legend which arrived in the Blitwanen classrooms several weeks before Kristian made his appearance in 7B.

"Why have you changed schools?" the new head teacher, Gasparinis, inquired sternly and officiously. He was a peasant from the Mazurian marshes, a fool who, until he reached the eighth grade, had pastured goats and instinctively hated the so-called urban, well-to-do, spoiled children, since they were not fluent in Blitvinian and in their wealthy homes spoke Hunnish. Barutanski's father was an engineer in the Ankersgarden arsenal and his mother came from Kurlandia, an Ingermanlandian. Barutanski spoke Blitvinian with an Ingermanlandish accent, like someone who had learned his Blitvinian only in school.

"I asked you why have you changed schools?"

"Because I couldn't be at the top of the class!"

Laughter in the class.

Indeed, Kristian Barutanski's reply couldn't help being funny to 7B. It was known that he was a bad student and had already repeated two classes: the fifth and sixth. He had failed in his first term at Ankersgarden, from where he was expelled for taking part in the plot against the Grand Palatine, yet here he was telling Gasparinis that he'd changed schools because they hadn't made him first in his class.

"Oh, really? And what about that chocolate they found in your landlady's house?"

Silence, a pause. (There were rumors that the dynamite had been hidden in chocolate.)

"All right, then! And what did you get for the Blitvinian language?"

"Always A-minus!"

"Really? Naturally. You haven't a clue about the Blitvinian language! Who was your teacher?"

"Kraus."

"Kraus! He hasn't a clue about Blitvinian either! He comes from Kurlandia. A Schwab!"

"Yes, a Schwab of the Augsburg persuasion. A Protestant!"

Laughter in the class.

"And you? What are you?"

"I'm a Protestant too!"

"What does that mean?"

"I hate Huns! I feel like a Blitvinian! My mother tongue is Inger-manlandish, but my father is from Plavystok."

"Oh I see. A Szlachta."

"No. Blitvinian aristocrats from thirteen hundred. All the Baru-tanskis were Blitvinians!"

"Then it's doubly disgraceful that you failed in Blitvinian!"

"Kraus didn't fail me because I didn't know Blitvinian, but because I wrote in a school essay that Europe was a whore and should be shot down like a whore!"

Gasparinis rose up from his desk and covered the distance to Barutanski in a single leap. "What was that you wrote?"

"That Europe should be shot down like a whore!"

For the moment it looked as if Gasparinis, a peasant giant of a man with massive peasant hands, would smash Barutanski with a single blow. There was a pause, full of silence and anticipation.

"Sit down, Barutanski! You don't know what you've said. You ought to be ashamed of yourself!"

The night before, Nielsen had dreamt of Barutanski. Heavy, majestic fir trees were reflected in the ashy half-light, in the crystal emerald silent mirror of a deep and dark Alpine lake. It was the silence of early morning. A calm, cloudless, summer sky. A naked young woman was bathing in the clear Alpine water. A girl. A blonde. This was Europe. And Barutanski, barricaded behind bundles of newspapers, in ambush from his shelter, armed with a Hotchkiss machine gun, was aiming at this young, fair, and lovely blonde girl, and it would take only a second for the crystal emerald water to be reddened with the warm, European blood of this strange, young, golden-haired maiden.

"Hold it, for God's sake," Nielsen shouted in deadly terror, rushing madly to prevent Barutanski from opening fire. The terrain was rocky and stones rolled down the steep slope under Nielsen's feet and he was hanging over a precipice, between life and death.

"What do you want?" Barutanski turned to Nielsen, regarding him with his cold, transparent, Ingermanlandish eyes, and beneath his gaze, somewhere in the depths of the irises, Nielsen sensed the sparkle of a boyish sympathy for his person.

"There's no point. Leave it!"

As though he himself saw that there was no sense in shooting at the girl in the lake, Barutanski waved a hand and got up from the machine gun. "Got any cigarettes?"

"Yes."

"And what's happened to you? You're bleeding. Your knees are all covered with blood."

True! Nielsen's knees, trousers, and shoes were all covered with blood. His hands were bloody, the cigarettes, his shirt, everything was sticky with black greasy blood. Barutanski, pimply-faced and nearsighted, with black-rimmed spectacles and with the boyish face of a member of 7B, but completely gray haired, got up and undid one of the bales of newspaper that had served as a barricade for his Hotchkiss, and began to wrap Nielsen's open and suppurating wounds in dirty wet newspaper.

"What's the matter? There's no need, don't cry, why cry?"

Barutanski began to embrace Nielsen, trying with his thick, sensually swollen lips to suck up his tears. But it was not Barutanski. It was Europe, that young, pure, golden-haired Europe, bathed in the crystal clear emerald water, and all the terror of his deadly running along the edge of the precipice, of the dirty bale of wet newspaper,

Barutanski in his brown legionnaire greatcoat, the smell of Russian leather and tar, the ash-gray dawn of an Alpine morning, all this was spilt out in a flood of sweat, bloody mucus, tears, and other such protein. Nielsen started from this nightmarish dream, feeling his heart beating against the pillow and echoing like thunder in the mattress springs, the floorboards, the entire flat. Wet with tears, with his tongue and sweaty sleeve wiping away the saltwater that was dripping down his cheeks into his mouth, Nielsen lit the lamp and got up.

Half past two.

Through the open window someone could be heard passing down the yard.

Footsteps. Quiet, rubber soled on the gravel.

Silence.

Someone had stopped under the window and was waiting. Nielsen had enough presence of mind to turn off the light and throw himself down on the floor.

A long silence.

Nothing.

Not a sound.

Somewhere distant, in the town, a clock struck from a tower.

One.

Two.

Three.

Three-quarters.

Again, footsteps in the yard. Now moving away, step-by-step, toward the warehouse on the other side. Thoroughly alarmed, Nielsen dashed to the window and yelled at the top of his voice: Who's there?

Nobody.

Nothing.

Not a soul.

He waited.

Not a move.

In one of the neighboring buildings, on the other side of the fence, behind the wooden sheds and henhouses, an orange rectangle of light shone from a window. Somebody had lit the light and there was the sound of a flushing toilet. The sound lasted some time. There was no one anywhere.

"This is panic! Nerves! I'm scared to death!" Nielsen repeated to himself, half aloud, closing the window and lowering the curtain.

"There's no sense in going on like this! I must get away. Settle everything and go. This way I could go mad!"

The room was stuffy. Locked. Everything in that stinking ground-floor room was squeezed under such an unbearable pressure that it felt as if it were under some hydraulic press, as if the ceiling, floor, and all four walls were contracting, as though those stupid surfaces were moving concentrically and would crush Nielsen like an old coat at a dry cleaner's.

"How did Georgis put it? That I'd end up like a bullet-holed coat before he'd swing thirty centimeters above the ground according to the strict regulations of the Blitvinian criminal code?"

Nielsen got dressed and lit a small Coleman stove to make some coffee, lit a cigarette, and began to walk nervously, from wall to wall, like a hyena, in agitated turns, like a wild beast. Nervously smoking one cigarette after another, he circled this locked cage up and down, for what seemed an eternity. Dazed. The first signs of an excited and upset digestion. A clock struck in the tower. Twice. Half past three. Morning. Soon it would be a dirty, foggy, Blitvinian morning.

"This is panic! Nerves! I'm scared to death! This is a disgrace. Unheard of! And how long can it go on?"

It was exactly like this ten years before, when Barutanski was sitting in the Hotel Blitvania in Anderson Park. The Hotel Blitvania was a center for killing then, both by day and night, for a whole year, and mutilated and headless corpses floated down the dirty, yellow Blitva River. Now that bloodstained Hotel Blitvania had moved to Beauregard! What difference was there between the Hotel Blitvania and Beauregard? Then it was a case of canine psychology and tails between the legs, and today it was the same. Tails between the legs and fear! Fear and tails between the legs! Eight years! Everyone was avoiding him, as if he had the plague. They all crossed the road to escape him, swimming like dogs across to the other side of the street, only to avoid being compromised by being seen with him. Not a single person had come to shake his hand. No one had written to him. Nobody. Nothing. And these Blitvinian progressive characters around him believed in God, but turned their eyes away from the warm pool of human blood. "Oh God, human blood has flowed from time immemorial!"

Nielsen stopped in his circling in front of Buryanski's note. In a dark frame, with a sprig of evergreen, Buryanski's note hung there on the wall, a piece of paper no larger than three centimeters, torn from an apprentice's squared notebook and, on that crumpled and yellowed scrap of paper, today almost completely faded, was written in human blood: "Buryanski, to everyone! This is our last night, God have mercy on us, we are being tor . . ." A document from the Hotel Blitvania. The mists had consumed that Buryanski, Blitvinian legionnaire, student of agronomy, whom they'd arrested on suspicion of planning the assassination of Commandant Barutanski and who, after this note, had vanished without trace. This Buryanski was the real reason for the end of Nielsen's relations with the Commandant. It was then that Nielsen quit the Legion, relinquished his rank of lieutenant colonel, and returned his medals to Barutanski and opened a solicitor's office, whereas the plan had been that he should go to London, as Barutanski's envoy. "From Buryanski to the death of Dr. Nielsen," so someone would write in their historic study of present-day Blitvinian reality, nor would it be of any great interest, since today this was spreading like a flood over all the continents. Buryanskis and Nielsens were borne on the wind in their thousands and millions, like dead birds, in all directions. Today the whirlwinds were howling over Blitva. This was already utterly boring today and in a hundred years' time would interest no one. Dead details, such as one reads in Herodotus. But out of this concrete Blitvinian situation, this locked ground-floor room in which a man dared not sleep beside an open window, out of this lift which day by day descended lower into the bloody sediment, out of this spoiled digestion that made itself felt in the audible rumbling of bowels and stomach, that the arse might give directions to the brain, out of this unworthy status quo arose the question: What should one do?

Write? What? Phrases? Stupid bombastic phrases? All that had been written immeasurably better in the past in different variants, completely without success. Speak? To whom? The whole of mankind had done nothing else but speak for the last ten thousand years. From Socrates to the Vatican, nothing but speeches and sermons. Publish? For whom? Prove? To whom? To dear Mrs. Karin Michelson, who listened all night to a man, swallowing her tears, and then went and gave a copy of their conversation to Georgis? But this way—sensitive, agitated, distraught—was just as senseless. What was left? To lie? A hypocritical bastard, a man in a dinner jacket, whose only worry was that the burgundy should be at the right temperature and that his cognac should be served in such balloon glasses as to concentrate the aroma on the narrowed edge, like the scent of an orchid from its box? Where were the bridges over which a man might escape? In the truth? But truth—what was truth? The truth was all that a man felt to be inadvisable to express, inopportune to utter, for such a word, once uttered, would never coincide with our petty, egoistic, momentary interests! That was the truth! The truth was when one felt the need to say something that, from the point of view of one's own gain, one would be better, wiser, and more discerning to swallow. That was the truth! Was there ever generally any use to be gained from spoken truths? No, since, for centuries, there had been a Wanted notice posted for the truth as such. For centuries, the truth had moved like this through ground-floor rooms and waited to be shot. From Giordano Bruno to Buryanski!

Above the blood-written note of the late Buryanski with its frame and evergreen branch, above this signal, so to speak, from beyond the grave, above this ghostly letter from that world, there hung Knutson's painting: Giordano Bruno on the eve of his death. Giordano Bruno was looking at the starry sky and below, in the courtyard, the red flames were licking the stake.

There you had it! Human stupidity was conquering in all directions, and that human stupidity, like a canonized view of the world, possessed an entire series of not only brilliant painters, but indeed whole schools of such painting. And on the path of so-called progressive human intelligence, all that had been painted to this very day were various forms of fish or three apples on a plate or such awful, theatrical, dilettantish kitsch as this picture of Knutson's. This picture of Knutson's could be a scale model for the set of the third act of *Tosca*. Apart from this, all that had been written on the subject of human dignity and human reason, none of this was reflected either in painting or in European politics. What Giordano Bruno? Cardinal Armstrong called his monkey Giordano Bruno! Cardinal Armstrong had given his ape the name of Giordano Bruno out of spite for the dignity of human intelligence!

Cardinal Armstrong was the reality of current Blitvinian politics and not Nielsen who, like a keener, wailed over a torn bit of paper from some nameless and utterly insignificant Buryanski!

Feeling something pressing in his throat, on his heart, as though he would choke among those cupboards, icons, death masks, amid that rubbish of humanistic prejudice, Dr. Nielsen grabbed his trench coat and rushed out onto the street.

CHAPTER 4

A Dead Man on a Trip

Everything that had happened to our Dr. Nielsen during the past days had been a highly tense, grossly excited conversation with himself. In this confused monologue (on that vague border of the last rays of consciousness, when reason and madness, death and the wounded awareness of this real, earthly life, combine into a strange state of desperation like narcosis, when the body is still conscious of reality while in one's sight, thoughts, and images there appears the gray, melancholic shadow that accompanies death). This man had wandered the streets of Blitwanen in complete isolation, five, seven, ten days, from one café to another, as though life flowed normally on its way, as though he, Dr. Nielsen, did not present a person who trod these Blitvinian boards only until that mysterious moment when the invisible producer of that Blitvinian drama should give the arranged signal to the assassins and the affair would end at that very moment, as it had begun: backstage, concealed, in a canal; gondolas, distant thunder, the fall of a dead body into the dirty water to the accompaniment of a soft cantilena from the first violin of the orchestra: "Hey, Blitvinians, still the voices of our ancestors go on!"

Dr. Nielsen felt the reality of Blitva like a heavy, dull, and hungover headache. A ghostly, muddy vision, that accursed country, in which he'd arrived like a dead man on a trip, without any deeper moral or intellectual motive, without any particular mission, to exist in slaughter and to return, murdered, among the stars. When it had once been fated that one day in the universe it should happen that, among the 777 billions of suns, he should be conceived at one time in one solar system, and that a certain womb should deliver him as a being, as a personality, as a subject, as "him himself," that from that embryo he, Dr. Niels Nielsen, should come into being, then, by this same incomprehensible universal higher law, it had been fated that such a Dr. Nielsen should be born in that very Blitva. According to the logic of this undoubtedly universal fortune, that man should occur in chaos only once, he had been fated to arrive in Blitva and to be born in that unhappy land, and now he had lived in Blitva a whole forty-nine years, and the earth, together with that wondrous chosen Blitva, had circled the sun forty-nine times, for Blitva and for the earth forty-nine brief moments, but for our Dr. Nielsen an entire life, which would never return in any solar circling. Dr. Nielsen had made his appearance in that Blitva on his life's journey. He was fated for one universal moment to peep through life's crack into the universe (through the windows of the Blitwanen cafés the Savoy or the Valencia, the Kiosk or the Elite), and now the time had come for him, as a dead man, to return from this short earthly furlough from Blitva, back to the stars. This political astrology was not exceptionally witty.

Now it was late autumn. The Blitvinian waters had burst their banks and Blitva swam in mud up to one's knees, and he, a born Blitvinian, on the eve of his return from his life's furlough knew much less about Blitva than in that long-gone, forgotten time when, as a foolish and ignorant child, he first appeared in that mysterious country, catching butterflies and pasting the blue petals of an orchid in his herbarium. If anyone on the other side were to ask him, and God knows who that would be, perhaps his late mother, perhaps Buryanski, perhaps Muzhikovski or even old Flaming-Sandersen, to tell them about Blitva today, what its significance was on earth, in Europe (in that concert which some Westerners, why and for what is unknown, refer to as European and which had been playing so harmoniously to Europe's satisfaction for more than twenty years), today, having completed Blitvinian life, he wouldn't be able to say a single sensible word about it.

What was Blitva? Blitva was a gray blizzard in the dense northern mists, an endless muddy plain on the shores of a cold, rough sea that had the color of a dirty, ink-soaked rag, with its sickly yellow mornings, and this dark, dangerous, antipathetic Blitvinian sea roared in the half darkness like the sound of an organ in an empty, burned church. Everything in Blitva was muddy and frozen. Everything in Blitva was merely hoofprints on the empty Blitvinian road, when the blizzard howled and the frozen cod rattled against locked shop doors. In Blitva there were no men! Who was a man in Blitva? Where were there people in this land? The wind whistled against the signboards and the barbers' bowls that hung at the end of the street, and from behind the fences came the sound of a woman weeping. A police search had taken place in one of the buildings in the courtyard. There was shooting and a patrol had just disappeared in the blizzard, together with bloodstained and wounded prisoners. Women were crying. Somewhere in the distance a dog barked.

It was night. The streetlights trembled in the park of the ancient Blitvas-Holm fortress, which, to that very day, towered above the miry, flooded principality as a memory of those far-off days of Kurlandia and Hunnia, when, for centuries, the words of the Finnish conqueror of Blitva, the Prince Elector, were valid: "Blitvas-Holm is the key to the Karabaltic."

On the steep, seventy-three-meters-high, almost sheer cliff slept the ancient fortress of Blitvas-Holm above the town of Blitwanen, like a fortification on a hill set with dense fir trees. In the utter darkness of a muddy autumn dawn, the dark walls and towers of the old fort were still outlined, lit from time to time by a silver shower of headlights that slid silently down the curving paths of the fortress park, with the white, magnesium gleam of their long and mysterious tentacles lighting up now Beauregard with its or-angeries and arcades on the height of the vast Swedish park, and now the complexes of towers and ancient walls of the medieval Jarl's fortress. A lot of cars . . . returning from a Beauregard bridge party which usually lasted till three or four in the morning.

Dr. Nielsen stood on the small grass plot surrounding the statue of Waldemaras and, as if enchanted by the magical glow of the streetlights, counted the cars as they descended from Beauregard and, above him in the greenish light of the gas lamps, dressed in his bronze frock coat, towered Andria Waldemaras, the greatest Blitvinian poet of the nineteenth century, who had mourned his fa-therland with the well-known opening line "Blitva, my fatherland, thou art a poisonous disease." Andria Waldemaras stood there, with his frock coat down to his knees, his trousers creased, in mas-sive, elephantine shoes (that swelled like heavy loaves), and stepped merrily forward with his right leg, bareheaded, young like a high school reciter, and who read to the Blitvinians a book of his verse held in his left hand while, with his right hand, he held the fob on his watch chain on the right pocket of his bronze frock coat. That fob was in the form of a horse's head to which the gifted sculptor had paid great attention and modeled down to the last de-tail, one might say, perfectly.

Andria Waldemaras, who died in his twenty-seventh year from tuberculosis, signing himself in his love letters to Miss Hildegarde, the first among Blitvinians to do so, as "a dead man on a holiday to Blitva," he, the first among the dead Blitvinian holidaymakers, stood there like a monument on his granite pedestal, and a bronze Blitva knelt like an Oriental slave girl in front of him and offered him as a gift upon a velvet cushion a lyre, to him, Andria Walde-maras, the laurel-crowned genius, whose right hand held the horse's head of his fob, stupidly and naively declaiming his historic reveille: "Blitva shall not ever perish, while we, her sons are yet alive."

But who are we who live while our Blitva has not perished? I, Nielsen, and that Blitvinian they've arrested and whom they're leading in chains across the empty square, under the monument of the Blitvinian genius. In a rubber raincoat that poor bugger passed by, pale and upright, defiant, surrounded by a patrol of cuirassiers, and from under his left shoulder blade, as though drawn in bright red lipstick (almost cadmium), over the muddy and drenched rubber flowed perpendicularly an intensely red stream of fresh human blood. It was morning. A gray, dark, guttering, slimy, antipathetic, muddy Blitvinian morning, and in the distance, from around the corner, where stood the frowning scaffolding of a new five-story building, from the new Blitvinian *corso* came the sound of "Tango-Milango" from the Hotel Blitvania. That the Hotel Blitvania, as Barutanski's headquarters, had served as a central torture chamber during the years '17, '18, and '19 and that in the cellars of that accursed hotel several hundred people had been slaughtered was known to all in the city and over the whole of Blitva, and for years people made a detour around it in silence and with bowed heads, but today, on that very same place of execution, they were dancing the Tango-Milango.

In the newspapers of that mythical period, when Barutanski ruled from that accursed hotel as the first Protector, one might read in some texts consisting of cleverly infiltrated lines, between two or three words, timidly and cautiously, hints that once again someone had been massacred in the Hotel Blitvania, that someone had given evidence in court from a stretcher, that someone had been blinded, that someone had had needles stuck under his nails, and another with broken joints, but today it was all forgotten, today the Hotel Blitvania had been renovated as a first-class hotel. Today the Hotel Blitvania was a center for tourist traffic. Today rich foreigners and foreign diplomats of high rank stayed there. Today, for whole nights, they danced the Tango-Milango. And in general, in all Europe there wasn't a square centimeter on which somebody had not been blinded or had his joints broken or been beaten to death like a dog. On the entire globe there was not a single meter of ground that was not soaked in human blood, that was not a graveyard and a place of torture and execution. And mankind blew drunkenly into its saxophones. Day by day, mankind was becoming increasingly gorillaized, and that glorious Europe, instead of Europeanizing Blitva, on the contrary was itself becoming ever more Blitvinianized, and, Blitvinianized to a point of pure animalism, it played "Tango-Milango" in the Hotel Blitvania and this, today, had become the sole aim of its European Blitvinianization.

What did this herd of Blitvinians around him mean? The truth was: Blitva was disorder and misery, and therefore an unending succession of cause and effect, of disorder and misery. And the truly legendary Blitvinian lack of understanding for even the most insignificant order and pattern of phenomena—doubtless—logical, normal, and natural, was conditioned by the wretched circumstances in that wretched country of winds, rain, and bedbugs. Blitva was a dark and utterly unpleasant area, where the concept of good and of evil in its Western European sense had lost even the slightest so-called ritual value, and where the human heart was a dead nag, frozen hard and left on a Blitvinian road until the spring flood might carry it away. But the fact that, lately, a complete vacuum had opened up around him, Dr. Nielsen, that people simply vanished from his presence as though he were an escapee from a leper colony, that signified in these apes a panic, a fear of death. He, Dr. Nielsen, was considered to be dead. For them he was only apparently alive and no one, it would appear, could possibly grasp how it was that he continued to circulate in the world of Blitva and demonstratively put in an appearance in cafés. In his presence one noticed a semisilent movement of lips. There was a flash of glassy looks, and the touch of his hand, apparently, acted coldly and unpleasantly on his personal acquaintances, like a touch of death. And in those looks around him there hovered a tired human conscience, like a large, gray fly, dying in the cold of a Blitvinian November wind.

"You are mistaken in one of your basic propositions," Dr. Burgwaldsen had said to him, Burgwaldsen, who, for decades, had lectured in Vayda-Hunnen on the legal history of the Scythian, Carpatohunnish, and Karabaltico-Finnish peoples. "You're forgetting that Blitva doesn't live in the twentieth but in the fifteenth or in the sixteenth century at most. The fact that you have rebelled in defense of free civil dignity, in the civic, Jacobinian, *citoyen* (so to speak) sense of this obscure concept, that is what I call a false supposition, *amice,* and false suppositions inevitably produce poor conclusions! For this is how things are with us: that people are beaten during police inquiries, that, certainly according to the better, so-called European customs, could not be justified. In no way! Yet, after all, where today is that Europe where 'the better European customs' are valid? Answer me that question, my dear friend! Yes! Indeed! I ask you! Beating, typical Blitvinian beating, as an accompaniment to administrative functioning, that one could somehow explain: by means of hints from above and the excessive zeal of our common people, of the so-called lower, subaltern organs, as also so many other negative phenomena, by examination of causes and grasping of effects. This pathetic fact might gain its interpretation only in that sense which I, in the beginning, had the honor to quote, and that is that we are living in the fifteenth or, at the most, the sixteenth century. And consider this: Whether Barutanski, as a phenomenon, is to your personal liking or not, he is an organic phenomenon! His every act as a ruler is dictated by a deep, inborn awareness that he's acting not in the twentieth but in the fifteenth century. That, generally, is exclusively political skill: to manage in space and in time and act with the means which suit the needs of a particular time in a particular space. Yes! Nature, as is well known, does nothing by leaps or bounds, my dear young friend, and it is an old and well-tried piece of wisdom: *Naturae convenienter vivere!* And what you are seeking in this 'Open Letter' of yours is, for our circumstances, *rebus hic et nunc stantibus,* here, today, in Blitva, a demand which is against nature! You're looking for a leap, a *salto mortale,* from the fifteenth into the twentieth century! That is an intellectual supererogation, my dear friend; a state cannot be governed like that."

"So, Professor: The world has to be ruled by the bludgeon and I have to be beaten to death by that bludgeon simply because I don't think that the bludgeon should be *ultima ratio?*"

"Give me just one example in the history of civilizations that was not built on similar means of persuasion," Burgwaldsen replied. "The pharaohs, Pericles, the Rome of the Caesars, Borgia, the papal see, the East India Company, the Transvaal? According to you, Blitva should be the one exception? Forgive me, but that's naive!"

"Yes, my dear professor, I am naive, that much I admit. But do you know who it was who brought me up to be naive? In other words, who is responsible for my naïveté? You personally, you and your naive principles, which you naively preached from the rostrum and to which I naively listened through the course of several naive semesters, as you should well know! You taught us, together with the naive Cicero, that human communities should be ruled by that naive spirit of communality, that by the law of natural social instinct, people should be bound in naive organizations, according to the law of an instinct which Cicero naively called *naturalis quaedam congregatio,* and you yourself insisted that social groups should be naively similar to Cicero's naive *civitas* and to that naive concept which Cicero naively called *constitutio populis!*"

"Yes, very good, young man, but, if you haven't forgotten, I also taught you that people were hostile animals: *Sunt homines ex natura hostes,* by nature and her laws enemies, *ex natura hostes,* and, in addition, I also taught you this, that *salus populi suprema lex,* and there you have it! Blitva has not fought for its freedom for centuries to fall victim today to its enemies, spies, paid agents, and ordinary criminals!" Burgwaldsen declared.

Watching the convoy of cuirassiers crossing the empty Waldemaras Square and disappearing into the tree-lined Jarl Knutson Boulevard under the Kristian Barutanski Bridge, Niels Nielsen recalled that conversation with his old professor, Burgwaldsen, and, repeating "Blitva has not fought for its freedom for centuries to fall victim to criminals," set off, mechanically, limply, and automatically, following the convoy across the square, and then turned across the bridge to the other side into the park beneath the old fortress. To rest from the increasing pressure, to find peace in the woods among the centuries-old trees from which water dripped and its sound was irregularly disturbed. The rain had stopped, but one could hear the drops falling from leaf to leaf like tiny, independent worlds that had arrived out of the dark heights, and now, after their brief earthly existence, rolled, one after another, from leaf to leaf, from bough to bough, into the ditches, the mud, the Blitva River which, swollen, rustled under the bridge, dark and mucky, like the threat of an oncoming storm.

In the woods it was dark. Above the saplings in the rides, in the silvery level ground, there swirled a dense veil of mist that steamed up amid the mass of the trees, wrapping trunks and branches with its wet shroud, and here and there one could hear the fall of soaked leaves, heavy, vertical, dead. As though someone were squelching through the undergrowth. Plop, plop, plop. Down the main asphalt road came a company in full field equipment. Helmets, bayonets, boots, long Blitvinian greatcoats, and here and there the glow of a cigarette. A young officer at the rear of the company looked back in curiosity at the lonely passerby and that had a strange effect on Nielsen. A young, happy, smiling, and curious face, and he was wearing white gloves, so intensely white that they gave an impression of ghostliness. He was wondering who could be strolling in the woods at such an early hour. The dull tramp of the soldiers could be heard far below on the second and third curve of the serpentine. A raven cawed frighteningly among the treetops and the flutter of wings among the wet branches caused a whole minor cascade of drops that had wisely hidden themselves beneath the stalks, and this seemed to alarm the whole forest. A migration of tiny watery cosmoses began to move and spill hurriedly and excitedly on all sides. So did unknown, winged creatures bathe in the starry milky ways and then, from a single blow of a wing, billions of suns pour, burst, and flash on all sides and then everything is again silence, Nielsen thought, looking down through the branches at the lights of the town shining in straight lines and shimmering in the distance, like stars. Over the factory chimneys, beyond the railway bridge, the first specks of dawn were appearing in dull horizontal patterns and here, in the ashy darkness, slept the old Blitvas-Holm fortress in the silence of the gloomy, locked, and unpleasant barracks. Gray windows, damp, rain-washed walls, the clinking of chains from the stables, somebody carrying a lamp in the yard. The neighing of horses from beyond the walls.

The old fortress had constantly been added to over the centuries. The foundations of the present towers had been laid already in the eleventh century on the site of the wooden fortifications of Dimitry Blatvinsky, when the whole of Blitva, right up to the Finnougrian marshes, lay as a grand principality under the Carpatofinnougrian Hetmans. Under the Aragon occupation, between the seventh and eleventh Swedish wars, the fortress was renewed by Rodolpho Visconti, of whom it was written in the Blitvinian chronicle that he was a man of great versatility. He painted the portraits of saints in the churches, organized artillery for the Aragon irregulars, trained the Blitvinians in the art of ballistics, was court armorer and treasurer, wrote sonnets, engaged in sculpture, and Pietro Antonio Mediolanensis spread Visconti's fame, constructing fortifications and dungeons in Visconti's Blitvinian style from Riga to Ankersgarden. At that time, Blitwanen (which the Imperial Aragon governors, two or three centuries later, called Blitvinska) still bore the folk name Blitvas-Holm, and the illiterate peasant masses believed that in a pit under the fortress was a mysterious and gigantic monster that devoured entire nations, just as the Blitvinian peasants themselves devoured frog goulash, the favorite and most popular Blitvinian peasant dish. The famous work by Du Bois, *Les premiers temps de l'état blithuanien,* gives documentary proof that for centuries Blitvas-Holm was indeed a graveyard of nations. Whoever found themselves in those misty marshes would be drowned and vanish without trace. That Gepids slaughtered Saracens, that Scythians, Sarmatians, Celts, Balts, and Normans perished there for centuries in what were today unknown, drawn-out, and tortuous agonies, and that Huns and Finns, Hungarians, Mongols, and Slavs, beneath these battlements, destroyed Vandals and Barbarians, Saracens and Avars, today was a mere whimsical mystery for philological pedants, but yesterday it meant dread, fear, fire in the night, and the shriek of the mortally wounded and the drowning. Bloodstained Blitva, Blatvia, and Ilmenga, the bloody marshes around the ancient towns, through which, today, express trains thundered right up to Plavystok, all this, for centuries, had embodied a deathly wailing, which today the wind carried like the song of the storm-stricken trees in the ancient forests around Ankersgarden, where the steam saws of the great Blitvinian-English Export Limited moaned, and where today, in the bars, among dialectically educated workers, the fact was declaimed that "art must be tendentious in the dialectical sense," as was preached by the class-conscious poet Tamyan Apolonski, whose verses were chorally recited from Nyborg to Nystad. Swedish barons, Kurlandish adventurers, Blitvinian nobles, Swedish Protestants, and Aragon, Latin, and Southern Palatine Counter-Reformationists slew one another behind the walls of this ancient fortress for fully 350 years and, today, what remained? Jarl's tower and within it the barracks of Colonel Kristian Barutanski. According to Baedeker, Jarl's tower, that "legendary key to the Karabaltic," represented a truly independent architectural work by Visconti. Its weathervanes, its towers, its triangular facades with their covered staircases beneath the rich late-Renaissance arches of its arcades, the heavy, massive turrets of its bastions with the mouths of their cannon that yawned from the dark cellars, all this constituted a masterly building which, in tourist brochures, resembled an excellent toy for children, and, in fact, was a greasy slaughterhouse, soaked in human blood, standing today just as it stood in the time of that Kurlandish adventurer who, in one single day, widowed seven thousand Blitvinian women, when he had seven thousand Blitvinian soldiers shot for taking part in a conspiracy.

Covered in ivy, above the second gallery in the arcade, grayed by wind and rain, was a stone medallion portraying Jarl's head: in armor, a smiling face with thick, sensual, protruding lips and long curly hair combed after the Renaissance style: right and left from the parting, so that it fell like a rich drapery over the prince's armored shoulders on which, like epaulets, danced two pairs of lizards.

Iaromalius, Knutsonius, Dei Gratia Magnus Dux Blithuaniae, Novogorodieae, Huniae sarmacensis, Vogariae et al., totius Sarmatiae Dominus Anno VII Imperii Sui, so did he announce himself today to the unknown foreign tourists who, carrying little red guidebooks, lurked in the shadows of those mildewed towers, telling one another how Bonaparte stood under this stone arch after crossing the Neman, and how today the brilliant statesman Kristian Barutanski, from a nameless race of Blitvinian slaves, was building a nation before which lay the enviable future of a young, European, industrialized, and well-adapted organism.

Nielsen had climbed to the highest avenue of trees that led up the battlements of Jarl's tower, from where, on one side, there opened up a free prospect of the Blitva River that wound beneath the rocks, of the Waldemaras Park with its bronze statue, of the idyllic view of narrow paved streets, with their steep, old-fashioned Kurlandish roofs, on which moved weathervanes in the form of iron knights with banners, while, on the other side, stretched the majestic Swedish park right up to the monumental entrance to the palace of Beauregard, where, at that moment, the horse guards were changing. This was the famous sight which the maestro Roman Rayevski had chosen for the equestrian statue of Kristian Barutanski. From there opened a view of Colonel Barutanski's lifework: the modern architectural vistas of the new, modern Blitwanen, with their broad avenues of trees, of the massive square of National Liberation, with its seven or eight monumental ministerial palaces in the style of Corbusier, of the huge equestrian statue of the Prince Elector Jarl Knutson at the entrance to Jarl Knutson Boulevard. In Nielsen, lost in these views of objective history, as if he were no more than a wavering phantom, with every beat of his heart came idiotically, like an echo, the words of the senile Professor Burgwaldsen, that Blitva had not struggled for its freedom for centuries to fall victim to criminals. And one of those criminal types was he himself, Niels Nielsen. Blitva had not struggled for its freedom for centuries to fall victim to him, Niels Nielsen, a criminal foreign agent, in the opinion of the historiographer Fernandis.

Indeed, Blitva had fought for its freedom for centuries, but for that freedom Nielsens had fought and among them not a single Burgwaldsen, nor a Fernandis! Blitva had dreamt of its freedom for centuries, while the Burgwaldsens, Fernandises, and company had taught stupidities at Hunnish universities. That idea of Blitvinian "freedom" was a sweet self-deception with which a man lulled himself to sleep during endlessly long nights and the long, silent lonelinesses were filled with dreams of Blitvinian "freedom," which appeared to people as a soft chorus that accompanied them like the rhythm of beloved footsteps, like music in the twilight, when in the depths of human isolation the lamp of this strange and insane idea glimmered and, over the harsh reality of the truth, cast warm shadows of illusion that one day everything would be turned into the eve of a majestic, unheard-of festivity, when the pine trees' scent would be overpowering, when all the windows would be lit, the houses filled with expensive gifts and no school tomorrow, nor barracks, wars, or debts, and one might sleep in bed till breakfast time. Wonderful! It was not just a childish hatred of oppression, nor of the sight of foreign cavalry, of foreign commands, and of the antipathetic sound of Hunnish, Blatvian, and Imperial Aragon trumpets which, like a devilish fanfare, glorified everything that for Blitva and Blitvinians denoted a centuries-long defeat and shame. The great Blitvinian orators, the Jesuits, foretold the end of Hunnia and of the Aragon Empire and the rebirth of Blitvinia three hundred years ago, and the pastel blue satin dinner jackets of the Blitvinian nobles in Swedish exile formed the sad motifs of Blitvinian lyrical poetry of the nineties, when the youth was being born who was fated, restrained by slavish silence, to march in the ranks of the high-imperial armies of General Germansky, marching to the squeak of foreign flutes and the thump of enemy drums, beneath the imperial banners, against their free and patriotic will, and against Blitva. In those days the thought of "freedom" was a tired melody that trembled above the low, daily sufferings, above the Blitvinian mud, beneath the mouths of foreign cannon, in the barracks and the prisons, like a strangled verse concerning the Blitva that "had not yet perished . . ."

That song expressed a hope, completely muddled, like an undetermined negation of everything that, in fact, represented hellish reality: in the dark onset of evening in that obscure Blitvinian garrison, when the lamp flickered before the crucifix, the one symbol of Blitvinian suffering, and out of the semidarkness of the avenue of trees, together with the glow of a secretly lit cigarette, someone could be heard singing sotto voce about Blitva in which the spirit of its legendary heroism was not yet dead. This was Blitvinian youth, clad in an Aragon greatcoat and fated to die in foreign barracks, yet still they sang, in their melancholic loneliness, of a Blitva that had not yet perished. The weeping for an imaginary Blitvinian freedom, this was the weeping of inexperienced youth who flinched before the cannon. It was the revolt of healthy, boyish flesh against cannon as the only method of conviction among nations. Out of these naive and dilettantishly contrived verses of Waldemaras spoke the sadness of a cruelly crushed youth, sickly, tubercular, hungry, suffocating in the lice-ridden imperial barracks, yet which desired something less filthy, less disgusting, less unbearable. And that song of "freedom" was a sentimental, adolescent, youthful revolt against the mammoth insanity which, with its Aragon and Hunnish iron-shod *Feldwebel*'s boot, crushed everything that could be crushed in Blitva. That sentimental *Stimmung* was the trembling of a tiny, almost negligible light on the troglodyte wind of human stupidity. Perhaps it was no more than the glow of a sulfur match and only for a moment, and at an inexpressibly great distance, such that afterward, for an entire life, people moved under a false supposition that that light shone in this direction (in fact, it shone in a direction that was quite the opposite), but in such disasters and calamities as surrounded Blitva, it was still a signal, from a great distance, that all was not yet lost and that a man might yet be saved. That idea of Blitvinian "freedom" (insofar as it was an idea at all) consisted simply of a negation of negative Blitvinian reality. On the one side, it was a lamentation at inevitability in general, while on the other, it was a dream of new and unclear hopes that, for certain, the day would nonetheless dawn when it would not be so dark, so bloody, and so hopeless as it had been for centuries.

In those days, when Niels Nielsen decided to don the greatcoat of a Blitvinian legionnaire and, under the threat of the Hunnish gallows, sacrifice himself for Blitva, come what may, he had thought the same way: that the time had come for Blitvinian man to walk upright, to become the controller of his own fate, sensing that his will had become the word and the word a signal for action, for the realization of "freedom," for discipline, and for death, if necessary. Only that death had to serve one single idea: Blitva and its freedom. Such thoughts, such flickering thoughts, woven from dreams, hovered at that time like a film around the moods of Blitvinians. They appeared like a flame on the Aragon, Alemannish, Hunnish, Swedish, and Mongol Blitvinian sufferings. And those thoughts sought, in the greatcoats of their own legion, in their Blitvinian leather, in their rags, in the mares they rode, in the camps and the camp kitchens, one single possibility: that this mad slaughter on another's behalf and this provocative gambling with Blitvinian flesh would one day cease forever. This Blitvinian flesh, stupid, lousy, filthy, this backward, despised Blitvinian flesh, it needed to wrap itself in its own condottiere rags, to equip itself with carbines, sabers, and spurs, not to rattle them for the sake of rattling but, if cannon were the final means, then to fire them in its own interest and in that of its own roofs and homes. If it had to die like a lump of horsemeat, then let it die for itself, for its own Blitvinian causes, and not be a parceled mute corpse in a foreign post office, franked by foreign powers as fodder for foreign cannon.

It was all, doubtless, logical, but as usually happens with logic, the first crack in that logic made its appearance. They were in front of Plavystok, sometime at the beginning of '17. Nielsen was sitting in the snow, in the Blitvinian camp, together with his batteries, under the tails of Blitvinian mares, in the stench of Blitvinian closets, and no longer a monkey on a foreigner's chain, but now his own man, a Blitvinian, with his Blitvinian cannon and shooting for the sake of his own Blitvinian cause. Here Blitvinians had, for centuries, been slaughtered by Swedes, Visigoths, Trans-Moscovian Tartars, and Huns, but Nielsen, with his peasants, had advanced so that today he was seated with his Blitvinian battery in his own camp, had occupied Blitvo-Palatinsk, and was bombarding Plavystok. He was cooking his rebels' potatoes and there was sausage and vodka and, one day, he would cook those Hunnish cats in their citadel such a kettle broth that they would undoubtedly die of this, his Blitvinian concoction. It was a wonderful feeling of being one's own person, of free independence, even more, an awareness of sovereign existence! The artillery bombardment of Blitvo-Palatinsk lasted fully five days and nights. The town was held by first-class Kurlandish units, and Nielsen and his men lay in the snow, in plowed fields and mud around Blitvo-Palatinsk, as on a chessboard. The enemy was firing directly at their backs and more than 40 percent of the wounded remained lying shot through the shoulder blades, but one morning he, together with his peasants, with bared sabers attacked and entered Blitvo-Palatinsk, madly but successfully, against all rules of human common sense. He became the conqueror of Blitvo-Palatinsk. He remembered passing through it: nothing but the fat carcasses of Kurlandish horses, the blue vests of Kurlandish uhlans in the muddy snow, all yellowed with urine and horse droppings. The bells were ringing. At the end of the street a whole row of Jewish hovels was alight and in the half-open eye of a dead Kurlandish uhlan gleamed, in the morning sun, a greenish-blue light, strangely greenish-blue like blue vitriol. It was an experience of life at its fullest. "Man moved through the world like grapeshot, leaving behind him a tail of fire. Bells rang, women wept, Kurlandish corpses were scattered in the snow like blood-stained trousers, and the fact that the towns were crowing for us and the women were crying and the bells mourning for us was unimportant. Blitva had become a comet. Blitva had become our 'I.' It was the rattle of cavalry sabers, the flashing of helmets, the neighing of horses, the advance of Blitvinian flesh that had become self-aware. It was the victorious awareness of one's self. It was the historic passage of the Blitvinian panther, lithe, bold, the pantherish triumph of the Blitvinian idea."

In the midst of all this, Kadosh appeared, having that very moment received a telephone message from the Commandant ordering Nielsen immediately to surrender command of the entire Plavystok sector and to report at once to him, concerning the Rupertis affair. Kadosh, as his battery commander, had wanted to have this Rupertis shot. To shoot a baby, a sixteen-year-old high school boy, because he had received a letter from his mother in Weider-Hunnen saying that he, together with all his commanders, would be hanged as traitors, that the Blitvinian cause was lost, and let him come back to his mother before it was too late! This mother's boy began to cry and plead to be allowed to go back to his mother, since all was lost. His mother wrote that in Weider-Hunnen they were hanging Blitvinian legionnaires every day; in a word, the lad was spreading nonsense in the battery and Kadosh condemned him to death by shooting. The sentence came to Nielsen, as sector commandant, for his signature. He summoned the boy to report, gave him two or three slaps in the face, and returned him to his battery. Nonetheless, they shot the boy without Nielsen's knowledge and he, Nielsen, was relieved of his command and was summoned personally and immediately to report to the Commandant. He explained the whole matter to Barutanski in two or three words, but to the end of his explanation Barutanski remained silent and frowning, aloof, and maintaining his commandant's distance to the end: Nielsen had been wrong. One did not smack deserters in the face, one shot them. It was outside his competence according to the Legion Regulations to alter the decision of an officer, when it was a clear and indisputable case of insubordination beneath the flag and in action against the enemy.

"Yes, but he was a mere boy, a high school boy . . ."

"High school boy or not, he was a soldier of the Blitvinian Legion, and that's that!"

"In one sense he was quite capable of fulfilling the function of a legionnaire, but in another, more human, sense he was just a little mama's boy who fell on his knees in front of me and returned to his battery like a schoolboy after correction. He gave me his word of honor not to do it again and kissed my hand like a real baby boy."

"I'm surprised at you, Nielsen! What you're saying is pure defeatism! And if you weren't Nielsen and I didn't know who you were, I'd have had you shot immediately, do you understand? In my legion I don't need old maids, I need officers! Soldiers! Orders are orders and regulations are regulations, no matter whether we're high school boys or sector commandants. Do you understand, Major?"

"I beg your pardon, sir! I do not understand. We do not understand one another! To hell with your logic! I'm not in the Legion to be an executioner!"

"Really? And I don't command the Legion in order to hold utterly senseless conversations with defeatists!"

Plunged in dark and unpleasant thoughts, Niels Nielsen stopped in front of the main entrance to Beauregard. Through the huge, monumental gateway of heavy cast iron in the shape of larger-than-life irises and acanthuses, one could see the long yellow avenue of plane trees with vast lawns to the right and left. At the end of the avenue an asphalt road divided around the large stone circular fishpond and then came together, in a symmetric circle planted with rose bushes, in front of the huge, glass-covered platform at the main entrance to the palace. Everything here was redolent of the proud aristocracy of the baroque Hunnish governor's residence: the rhododendrons, wrapped in rags, on the wet green carpet of the Swedish lawn and the oleanders ready for transfer to the green-houses, the huge bushes of autumn chrysanthemums which bloomed as a sure sign that over all hovered the quiet yet skilled hand of an invisible gardener, that mysterious, poetic shade, that ac-companied every external, theatrical, decorative side of a triumphal, genuine imperial estate. One could see through the cast-iron acan-thuses that, in the garden, in the avenues, across the lawns to the fishpond, everything was in a great state of autumnal migration: there were rows of large baskets full of rotting leaves, whole rows of wooden boxes containing sensitive plants, and planks were placed over the stone circle of the fishpond and around the fountain. The vast fan-shaped leaves of fleshy tropical water lilies were awaiting their return to the shelter of central heating, and even for the fa-mous statue by Rayevski, depicting a naked dying warrior, there was prepared a small wooden house with a roof, like the idyllic nest boxes spread through the parks.

Perhaps that's the little Rupertis whom they shot before Plavys-tok, Nielsen thought, looking at the naked marble body of the wounded youth who had stumbled, mortally wounded, holding on to his shield with the last effort of the dying young organism.

In the ashy dawn of a dull northern morning, on the huge green lawn, amid that wet carpet, on its square of black granite, that myste-rious headstone acted like a ghost, like a warning to all passersby to beware, since to serve the Lords of Beauregard meant a theatrical death. In the palace all was quiet and still. There was not a soul about. Under the tall mezzanine was the entrance for coaches and carts, beneath an arcade that was as dark as a tunnel, and above the staircase of that monumental entrance, like a veranda enclosed in glass, stood an immense and gleaming platform of crystal with a rich, luxurious drapery of metal scallops. Lit by chandeliers, with purple carpets on its broad staircase, with shining brass bars, curtains, and tropical plants, that aristocratic glass platform in front of the main entrance, the huge high curtained windows on the first story, the steep lead-covered roof of this mysterious home, it all resembled a set for some strange dress rehearsal on a bare and empty stage.

There lives the man who, like a dark cloud, whirled me into the secret realms of most shameful fear, Nielsen thought, staring fix-edly at the same spot through the iron railings of the main entrance to the avenue, into the lighted platform of the palace of Beauregard, over which, second by second, the morning light was growing. In the tops of the plane trees, here and there, was heard the twittering of sparrows, together with the first drops of a fine, misty rain.

That confidence trickster had made it to Beauregard! He always had a blind self-assurance, and even in his school days he knew how to make his contemporaries believe that one could leave reality and journey into dreams, into an illusion of a dream. When his profes-sors at the university questioned him about real facts of so-called ac-cepted, verified knowledge, he never really knew how to answer a single question. In the framework of such school examination, he would lie impertinently, assuming a proud and self-conscious atti-tude like that of a true madman, and would thus conquer, by the cheapest means, by bluff, while in fact he was an incredible ignora-mus. The man bore in him such a wild temperament that by the senses of his diabolical dialectic he always guessed how to place his adolescent arguments like chessmen on a board and to create around him a mood for winning—not by force of intellect, but by any im-posed trickery. In those days, when Blitva was truly of no interest to anybody, when no one believed in it, he spoke of Blitva and spoke constantly and tirelessly from morning till night: with apparent courtesy, flatteringly, in friendly tones, he recruited adherents on all sides to his cause of Blitvinian liberation. A fanatic who made speeches (always somewhat theatrical) concerning the sufferings of Blitva, this man played the assumed role of a malcontent whose pockets were ever full of newspaper clippings concerning the sufferings and the persecutions of the Blitvinian people, of maps that called for a new partition of the Karabaltic, new stamps, new ships, new crests, new armies which, at that time, seemed, to a normal mind, a heap of senseless children's playthings. This semi-intellectual constantly, like some automaton, threw out ever newer masses of statistical and historical facts of which not a single one was true, but which all proved that Blitva had a right to its sovereignty, that Blitva was already a sovereign state in the eighth, ninth, tenth, eleventh, and thirteenth centuries, that it had been the victim of a false balance of power, and that Blitva would become Blitva again, once it was awakened. Regardless of whether he employed left-wing slogans or right-wing methods, often (too often) obedient to the "upper" as if he were their born servant, while to the "lower" arrogant to the point of intolerance, ever ready to give in and apparently to bend the knee and bow like a born opportunist, so that in situations where there was no other way out, he'd surrender unconditionally like a bedbug dug from its hiding place. He knew how to withdraw into himself, to hide, to smuggle himself through a keyhole, to disappear, simply to evaporate for a time, only usually somewhere distant, in the far Hunnish lands, to reappear like a massive smoke cloud and, in the fog of explosions, one would hear the whisper that Barutanski was moving like a threat through Blitva. A burglar by nature, he possessed a certain characteristic ability to squeeze through the most incredibly narrow cracks, and in him, as in a seashell, the murmur of the ocean could be heard in those days of most improbable dreams and illusions. Kristian Barutanski listened to the voice within him, the voice of this mighty and dark imagining, as to the call of distances, and was always sufficiently unintelligent not to doubt, even for one moment, in the profounder meaning of his confused fantasizing. In one sense, he saw further and more clearly than others of his stupid contemporaries, who regarded matters according to the rules of the general, accepted ways, usually seeing no further than their own noses. For Barutanski, only a single thought existed: Blitva. Blitva, for him, was the concept of this, the governor's, Beauregard, with him as commandant, and this was his ideal of a liberated Blitva. As a drowning man dreams of a ship, so did he dream of his beloved Blitva in the face of all realities, insane, half crazy, eccentric, overwrought, and unbalanced, yet in this, his intoxication, inexpressibly naive, indeed stupidly shallow. He lied greatly and incessantly and, like a dog after a shower of rain, he would shake himself free of his own falsehoods only in order, at that same moment, to continue to lie and, what was worst, in his false inspiration he truly believed that what he said was the truth and, soberly aware that he was not speaking the truth, he deceived himself with his own lies, given that it was convenient. This adventurer, bounder, place seeker, and beggar appeared before the Parisian experts as a specialist in mineralogy, assuring the parrots who sat behind the green table at Versailles that Blitva was so rich in ore of every type, with its platinum and oil he would earn billions and buy up complete streets in Paris. A fanatic, limited, blindly one sided, undaunted, a typical gambler who put his all on a single card and won, throughout his life he played the role of the lovesick troubadour who struck his mandolin beneath the balcony of his beloved Blitva. And when that hypocritical, soft-spoken magpie perched upon Blitva's balcony, then blood flowed in Ilmenga, Ladonga, and Blatvia, as never before in Blitva's past. He had one advantage over all other people: Of "Man" he had no illusions and was convinced of human stupidity, had been convinced from the very first, namely, that it was a mare which one might very comfortably mount. Feuerbach's concept of the idealized "Man" with its romantic formula Homo (H) he contemptuously pronounced HP—

not Homo Politicus but Horse Power. And see how far this rider of human stupidity had come! "The point at which I visit the forecourt of his aristocratic, Swedish dwelling, to peep through the cast-iron acanthuses of his park gates, at the drawn curtains of his feudal home, dragging myself around his lordly windows like a rain-soaked cur! For more than a week in my thoughts I have been visiting this madman, like a man who has lost all sense of shame and all dignity. I feel somehow drawn to him. He is a Barutanski. In him there is blue blood! While the Nielsens were nothing but centuries-long Kurlandish serfs around Ankersgarden. And what would happen were I to kiss his hand, as that little schoolboy from Weider-Hunnen did to me? He'd have me shot, because what he needs are officers and not sentimental crybabies! He requires legionnaires and not defeatists!"

"Excuse me, sir, loitering here is forbidden!" A frowning, well-dressed individual approached Niels Nielsen. In a black overcoat with a hard cloth hat on his head. "Be so good as to leave!"

Niels Nielsen gave a shiver, nodded, and moved off into the dark avenue of the park, with a tired and heavy tread. From the Jarl barracks came the joyful ring of reveille. Somewhere in the distance, over the plain, like a siren on a ship, came the wail of a locomotive. Silently, inaudibly, almost snakelike, two sentries on bicycles passed by, and looked back for some time at the pale, suspicious figure wandering around Beauregard at such an early hour.

CHAPTER 5

Larsen's Nocturne

In the great hall of the Blitvinian Academy of Arts and Sciences the opening was taking place of a posthumous exhibition of the works of Sigismund Larsen. Sigismund Larsen painted pictures of which the Blitvinian press wrote that they were works of genius and then, one day, he hanged himself in his studio, without any real reason, in all probability in a weak moment of "temporary unbalance of mind," as stated in the Blitvinian newspapers, pissing over this youthful and gifted grave whole cascades of the warmest tears. Sigismund Larsen took down one of his paintings from a nail in his studio, knocked in another nail beside it, and so hanged himself on two nails, to make sure, leaving no letter or explanation behind him. Mainly he'd lived on his own and he hanged himself when he was completely alone and the fact that he'd announced a few days before his death, to a circle of café acquaintances, that painting pictures in Blitva was an occupation worthy of fools was merely to repeat an everyday phrase and no one would seriously see any reason whatsoever for such a common, flippantly superficial phrase to be taken as a possible motive for such a capricious, indeed hysterical, suicide. The event itself did not upset Blitva as being a sinister event, but rather as a more or less exciting sensation of the day, such as occur in all the artistic centers of Europe, which was just another proof that, in this respect, Blitva was becoming more Europeanized with every day.

The posthumous exhibition of Larsen's work was organized under the gracious patronage of Her Highness Ingrid Barutanski, the famous Blitvinian poetess, the wife of Kristian Barutanski, herself a full member of the Blitvinian Academy of Arts and Sciences, who in fact had founded the Academy, having persuaded her husband to provide for such a cultural purpose the necessary funds in the budget and to present to the Academy the palace of Count Thorwaldsen, a count of some seventeen titles (ending with *et Silva Blithuanica*), so that the immortals of Blitva might be able to work and create in elegant and indubitably European surroundings. In front of the Academy park, two fountains, lit by green lamps, lent a magical aura to the whole sight, with the murmur of their greenish transparent jets, as the procession of the most select Blitvinian elite climbed the broad marble stairs toward the rich empire colonnade, through which the light of massive chandeliers spilt in an orange stream from the vestibule decorated for that evening with large, valuable Flemish tapestries. Like a mysterious symbol of the hyperborean and Pan-Karabaltic mission of the so beloved Blitva, there, in the Academy vestibule (in the likeness of the mysterious Californian Miss Dolores), stood Blitva the Golden, like a laurel-crowned Pallas Athene, presented to the Academy by its first president, the gifted sculptor Roman Rayevski, who appeared that evening in his gold-braided Academy dress suit with all his honors, playing the role of the host of this immortal house at this reception of the noble patroness. Behind Roman Rayevski, in a group, stood eleven academicians clad in new immortal dress suits, with three-cornered hats and swords, and, to the left and right, were lined up the Academy lackeys in pumps, white stockings, and powdered wigs, mustachioed and ill-shaven savages, like extras in a performance of *Traviata*. All the immortals were present, including the most distinguished, the builder of the church of Saint Paul Blithuanicus,

Blithauer-Blitvinski, husband of Ariadna Vosnesenskaya, the new Blitvinian coloratura nightingale; the monocled numismatist Count Thorwaldsen de Palatinsk, de Holzexport, de Svenska K.G.F., etc., etc., etc. . . . and de Silva Blithuanica, then the cultural historian Vanini-Schiavone, who recently, in the name of and by the order of Cardinal Armstrong, had discovered abroad and purchased for the Academy collection, as a gift from the cardinal, a Virgin by a certain Giovanni Gualtieri, and a Cimabue, and yet another Virgin by Pietro Vannucci, the artist who was nicknamed il Perugino. Between the twelve lackeys in their dark coffee-colored livery and the twelve immortals in their velvety-gray dress suits, in the rich iridescence of lacquer, gold, jewelry, moiré and glacé silk, towering a head higher than all the rest, was His Eminence Cardinal Armstrong, accompanied by his private secretary Monsignor and thrice Dr. Lupis-Masnov. Cardinal Armstrong, in his violet cassock, stood head and shoulders above the rest, with his lithe, slim, indeed ascetic appearance, with his bald, gothic pate, with his eaglelike nose and sensual, fleshy, swollen, almost Negroid lips. Standing a head above all the others on massive peasant feet, as on his own monument, this man offered to those present a fine, soft, well-manicured hand to be kissed with the routine spontaneity of a skilled actor, for whom it was easy to play a dignified role, when he outstripped his partners not only with the part he played, but also with his size and income. It was said of Armstrong that he'd been the lover of Countess Thorwaldsen, etc., and that the Holy See had appointed him Eminence more because of the political line of Blitvinian prestige than of the importance of that small flock which the cardinal, with his several hundred thousand Blitvinian faithful, represented. Armstrong bore his dignity with the full confidence of a feudal, ecclesiastical lord, with his every word and movement stressing the distance that divided a mere Blitvinian academic immortal from the bearer of princely purple. Armstrong enjoyed the reputation of a great orator, but it was whispered around town that the cardinal learned his speeches by heart and that his personal secretary, Monsignor and thrice Dr. Lupis-Masnov, actually whispered the salient phrases, playing the part of the perfect prompter who carried all the cardinal's speeches in his head. Malicious Blitvinian gossip went so far in its negative exaggeration that it was said in the cafés His Eminence, the exemplary spiritual leader, practiced his speeches at home in front of the mirror, which was a piece of completely unnecessary libel, and which, even if true, would still be proof of how Cardinal Armstrong understood, with great conscientiousness, his role of spiritual guardian in the contemporary shaken and disoriented Blitvinian society. Be that as it may, Armstrong arrived at this ceremonial *jour de vernissage* in the company of his personal secretary, Monsignor and thrice Dr. Lupis-Masnov, without his favorite, his pet monkey Giordano Bruno.

His Eminence's monkey, Giordano Bruno, belonged to the category of a devilish jester, *Pithecia satanas,* with a dense, hairy, massive, and jet-black tail, jet-black like the tails on the helmets of the Madrid palace guards, with curly Negroid hair and with a beard à la Sâr Péladan or Landru. It was an ill-tempered, impertinent, and ill-tamed beast. While abroad, purchasing paintings for the Academy, studying the works of Ceni di Pepo and Perugino during his preRaphaelite peregrinations, Armstrong bought his monkey in Sicily and thence took him everywhere as an *argumentum ad hominem,* that Darwinism was pure blindness and merest stupidity. Whether Cardinal Armstrong really hated Darwinism or wanted, by means of this stinking shaggy monster, to increase the distance between himself and his common men was not clear, but that Giordano Bruno with his African stench regularly made the cardinal's guests vomit and by means of certain innocent, but monkeyishly immoral, gestures insulted the sensitivity of the well-mannered ladies present was beyond doubt. The entire elite of Blitwanen was revolted by this act of the cardinal, but no one had as yet dared to say a single word on this subject to him. On the contrary, the cream of Blitvinian society squatted on its hind legs in front of Giordano Bruno, ingratiating itself before the princely favorite with bananas and sweets, and even that evening several academics respectfully inquired after the health of the worthy cardinal's favorite, almost one might say of His Excellency Giordano Bruno, and being most humbly satisfied by the monsignor's information that Giordano Bruno had not appeared in the Academy vestibule at that *vernissage* due to technical reasons ("it was raining and he didn't feel his best"), but that he was down there in the heated Packard, listening to the broadcast of Beethoven's Fifth from London, conducted by Toscanini. Apart from Giordano Bruno, everybody was present in the vestibule of the Academy of Arts and Sciences: the ladies Dagmar Baltic, Ingrid Chevrolet, Karin Mercedes-Benz, Kristina Blitva-Spranex, Blithuanian Oil Depot Eleonora, Blithuanian Business Company Charlotte, Henrietta Tiepolinis of the Blithuanian Climatic Rampassing Limited, Danitti-Stöwer of the Companie Générale Transatlantique Blithuanian Line, the wives of General Sandersen and of General Andersen, and the wives of the Blitvinian senators Peterson, Jensen, and Krakovski, husbands and wives from seven faculties and of other higher administrative institutions, several actors and actresses from the Academy National Theater and two or three reputable painters, with academic rank and with purple swollen noses, old, insignificant, myopic drunks in borrowed dress suits with the Blithuaniae Restitutae of the eleventh grade for service to society in their buttonholes.

Last of all, yet with impeccable punctuality, arrived the Lady Patroness Madame Ingrid Barutanski, accompanied by her close friend and wife of the candidate for the post of president of the Republic, Silva Rayevski, and the cavalry captain Flaming-Sandersen, and after the president of the Academy and candidate for the presidency of the Republic, Roman Rayevski, had presented to her the ladies and honorable members of the Committee for the Organization of this Posthumous Exhibition: Dagmar Baltic, Karin Mercedes-Benz, Eleonora of the Blithuanian Oil Depot, the wives of generals Sandersen and Andersen, the wife of the deacon of the Protestant Theological Faculty and the wife of the rector of the Technological Institute, and, when she had received the respectful bows of the eleven immortals, with Cardinal Armstrong at their head, Ingrid Barutanski moved graciously through the ranks of mustachioed lackeys with their wigs and white stockings, up the decorative marble staircase into the ceremonial hall on the first floor, and when her patroness's foot, in its perfect Potsdam shoe, the creation of the virtuoso Goloveychik, crossed the threshold of the ceremonial hall of the palace of Count Thorwaldsen et Silva Blithuanica, the posthumous exhibition of the paintings and sculptures of Sigismund Larsen was open. She was followed, as in a fairy tale, by the ladies' whispers: Who made her shoes? Goloveychik, 11 Jesuit Street! After Ingrid Barutanski, in her perfectly made shoes from Goloveychik's at 11 Jesuit Street, came the entire cream of Blitva. She was immediately escorted by Madame Silva and her husband Roman Rayevski and the uhlan captain Flaming-Sandersen, grandson of the great Blitvinian ideologist Flaming-Sandersen, followed by the immortals, together with His Eminence Cardinal Armstrong, and, after them, the ladies of the Honorable Committee, all the representatives of the Blitvinian economy and intellect, and lastly several hundred less outstanding guests, who, till then, like common mortals, had been waiting under their umbrellas in the park or under the roofs of their limousines on Jarl Knutson Boulevard, where the cars were stretched, without a break, from the avenue of plane trees all the way to the Blitvinian bridge.

In that crowd, one of the invited was Nielsen. Nielsen was acquainted only superficially with Larsen, more through his canvases than personally, but that quiet man, with his intensely blue eyes, with his blond Swedish beard, and with his canvases which were not as interesting in an artistic sense as in their subjects, had always awakened in Nielsen a deep affection. From Larsen's every line flowed a harmonious, balanced, yet imposing peace of evening, and his subject was always obsessively the same: the afternoon silence of an empty Mediterranean town, when the sky was a dark steel-gray and orange and white striped awnings fluttered in the warm breeze. Always those narrow empty streets of Mediterranean towns, with their sails, awnings, or silken scarves fluttering on the afternoon breeze. But what was of greater value than these lyrical paintings was the result of his last days. In the thirty or forty days before his death, this man had sculpted in wax some seventy or eighty sculptures, seventy or eighty statues, some life size, and some as miniatures, tiny wax figures, leaving behind him a work that was utterly insane and unbalanced, yet so ingeniously rich that this undoubtedly sublime, exceptionally gifted legacy inspired all the Blitvinian artistic circles, otherwise as immune as crocodiles to anything that took place in the sphere of artistic creation that was not either gossip or slander.

At the back of the large hall, in front of a sort of canopy that sheltered it in rich gray velvet pleats, stood the deceased's bust crowned with a laurel wreath from which fell a double black silken ribbon, symmetrically, with one end to the left and one to the right, so as to show clearly and legibly, in antique golden letters, a verse by the lady poetess Ingrid Barutanski: "All glory smells of bitterness and death." On the walls also, for that evening, draped in gray velvet, shone some thirty newly varnished sunlit landscapes and several hundred drawings and etchings, but what filled the hall, like the chiming of golden bells, were the last works of the deceased, tastefully arranged on gray-velvet-draped columns, works that were unknown to the wider circles of Blitvinian art lovers and were presented to the public, as a

gift, in the richly designed and illustrated catalog with its enthusias-
tic introduction by Ingrid Barutanski. Larsen's wax figures were divided, in practice, into two groups: wax figures in very intense colors and statues gilded in a gleaming gold patina, such as is used to
gild Christmas walnuts. The colored wax busts resembled the baked
clay of Renaissance sculpture, but the mysterious terror evoked by
those colored heads lay in the fact that they were all the heads of
wounded men. The wax faces on their velvet stands, with their
deeply gouged dark eye sockets and blood-red lips, in deep contrast
to the hot, lyrical, sunny, and balanced landscapes on the walls, gave
the impression of devilish toys. The gilded heads were those of angels and saints, just as hellish in their movements and hopelessly pathetic in their agonies, with a lily in hands clasped in deathbed
prayer, from which a chameleon thrust its long tongue, with a grinning mask of malice, falsehood, hypocrisy, and human lust. This
hellish demonic chameleon held in a golden, angelic hand was completely green, with a turquoise glint of blue vitriol, with sparkling
emerald eyes, and with a tongue half a meter in length, which, from
the chameleon's jaws, curled around the dying angel's face in a
gleaming spiral, and on this greenish, metallic wire was wound an
endless mass of symbolic mascots relating to the most everyday life
of the average contemporary man: a toilet bowl, dentist's instruments, a hearse, cats, cars, guns, naked women, church organs,
boats—in other words, everything that troubled every living partic-
ipant in modern civilization, such as toothache and bad conscience.
This included a sketch for a monument to Jarl Knutson: a knight in
armor, shining, gilded, and all loosely covered in fine gold leaf, and
in his hand a flat knightly sword covered in red tissue paper. Above
all, on a black velvet cushion, shone the silver head of Blitva's glory,
Andria Waldemaras. There, on its black velvet cushion, slept the silver head of the poet Andria Waldemaras, who died of tuberculosis
in exile at the age of twenty-seven, but here, on his black cushion,

slept like some Blitvinian *nostromo* an old sea dog with a Swedish sailor's beard, with the well-modeled face of a genius who had perished tragically but had not surrendered. All the symbolic, historic shame of defeat was dominated by a higher, mysterious, poetic, and clairvoyant smile, as may be seen on the lips of victors. But beside this silvery smile, beneath the strong, firm, monumental arches of the silver bushy eyebrows, deep as bottomless wells, yawned the eye sockets gouged out with the chisel and pasted with tar, with a mass of congealed tar that dripped from the eye sockets and flowed, dark brown, like chewed tobacco, into the poet's mouth, which smiled with its inner, superior, and clairvoyant smile, and on which, by all appearances, there trembled a verse! That Andria Waldemaras, on his black velvet cushion, was, in reality, Sigismund Larsen *in personam*! It was, in fact, a self-portrait, a confession of his own life, of his own tragedy, of himself, his most intimate and secret self, the intellectual-moral scalp of the Sigismund Larsen who had taken down his last painting from the wall and hammered in an extra nail to make his death more certain!

Niels Nielsen stood fascinated in front of this silver mask on its black velvet. He could not drag himself away from those strange, dark, blind, and bottomless holes from which dripped tar, stinking, glutinous, resinous, brown with the color of Blitvinian mud that squelched on all sides, under every foot, dissolving, like a grave, beneath every silver, superior movement and swallowing every power that had ever tried to defeat and overcome that muddy Blitvinian graveyard.

All the same, it's no small thing, Niels Nielsen thought, looking at Larsen's mask, to create in such a lost and out-of-the-way corner, to create, so to speak, in the despair and loneliness of one's own anonymity, to work one's entire life, not indeed to be anybody, but to be of a superior personality, more even than that, to be a gifted, unusual phenomenon, to despair of oneself and kill oneself because of the utter hopelessness of one's artistic efforts succeeding, and here, now, a committee of gentle ladies arranged a tea with snacks in Beauregard. They'd serve pâté de foie gras and jellied salmon, and the gentlemen from Mercedes-Benz and the Blithuanian Oil Depot would drink their own product, Baltic Cherry Brandy. A Blitvinian quartet would play, and in all the quarters of Blitwanen they would collect money for a worthy memorial to a dead Blitvinian giant. Roman Rayevski would earn several hundred thousand Blitvinian lei, and again they'd serve crabs and fish in aspic. And so the show would go on, the show that bore the name of the construction of a new European civilization, somewhere in the forests between Plavystok and Hunnia, where the devil wished all his acquaintances bon voyage into hell! And the face on that black velvet was the face of a man who, before all Blitva, shed his blood for the love of an idée fixe. Beneath that snobbish and ceremonial parade flowed the blood of a living and gifted man who had killed himself out of despair, just as did Andria Waldemaras, the talent over whom Blitva had mourned and wept like an old woman for more than thirty years! Those Waldemarases, those Larsens had ceased to be the individual victims of individuals. It was a picture and allegory of a common situation, of a common fate, Destiny, that had no deeper meaning than simple suffering, that was called Blitva! And there, in front of everybody, at the head of this select entourage came Ingrid Barutanski! She, the poetess, the gifted woman, she had had a sense for the symbolic meaning of words, she had once lived intensely for the sake of her hendecasyllabics and terzinas, and what had become of her? A boring, mundane doll, an antipathetic bluestocking with nothing in her head but the external, formal sides of a diplomatic protocol reception. And here too was her maître d'hôtel, her chancellor, her "peripatetic hanger-on," Jules Dupont! A disgusting pimpish snout of a foreign lackey, who was certainly working for some intelligence office abroad!

How people change! It was back in the days of the parliamentary era of Muzhikovski that Nielsen had last spoken with Ingrid Barutanski, in Beauregard, on the occasion of the state celebration of the Constitution, when Madame Ingrid had cast a glance from the stage at the brilliant circle of lady patronesses clad in patent leather and in the multicolored fabrics of generals' wives, and ironically remarked that always, since her youth, she'd had the ideal of marrying a real, genuine, legendary hero, while in fact she'd married a type of police functionary!

"You mean an agent, Ingrid," Nielsen had remarked sarcastically to his once intimate friend of long-gone prewar days, when, as students, they'd made tea together on a spirit stove and chewed bacon for supper, quoting Stirner and Nietzsche.

"Yes, Niels, a police agent! If you like, an agent provocateur!"

And today? There she was, together with the director general of the Finsk-Svensk-Blithuanian Society, examining Waldemaras's bloodstained head on its black velvet, explaining to that senile cretin routinely and snobbishly the daring impertinence of depicting "in such a way" the greatest product of Blitvinian Romanticism: *unmöglich*!

"What do you think of all this, Nielsen?" a quiet voice said behind him and he felt someone nervously take hold of his arm. It was Olaf Knutson, the right hand of Roman Rayevski. A sculptor of some fame and reputation, a neurasthenic talent who had completely given up and today worked for Rayevski in his studio as a technical assistant. Olaf Knutson, a man who had announced himself as "finished," as *raté*, as the shadow of something that had no reason to live, but whom Nielsen knew as a thinking man, indisputably honorable and unfortunate. The mere fact that Olaf Knutson had risked approaching Nielsen at such a time and in such a place was clear proof that Olaf Knutson could not care less how that exclusive gathering of Beauregard toadies and detectives might regard his gesture. It was Olaf Knutson who had sent Niels the invitation to this sickening occasion, in the certainty that he would not reply, and now, seeing him in the crowd, was delighted.

"What should I say?" said Nielsen, cordially shaking hands with him. "There's nothing to say! I look and wonder! I'm still sufficiently childish to be forever wondering! As things are today, it looks to me as if Larsen did the only thing worthy of a real man in these caveman conditions of ours: he went without a good-bye!"

"Look, for God's sake, come with me! I'll go mad if I have to spend this evening alone! I feel as if my guts are turning over! If I have to stay here another second, I'll puke!"

Nielsen had had enough of the crush and bustle of this false and stupid hypocrisy and so, quietly, they crept out and found themselves outside in the rain, beneath the awning of a dark autumn Blitvinian night.

"We're being followed, Nielsen!" Olaf Knutson warned him, nervously regarding some obscure figures walking parallel with them on the other side of that narrow and badly lit Jesuit Street.

"No one's following us, my friend! They're just ordinary pedestrians! It's a woman carrying a parcel and dragging a child behind her!"

"You're being watched, Nielsen! I got mixed up with some senators behind the headquarters and heard a man I didn't know warning an agent about you! At this do, there were at least as many agents as there were guests!"

"Yes, after my 'Open Letter,' I've become a stupid and pathetic sensation in this part of the world! Like a lot of frogs scared by a dog, my most intimate friends dive headlong into the water to avoid me! Cabbies and market women point me out! Ministers too! Naturally!"

"But no! You're being followed! Look at those two under the arcade!"

"They're just a pair of street musicians, Knutson! What's the matter with you? Your hands are like ice!"

"I've had it, Nielsen! If this goes on I'll go mad!"

They turned down Jesuit Street to Andria Waldemaras Square, where, around the monument, garlands of gas lamps wavered and where, in the darkness above Jarl's citadel, one sensed an impenetrable, fog-laden Scythian night that now lay like a depression of massive cowpats stretching from Vilenyska and Rungen all the way to the Hunnish tundra on the Blatvian border. In front of the baroque facade of the Bernardine monastery, in the center of the darkened square, stood Andria Waldemaras on his granite pedestal, the work of a Kurlandish academic sculptor, far more banal in its conception than Larsen's inspired portrayal. That bronze schoolboy on his stone cube, lit by the greenish light of a gas lamp, like a dummy in a badly lit provincial window of a store selling wholesale housecoats, and, seventy meters above the bronze poet, one felt the outlines of Jarl's citadel with its cannon and with Barutanski's machine guns.

"On this very spot three years ago, I went through a demonic scene with Larsen," Olaf Knutson said, casting a melancholic glance at the bronze Waldemaras and the marble Blitva beneath him, bearing his lyre on a velvet cushion. "It was that same night when Barutanski burst into Beauregard and when his drummers proclaimed a state of siege all over the town. I was standing with Larsen under Waldemaras's statue and he spoke about the elegiac nature of our Blitvinian reality. 'There's been a state of siege in Blitwanen for at least three hundred years, and should anyone in this provincial backwater of ours even have dared think of making a move in this general stagnation, the heavy Meklenburg cavalry would set off from this accursed Hunnish-Aragon citadel and one would hear the tramp of Hunnish hooves echoing down the streets between the cathedral and Jesuit Street. For centuries, the Huns were shooting over Blitwanen, the sound of broken glass, of empty burgled flats, terror, nowhere a sound except for the howling of a desperate dog, crying over our shattered Blitva.'

"It was a foul, windy, dark night," Knutson went on, "when I stood here with Larsen, and at that very moment when Larsen mentioned the dog howling over Blitva, in the distance we heard the howling of a dog, scared by the shooting, which grew ever fainter. Over there, in that single-story house, that third window from the left of the balcony was open and one could see the reflection of candlelight wavering on the ceiling and I and Larsen both had the same sense: that in that room, where the candle flickered on the ceiling, a dead man lay and the dog was howling in the night over his death, in the distance, in the fog. Many a dead man lay that night in his room throughout Blitwanen, and the Blitvinian kitsch artists of the sixties could find no other motif than dogs howling over the graves of Blitvinian patriots. It was the only theme of Blitvinian painting seventy years ago and Blitvinian lithographers made a good living out of it: out of dogs over Blitvinian graves and under Blitvinian gallows. And today? Today, this evening: Beauregard and the citadel are in the hands of Barutanski. Today, this evening, tonight, at this very moment, blood is flowing in Blitva just as it did under the Huns, only perhaps more so. Tonight again the dog howls under the window of the room where a dead man lies. Tonight Blitvinians shoot at one another, and what is the gain? Tonight Blitvinian flesh is crushed and bloodied, houses and flats are riddled with bullets, feathers fly from ransacked houses, and that howling of a dog over our burnt ruins is the sole Blitvinian motif that is worth portraying. The question is how? Who of our contemporary artists in Blitva possesses the ear to sense the sole human voice in this contemporary Blitvinian ballad, that sole human voice that is, in fact, the howling of a dog! That was what Larsen said that foul windy night beneath this monument, and that's how he gave the Blitvinian nocturne we saw tonight, sealing his farewell letter with his own blood. All this, our Blitvinian, Akhasverian, alienated, ephemeral condition, neither here nor there between two shores, in two severed halves, that deracinated decomposition, that suppurating doubt of the aim of one's own existence, that painful cutting off of rotten prejudices, that constant slithering from one to another ever greater lie, those painful wounds, those harsh blows of the mind and conscience, those dread and secret sufferings within oneself and around oneself, and then, one day, capitulation and death. And after all this, an apotheosis in Thorwaldsen's palace or a foul bronze statue like this! Despair! Please, come with me! Let's have a drink somewhere where there's light, music. Here it's awful! The damp gets right to your bones, as if you were catching fish in a cellar under the Lethe! Let's go to Dominic's! There it's warm and merry. They serve pheasants on the spit! Dominic has real French cognac!"

Nielsen too was glad to go to Dominic's. "There are open fireplaces, and fair-haired, good-looking Scots girls play the harmonica. At Dominic's one can really eat well." At the corner of Bernardines they took a taxi and set off down the narrow streets into the center of town to Dominic's.

CHAPTER 6

At Dominic's

At Dominic's the atmosphere was both comfortable and jocular. It was warm. The flames licked up in the old-fashioned Swedish hearth, and against their reflection sizzled roast suckling pig, pheasants, and small gray hens, a special type of Blitvinian chicken that is eaten with *blitvanchik,* an extremely tasty porridge made of buckwheat, the favorite flour of Blitva, used for *blitnya,* bread made of pancakes, soaked in a mushroom sauce. These were all Dominic's specialties, which, under the old, smoke-blackened beams of this cheerful Kurlandish inn, he served to Blitvinian gourmets with his famous Mediterranean wine in its original demijohns. Here steamed entire legs of veal on massive silver plates, served in the Flanders style, in thick slices with bacon. The tables around the buffet were laden with beluga, sturgeon, and pink salmon. There chefs in their snow-white caps busied themselves, delivering long-whiskered lobsters, salted beluga, sausages, and cheeses to all sides of this food fair which bustled and hummed around the some thirty tables in the main dining room. On a stage six good-looking and attractive young girls were singing naive American popular songs to the accompaniment of an accordion, repeating the same thing in many variants to the point of childish monotony: Spring is here or spring is surely coming, for my love waits for my first letter in spring—accompanying it all with the banging of drums and other such Negroid instruments.

Summer days are coming,
Winter days are gone.
Merry birds are singing,
In the flow'ry dawn.

Olaf Knutson and Nielsen downed five or six rums and five or six glasses of Blitvinian oat brandy, a vintage spirit that burned like the devil, and ordered a real common dish of Blitva, Viking Stew, which was served as a starter with spicy sausages poached in *varen'chik,* an unusually complicated sauce with thirty-three ingredients, of which the most important were pig's trotters and calf's intestines, all finely cut up with various spices and fried in wine.

After the third or fourth rum, Olaf Knutson began to feel the effects, and since both were still under the influence of Larsen's *jour de vernissage,* Knutson began immediately to rage against Rayevski with such ferocity, it was obvious from his first words that the figure of Rayevski irritated him to the point of mental unbalance and that Rayevski dominated Knutson, not merely as a source of constant anger but also as an idée fixe.

"Did you see him this evening, the old bastard, looking so sourly at Larsen's waxworks? I tell you, if that bluestocking, that little snob Ingrid Barutanski, hadn't wet her knickers over Larsen's last works (by whose suggestion God alone knows), there'd never have been an exhibition, believe you me! Rayevski was green with anger and envy when Ingrid Barutanski called him over to look at Larsen's figures! He took it personally! Green with anger and envy! Rayevski immediately said that he and Larsen stood for two quite different things, two different capacities. In Larsen's final inspiration there was that power which, to put it vulgarly and in one word, is what they call—genius!"

Niels felt the need to contradict. Not because he was convinced of Rayevski's talent, but because, that evening, after his sixth rum, he felt that Olaf Knutson was expressing the normal human envy of a less gifted hairsplitter.

"You must admit: Larsen and Rayevski, to say the least, are two completely separate and different talents."

"They're nothing of the sort. Larsen represents the inspiration of a real creator, a true poet, a genius with insight, a one hundred percent sincere artist, and what Rayevski does is just bluff! I can't understand how it is that none of you grasps that Rayevski's work is nothing but the most blatant impertinent fraud! I'm surprised at you, Nielsen! For instance, you can see clearly that Barutanski's a cheat, an impudent bluffer, a murderer! And see here: I endorse everything you wrote in your 'Open Letter.' To the last line! But all the same! Barutanski is nothing but politics! The usual, every-day, stupid or criminal (it doesn't matter which) politics! You have no idea to what extent Barutanski's actions are more honest, more virile, yes, if you wish it, more positive than what Rayevski's doing! For politics is a whore by profession, whereas art ceases to be art the day it goes to bed without love!"

"I don't agree with you. Politics is just as ideal an occupation as art! And the question of Rayevski's talent is an open one. But any-way, as you see, he has excited immense interest abroad," Nielsen replied.

"What talent? It's not a matter of talent causing interest, but of mystification! Who attracted attention abroad? Rayevski? Go to hell! I'm surprised at you, being a relatively intelligent man, expressing yourself in such a primitive way. What sort of attention did Rayevski attract abroad? As an artist? As a painter? As a sculptor? No! He is accepted abroad as a politician, not as a painter. He repre-sented Blitva in Paris, and now he'll soon be elected president of the

Republic and all those old millionaire American spinsters who come to Blitva to have their portrait painted by the president of the Republic and who'll pay him a thousand quid for each portrait, they'll be a certain proof in our Blitwanen backwater, to you and those like you, that Rayevski 'has attracted immense attention even abroad.' If Barutanski were a painter, his paintings today would sell to the English old maids just as well as Rayevski's, and what proof would that be of the inner value of Barutanski's pictures? God's truth, you talk like the most ordinary philistine! You politicians haven't a clue that for artistic creation, morality comes first. Rayevski is an immoral swine, and Barutanski isn't exactly a Catholic monk."

"Does that mean you refuse the artist the right to engage in politics?" Nielsen asked.

"No, my dear sir! That's not what I said! Is what Larsen expressed in his wax figures politics? Yes! That's politics in its highest sense! Only that 'politics' is expressed in a spiritual way which has found its adequate form! I deny the right of an artist to gain any form of quasi-artistic success by political means! That's it! For Rayevski abroad, Rayevski in the foreign press, Rayevski in the introductions to his catalogs for the foreign public, presents above all propaganda for Barutanski's Blitvinian enterprise! Rayevski signed the peace in Blato Blitvinsko. Rayevski was the president of the first Blitvinian Constituent Assembly. Rayevski was the expert on Blitvinian affairs at the Paris conference of ambassadors in 'eighteen. Rayevski is the candidate for president of the Republic. Rayevski is the most intimate friend of Barutanski, the dictator of Blitva. Rayevski is raising a monument to Barutanski. Rayevski has designed the church of Saint Paul of Blitva. Rayevski has painted the pope's portrait. Rayevski plays mah-jongg with Cardinal Armstrong, Rayevski is the president of the first Blitvinian Academy, and so on and so forth. And when people approach Rayevski as an artist, they—in that very act—really approach him as a political gambler, a cardplayer, a political ace, a man who has Beauregard in his side pocket and who sits above Blitva like some form of super-man! People don't flatter Rayevski as an artist (for people generally have no interest in art as such), but because they think that by means of our national Blitvinian genius they'll be able to sign fa-vorable trade agreements with Beauregard. All that scum of inter-national commercial travelers who come to Blitva to sell sub-marines or steam plow or sewing machines go to pay their court to Rayevski. Well, you've been at his social receptions and therefore know very well what the parties given by our Sunday-best 'Genius' are like," Knutson said.

"Yes, I have, but I don't think this should be decisive in assess-ing a work of art. In any case, I'm no expert in such questions. They seem to me to be too complex and unclear. But one thing is true: After every such solemn reception at Maestro Rayevski's, I returned home with a heavy moral discomfort, whether of con-science or taste I don't know. In any case, I'll give you this, with a feeling of disquiet and disharmony. . . . But I still say: I can't be a judge in these matters because it's hard to talk of something when one lacks a sufficient knowledge of the facts!"

"I see. You refuse to judge? But as for Beauregard, you consider yourself an expert? When it comes to Barutanski, you think you're competent, but not when it concerns Rayevski? What wonderful logic! Congratulations! Well done! You know all about politics, but Rayevski isn't politics? Bravo!"

It was Olaf Knutson's eleventh or fifteenth rum and he was cut-ting pieces of salmon, as wide as your hand and thick as your thumb, from the silver tray and the pink fish melted in his mouth and disappeared as if it were Neapolitan ice cream.

"In other words, when it comes to the artistic value of Rayevski, you don't feel competent?" Knutson continued. "When it comes to that, my dear Dr. Nielsen, you can't judge? Marvelous! But those

Protestant elders of the church who admire Rayevski's Counter-Reformational, allegedly hundred percent Catholic angels, those Protestant, Lutheran theologians understand it, one has to give them credit! One has to give it to our provincial Blitvinian ministers who know Western European civilization only from the point of view of American shaving cream or this or that brand of condom, to those cows on sale to the highest bidder, those miserable bastards. One has to admit that they really understand the point of Roman Rayevski's art when they look at the horse for the equestrian statue of Kristian Barutanski and say: Maestro, you've exceeded your wildest dreams! *Magnifique!* Those ridiculous, semiliterate lawyers of ours who squint their left eye when faced with a naked woman's body in marble, thinking they've fooled somebody, when they utter the word *marvelous,* like muck out of a force-fed goose, they're the only competent people to judge such matters, and they're the ones we should ask, in the form of well-organized opinion polls, for such gentlemen are competent to give any final conclusion! To blink their eyes and squint, to scratch their heads, sniff, pick their nose, scratch themselves between their legs through their trouser pockets, spit out a toothpick, throw away a cigarette and light another, and all this in front of Rayevski's monumental statue which depicts the half-naked figure of Dolores as the armored symbol of Blitva. To behave like this before a work of art, as does our Blitvinian scum 'that understands art'—Christ, my dear chap if you consider yourself less able than these, as being no specialist, that, my dear friend, isn't resignation, it's just bloody intellectual laziness! If you think it's important to settle accounts with Barutanski, as you do, and I agree with you, then for me as an artist, as one who believes in the purity of creative morality, then for me it's immeasurably more important to come to grips with Rayevski! For you, clearly, Rayevski is unimportant! But what would you say to me if I said that this Barutanski of yours is unimportant? 'That I was not competent to make a judgment regarding Barutanski, because I was not qualified to deal with such complex political questions.' What would you reply? That I was a morally and intellectually lazy bastard! And you'd be dead right! For that's the whole point! Barutanski and Rayevski represent one and the same thing, one and the same phenomenon: the present mess that's Blitva under Beauregard! They're just two symbols of Blitva! If the moral question of Blitva gets to you, how can you be so bloody lazy regarding Rayevski? Cheers! My dear Nielsen! See, faced with this posthumous celebration of Larsen, I raise this glass and toast you for your 'Open Letter' and all honor to you! Hats off! I'm no chameleon with a different opinion about everything with a respectable intellectual and moral reserve, to tell you that politics isn't my field and that I'm not called upon to make a decision, since I don't understand the question of Barutanski! I understand the question all too well and I admire you because, amid all this shit, you're the only real man, and I raise this glass to your health and I give you my most profound and sincere respect for your heroic gesture! But look here, in return, logically, I demand that you listen to me, that you grasp, once and for all, the need to understand this question correctly, which is in no way less important than your Barutanski! Your health! Life, you see, wouldn't be so foul if we didn't have such hellish vampires on earth—summer days are coming, winter days are gone. . . . Your health! Listen, Nielsen, for God's sake! Did you know that that same Roman Rayevski ordered from Paris five hundred silver cigarette cases with his monogram and crest and that now he'll have the date of his election to the presidency added, and that then there won't be a man in Blitva who doesn't have a presidential cigarette case? Perhaps even I'll get one! Who knows? I might even get a gold one with his monogram if I go on serving him like a faithful dog for another fifteen years! As it is, I've lived in Rayevski's shadow for almost two decades, and when we walk down the street you can hear the whisper behind us: 'Psst, that's Rayevski,' and then from time to time somebody remembers to ask: 'And who's that with him?' and then one hears on the public's lips: 'That's Olaf Knutson.'

"'Who?'

"'Olaf Knutson.'

"'And who is that?'

"'He's our maestro's personal detective'—that's what I heard an old lady say about me when we passed her. And so Olaf Knutson faithfully accompanies his master on the way to his master's apotheosis, and so Olaf Knutson has become a candidate to be one of the immortals of the Academy, only he has to wait humbly in the antechamber until one of the chosen twelve renders up his immortality to God. The other day I read in the *Tigdende* that Rayevski truly represents 'a synthesis of the national Blitvinian mythos'! He, said the *Tigdende,* is 'the Messiah, Prophet, and Victor and the Blitvinian national mythos'! He is the Blitvinian soul incarnate! The guardian angel of the Blitvinian race! And I? Who am I? I'm a man without any special abilities, but it makes me want to vomit! Rayevski has walked all over me, I know it. I'm just a nobody, nobody and nothing, while Rayevski has truly achieved 'the Blitvinian synthesis, the Blitvinian national mythos'! I'm just a type of liveried servant in his house, and I know that man hates me to such an extent that he'd like to have me killed, because that cunning, clever, and introverted prophet, who has donned the worthy gown of aristocratic silence, knows very well that I've had the honor of seeing through him and his tricks! That rogue needs undressing, analyzing down to the last element of his idealless nakedness, and then one would see that there was no more to him than that pathetic, gold-braided, tasteless academic frock coat which he designed for himself in front of the mirror, and I had to sketch some eleven versions from various textbooks on diplomatic protocol—eleven gold academic frock coats, so that Roman Rayevski could fittingly disguise his Blitvinian academics! Mindless stupidity!

So there you are: two or three presidential cigarette cases, silver snuffboxes, teas, receptions, soirees, and little Dolores as Blitva, and there you have it! In all that, there's not the least inner value! It's without power! All on the surface: mere reflection, imitation, copy, transposition, plagiarism, nothing, a melange, a disgusting melange. That idiot takes more than half an hour every morning to tie his tie in front of the mirror, and the glass in his spectacles gleams so emptily that one never knows whether it's just the glass that's empty or his expression. His wife Silva is the most everyday type of career lady, and believe you me, Doctor, they're so mean with their housekeeping budget that the food they serve is beneath criticism! Everything in that fine home is badly done, illogical, exaggerated, unintelligent, distorted. Lately it all seems to me too much in the style of Beauregard protocol. Now all of the male household take half an hour to tie their ties in front of the mirror. The whole atmosphere gets more unbearable with every day! I know you'll think I'm being prejudiced! I have the impression you think I'm being unjust! That I see nothing positive in the man. I recall that two or three years ago you used to visit him from time to time and your whole attitude toward his artistic work reflected a deep inner respect! But in what way, I ask you, is this 'sculptor' any different from me? His modeling is good and correct? And mine isn't? Such correct and faithful modelers as he or I come in thousands in the world. To be a good modeler presents nothing in particular. It's like stuffing birds or designing furniture. And the fact that he has stood out above us other several thousand modelers, stuffers of birds, and hired draftsmen is not due to the fact that he's a better modeler, but that he's a gambler, and a lucky one! Am I not as good a modeler? Wasn't it I, for instance, who modeled the horse and rider for Barutanski's monument, entirely on my own (to his so-called design), and everybody marvels at 'his' power of modeling! And then the pedants say: 'Ah, yes, my son, it's true, you do the work, but the ideas are his!'"

Pause. Cognac. A cigarette. A puff. Two or three more puffs. Cognac. A glance that circled with the smoke and was lost in the distance, and then Knutson's voice returning out of a great height and circling around the inn like a tired bird, to sound once more in a muffled minor key: "For God's sake, don't any of you see that these 'ideas' of his aren't 'ideas,' but the merest deceit? And do you know what's amazed me for years? It's the fact that that man has the moral nerve to look me in the face. He is the 'master,' who has his own 'ideas,' and my job is to realize his 'idea,' as my drawing, as my maquette, as my clay version, as fresco, as stone, as wood. I have the job of dealing with workmen, to be present at the molding, to work and toil for days and nights together (twenty-four hours in his service), and he plays the master, the prophet, winks slyly and scratches his bottom. He signs the orders, builds the houses, and I'm just a drunk, a nobody, a man of no talent, a miserable failure whom he, like the generous patron he is, supports. I tell you, I just don't understand it! But I know this! One might easily say: Why go on for years wailing like a childless woman? Why didn't you pull yourself together, spit on your hands, and go your own way? By today, you'd have been your own master like him. You too could have become a prophet and built fountains and churches, molded a bronze horseman on your own account, and not gone on grumbling for years about how the man for whom you have slaved and toiled for years cheats you! Yours is the voice of weakness, and right is on the side of the stronger! Yet you play his game, you're just a type of uniformed lackey, a dog that wags its tail in front of its master. You eat out of his hand and you'll never dare to fling the truth in his face, because you haven't the guts! Yes, that's the truth! I haven't the guts! And do you know what should be done to him, if one had the guts? He needs killing like a mad dog! Two years ago when we were on his famous tour of America, there was just such a dramatically obvious moment, when I should have killed him and I didn't do it, because I hadn't the guts, because I'm a louse and not a man, because I was born the way I am: a stutterer, an idiot, with water in my veins instead of blood, a pathetic creature! I don't know whether you remember Rayevski's tour from New York to San Francisco and then in the South American republics, his triumph in Rio de Janeiro, for instance? In Ankersgarden we boarded the *Blitvania*. It was her first transatlantic voyage. It was, so to speak, a double occasion: the first voyage of a Blitvinian transatlantic liner, with the first Blitvinian genius, who was carrying to the Anglo-Saxons and the transoceanic Spaniards a greeting from Barutanski, together with his, today, historic phrase, concerning the Blitvinian Quattrocento! In Bremen and, especially, in Southampton, we took on a crowd of American passengers on their way home. Those millionaires, God knows why, had a weakness for the maiden voyages of certain ships. They were a band of perverse robbers! It was a sort of millionaire rape of a ship! This mass of gentile nomads stuck to our *Blitvania* like flies to a beefsteak and, naturally, Roman Rayevski, the well-known Blitvinian genius, acted, for this lot, like a first-class sensation. As you might expect, being the Sancho Panza of this our 'synthetic national prophet,' this pure genius, I published an article about him in the ship's newspaper: who he was, how he was making his triumphal tour, how his pictures, his compositions, represented a Blitvinian epic, how he was a type of prophet, since in his pictures made in the long past prewar days he had foretold the collapse of that great whore of all whores and Babylon of all Babylons, Hunnia, and so, with his portrayal of our legendary heroes, eternalized our centuries-long Blitvinian sacrifices, our patriotic striving, our thousand-year-old ideals, that is to say, he had realized the dream of generations of Blitvinians, how he was the true Blitvinian prophet, that he was the architect of our ideals, the dove and the eagle in a single marble dream, and so on and so forth, just as they write about him in the catalogs and monographs, in a word, in history. Whenever Rayevski appeared in the huge Louis Fifteenth salon of our *Blitvania*, the band played a fanfare and all the lorgnettes turned toward that celestial figure of a prophet from an unknown and mysterious European land, one who passed through the millionaire ranks as if they were chaff, always carrying three or four thick volumes as though forever engaged in the study of deeply significant and profound questions, as though for days he did nothing but absorb books! Absorbed books even at sea! (And this, remember, a man who hadn't read three books in his life!)

"So then that is interesting! A phenomenon! A giant! A prophet! A racial synthesis! He predicted a whole national liberation! He is traveling to New York! Broadway! A single portrait painted by him costs seven hundred pounds. He is a personal friend of the dictator of Blitwania, of Colonel Barutanski, who delivered the Karabaltics from the red hell. Yes! Morgan, Rockefeller, and many others want to have their portraits done by him. He is a religious sculptor! He is a friend of Bishop Armstrong! He is not only an artist but also a prophet! In fact, he is the first man who presented to Europe a young unknown interesting Karabaltic race! 'Grand! Karabaltic, what does Karabaltic mean?' Karabaltic is a kind of milk separator.

"Belowdecks, in the third- and fourth-class sections, where several hundred of our Blitvinians were emigrating in order, as the poorest of the poor, to become slaves on American soil, slaves of the lowest order: Japanese and blacks. Nothing ever struck me so hard as the stink of our Blitvinian lower decks, and no matter how little, either by nature or by character, was I prone to exaggeration and, least of all, to demagogy, that very contrast between those Blitvinian stinking rags belowdecks and the golden saloons abovedecks so got to me that I could not restrain myself, without any ulterior motive, from feeling, as one does sometimes feel, that the whole of this buildup of our Blitvinian civilization was heading basically in the wrong direction. What's the point of our luxury Blitvinian transoceanic liners when beneath their decks Blitvinians travel on the level of poultry, in their own shit and their own stinking rags? Nonsense! And all our present intellectual views, our propaganda abroad, our art, particularly our glorification of the so-called higher, metaphysical calling of our Blitvinian race, our racial messianism—all that amounts to nothing but placing cheap plaster decorations in a flat where what they need is not decorations but bread! Roman Rayevski, from his superior height, above any of my most convincing arguments, interrupted me with the statement that I regarded everything from a too pessimistic point of view. That our people were poor was true, but that was why they went to America, to stop being so, and there, on the other shore, they would become house owners in the second generation. And just think, Rayevski's very words, that in two or three generations one of the descendants of these Blitvinian émigrés of ours would say: My grandfather came to America on the same boat that carried Roman Rayevski on his first tour of America! Of all that I had seen belowdecks, nothing would remain in future history! History would record not a line concerning the stink and hunger! For history does not sniff the backside of every detail. History paints a broad picture, a decorative picture, in large, synthetic lines! All that would remain in history would be the journey of Roman Rayevski! And nothing else! Neither what it looked like belowdecks, nor what I thought of it! And that was how one should look at it."

It was as if an earthquake had struck that moment beneath the foundations of Dominic's old-fashioned inn. In a single second all the guests leapt from their chairs. In the sudden tinkling of glass, crockery, silver, amid overturned tables, amid fish, roast veal, beluga, aspic, in all that chaos, everybody was at a loss, nobody realizing, for the moment, what had happened. From the upper gallery above the stage where the girls were playing their accordions, two strangers opened fire with automatic pistols at one of the tables in the central section, and this rapid fire whistled above the whirling mass of tablecloths, broken crockery, spilt wine, broken chairs, and the cries of the wounded with such a sudden and horrifying speed that in the disordered and terrified rush and outcry nobody knew where they were: what was this drumming, this falling of glasses and crashing of chairs, who was wounded and crying for help, and why was there such a mass of spilt borscht?

"That's not borscht, it's blood! Somebody's shooting! Help! Police! Waiter, bill, please! Help! Blood!"

"What's happened?"

Olaf Knutson leapt instinctively toward Nielsen, who was frozen to his place, pale, cold, without a drop of blood in his cheeks but completely calm, looking around him at the confusion, as if absentmindedly.

"It's nothing! It was shooting. I modestly think their bullets were meant for me!" Nielsen said.

"You're bleeding. There's blood coming from your sleeve."

"No, I'm not hurt. Somebody spilt some pickled beetroot over me!"

"I told you, Nielsen, they were following us! It was damned silly of us! We gave those bastards a perfect target!"

"What of it! They'll shoot us anyway, sooner or later! So what the hell!"

"Let's go! Right now! Come on! No point in doing the bastards a favor! You mustn't go home! You can sleep at my place! Christ almighty, I've been blabbing all evening like an old woman, while your life was in danger!"

Knutson took Nielsen home to his flat, refusing to let, as he put it, "a man condemned to death" go home. After some discussion, they agreed that Nielsen would spend the night with him, and that Knutson would then take him to his godmother, Mrs. Gallen, who was stone deaf but otherwise a highly intelligent woman. She'd been a piano teacher. She'd had an only son, Sigurd Gallen, a captain on the general staff who'd fallen doing his duty in defense of the legitimate government of Muzhikovski in the year '25, when Barutanski's artillery bombarded the citadel. Ever since then, Mrs. Gallen had fallen into a quiet state of depression, broke all the strings on her piano, and, being stone deaf, she now played on a silent piano, so that no one could hear. This was her only eccentricity, but this would not bother him since it could not be heard in his room, and otherwise he would be quite comfortable. And then, in a day or two, when things had calmed down, he should go to Blatvia, which was the most sensible thing he could do, given the situation. There was no time to lose.

CHAPTER 7

Rayevski's Triumph

The third day after the shooting at Dominic's (two dead and several badly wounded), the legal representatives of all the Blitvinian corporations gathered at a plenary meeting in the old Palace of the Principality in order, unanimously, to elect and recommend Roman Rayevski to Barutanski as the candidate for the presidency of the Republic. That noble gathering of all the various Blitvinian professions, guilds, and institutions sat in the main hall of the ancient Princely Residence, on the first floor, from where, through the massive balcony windows, the Blitvinian dignitaries had a view of the rich crowns of centuries-old plane trees, tinged with the dark copper gleam of late autumn. In the oval baroque hall in the style of Stanislau Augustus, behind a massive bronze inlaid table, a myopic, gray, anonymous figure, resembling the perfect lackey with sidewhiskers, played the part of president. Above this pathetic lackey figure of a president there hung a monumental square of pale gold, translucent pastel tapestry on which, in fantastic, phosphorescent-greenish distances, galloped naked cuirassiers with shining, emerald-green helmets, framed in rich motifs of melons, fish, dark blue waterfalls, and a background of stars, through which shone suns like golden apples. Above this select gathering of Blitvinian high clergy, representatives of science, trade, industry, and the free intellectual professions there dominated the frowning figure of the governor, protector, and actual ruler of Blitva, the portrait of Colonel Barutanski in a rich and heavy frame, ornamented with bas-relief of symbols of war: cannon, swords, maces, banners, and crossed muskets, all decoratively bound together by cockades and garlands of laurel and oak leaves, which lent to that dark portrait a particularly serious, martial appearance. On the president's table, bathing in the polish of that gleaming board, smiled the plaster head of the Republic of Blitva: the head of the charming, mysterious Dolores, a smiling young lady with a laurel wreath, of whom all that was known in Blitwanen was that she had arrived from California and enjoyed one hundred percent of the sympathy of the dictator Barutanski and that the new series of Blitvinian thousand-lei notes was to bear her head in the person of Blitva Reformed, wearing a golden helmet, in armor, and carrying a lance, representing in neo-Hellenic style the stock exchange equivalent of a thousand golden Blitvinian lei, payable to the bearer at the counter of the Blitvinian National Bank. According to a prearranged protocol, a representation of that noble Blitvinian assembly of all estates (among which, at the very end and in the lowest place, was mentioned a delegation of workers) was to present itself at Beauregard and there, in the name of the Blitvinian Plenum, assembled in the Prince's Electoral Palace, to inform Colonel Barutanski of the preelection result and, having received the Protector's confirmation, that same delegation was to proceed under the escort of a squadron of uhlans to the candidate Roman Rayevski and to hand him a form of decree by which the assembled estates unanimously elected him candidate for the presidency. Under the leadership of the architect Blithauer-Blitvinski, the delegation consisted of five members: a representative of the Catholic and of the Protestant churches; old Burgwaldsen, as the Nestor of Blitvinian scholarship; the president of the Supreme Court of Blitva, Fortis-Valetzki; and the president of the Blitvinian Legion, Lieutenant Colonel Kardosh.

In expectation of the formal delegation from Beauregard, the nominated candidate for the highest honor in the Republic, Roman

Rayevski, invited some forty most distinguished guests to a gala luncheon at his villa. Apart from Ingrid Barutanski, who, in herself, represented the center of this noble gathering (worthy of the deepest and most devoted respect), there were also a number of Anglomanic snobs, headed by the leader of the Adagio Freemason Lodge and the editor of the largest Blitvinian daily, *Blitwanen Tigdende*, Wernis. All of them bold, castrated vegetarians who, in principle and exclusively, drank only mineral water and, equally in principle, never signed promissory notes, who judged the position of others according to the *Times* editorial and who otherwise snored happily on solid interest, never less, if possible, than 18 percent. Dr. Willumsen, head of the section for the promotion of Blitvinian interests abroad, a gentleman who declaimed histrionically about the patriarchal cult of the family as "the only basis on which the destroyed Europe might be restored," brought with him to this gala luncheon an ancient English mummy, the senile Lord Butler with his wife, and, in conversation with the said Lord Butler, spoke of Blitvinian shoots (that abounded with vultures), declaiming in a loud voice into his lordship's hearing aid that the cult of the family was the sole patriarchal basis by which one could decently hunt in the unspoiled hunting grounds of northeastern and Karabaltic "Europe, unsullied by Western materialism." Talking daily to deaf French academics, English and American Quakers, and other various such benefactors of the world, who for years had come to Blitva to study the Blitvinians from the point of view of anthroposophical wisdom and the semireligious and relatively profitable zeal of the Salvation Army, he stated coldly and absentmindedly that the Blitvinian people were, in essence, completely healthy, since for the Blitvinians the cult of the family was highly developed, and that the family "was that patriarchal base on which the postwar demoralized and materialistic Europe might be restored."

"Indeed, indeed, that's good thinking," Lord Butler nodded, "and we as the pillars of good society, the cream, the elite, by all means the best of society, we should be aware that shooting in such poor countries as Blitva represents indeed an institution of social charity. It brings in foreign currency and raises interest in tourism, and from such charitable hunting and shooting the Blitvinian peasant can only profit. Apart from this, one should never lose sight of the fact that, in this way, the uncivilized Blitvinian masses come into contact with representatives of the polished world, with the hunting elite."

In the vast Kurlandish hall, around an open Blitvinian hearth, there gathered the intellectual elite of the town of Blitwanen. Following a rich and leisurely lunch there, with cognac and black coffee, stood two ex-political governors, several ministers without portfolio, a forensic anatomist with his wife, a ship owner, also with his wife, all of them excited and apprehensive, with a single thought, namely to place themselves as near as possible to the future Bearer of the Highest Blitvinian Honor when he received the Address of the Estates, just as guests jostle around distinguished citizens five minutes before midnight so as to be face-to-face with the chief and secretary general in the New Year when the lights went on, and be among the first to wish their chief and secretary general all happiness, for the happiness of Roman Rayevski, in this case, meant happiness for their ships, for their factories, for forensic anatomy, and for the rather empty wallets of the ministers without portfolio.

From the hall a double three-winged door opened into a winter garden, where among huge spreading rubber plants, palms, rhododendrons, and monkey puzzle trees in the full afternoon sunlight it was several degrees warmer than in the hall, which, seen from this intensive sunlight, seemed like a dark and smoky place where a fire flamed in the half-light at the back, and where people loomed through the violet clouds of cigarette smoke more as the outlines of various colored fabrics, silks, and uniforms than as individual persons.

In the winter garden, in the massive walnut relief by Roman Rayevski, the Assumption of the Blessed Virgin, depicted at that very moment, redolent of an unworldly excitement, when two angels, in a single vertical movement, raised the earthly remains of the Virgin to heaven, to the terrified bewilderment of the Apostles, who wrung their hands and wept for the Virgin, there, beneath the palms and rubber plants, stood the painter Vanini-Schiavone with Jules Dupont, a pedant and a witty conversationalist, who moved about the world of Beauregard as the favorite equally of Barutanski and his wife. Jules Dupont was present at this formal occasion as the semiofficial escort of Madame Ingrid Barutanski and, settling himself comfortably in the cushioned California hammock, he had been expatiating to Vanini, for the last half hour, his criticism of Rayevski's bas-relief: It was unconvincing, utterly empty, insincere, unintelligently rendered, weakly constructed, sloppily drawn, and, what was most important, it was like a banal phrase, absolutely boring, unoriginal, unpleasant, yes, one might even say irritating. Discussing this well-known and recognized masterpiece of the future president in this well-intentioned and friendly manner, Jules Dupont, suddenly and without any warning, asked Vanini whether he thought Roman Rayevski really believed in God. Perhaps the question was superfluous, in no way appropriate, but for him, an old, so to speak, experienced atheist, of some interest. Silence!

Vanini puffed on his thick Havana. In front of him on the table was a mass of silver, dishes, silver jugs with black coffee, decanters of cognac, crystal with sweet cream, tins with originally packed Havanas. Everything on the table in front of him was rich, overloaded with massive carved silver boxes, with silver-mounted crystal ashtrays. Everywhere there was the scent of first-rate Courvoisier, of a solid meal. The entire conservatory with its doors opening on the park shone in the rich sunlight. There was the murmur of fountains, the buzz of the guests from the hall, and, from somewhere in the distance, the muted sound of a foxtrot from one of the rear salons, a completely lazy, sybaritic, pleasant, and sleepy boredom, in which one could doze without a care, while here was the unpleasant, tedious voice disturbing one with its stupid nagging.

Who anyway was this Jules Dupont? This mysterious Jules Dupont, what role did he play? In whose interest was he sniffing about? In any case, wasn't this whole conversation just a form of provocation? Why then these tendentious and stupid questions?

"However: why ask me whether Rayevski believes in God? What's the point?" Vanini said, handing off the indiscretions of this importunate foreigner.

"My very question makes the point clear: What interests me as an authentic atheist is how can anyone create religious motifs if he doesn't believe? You're a religious painter too, Monsieur Vanini! All the churches in Blitva are full of your paintings: your Gethsemane in Armstrong's bedroom, your Blitvinian Apotheosis in the Jesuit dome, with Christ the King as the universal ruler over the insignificant centuries of Blitva, your saints on altars, your Madonnas, your angels, all this goes to prove that you are an ecclesiastic, that is to say religious, painter, so what's so illogical in asking you your opinion as to whether Rayevski is truly a believer? Is this Ascension really the fruit of religious inspiration or just routine? As mere routine it could hardly be justified, so all we can do is to assume that Rayevski really does believe in God."

As though brushing off an annoying fly, Vanini absentmindedly repeated his question to Dupont: "All right then, what about you? Do you believe in God?"

"I've already told you: I don't believe in anything, not in God, not in people, and I think the whole thing is a long-outworn prejudice.

That is to say, I use the word 'prejudice' in a mitigating sense for those who really believe without any ulterior motive or purpose; in other words, those who are true believers."

"Then you're convinced that there are such people who believe, just because they believe?"

"Don't be ridiculous! How else can one believe? If someone were to believe just in order to sell his Gethsemane to Armstrong, then his faith is that of a seller of pictures, not that of a believer! At least that's clear. The only way to believe is naively, without any hidden motive, without any scheming."

What's this guy going on about? Vanini grumbled to himself, brushing aside in his thoughts this shadow of a man, as though, half awake, he were brushing off a spider's web of uncomfortable forebodings. This Dupont has lately grown too inquisitive about everything: who thinks what, who's going where, and why this and why that? Roman Rayevski is an artist, that is to say, a painter, a creator, which is true, up to a point . . . And to slander or criticize Rayevski before today, that was one thing! But Rayevski today has ceased to be an ordinary artist! Today Rayevski is in the process of becoming the highest dignitary of Blitva. Today one must consider the matter from quite a different angle.

Slyly squinting with his left eye and clicking his tongue in satisfaction that he'd found a good way out of this doubtful and unclear situation with this doubtful and in every way mysterious Jules Dupont, Vanini licked his cigar, poured first himself and then Jules Dupont a glass of Courvoisier, and, with two fingers, took a grape from a silver tray in front of him, ate it and then another, and then mechanically wiped his fingers on a towel and then, wiping his lips with the same two fingers he'd used to pluck the grapes (with his thumb and forefinger as the market women do when they wipe their mouths), he inhaled two or three deep and luscious puffs of his Havana, and, leaning back once more on the soft cushions of the

California hammock, rather lazily, like a rhinoceros in warm water, turned toward Roman Rayevski's relief which portrayed the Ascension of the Blessed Virgin and, examining that well-known masterpiece of his friend and future president of the Republic, it seemed to Vanini, at that moment, that everything he and that Jules Dupont had been saying was exaggeratedly negative! "All right! All honor to objective criticism, but there's no need to exaggerate. Not everything in that relief's so bad. Rayevski's a routine artist, that's true, but still it's all done with the sure hand of a master! See how his John the Apostle is dramatically bent forward, how his left elbow's pressed tight to his side, which gives his entire outline that necessary movement to emphasize the impression of sadness and despair. Truly, the trick of a master!"

Once again Vanini squinted and, covering his right eye with his hand so as to get a better view, he again fixed his attention on John the Apostle on the walnut relief, thinking that that John the Apostle would indeed have been better on a canvas than on a relief: if the fabric of his toga had been scarlet red, and if, behind it, there had been a dark Berlin blue sky, this would have raised the tragic devastation of his movement.

"And why are you bothering me about whether Rayevski believes in God or not?" Vanini continued. "What's it to you? Or are you one of those people who have been saying lately that Rayevski has no talent? You see I couldn't agree with you on this! It's unimportant what the artist thinks or believes while creating his work! What is important is that the work is of value, and that, you see, is the main question! If someone signs a religious work, then no one has the right to doubt it. A man guarantees his political, aesthetic, or religious convictions with his signature, just as he does his checks."

"All right, but if there's nothing to back up his check," Jules Dupont interrupted ironically, "what then, Monsieur Vanini?"

"As regards his religious capital, of that, my dear sir, I do not feel competent to express a judgment, and as regards the aesthetics, there too I cannot agree with you. Look, I ask you, be good enough to turn your rather arrogant and somewhat limited attention to the life of the small details, which don't leap to the eye and which live with their own hidden and mysterious rhythm beneath the surfaces of every work, naturally, that has arisen organically, from need, which is not cliché! And look, this John the Apostle, for instance, is no cliché!"

With a single movement, Vanini-Schiavone overcame the entire sloth and languor of a sated siesta, and, driven by the desire to lend his words the temperamental conviction that usually worked when one wished to express one's enthusiasm regarding certain so-called creative inspirations, he leapt up excitedly, like a young man, and in two or three steps stood beneath the relief of the Ascension. Caressing certain forms and pointing with a gesture to the various figures and movements of the relief, he plunged headlong into a noisy cascade of verbiage that recalled the shouting of Italian street sellers, crying their goods, praising some to high heaven, almost with the skill of a juggler, by which individual words lost their inner value, becoming transformed into a masterful, brilliant hovering above all things, truth or lies.

At that fatefully fortunate moment for Vanini-Schiavone, luck had it that the master Roman Rayevski himself appeared at the winter garden door in the company of Cardinal Armstrong, Lord and Lady Butler, Count Silva-Cacarucca, and Professor Gyeleskehlis, the well-known Blitvinian historian, descending the sunny veranda steps that led into the studio situated next door, separated, like an atrium, by a glass partition curtained off by heavy dark brown curtains.

"Don't let us disturb you, gentlemen," Roman Rayevski greeted his guests in the winter garden jovially (leading the cardinal and the noble visitors into his studio in order to show them the monumental statue of Colonel Barutanski), halting a moment on the staircase, amid the torrent of Vanini's words, to hear what Vanini was expounding so passionately to Jules Dupont, who listened with deep interest, clearly impressed by Vanini's loud and excited rhetoric.

"Ah, Maestro, we were just admiring your John the Apostle! For anyone to bend the human body in such a way and at such a moment, when it was organically necessary to emphasize the impression of general bodily exhaustion, it is not the precondition for such a trick simply that the artist has a masterful and absolute command of all the anatomic details of the human body. Rather, it is a matter of intuition and gut feeling, which guides the creative hand, blindly commands that those biceps show the sinews, and fall, limply, almost as if dead, onto that very spot where, beneath the walnut wood, one senses the softness of the fabric under which the clinging flesh quivers, stirred by unbelievable pain. This one cannot achieve by some external, technical routine, for mere routine is in itself a dead force. Mere skill cannot achieve that degree of conviction that makes a wooden relief become so alive that it acts with the solemnity of a funeral drum! For John's broken movement is like a *marcia funebre, altroché marcia funebre.* It is the funeral incarnate. It is the weeping over the open grave. It is the embodiment of true unadulterated human pain, adequately expressed by the pure technique of a sculptor, by a single stroke of the chisel, a masterly treatment of the wood in the right place! An academic example of perfection, showing how a single detailed movement expressed in relief may dominate the entire composition and become, so to speak, the dominant feature!"

"Bravo, Vanini, well said!" Rayevski gave a patronizing clap of his hands. "Please, carry on, gentlemen; don't let us detain you!" And then, with a soft and supple gesture, he gave a low bow to his company and, pointing in the direction of his studio, led the small procession toward the curtains, behind which one could see the shape of the hidden form of a massive horseman. Pale with admiring excitement, Lord and Lady Butler, Count Silva-Cacarucca, and the professor and historian Gyeleskehlis disappeared behind the curtain from which came a murmur of sincere, almost ecstatic delight and admiration dominated by the repeated chorus of the vowel "Ah."

"Look here, Vanini, I know people have to lie! Lying is, so to speak, a cosmic medium. In the universe the stars drift in lies. Worlds and centuries are made of them. I personally am a most pious admirer of the lie as such. In the anatomy of urbane society, the lie is the type of flesh that pads the bones. Without lies, everyone would appear as awful as bare skeletons! But such impertinent lying I haven't heard for ages! People lie like that only in the Levant. Where were you born?"

"I was born in Bologna! But my ancestors came from Cyprus, and, Dupont, I am proud of it!"

"I congratulate you!" Demonstratively discarding his newly lit cigarette into a large crystal ashtray, Dupont turned away and followed the lordly company into the studio.

There, beneath a glass cover, in the center of the vast space, stood the unnaturally huge equestrian figure of Barutanski. In the form of an ancient tribune in armor, mounted on a heavy Blitvinian stallion, more like a tyrannical Electoral Prince than the Commandant of the Blitvinian Legion, Barutanski sat his horse in armor. His legs, beneath the tunic, were bare, in ancient sandals with richly decorated buckles, on which eagles' beaks mingled with the heads of dragons into straps that bound the Commandant's ankles so as explicitly to emphasize the bony, well-modeled, and well-shaped foot, of which it was said in bohemian circles that Olaf Knutson had modeled exactly from a plaster cast taken from life.

The breastplate was decorated with an endless abundance of ornamentation, which ran over the knightly steel like snakes, lizards, grapes and vines, encircling, like garlands, various medallions and cornucopias. In the framework of this decorative wealth and abundance, in these bas-relief medallions, various scenes were enacted: Barutanski entering Blitwanen at the head of his Legion, Barutanski under a rich purple canopy reading the Magna Carta Regni Blithuaniae in '17, Barutanski building Ankersgarden on the Karabaltic, Barutanski sitting on the throne of Blitva and governing, and there were seven of these medallions. Two on the front, two on the shoulder blades, two on the shoulders, and the central and most important on the chest. This portrayed Barutanski's apotheosis: Barutanski, like a demigod in the clouds with Jarl Knutson crowning him with the laurels of an immortal. Kristian Barutanski's head, bold, oval, the truly noble head of a Sigismondo Malatesta, directed its steel-gray glance into the distant future of Blitva. The hair was rich and curly (perhaps even slightly Negroid), decorated with Renaissance ribbons which fluttered in the wind. It was crowned in laurels, as became the man who had made Blitva a free state after a thousand years of slavery. The steed of this bronze horseman reared up in a wild prancing, held in by a masterful grip so that, with its slightly bent back legs, it sat on its massive bronze tail, which spread over the plinth at the back as the sole support for this great mass of clay, raised in a banal and hackneyed movement of this quadrupedal animal which (why, God knows), faced with the pathos of centuries, had come to symbolize strength and power, usually thus placing the horse before the rider. On this academically well modeled horse, which by the naturalism of its shanks and thighs, its maddened and foaming muzzle and gaping nostrils, did not exceed the average, commonplace, everyday piece of sculpture, sat the rider whose head bore the character of an extremely well wrought and convincing portrait. It was really Barutanski! With his fine, scarcely defined lips, with the tired, dark circles under the eyes framed in a rather melancholy expression, with his supple, bony limbs and strong and energetic right hand that restrained the restless stallion with a single movement, touching the saddle with his left hand, lightly and scarcely noticeably (as if in that relaxed, almost careless passivity of the left hand was portrayed the complete, indeed sovereign, superiority of the rider over the great mass of equestrian power beneath his legs). Barutanski on his Atlanta truly represented that real Barutanski from Beauregard in a larger-than-life and monumental proportion.

Like tropical snakes in some provincial menagerie, this massive clay figure was wrapped in damp cloths. Two workers, under the direction of Olaf Knutson, were unwrapping the statue so that the monumental imperial figure could be exhibited to the noble guests in all its imperial glory and Renaissance. There was something un-usually bizarre in the careful unwrapping of the damp cloths, as though the rider suffered from a rare but dangerous inflammation and they were removing his bandages and a doctor was washing him down with a thin jet of water from an orange-colored rubber hose. Beneath these damp cloths and the shower of water that gushed down the horse's huge thighs and flanks, that massive rider reared over the rheumaticky and deaf lords like a muddy phantom, and, in that silence, full of an anxious respect for the majestic mas-terpiece, one could hear the water dripping down the wet clay fig-ure and pouring out into a metal drain which had been placed be-neath the wooden plinth.

Confused, agitated, absentmindedly, Olaf Knutson supervised the unwrapping of the cloths from the equestrian statue and lis-tened, as through half sleep, to Professor Gyeleskehlis expounding to the assembled guests the emotional symbolism of the moment when, in a few minutes' time, a delegation of the Estates of Blitva would appear in this noble house to present to the master Rayevski the address by which the greatest treasure of the Blitvinian people, its sovereignty, would be given into his keeping! There had been three such dramatic moments in the later history of Blitva. The year 1424, when the representative of the Aragon dynasty read his *Oratio ad Nobiles Regni Blithuaniae* to the Blitvinian Diet and at that moment fell, cut down by Kurlandish plotters and rebels; then the year 1518, when Sigurd Oranyski published his *Status Blithuanicus* and fell at Plavystok from a bullet (which strayed from a forest where he was walking in the moonlight), young and healthy and full of hope, when he had beaten the Swedes in a whole series of battles and twice taken Blitvas-Holm. The third and final attempt to establish sovereignty ended tragically with Isabelle Blatviska in the year 1643, when she returned the *Address ad Regentem Regni* and was condemned to death by the Ingermanlandish Catholic regent and was executed a year later and, after the unfortunate episode of Flaming-Sandersen, who was shot by an agent provocateur, today the creator of this masterpiece had lived to receive, from the hand of this brave horseman, the golden apple of Blitva which, to the honor and good fortune of future generations, he would guard and hand on to his successor more shining than when he received it. And that we had been able to see this, to partake in this great event, was due exclusively to the Protector who today was rightly numbered among the greatest Blitvinians in the pantheon of Blitvinian history. His place was with Jarl Knutson the Great and the Prince Elector Sigismund of Kurlandia.

Olaf Knutson listened to Professor Gyeleskehlis, vaguely feeling one and the same thing: that he'd been born a servant, lived as a servant, and would die as a servant! There, beside him, stood his employer, Rayevski! Surrounded by counts and lords, standing in front of Knutson's horseman and awaiting the delegation of the Estates to present the address to proclaim him sovereign. Rayevski had been born the prophet of Blitva. Rayevski had done the pope's portrait. Rayevski had dined with monarchs. Rayevski himself today would become the equal of kings! Till now, he'd ridden in the stagecoach of his talent, but henceforth, Blitvinian uhlans would sound fanfares in front of his presidential coach and the lords and counts of the Estates and all Blitva would kneel in front of him! He would live in the Electoral Palace, in the aristocratic center of Blitwanen, where the streets were quiet and the ancient copper Kurlandish roofs were green with the coating of many centuries. In the old prince's park were many doves. Fountains splashed. There was an aristocratic silence, and there Rayevski would create his majestic masterpieces. He would be surrounded by young and beautiful women. Great actresses and poetesses would weep in front of his religious works and Vanini–Schiavone would write his thirty-third book about him. Roman Rayevski would play his chemin de fer with bishops, cardinals, barons, and generals; the sovereign creator, above all criticism, he would doze happily on his dividends, like a retired mandarin.

And he, Olaf Knutson, would go on tirelessly modeling, carving stone, kneading this wet and sticky clay. And he would vegetate in the shade of Rayevski's greatness, for his own satisfaction paint two or three sardines or two or three apples, live off coffee with cream, his teeth would fall out, and he'd be happy that fate had allowed him to rise to such heights as to be able to remove coverings from such inspired statues, that it had been given to him, as a nameless hired hand, to model according to the Idea of the Great Master. And just so, as he stood there today, among those lords and cretins, a nameless unknown, in the background like an employee of a workshop, like the slave irrigating Barutanski with a rubber hose, so he would stand by the wall like a servant, like a liveried lackey all his life, for he was worth nothing else, when he had been born to be nothing else but a servant! All those English ladies and spiritualists, numismatists and barons, all that ship-owning rabble of adventurers and French babblers (like that unpleasant Jules Dupont), they'd all pass him by as one would a servant, and he would doff his hat, open the

doors for them, and unwind the cloths from the clay models, whenever their honors might so desire, and no one would ever explain to
these fools, wasters, adulterers that all it was was a cheat and a scan-
dalous lie! On the one side Larsen's deathly grimace—and here this
apotheosis! There the repulsive, criminal shooting at Dominic's and
poor Nielsen running around like a hunted animal, and here that
ape Gyeleskehlis, with his pathetic "historical dates," and that stupid Malatesta on that stallion from the Blitvinian stud which Knutson had visited for a whole year, modeling horses in various movements, in order to create that disgusting kitsch that portrayed a
burglar as a victor!

Olaf Knutson felt these contrasts rumbling beneath him like
some deep, subterranean roaring of lava somewhere in his being.
He felt himself being separated from his sober, balanced, and normal state (which appeared as a gray and passive standing in the
background, by the wall) by only a minute, infinitesimal, scarcely
noticeable margin, from being carried away by such a wild tornado,
with such a thundering, that all would be over in a second, finally
and bloodily. For what was this going on around him, and what did
it mean? A mad and disgusting dance of phantoms, a wise exchange
of wit, sly, cross-eyed, a shameless lying in the teeth, a stroking of
beards and fat double chins, a self-satisfied burping after a well-
performed murder, the wagging of tails, the usual, everyday, and
disgusting bowing to success. And success, that was this studio, this
deaf Lord Butler, this Barutanski sitting his horse in armor, money,
palaces, academies, a mass of money that rained down like a shower
of sequins, victory, courts, Beauregard, the Address of the Estates,
triumph! And in all this, Blitva was forgotten! Blitva lay together
with Larsen. Blitva gnawed its fingernails in fear, together with
Niels Nielsen in the tiny room at the crazy old Mrs. Gallen's, she
who all night played on her soundless piano for the sake of a son
whom they had also murdered. A dear lad, the twenty-eight-year-

old Sigurd Gallen, who fell defending Blitva! What was happening to our poor, bloodstained Blitva? There, from the street, came the sound of silver fanfares, the arrival of a squadron bringing the Address of the Estates, the shouting of the crowd and he, Olaf Knutson, stood there like a servant guarding the clay Barutanski and wrapping him in wet cloths until the day when that criminal type should be cast into bronze, in bronze to outlive the centuries.

What was it Rayevski had said that night on the *Blitvania*, when the poverty of the third-class Blitvinian émigrés stuck in Knutson's throat? "History works in broad lines as in a fresco. History paints decoratively!" History didn't ask for Olaf Knutson's opinion on the day when the Estates presented their address to the president of the Republic, Roman Rayevski. History viewed the various ages synthetically! That was how one should look at things: synthetically, and not like some nervously disturbed pedant! Synthetically! Decoratively! As decoratively as are the frescoes in a church. In broad lines! In the name of eternity, of glory, and of triumph!

Book Two

CHAPTER 1

Panic at Beauregard

Kristian Barutanski controlled the anxieties that had lately troubled him more and more, by speed. Behind the wheel of the latest expensive version, the 1927 Peugeot Grand Luxe Coach, with its doubly upholstered beige seats of chamois leather, with its silent floating movement on the very latest tires, in a cabin specially placed on movable springs, with the massive engine tuned to balance the vehicle so that 105 kilometers was attained without effort, to the monotonous sound of the wind against the windshield, with the hum of the complaining road as it unwound beneath the wheels (so that it seemed as though the waving treetops, road signs, and bridges flew furiously into the jaws of the shining vehicle), with his hands on the wheel and his gaze fixed in one straight line toward the distant peasant carts on the road, which, in one moment, grew visibly into the outlines of horses' rear ends and the highly polished dashboard, Barutanski drove down the macadamized Ankersgarden highway, his entire attention on the speedometer, which, as though with the shaking and trembling of a wound-up spring, climbed ever higher and more dangerously, its vacillating red indicator wavering between the numbers 130 and 135.

The boredom of everyday life is killed by the normal modern European imperial method, by golf, horses, cocktails, tobacco, women, expensive articles, elegantly tailored clothes, wit, or worry over one's esteemed digestion, but Barutanski had begun to kill it through speed. Flying along between 130 and 140 kilometers an hour on his well-polished expensive petrol can, like a load of grapeshot, in a cloud of sooty smoke and dust, one could feel how a dark and strange tension grew in Barutanski and, like cocaine, heightened the élan vital and a man's worries remained behind him in the mud, like run-over hens, and all that could be heard was the whistling of the wind and the murmur of the wild careering that raised a man above his nervous anxieties and uncomfortable headaches, like a dream.

Lately, Barutanski had felt ever greater depression. Against his better judgment, that one should hold firmly to one's own direction and to avoid "psychologizing," he had sunk into the morass of an aggressive neurosis of suspicion. He felt increasingly that he was losing the certainty of his convictions. As though he were split between innate contradictions, and his entire life seemed only an obscure and nebulous confusion of open questions.

Not even smoking helped anymore. Sitting in the library at Beauregard, watching the smoke of his Maryland-Jaune cigarette, he would be lost in endless conversations with himself, occasionally uttering, at moments when the dialogue became acute, the odd word aloud, so that the sound of his own voice returned him, like the sudden crack of an explosion, to reality. Petrified by the sound of his own voice, Barutanski would feel a shaking in his finger joints, feel his knees giving way, as if his entire body were a vibrating nervous cord of incomprehensible, morbid stress. The smoke spiraled from the glowing end of his cigarette, and these transparent, bluish whorls turned into a wavering veil of agitated mist that, to the rhythm of the heartbeat, flowed upward like a vertical screen, melting into long, fanlike, horizontal curtains, which slowly sunk above the parquet and carpets, embracing the entire space around him with cloudy iridescences of vague and unclear images that fatefully corresponded with his general grasp of events.

And events as such had no profounder meaning than the smoke of a fortuitously lit cigarette! True, looked at from this worldly point of view, without self-deceit, lies, or sentiment, from the point of view of tiny, worldly truths (which indeed are inexpressibly tiny and fatally relative), one might give events a certain "profounder" sense, but the open question remained: What sense and what "profounder" sense? The sense of smoke, of blood, of a single individual human body, of human bodies as corporeal masses, as vast quantities, as humanity? The human sense of events in the name of the individual or in the name of society? The human sense in the name of the "development" of that human society? In any case, what did that banal and overused term "the development and progress of humanity" mean? Ever superficial in his acquiring of knowledge, Barutanski considered things with a definite shallowness, in generalities, *à peu près*. To tell the truth, he had never come to a clear understanding of the most basic ideas. He liked to think as in a dream.

They said there were changes on the earth's surface. In "this" or in "that" direction certain "movements" continued, and for a considerable time at that. Several thousand years. Whether this "movement" continued in "this" or "that" direction, "forward" or "backward," that was a question for the poverty-stricken, limited, and stupid human assessment. Once man grasped this pathetic earthly mechanics, there was no God, morals, nor ideals. Everything became indeed the smoke of a fortuitously lit cigarette, the dream of a dead conscience, murder as a respectable civil occupation, a delirium of morality and intelligence. Everything was as stupid as a lit cigarette, indeed no more than the twisting of a transparent, hazy cloud in an empty room. Man was still a wolf to man and that, they said, was what remained to us from prehistoric man, from chaos, from nature, from that animal and cannibalistic element in man, which, according to those old time wasters who professionally expressed wise saws concerning the fate of mankind, remained in us from what was (according to these bureaucrats of human thought) the dark and repulsive, truly cosmic element in man. As though man could abandon himself, liberate himself from his own being, his human, chaotic, cannibalistic, that is, animalistic, substance, free himself from his one single basis of life, that is, the animal. Ridiculous! An animal himself, Barutanski genuinely despised every form of thought other than the animal.

The Dominican father Bonaventura Baltrushaitis, a man of undoubted learning, even intelligent in the various spheres of moral philosophy and of his so overestimated neo-Thomism, this in every detail elegant monk, with whom Kristian Barutanski had lately spent endlessly long nights in futile conversation, this learned Father Bonaventura maintained the opposite view: that man had appeared on earth, above all, to create the divine order within himself and therefore, logically, in the entire menagerie around him, that is to say, in nature. Man, according to Father Bonaventura Baltrushaitis, appeared in nature as the voice of the harp of the Lord among the apes and tigers, and the meaning of his human dignity lay truly in the fact that he should become the divine Orpheus among the dumb creatures around him and turn nature into the finest of David's psalms.

Doctor of theology and philosophy, Father Bonaventura most definitely refuted any human significance in the concept of "development" or "progress." The man who did not know God (according to Father Bonaventura) was still a prehistoric man, regardless whether, like a cannibal, he dined on his neighbor's kidneys or examined a patient's bowels by means of X ray. To travel by air or by car, to listen to the radio or write articles on atomic physics, without belief in God was—according to this witty Dominican—to live still in the period of prehistory, in the state of an animal, in a moral diluvium. Politics and political structures he considered of no significance whatsoever. For Bonaventura Baltrushaitis, the whole of history from the pyramids to Washington was a mere cloud of sand and dust.

"Listen, how hollowly that echoes, that knightly armor of your ideals, Excellency!"

Father Bonaventura halted one night in front of an armored figure in the corridor of Beauregard where he was walking in Barutanski's company through the gallery. While discussing such dark and obscure questions with the autocrat of Blitva, he had paused before a metal knight and, percussing his knightly armor, like a doctor, smiled at Barutanski ironically as one might to a child in front of a shopwindow. Outside, the north wind howled and one could hear it beating on the plane trees in the park. In the pale light of the candelabra at the end of the corridor, bent in front of the shining steel of the mute knight in armor and with the heavy winged helmet, the figure of this monk, clad in his white habit, reflected something both exalted and decorative, so that it seemed as if some mysterious magician in a white burnoose was tapping upon a corpse which had taken on the knightly worldly figure of a warrior and, in fact, was nothing more or less than a simple dead metal toy.

"All that is happening today in European politics, Excellency, all this armed upheaval with us in Blitva and throughout the world is nothing but an utterly empty, soulless, godless agitation of such iron toys! These metal Kurlandish knights in their steel armor move about the earth like goblins, operate state machines, sit beneath radio antennae, and thunder with artillery, taking a knightly view of things around them, as generals with naked swords in their hands, while, in fact, they're just dead barbarous toys, utterly empty, and listen, I beg you, how desperately hollowly they sound, like tin boxes! All the navies of the Great Powers are nothing but a pile of scrap metal which, without awareness of God, will be thrown on the rubbish heap like used sardine tins! And that atheistic mob that would throw your knightly, idealistic steel armor through the windows of the Beauregard palace, that hungry, barefoot, and nameless rabble that has no other thought in its head than to stuff itself with roast meat and guzzle the Malaga from your cellars, those intellectual rebels from the cafés of Blitwanen, who threaten our authorities in the name of 'the people and mankind' with 'Open Letters,' they are just a stupid and godless crowd of hungry cattle, and their sole ideal is diluvium, pogroms, criminality! Without God, Excellency, there is not and cannot be any sense, be it earthly or spiritual. Without God, life is just a monstrous, hollow dummy in the empty corridor of an empty palace, on a dark windy night, like tonight!"

True, up to a point Father Bonaventura was right! It was empty in Beauregard as in some medieval castle. One needed to go down among people, into the cafés. One needed to go down to Dominic's, get drunk, "decastleize" oneself, to make friends again with those weak-minded, liberal café philosophers, to ask those fools down there in the cafés what they thought, what they wanted, how they saw things: What should the mission of our newly born Blitva be? What should be done in the name of Blitva? Was Blitva in any way on the path to fulfilling its historic task? Was it really possible that those cretins in the cafés unanimously considered Barutanski as the resurrected autocrat, the bloodthirsty specter and ghost of a present-day Jarl Knutson?

Faced with a pile of most varied and, at first glance, invisible responsibilities, Barutanski had lately more and more pessimistically felt his awareness faltering in the midst of a vast multitude of ever less pleasant questions, and in the sticky conglomeration of mud and murder and blood and corrupt stupidities he felt himself increasingly uncomfortable, like a sick man in a sweaty nightshirt, while his heart beat more and more agitatedly and the fever slowly penetrated his brain so that his vision of things grew more and more obscure. There was a time when, due to the overloading of his schedule, his life was so full that he had little more than five or six hours' sleep, and he rushed frantically from one representative duty to another, so that he had not a single second to waste in speculating about the stupidity and senselessness of life "as such." He pulled his load like a harnessed nag. He visited five or six European capitals on so-called diplomatic missions. He negotiated with European moneylenders and statesmen from Stockholm to London. In Paris he spent a wild, drunken spring with the dotty, mysterious Dolores de Janeiro. He had sat bored stiff, night after night, in Ingrid's snobbish circles. With Bishop Armstrong he had built churches. With Bishop Armstrong he had gone to Castel Gandolfo. With Bishop Armstrong he had been received by the secretary of state in the Vatican. Together with Kavalierski and his gang, he'd purchased submarines. He had been to Spitzbergen on the *Blitvania,* the latest Blitvinian destroyer of five hundred tons. But all this gave him a sense of sickly satiety, to the point of exhaustion, of physical disgust. Bonaventura Baltrushaitis was right! Everything in Beauregard sounded as empty as a tin toy!

What was the point of buying Hotchkisses, Rolls-Royces, Peugeots? A rain of gold had showered on a few favored individuals, on certain special favorites of fortune, while he today, beneath this cascade of wealth, yawned from utter boredom. Now he drank his thirty-fourth coffee and smoked his seven hundred and seventy-seventh cigarette, traveled by night in the first-class luxury of a wagon-lit while beside him snored the twenty-three-year-old beauty Dolores de Janeiro? But where had the time gone when he thought to find under her brassiere a luscious and juicy peach? Beneath the corsets and bras of these ladies, everything was always the same: a rotting sack of hot, decaying marzipan that bore the sickly smell of hay, of cinnamon, of Houbigant, and, for this, one had to shave with special razors, massage oneself with special cologne, eat only grilled steaks. One had, on occasion, to sweat in embarrassing situations, and it all ended so pathetically, like a small boy pissing. Everything was what it was: the imperative of the digestive organs. A hundred and thirty-seven kilometers in fifty-three minutes yesterday on the

Ankersgarden motorway, and today, after lunch, Armstrong with his new cathedral; Rayevski with the statue; the special report by the chief of the Blitwanen police, Kantorowicz, on the latest attempt at a plot on the Blatvian border; that evening a performance of Scriabin at Ingrid's; the report of the director general and governor of the National Bank, Maimonides, concerning the state of currency stock in his personal accounts in Amsterdam and Zurich; his trip to London regarding the 7 percent Blitvinian national loan; then the open question of Dolores de Janeiro, who impertinently, one might even say aggressively, was arguing for her demand for a payoff; Jules Dupont's book of conversations with him, as the dictator of Blitva, regarding the Blitvinian question; the possible purchase of new submarines in London, and for his personal Chevaux-Légers brigade the new submachine guns that were waiting in Pilsen for transport; competitions; the election of that ape Rayevski as president of the Republic; the question of the new and so-called basic parliamentarization of the Blitvinian political machine; night walks, dogs, Great Danes, guards, the call of sentries, endlessly long nights; in a word: the Beauregard prison without remission. And in all this and above all: his teeth were loose, his left eyetooth, his wisdom teeth, his two lower front teeth. His whole skull was loose. Blitva was loose. The international situation was utterly obscure. His physique in general, of late, showed a great mass of ailments. Something was happening to his appendix. His tonsils were rotten. His nerves were giving way. Acids were accumulating in his joints, and those boring visits to the dentist's chair, the indiscreet palpation by doctors, those mysterious Aesculapians who whispered whole tomes of phrases about blood pressure, the essential need for rest, the possible need for an operation on the appendix, diet, tobacco, whiskey, ulcer, hormones, vitamins, it all became more and more empty. All this stupidity grew to incredible proportions, while, in the background of it all, unmoved and aloof, stood Father Bonaventura Baltrushaitis, who had so enveloped him in his convincing rhetoric that Barutanski felt he no longer had the strength to throw this tedious and insistent friar out the door. Amid the boring and obscure stupidity that surrounded him, in the killing loneliness about him, that charming Dominican had become a daily necessity and, listening, half asleep, to Bonaventura's constant flow of words, Barutanski felt that Bonaventura's theories in some way relieved him and that Bonaventura's imagery served as a pleasant relaxation, without realizing that this apparent comfort in his poisoned state of vulnerability had turned into a need that grew from day to day . . .

Father Bonaventura had introduced him to Pascal, and in Barutanski's ever deeper and angrier disgust at his own surroundings Pascal appeared to him as the powerful and exalted light of the gentle brain who penetrated to his God in his own original and knightly way. Reading Pascal, he ordered to have written out on a parchment lampshade, in black and white stylized Gothic letters, Pascal's famous phrase concerning loneliness and the fact that man dies alone: *Nous sommes plaisants de nous reposer dans la société de nos semblables: misérables comme nous, impuissants comme nous, ils ne nous aideront pas; on mourra seul. Il faut donc faire comme si on était seul!* How much more intelligent than Ingrid's Scriabin! Than her statue of the Virgin in front of which—on her orders—her maid Olga had to light a hanging lamp! All of Ingrid's lyrical, academic, literary crowd in her stupid Louis XV drawing room, with M. Dupont at their head, of whom Georgis insisted that he was certainly acting in some foreign service. Pascal said that a man dies under the stars entirely alone and that was the only certain truth! Bonaventura Baltrushaitis believed that it was possible to achieve a degree of perfection with God's help. OK, without hunts, dances, without banquets, without gifts and whiskey, without horses, cavalry, and Peugeots! But what about Dolores?

Dolores had seemed the one woman whom he sincerely, directly, sensually, physically desired, and all this had so quickly changed into the most usual, banal, fleshly satiety of the brothel. How little, indeed, could a woman give a man. "Women are as helpless and miserable as we are, women cannot help us," as Pascal rightly said. "A man will die utterly alone!" Why then this pathetic drooling with women in hotel beds? Women were corrupt, disgusting, laughable; with those chatterers it was always the same thing: they'd sniff around a man's trousers, squat, kneel, wink, fuss with their suspenders, melt like oysters beneath a man, and that doglike exhibition of the digestive orifices, that pathetic raving around a bed pot, all that ended with checks at the Crédit Lyonnais. All that was more or less an expensively bought Blitvinian secret, but it could have been beautiful, adolescently romantic, in the moonlight of some Swiss lake, on a clear summer night, when the glaciers gleamed in the distance. Dolores played the part of the warm, young, and happy innocent girl in love, but in fact she was the most ordinary sophisticated whore, a transparent, antipathetic con woman who'd now have his shirt off his back, and Georgis might well be right that she'd been a foreign agent from the very start. Why had they put her picture on the thousand-lei notes? That was bloody stupid! Georgis (anyway) saw an agent in everyone and, when one thought of it, he was not so wrong. Innocent and spontaneous was something only children could be! Little Solveig, the only daughter of the Beauregard head gardener, a fair-haired schoolgirl, there was an example of an innocent, laughing, and carefree child! He'd already told Georgis that he'd taken a great liking to the girl and that it would be a good idea to send her to Paris, to some institute, at his expense, as his protégée! But Georgis had replied that this was the first sign of senility!

Georgis was a cretin! Why shouldn't they send little Solveig to Paris at his, Barutanski's, expense? Morgensen's little Solveig could have gone to some French Carmelite institute, and he could have come for her around Easter. Good God! A seventeen-year-old woman—was that anything unusual? And physically she was no longer a child! Her hips were well developed; she could have a child. A healthy young mare! He'd have wrapped this small, wounded, bleeding little doe in a warm plaid, sat her beside him in the train on the red velvet and peeled her an orange to stop her tears. For heaven's sake, love takes its root in blood; without blood there's nothing!

And this way, here he was sitting in the dark, wasting time with Bonaventura Baltrushaitis and shooting hares and deer in the mud of Blitva! That autumn he'd killed 3,000 hares, some 270 deer, and 27 wild boar! And Bonaventura Baltrushaitis assured him that the man was not born who could achieve his life's aim on this earth without faith in God. He'd confessed to the priest that he felt an irresistibly warm, sincere, profound physical need to give a child to this innocent filly, and Bonaventura had simply given a superior smile, as people do when offered an undertaking that was not sufficiently promising to turn the head of an experienced confessor with its possibilities, but was still worth being given a chance.

Everything in the end was in God's hands! Little Solveig was a well-brought-up, devout girl, and Barutanski was living with his wife in a free, civil marriage. Regarding the state of legal marriage, in the eyes of Father Bonaventura all that mattered in reality was the sanctity of the marriage sacrament. In this respect, by his neo-Thomistic view there were no particular, insurmountable worldly obstacles to Barutanski's plans.

"For you see, Excellency! That highest, absolute supernatural and certainly superhuman Being above us, that sum of all the phenomena of varied and utterly varied earthly events, that power of supernatural Will above us, that heavenly ebullition of supernatural Reason and supernatural Intelligence, that holy mystery, superexistential concept, which is nameless and inexpressible, indefinable and incomprehensible in its endless Wisdom, that which may not be seen, for it is clearer than sight, *hic non videri potest: visu clarior est; nec comprehendi: tactu purior est; nec aestimari: sensibus maior est, infinitus, immensus et soli sibi tantus quantus est notus;* in other words, Excellency, the Lord of Lords, whom the learned Leibniz defined, indeed very well, as the Lord of all people and of all intellectual substances—*Chef de toutes les personnes ou sustances intellectuelles, comme le monarque absolute de la plus parfaite cité ou république*—should it please him and his providence that he should employ a small, dear, devout girl as a means of Your Excellency's sincere turning to his wise protection, then, for me, your confessor, as a healer of sick spirits who stray godless and without faith, there remains only once more to give thanks for yet another proof of his measureless mercy. If such be God's will, we shall submit. One does not believe because faith preaches the truth. One believes out of respect before the divine insight, through which he announced his apotheosis. In this sense, we must all be soldiers who blindly follow God's commands."

Apart from other morbid signs, Kristian Barutanski had begun to be troubled by the thought of death.

Everything that existed was immersed in death. It was a question that beat in every pulse, and the ear did not exist in which death's emptiness did not sound as did the distant, gray, dark sea in a seashell. Death traveled the blackness of animal guts in the darkness of circulation. It trembled in the least visible shiver of the leaf. Between things and appearances breathed Death. It filled the fates of everything, of the world, of the stars, with its dark breath. In a word, it was ever present. It was here, all around us; in the park of Beauregard, in its halls, its corridors, and in this gloomy, disgusting library. It sat there beside the fireplace, on a Regency armchair, melancholically staring into the flickering flames. Its cigarette smoked calmly, vertically, vertically as though there were no one else in the room. Far away, from somewhere in the park, came the excited barking of a dog. Bugles sounded in the cavalry barracks in Jarl's fortress. The evening silence that fell over Beauregard was absolute. Not a living soul moved, yet Death was there!

What did it mean, that Death was there? Did it mean fear? Was it horror at a failed life that was coming to its end? Why was it there?

There had been a time, the most dangerous, the bloodiest, and most fatal time, when Barutanski had daily sowed death, when his furied figure meant certain and cruel death for his fellow beings, yet Death had not been there. But now, for the last two years, it had appeared as terror before the chaos in him himself, before the inexpressible and fatal chaos, in which he could have died without accomplishing anything for himself in this world of Blitva, and it was not impossible (which Father Bonaventura argued and firmly believed) that there, somewhere far away, there might yet exist another shore, and when we crawled onto it like wet dogs, then possibly Someone might inquire of us: In whose blood had we wallowed and why? And what could he, Kristian Barutanski, answer to this undoubtedly logical question?

In that hellish abyss, in that, according to all descriptions, dark Underground, there where beneath all that was living flowed the cold and murky River Styx, that dragged a man by the laws of worldly logic into the muddy pit of his own grave, what could a Barutanski reply to such an uncomfortable inquisitorial question? Nothing! It was one of those final questions to which there was no answer!

All that really existed in life was the instinct to avoid Death. That instinct convulsively gripped every living thing, for while life continued, its entire mystery lay in the fact that it had not yet died. That living instinct hysterically clung to the sound of the accordion that wept beneath the fortress cliff, and that beggar's song one heard of an evening, that was the only living thread by which human thought might return out of the darkness to that empty room in Beauregard, into that reality around us.

Footsteps in the corridor . . .

It was Klement bringing a teapot and cigarettes on a silver tray and lighting the lamp.

A yellow circle of light lit the half-dark space of the library, and in the brown half-light from out of the grayish dusk in which there was nothing flashed around Barutanski a mass of books. All those Petrarchs and Aquinases, like plants in an herbarium, like dried flowers stuck between two sheets of cardboard, like insects, butterflies and bedbugs, all the Tacituses and Senecas! They all wrote books and then died and were no more! They moved around the world. They killed, killed one another, prayed to God. They were crowned on the Capitol with laurel wreaths. The bells from the Ara Coeli rang in their honor, and now they were dead. Their wisdom in its pigskin binding was worm infested; moldy, dusty volumes in the Beauregard library, in the twilight, in Blitva, in the nothingness full of headache and stupid thoughts, and, over all, the sound of the accordion in the distance and smoke. And smoke. The clock on the tower . . . the chimes of Blitwanen. Seven o'clock. Hail Mary. The bell on the Jesuit Cathedral. The bells of Blitwanen.

This Blitvinian stew we'd cooked was not bad! Perhaps a bit too bloody? Perhaps we did cut off slightly too many people's heads?

The bells rang the Hail Mary in Blitwanen, and Barutanski felt his knees giving way (from too many cigarettes), and that it would be not a bad idea were he to take Bonaventura's advice and—pray. But on the other hand, he heard his stubborn and rational voice with its human common sense: Life was pure hell and Death the sole liberator from that hell! If you had killed anyone, then you had rendered them a service! In that lasting insomnia we called life (full of a cursed and often strange vigil), Death came as a final dream, and therefore Father Bonaventura's babbling sounded utterly illogical, as though Death were not the "final dream," but after this physically unpleasant procedure there followed "the true awakening." According to that one-sidedly educated and pedantic friar, it would appear that our entire physical, earthly life were nothing more than a type of rehearsal before the main hearing, in which we would be judged by this neo-Thomistically educated doctor, the theological referee, according to the relentless, indeed cruel law and, at that, on the tiniest, most secret, almost invisible offenses not only of our hidden motives but even of our instincts.

According to Bonaventura, we were nothing but a plaything of incomprehensibly inimical and adverse forces in the hands of God. All right then! If we were just a toy in another's hands, then, playing with the fate of others, we in ourselves were nothing but some dark entity which was darkness in itself. In the confusion of unfathomable rings and circles, in the mysterious iridescence of the dark outlines and circlings of endlessly confounded concepts, amid dangerous and obscure chaos, the death of a Colonel Barutanski would be nothing more than a first-class Blitvinian posthumous honor! Two companies of cavalry, the flickering of sooty torches reflected in the helmets and breastplates of the guard, black muffled drums: po-pom, pom, pom, pom! Chopin: tri-i-i-i . . . ra-ra . . . ra-ra . . . ra-ra . . . ra-ra—tardom, trom-trom-trom! And everything else, above and around it, just a chattering repetition of nonsense. A magpie that had learned by heart the mysterious words: "nothingness," "salvation," "eternity," "the starry sky," "the moral law within us," "the soul," "the moral responsibility of the individual." What moral responsibility of the individual?

The "I" was no constant, ever personal "I" that would be ever at one with its so-called "I-ness," for that damned, inconstant "I" was forever changing. It moved, and through this "I" of ours there moved and migrated countless other "I-nesses." The independent, isolated, separate "I" in itself represented a mass of its own graves.

This present, momentary "I" of ours marched on its own graves. The "I" sprung from itself, the "I" flowed like a flood. The "I" was both the river and the source in one person. The "I" died and was resurrected every day. The "I" pretended and disguised itself like an old, worn ham actor. The "I" changed its wigs and masks in an everlasting succession. The "I" fed and excreted. The "I" flitted by like a shadow. The "I" was like nicotine, like headache, like stupidity, like sex. The "I" was self-ignorance, confusion, both blind and clairvoyant, satiated and ravenous. The "I" rolled like a maddened herd of itself and its own curses, and through it all flowed a universal quantity of the same obscure and unclear "I-nesses," and our personal "I" flowed through innumerable other, similar "I-nesses," and in this tangle of fates and awarenesses who was to say whether this very "I" of ours, in one of its many and utterly fortuitous roles, had failed, cheated, or even killed, and that, for that very reason, was "personally" responsible for the failure of some entire highly moral performance that in itself fell into the category of utterly tasteless and drunken Blitvinian carnivals! Indeed, the usual, everyday memory of our so-called sinful and subjective "I" convincingly proved that our earthly and sinful "I" had died so many times and that in its petty Subjective Death it had vanished in the Lord so often that one would need to appear before the tribunal of one's personal moral responsibility armed with an entire detective apparatus, which, like some perfected English registration office, would be equipped with all the necessary proofs of the identity of our own selves. For our most everyday "I" was made up of a whole mob of the sinful deceased, and if we had died already countless times, how could we then answer for all the crimes of completely unknown, alien, far removed, and foreign dead men? And since we had already killed and buried ourselves time and time again, how could we be responsible for the fact that perhaps we had killed somebody not identified with ourselves? As though human death were not merely the extinguishing of a totally valueless match? And to put out a match, surely that was not a question of personal moral responsibility?

Lately strange things indeed had been happening to Barutanski.

People had reduced the concept of the universe to that of substance and force long before him and, before he had even been born, in the human universe everything had become emptier and emptier with every day. Goodness had gone and—therefore—sin too. God had gone, conscience had gone, and so, gradually, freed from specters and the medieval prejudices, man had remained alone on earth and in the universe and, in his godless isolation, he had invented for himself two or three consolatory truths and, in that Nordic mire, one of them was called—Blitva. For Kristian Barutanski, Blitva was such a consolation that, under the magic of this supernatural concept, he had come to the conclusion that, for Blitva's sake, one might kill without the slightest stir of the conscience. For the life of Blitva all around him and from the beginning had been so bloody that without killing it was unthinkable. The idea of death, in that Blitvinian interpretation of the mystery of life, was an idea that had no other purpose than to complete statistical facts regarding individual battles, individual death sentences, or secret murders. Seen from Barutanski's chivalrous view of the world, from that mass of flying machines he had purchased in various factories from Glasgow to Turin, from that endless quantity of murderous weapons which had occupied him, as a tireless traveler, and which he had amassed in his magazines from Ankersgarden and Plavystok to those around Beauregard, the way to doubt, to paranoia, to a state of morbidity, in which moral questions began to haunt him as reptiles do alcoholics in a state of delirium, the way to an excited consideration of the inner and deeper sense of such anxieties, the way to summoning the learned Dominican father

Bonaventura Baltrushaitis and to begin endless nightly talks with him regarding the futility of earthly life, that complex and apparently deeply confused path of Kristian Barutanski to repentance and to his first prayer was far away, yet logically opened and consequently developed as a perfectly natural result of an entire sequence of deeper, at first glance, unimportant reasons.

Nature "as such" was nothing but a collection of facts among which, in a mass of details, man, after all, existed. The total of such facts that revolved beneath the sun and around other unknown suns was in all likelihood enormous, perhaps immeasurably greater than could be conceived by the human mind, perhaps truly incomprehensibly greater, yet this incomprehensibility still did not mean proof of divinity, as Father Bonaventura Baltrushaitis interpreted it. For instance: A bug ensconced in the velvet of a theater seat in relation to the music of Richard Wagner in the second act of *Tristan und Isolde* would find itself, faced with the musical sense and artistic value of Wagner's score, at an inexpressibly great distance from its own bedbug's mentality, but were that distance perhaps to be much greater than it seemed to us from our human point of view, such distance between the bedbug and Wagner's instrumentation would still be no proof of the existence of supernatural phenomena in nature. Both the bedbug beneath the velvet seat in the opera and Wagner's score were the expression of one and the same vital force, which, in both cases, acted in differing quantities, yet in its essential content was identical. And it was not impossible (following the same logic) that between our human brain and the unfathomability of the planets around the various suns was a distance far greater than that between the bedbug and *Tristan und Isolde,* but this proved nothing except that the potentialities of natural unfathomability were truly innumerable. But one thing human experience did confirm: The facts that surrounded man in nature were not particularly favorable to him.

Whether their movement around man was correct in a higher sense, as Father Bonaventura sought to prove, or not, that was an open question, but that nature took a direction opposite to that of human interests, that was beyond doubt. Stomach ulcers, loose teeth, skin diseases, nerves, catarrh of the bowels, headache, lasting and utter boredom, which tormented Kristian Barutanski to the point of madness, all this was the clearest denial of the idea of divine harmony in the world around us, and, lastly and above all: the thought of death! Between Nothingness and Immeasurability on this muddy morsel of Blitva there burned one of the carbon compounds, between the sun and earth's gravity, and that tiny earthly, truly ridiculously pathetic carbon compound was called Kristian Barutanski and it was his fate one day to kick the bucket under a hail of bullets, like a dog, without a death sentence, and the day of that death sentence was unknown, for it could happen even that very evening!

Who'd do the shooting? Father Bonaventura? He was born in Blatvia. Had his identity ever been checked? What about Olga, Ingrid's maid? That was not out of the question. A Hunnish emigrant who opened her legs to Captain Flaming-Sandersen. And Flaming-Sandersen was the son of Dr. Flaming-Sandersen, who, after the fall of Muzhikovski, demonstratively retired from state service. They were all rebels, those Flaming-Sandersens! The bearer of a historic Blitvinian name! What crap! Those bearers of historic names were every one of them megalomaniacs! What Blitvinian history? The real Blitvinian history began with him, Barutanski! Everything before him was a pathetic nonsense. Georgis? Jules Dupont? Rayevski? Olaf Knutson, that neurasthenic fusspot, who was never satisfied with any solution? A Freemason! A crypto-liberal! A friend of Nielsen's! Apropos Nielsen? He'd vanished. In all probability he was already with Kmetynis in Weider-Hunnen. They were busy making bombs. As with that business two years ago at the Boule Blanche in Paris, there too Kmetynis had his fingers through the young Jensen! Criminal scum! They all needed crushing like bedbugs! Georgis did well to shoot the old Jensen! There was no place for sentimentality! Blitva needed cleaning of this infectious vermin, once and for all. And why did they reproach him that he'd killed a lot of people? Who had he killed, anyway? He'd been a sentimental and a Samaritan gentleman! And this, to-day, was his reward. He was held personally responsible today for all Blitva's historical, present, and future failings, as if any human creation in this life could ever be perfect. The truth was (as Nielsen had said to him several times, when they were still friends) that Blitva more resembled a miscarriage than a normal birth! That was true! And that damned Blitva had swallowed up his personal life ac-cording to the same logic and the same rules as it had the lives of so many other Blitvinians. For what hell of a dog's life was it, to be afraid of one's own housemaid? To chat for whole nights with an unpleasant friar, who was probably, under his Dominican habit, a foreign agent? To listen to the wind howling around Beauregard, to fear one's own nervous irritation, to drive at 130 kilometers per hour on the Blitvinian highways (an undertaking equal to the most stupid suicide), not to have one's own flat, to be besieged by foreign idiots, to be the Blitvinian spittoon for illiterate pamphleteers, and lastly: to bear the tedium of endless insomnia which had gone on for the whole of the last year. And why was he to blame for those lost souls around him, because they'd ruined their own lives? There wasn't a single man in his immediate vicinity whose life was worth living. Hyacinth Kerinis was a murderer by profession, a criminal type! Karin Michelson spied against her own principles, purely for materialistic reasons, and betrayed the man who was her lover. That poor fool Nielsen! A rotten business! Georgis, sooner or later, would commit suicide. His, Barutanski's, wife, Ingrid, was a nymphomaniac and a spendthrift, and if someone liquidated him before her, she'd die somewhere in exile, like a beggar. Armstrong, Rayevski, Blithauer-Blitvinski, Vanini-Schiavone, they were all just clowns! Kavalierski was mad, a sadist, a born burglar. Nielsen was an irascible onanist, an intellectual ape, a man who forever played a role beyond his power. And so as things were with his most intimate circle, so they were in life generally. States, the law, social and political organizations, all were riddled with defects, and what was lacking was due to a more profound law of nature, the law of that element to which people gave the banal title "the eternal human." All people in general were shipwrecked, and man's life was nothing but a constant shipwreck. And from the wrecks, all around us, floated irrigators, chocolate, toilet bowls, radios, pumps, pipes, books, guns, cannon, whole shipwrecked civilizations drowned around us, but Kristian Barutanski's cosmic task was at all costs to assure a favorable export of Blitvinian beer and Blitvinian sugar beets, and therefore he needed shooting down like a dog, for he had truly secured those exports by legal international trade agreements, under the jurisdiction of the court in The Hague. What logic!

He should be killed, they said, because he had killed. But what did it mean to kill a man, if one came to think of it? It meant to take his life. Yet life was nothing but the process of dying from one's first to one's last day, for, once a man was dead, the process of dying was at an end. That was logical. Death, then, meant the end of dying. To cause that end by some human means, be it a revolver or the gallows, meant nothing else but to liberate a man from the uncomfortable, long-lasting, and inevitable process of dying which was mathematically inescapable, tortuous, long-lasting, and tedious, often enervating beneath all human dignity! All people were mortal, so why was it a particular crime to hasten that mortality in individuals in the most exceptional circumstances? The usual, normal, accepted death was the result of sicknesses that developed with man from his birth, while the death sown by Kristian Barutanski was the result of circumstances that led to the liberation of Blitva. Why then should Kristian Barutanski be "specially" guilty, for having killed in such "special" circumstances? As though people had not killed in such circumstances, and for centuries at that? And how had he killed anyway? He'd had them shot, very simply! Was it painful to be shot? Absolutely not. The experience of many wounded people confirmed that the bullet was quicker than pain. Compared then with the various other possibilities of the so-called normal, accepted, clinical, pathological death, the youthful, patriotic, ideal death with which Kristian Barutanski had liquidated his clients was a true blessing. That here and there the odd body twitched like a headless turkey, that was only due to natural reflexes! In that twitching there was no consciousness. With a bullet in the heart or the brain, a man was surely dead. And once dead, he was gone. Never to return. And a man could kneel, pray, repent as much as he liked, confess, babble night after night with Bonaventura Baltrushaitis, listen to the bells, travel to Rome, put himself down for a papal blessing. A man could find a morbid relief in self-condemnation. He could find relief in the most minute analysis of his own stupidity. Instead of kneeling before bloodshed, guns, police, armies, he could kneel in front of altars to his heart's content. He could become a vegetarian, if it amused him. He could live according to the strict rules of love, honor, goodness, sleep the sleep of a philistine saint, and live all his life observing the strictest diet—the devil would get him in the end, no matter. And such an exemplary citizen would croak under the unremitting blade of death, just as Kerinis, Georgis, or Barutanski, who brought with them several solid brigades of the dead and numberless fires and atrocities. And faced with that fact, that one vanishes into the abyss, what was the sense of such empty human concepts as "healthy common sense," or "Blitva"? "Science" and "scientific proofs"? A laughable confidence trick and a lot of prejudices. And especially that "science"!

He'd spent an evening in the laboratory of the factory for chemical warfare, run by a Karabaltic Slav, Dr. Wystulanski. That Dr. Wystulanski, the hope of the young Blitvinian science, one of the most likely candidates for the Nobel Prize, greeted the head of Blitva with the pretended humility of a lackey and there, in this stammering and nervous man's office, the man who, for the Blitvinian army, was preparing poisonous gases, Colonel Kristian Barutanski, in the company of Bonaventura Baltrushaitis, hardly spoke a word the entire evening. In huge four-colored charts on Wystulanski's laboratory walls, like mysterious Chinese characters, in tangles of vertical and deathly formulae, there towered above the visitors' heads the posterlike symbols of poisonous war gases. Beneath those demonic methylchlorates, beneath the hundred-percent-lethal monochloromethylchlorophormiates, beneath the large red formula for phosgene ($COCl_2$), there sat a small, bald man with a stutter, that feebleminded hope of the young Blitvinian science, a fool dressed in his jacket and smelling of eau de cologne and expecting from this semiofficial visit of Colonel Barutanski a Blithuania Restituta third class. He talked of how poisonous gases and gases generally harmful to man were eternal. And that in the opinion of science it was an elementarily comforting fact, for instance, that nitrogen was indestructible. Oxygen the same. Oxygen was eternal. And so, in general. Seventy such nitrogens and oxygens forever, and chlorine and hydrogen gave off hydrochloric acid, and the sun's rays radiated carbonic acid from the air with the aid of chlorine, which the plants gave off and so one exuded the other according to the laws of nature. Europe exuded $COCl_2$ and monochloromethylchlorophormiate, and that all this was not only an utterly senseless, truly stupid radiation of poisonous gases (as Dr. Wystulanski expounded), this Dr. Bonaventura Baltrushaitis guaranteed, for this learned confessor sold, wrapped in his Roman Catholic silver paper, tastefully enfolded in the cellophane of a brilliant religious view of the world, his unique salvation and comfort, his centuries-long tried remedy against the fear of death! The seraphic and angelic faith in the supernatural meaning of monochlorophormiate. Gases moved in one direction and then in another, in the direction of Saint-Quentin, then in the direction of Arras or Ypres. This rolling of gases over the French battlefields in the year 1918 gave birth to Blitva, and Blitva today had its scientific hope in Dr. Wystulanski and in the vast nothingness of the universe, crisscrossed with the fiery, chaotic paths of the stars. One of those paths was that of the completely free and sovereign state of Blitva, which today, due to the concatenation of international affairs, was still a republic. Yet if little Solveig so desired, the completely free and sovereign principality of Blitva might become a kingdom and little Solveig might become Her Majesty, registered in the dynastic *Gotha Almanac* according to all the laws of international protocol.

Nothingness existed. In this nothingness there was Dr. Wystulanski with his monochlorophormiates, but, other than this monochlorophormiate, there was nothing, only those gases, poisonous, mustard, that killed rats in the laboratories as they would future soldiers. And, apart from them, there was nothing, since nothing was no more than a verbal concept, unthinkable to human experience. *Ex nihilo nihil fit, et in nihilum potest reverti;* that was utterly without sense. So? So there was nothing left but to poison oneself with gases, fire the artillery, rape dear little naive smiling Solveigs . . .

At the point of despair, in terror of the unknown and fatal bullet that could come at any moment, crushed by the realization that appeared to have grasped the senselessness of everything, in the utter emptiness of a boring, monotonous, and, in its monotony, fatally stupid and decorative existence, surrounded only by chimpanzees (who had no other aim than to receive honors), Barutanski, fleeing from his own private hell, regarded himself more and more with a certain warm sympathy, and as though he were his own confessor, he felt the need to kneel before himself, to pardon himself and to absolve himself as an unfortunate who repented, without knowing why, except that it took him by the throat and he felt that he might burst into tears.

"Man is a hellish column of lies and murder, a bubble of nasty diseases. He is carried, rolling like a blind torrent of instincts. He howls under the stars in a blizzard of stupidities, and where does he roll, where does he flow, where is his source, and where his destination? And why?"

"Ah, you see, Excellency, your 'why,' that's the basic starting point, by which man fell into his final error at that very moment when his own brain asked that stupid question regarding the expediency of life." So the doctor of theology Bonaventura Baltrushaitis replied, certain that he spoke the absolute truth. "Posing such a pathetically human question is to be blind with healthy eyes and to ask why do I look, when it's clear that I look simply in order to see. What one needs is to see and not to ask 'why do we look'!"

"In order to see what?"

"God, Excellency! Man lives in order to see God, to know God, and that is all! To ask oneself the unreasonably shallow question 'why,' that is to be lost in regarding the most banal surface of life. What you touch with a tip of your pathetic and pitiful question, Excellency, is no more than the dust on a butterfly's wings. One must look much more deeply, as did Saint Teresa. Our Lord God is a merciful majesty, and one should approach him on one's knees, as before the true throne, with hands clasped in prayer. Treason against the divine lawgiver is a mortal sin, but that wise and all-knowing sovereign willingly forgives all treason, and in that lies the mystery of his mercy: which means that his moral amnesty is, as it were, permanent. He dismisses treason with a single sovereign smile. And for man to gain from God this great and incomprehensible mercy, he must unite with him in his thoughts and that, Excellency, can be achieved solely through prayer. Apart from this, Excellency, one must always keep in mind that the devil, who is always among us, constantly fights with all his earthly powers against the purity of our heavenly inspirations and all the problems which have so painfully preoccupied Your Excellency lately: a general intellectual anxiety, a doubt of the worldly meaning of our physical life, vanity, an unnatural leaning toward carnal enjoyment, a sense of guilt, and the various degrees of human hatred within us, et cetera, et cetera, and that all these are simply the tarry hoof of the devil that treads around us, sensing, as he does, that a noble and gentle soul, one that thirsts for a knowledge of God, is escaping him. God may be felt, Excellency, after tremendous nervous exertion, and Your Excellency in every way has merited that someone should unburden you of an excess of worldly worries. For to be the supreme lawgiver and father of an entire people in such troubled times as ours, that is a task beyond the power of even a Saint Christopher! And Saint Paul also, by all accounts, had strained his nerves to the utmost, when, in a supernatural ecstasy, he came to the assurance that divine things are more important than worldly things, and when he wisely realized that we do not live as 'We,' that is to say, as isolated individuals in nothingness, but that God lives and abides in 'Us.' For as regards the most ordinary elements of human piety, as the prerequisite of a deeper and solely valid contemplation, by my own observation, Excellency, I see that in your personal life there has been a surplus of such elements. From the first day, when I had the honor and good fortune to be in your company, I noted that you belonged to the category of dear, kind, friendly, obliging people, that you loved those around you, that you bowed in humility to all those beneath you, that you were ever sincerely at the service of any who needed help, that you lessened human anxiety with selfless self-sacrifice worthy of admiration, that you had selflessly dedicated yourself to the cause of Blitva without any selfish motives, that you helped and comforted people, that you were a just, truthful, sincere, and good man, who modestly and piously lived according to God's laws! You, Excellency, are tormented by the question why life should have occurred on this planet and why man lives under the sun. The basic scientific question what is organic and what is inorganic is both ridiculous and pathetic. All that is organic and inorganic on earth bathes in the sun, and that sunbathing is no more than the sunbathing of sunbathing suns, if I may put it like that. All that is of the sun in us desires to return to the sun, and that is the reflection of the sun on the earth's surface, that which—in a word—is banally known as life. And note, Excellency, just as man bathes in the sun, so he bathes in divinity. And just as all the sun in us gravitates back to the sun, so all the divine in us gravitates to God. What is fundamental is this, which Saint Teresa truly noted: He who thinks to see himself with mortal eyes, he thinks only in an earthly and limited fashion. One may see oneself only with the eyes of the spirit, and who sees with the eyes of the spirit sees truly, and who sees truly has absolutely no need for reason. The feeling of God's presence among us is no more than the feeling of greater security in life, Excellency! One needs to believe, if you will, for Pascal's typically French motive, that a man might profit, *pour gagner*! Faith gives us and strengthens in us the intimation of a higher order among things and events! You yourself have admitted that lately all things disgust you. Women are abhorrent, the digestive organs offend you as the sole means of connection with women, Beauregard has become like a prison. You consider yourself personally lost, but I've noticed, for example, that you find peace in listening to organ music! Or do you recall how last Easter in the company of his eminence the cardinal in the Dominican monastery in Ankersgarden, you fell into an ecstasy at the truly supernatural beauty of the stone crucifix in the monastery corridor? The prayer that a man delivers with the concentrated intention of returning to God is a rising above things, and man may rise above things with the optical ecstasy over a crucifix and with church music and with wise reading of church thinkers. Prayer is contact with God, and contact with God, instead of the melancholy, revolting emptiness of the futility and vanity of life, returns to us our faith in life's fullness and meaning. Prayer, even at its least successful, is always a good and reliable means against moral headaches, and in every least significant prayer there is always, no matter how tiny, a shadow of hope that all is not yet lost, since there is always in our hearts room for the divine mercy that pours down from heaven, to use the metaphor of Saint Teresa, like heavenly rain. At one's first, most primitive, so to speak, introductory contemplations of God, one must always bear in mind, first, that man's means of awareness are extremely limited, and then, that all concepts of God that man is able to grasp are obscure and that it is important that they be constantly sought. On the devilish midden of our living reality God shines out amid the rubble of lies and prejudices like a phosphorescent flower. And one should wait patiently for the divine mercy in the anteroom of our Lord. For to be accepted into the divine audience is no small honor for an ordinary mortal! And what is of primary importance for the beginner in prayer: The way to the spirit is hard; it is no way for spiritual weaklings, for the arrogant or the hypocritical who think that their reason is their only lamp in the darknesses of life. God halts the action of reason the moment there is contact between him and the praying soul, and to enter the hall of the spirit before his angels who lead us through the labyrinth of the consciousness to his throne means to give oneself over blindly to the feelings of our heart which, in this case, is man's only relatively reliable guide. It is better then to be unlearned and simple and to have the feeling for God than learned and arrogant and thus plunged in lies and deceits. This, Excellency, is among the commonest failings of the human spirit! To this rubbish belong first those questions which, at first glance, appear to us to be intellectual,

philosophic, but which in reality are of less value than the silver sequins from ladies' discarded dresses! So, for example, to these belongs that apparently basic question: Has life any purpose at all? For
take this life around us, Excellency! Take this world of tortoises,
bedbugs, cockroaches, locusts, lice, carnivores, wild beasts, take
those distant diluvia and those mysterious Africas with their mos-
quitoes and diseases, tropical heat, poisonous snakes and sharks,
take that demonic world, the world of a Hieronymus Bosch with its
monsters and horrors, where one continues to eat the other for centuries—put yourself for one moment in that so notorious elemental
nature, Excellency, and you will agree that in this hellish chaos
man's brain is but a pitiful phenomenon! In the vast dark primordial
forests, in the blind cannibalistic abundance of flora and fauna, in
those limitless, bloodthirsty hordes of predators, of mammoths, os-
triches, lions, leopards, in those clouds of reptiles and monstrous
birds, in that horror of storm-tossed oceans, amid volcanoes, whirlwinds, and in thunder, this our glorious man stands naked and
alone, with three liters of water in his skull, and, if he compare himself with the life forces around him, he will inevitably come to the
conclusion that, as a living phenomenon, he has not and cannot have
any more profound meaning than has the tapeworm in his bowels or
any other skin disease on his epidermis! And you yourself once
deigned to remark that animal physical love takes place in parts that
nature employs for excretion and in this all too human, miserable
flood of fevers, colds, toothaches, rains, winds, and blizzards, man
has gone so far in his thoughts and deep observations that he has
confirmed that deep shocks to the brain result in an exaggerated secretion of alkaloid phosphates in the human urine. In this way he has
equated what goes on in our skulls to the secretions of urine. He has
explained murders, incest, lies, arson, killings, theft, robbery, and
human fraud as a form of chemical process, and, having reduced
himself and his human substance to a chemical formula, it is only

natural that he has rejected conscience also as a totally unnecessary chemical product! The most logical contradiction, truth and falsehood, honesty and dishonesty, mercy, the sense of justice, gratitude, duty, maternal instinct, feeling for family life—in a word, everything that is called human in the noble sense of the word—this man has crushed as outdated prejudice, and, thus freed from his human conscience, and himself an animal among animals, man has felt himself to be the most powerful of all creatures and so has begun his triumphal bestial progress, the beast above all beasts, the white, silken beast that moves victoriously beneath the stars to its victory over nature. Man flies like a bird. He is quicker than all animals by means of his machines. He has overcome climatic obstacles. He has conquered sickness with the knife and with medicine. Man is on the road to dominating the resistance of matter, to prolonging his earthly life by care of his body. He's gathered so much experience that, in this sense, he has outwitted all animals. Yet there you have it—despite all this, this same man is still ever the most ordinary, revolting, blind, indeed, mad and raging beast! Today, with such a rise of technology, this same man is closer to the prehistoric cannibal than to the concept of the man who can distinguish good from evil and who is aware that his neighbor is exactly such a man and equally valuable as he himself. This very conqueror of the animals is ever still himself an animal. He kills, steals, burns, makes war, slaughters, indulges in gluttony and in drink, tortures his neighbors and causes them evil at every step, betrays his comrades, cheats, swindles even his closest family, mocks, hates, envies, sneers like an ape at everything in life that is supernatural, and he's as daft as a young kitten that chases after every rustling sound, and more resembles Shiva's wife Durga (who shows us her bloodstained palms soaked in human blood and her only ornament is a necklace of human skulls) than the divine person of our Savior, who redeemed us on the cross by his own death. There you have the devilish, hellish, satanic view of life, which today's modern man uses to lighten the cosmic darkness in the miasma of ignorance and fear before the unknown. And believe me, Excellency, those dear, humble, good women, whom life has drained, who piously utter sighs in the dark pews in empty churches, in their prayers of repentance are far closer to wisdom than our modern thinkers who are convinced they have discovered the secret of all secrets by reducing human thought to a chemical process equal to the secretion of uric acid or salt. The way to God, Excellency, leads through the church. And the church is not only the singing of hymns, the attendance at early-morning Mass, kneeling in half-darkened places, where one plunges into the decorative side of the church service and enjoys the perfumes, the luxurious vestments, the organ music and the ringing of bells, the scent of roses, all of which certainly leads to the mood, the ecstasy, the inspiration, and which becomes a supernatural view of being, the precondition of relief that reassures and comforts us that we are on the best road to discovering the peace and harmony of that concept in whose framework God abides. One should not overcomplicate one's method of approach to these spiritual heights. One should begin very simply, like a peasant, with the rosary, and then continue with the Litany, attend holy Masses, recite an Ave Maria before going to sleep, one, two, three, thirty-three Ave Marias, and you'll see, Excellency, that one's anxieties melt away like the spring snows, that the waters of the resurrection ripple on the slopes of our spirit, that the murmur of heavenly streams washes away all the dark sediments of Satanism which, for years, have grown inside us, and one will learn by experience that the healing balsam of prayer is far more efficacious than appears at first sight. The way is not so obscure, nor so steep, as it would appear to laymen, but one must forever bear in mind also that these initial spiritual exercises are elements that serve, just as the rules of grammar serve, only as an aid to expression. Prayers are individual. Prayers lie before us like letters in a letterpress. What poem these scattered black letters will form depends on the skill of the individual. Somewhere Marx wrote that he had no intention of explaining the world, he wished to change it. Yet the dialectical thinkers refuse to admit that, before our eyes, God has been changing the world creatively for centuries. For us to change this evil world depends upon our prayers, and whether it be given to every man to do so is best proven by the hundreds of thousands of saints and those beloved of God, among whom there were thousands of utterly uneducated laypeople. It is given to every individual to liberate himself from the hellish poverty of our daily life. God is present in all things, and who has the eyes to see him feels the fulfillment of his presence. In the utter bewilderment, in the grip of uncertainty, in our prayers, our spirit cannot know whither it goes or whence it comes, nor what it desires, but praying sincerely and devotedly, the spirit feels prayer raising it above its everyday worries and, rising thus through prayer, man inevitably feels himself floating above earthly things. Saint Teresa felt from Jesus in her prayers that the culmination of her prayers remained beneath her like the tops of earthly hills and that an eaglelike power of consciousness carried her vertically upward to the supernatural mystery of the holy sacrament. I do not mean to say that it is given to every man to devote himself in such an exalted and poetic manner as did Teresa de Cepeda, for her inspiration was a mark of special mercy, but every man who desires to be freed from this satanic, evil, nervous state of anxiety, which modern psychoanalysis has named psychosis or neurosis generally; every such individual who, contaminated by modern life, troubled by the problems of our immoral times, feels at every step the thousand vacuums of the hellish porosity of our ideals; every unfortunate who feels the need for order in chaos and for a rising from the depths; that is to say, every one of us must be aware that the dignity of the spirit over the abyss would not be itself were it not beset by the gravitation of sin; that is to say, of the earth and of hell. What do the concepts 'earth' and 'hell' mean in the circumstances of our Blitva and of Europe in general? They mean the belief that on this earth one may achieve something only by earthly means for physical, fleshly, digestive, sensual, earthly ends. This includes politics and all political ideas, be they left or right. Regardless whether you, Excellency, rule our beloved fatherland here from Beauregard (which you do extremely wisely, with great tact, and, as concerns Blitva's national development, with true genius), regardless of the fact that such a hysterical humanist as Nielsen attacks you, first with open letters and even with mad attempts on your life, unworthy of man in any circumstances, yet either approach is vain and must be vain, if the cause be not under the banner of the Lord. For what can be the end of such humanism as that stupid so-called humanism of a Nielsen? Murder! Blood! Slaughter! Criminality! Apropos Nielsen: By sheer chance, Excellency, I learned, discreetly, where he is staying. Completely by chance, last night."

"According to my information, he's in Blatvia."

"No, Excellency! Dr. Nielsen is still in Blitwanen! He's staying with a Mrs. Gallen, the widow of Sigurd Gallen, the well-known exporter of salted fish and the former owner of the firm Gallen and Company."

Dr. Bonaventura Baltrushaitis rose to his feet and, with a furtive movement of his right hand, parting the rich white and heavy folds of his Dominican habit that, like thick curtains, hid his other clothes (as a mantilla hides a mask), he drew from the back pocket of his trousers a small gold-lettered book bound in soft crocodile skin and, jamming a pair of gold-rimmed spectacles onto his large, swollen nose, breathing heavily and rapidly like a rhinoceros, he leafed through the small gold-embossed crocodile-skin book, so that its soft, half-transparent leaves, as fine as cigarette papers, rustled beneath his fleshy, swollen, and somewhat sweaty fingers.

"Yes, here it is! Mrs. Amanda Gallen, 5A, the Promenade, first floor, right. That lady, if you remember, Excellency, is the mother of the Captain Gallen who died defending that hateful, demagogic, and godless band of Muzhikovski! During the last two or three days there have been whole conferences of such gentlemen!"

Barutanski got up and, with apparent calm, as though quite unconcerned, as if the matter did not seem to him of any particular importance, strolled over to his massive desk at the very back of the room, by the fireplace. There he sat down and lit the lamp, and Father Bonaventura appeared before the Commandant's desk quietly and with silent steps, still holding his tiny breviary, from which hung multicolored silken fringes; the burning red and emerald green of these silken fringes stood out against the white Dominican habit.

So, Barutanski thought to himself, Georgis is well intentioned, but as daft as a hound without scent. And his intelligence service isn't worth a bent farthing! Georgis is looking for the bastard in Blatvia, and he's sitting under his nose.

"What was that you said, what was the address, Doctor?" ("Doctor" and "Father" were two variations in their mutual ceremonial in their theological mystic seances in Beauregard. "Father" meant that the Lord of Blitva was paying attention, that he was well disposed and was behaving toward his spiritual instructor truly like a lost son who desired indeed to be reconciled with his spiritual father. But "Doctor," this was pronounced coldly and with the authority of the Commandant, from above, from the heights of Beauregard, just as strictly as when he called his favorite spaniel "Lord" when the old and deaf dog left a wet trace on the carpet beside the fireplace.)

"Amanda Gallen, 5A, the Promenade, first floor, right, Excellency!"

There was a pause. Barutanski got up and paced up and down the library, and in that brownish darkness his spurs sunk into the carpet and, as if muffled, skipping across the dark Baluchi carpet, sounded like tiny, mysterious ox bells. There was a long silence in which all that was heard was the hissing rumble of Bonaventura's stomach,

into which that pious soul had been pouring one glass of Martell after the other. Licking his drooling lips, Bonaventura lit a fragrant
Havana, as thick as a thumb, with a twenty-two-centimeter-long
match, and, regarding this burning column that smoked with the
scent of some tropical bark soaked in an aromatic oil, he poured
himself yet another glass of Hennessy and, smacking his lips in satisfaction, slumped into one of the armchairs beside the fireplace. A
burning coal collapsed on the pyre of logs that was the fireplace and
the dark red reflection of the flame licked over the ancient beams of
the library, casting its light with the strange hellish glow of a bonfire
over the white-clad monk and the scowling, silent horseman.

"Yes, that's how it is, Excellency. Of all the present errors of
modern man, one of the worst is undoubtedly vulgar materialism!
People like Nielsen with their hero Giordano Bruno think they've
swallowed all earthly wisdom like a flock of stupid chickens that
think the handful of grain scattered in front of them is the be-all
and end-all of the universe! From seed, say these followers of
Giordano, arises the stalk, and from the stalk the ear, and from the
ear we knead bread, and bread turns to blood, and blood becomes
man, and man, dying, decomposes into a corpse, and the corpse
returns to the earth, and from the earth springs the stalk, and from
the stalk comes grain, and thus this clever cycle ends in the demonic and satanic concept of 'the indestructibility of matter.' And
once this devilish matter is indestructible, then it's all the same to
us who kills whom. In other words, let's all kill and slaughter one
another! Yes, that vulgar materialist concept of the indestructibility of matter, that is the root of all evil among people of today's Europe! These shortsighted idiots have written great tomes about the
fact that this, their 'matter,' moves in the sphere of things, borne
by yet more blind forces, so that matter changes its form and thus
apparently passes, as does all else. Yet this is merely apparent, for
forms pass in the flow of events, but 'matter,' that ill-fated 'sub-

stance,' it remains. Everything, then, that has taken the form of any appearance of this, their 'matter,' all this persists only on the thousands and thousands of long-dead forms of this same 'matter,' for only the form of matter dies, but the essence of matter is 'eternal.' Thus death, as such, is merely a necessary change of material form, and so fear of death and mortality or of the vulgar ephemerality of form, as such, is utterly irrelevant, for it is one of the natural 'materialistic' laws (according to those learned gentlemen, our modern thinkers) that only the form of things changes, yet truly this is nothing but a variation of something that is indestructible and is known as 'matter'! When it is, thus, natural to die, since this is only the necessary variation of an ephemeral material form, what does it mean then to remove somebody from this earthly life, according to this same materialistic logic? To kill a man, to kill one's brother, one's neighbor, one's benefactor, to kill Colonel Barutanski, according to such people as Nielsen, means no more than, in the fatally necessary change of a given material substance, to perform the change 'of eternal matter,' that is to say, 'of indestructible matter,' in one of its innumerable permutations. According to these gentlemen, death as such does not exist, and, if there is no death, then violent death is no murder, and where there is no murder there is no guilt, naturally! Intellectuals like Nielsen, who are, heaven knows why, subjectively certain that they possess two or three grams of brain more than the rest of their fellow beings, such sick megalomaniacs are capable, on the false premises of their personal conceit, to wade in blood up to their knees, sure that they are thus promoting certain ideals of 'humanism,' 'fatherland,' 'the people,' and even entire 'humanity'! And were I not convinced that in this case (putting aside all others), it is a matter of the hellish, satanic errors of negative, criminal people, I would not have mentioned these individuals at all to Your Excellency, but in this case, I feel it not only to be my duty as a confessor but my duty as a subject to warn

Your Gracious Highness that it would be no bad thing for Your Excellency to pay particular attention to those surrounding you here in Beauregard, since, if I am not mistaken, Mrs. Michelson, for instance, belongs to the most intimate circle of friends of that gentleman. And then there is that Olaf Knutson, that disgusting intellectual, Freemason, agent provocateur. He too is a friend of Nielsen's, and it was he, Olaf Knutson, who hid Dr. Nielsen at Mrs. Gallen's, in her flat at 5A, the Promenade, first floor. Yes! That's what happens when people believe that human thought is not a gift of God, but the radiation of alkaloid phosphates in uric acid!"

In his nervous pacing between the fireplace and the ancient, smoke-blackened globe on which the continents could no longer be distinguished and the seas had long been melted with the land in a brownish mixture of dark chocolate, Barutanski, glassily clicking his spurs, halted in front of Father Bonaventura and, thrusting at the friar his dark and penetrating glance (framed by tired and sickly circles), he demanded to know whom he suspected in Beauregard, in the sharp, strict tones of a policeman, who was taking down the first statement of a detainee.

"Facts, Doctor, facts!"

Dr. Bonaventura Baltrushaitis was scared. He hadn't thought that this would lead to a detailed interrogation, and, feeling tiny needles of icy sweat breaking out above the wrinkles on his forehead, he rose from the armchair and stood in front of the Commandant at the regulation distance of three paces, with arms hanging straight at attention like two heavy weights. Along his left sleeve, his Havana smoked, and smoke from the cigar framed the outline of his Dominican habit in wavering vertical lines. It seemed as though this white-clad monk was himself smoldering like some old-fashioned gun fuse. There was a long pause. Barutanski, with his hands behind him, rubbing the palm of his left hand several times on the right, during the whole of this unpleasant policelike scene nervously jerked his left knee so that one could hear the spur on his left boot rubbing against that on his right, and this lent the entire scene the particularly unpleasant, indeed sharp, tones of a military tribunal.

"All right, if you have suspicions, who is it you suspect?"

"In fact, I suspect nobody and everybody, Your Excellency! I think I have a good sense for such things! I feel there's a plot somewhere in your immediate vicinity! Who this may involve in Beauregard I have no idea, but I sense it. . . ."

"OK, only none of your jokes, Doctor, I beg you! On what basis do you suspect the people around me, Doctor? And how did you find out that Nielsen was staying at the home of that old woman?"

"Please, Your Excellency, that is a secret of the confessional!"

"For God's sake, I'm not one of your first-year priests to be charmed by that type of joke. I want to know where did you get Nielsen's address from. From Mrs. Michelson? I'm well aware she is your mistress!"

"No, Excellency! I'm friends with Mrs. Michelson only because I suspect her. To me, Mrs. Michelson is a hundred percent suspect!"

"Oh, cut it out! You needn't bother your head about the Michelson woman! Who gave you Nielsen's address?"

"Excellency, I consider it's in the interest of the state that I tell you! And only because of such a matter of principle can I betray to you what was a hundred percent confidential. The old lady Gallen told me this during confession. She considers you personally to be the murderer of her only son, Captain Gallen. She is a bit senile, and since, in her confused state, she confuses the idea of anger with her maternal love for her dead son, her only mortal sin lies in the fact that he has lately involved her in the senile and maniacal hatred that she prayed to God for your death. She passionately desired your death, but at the same time sincerely repented for her mortal sin and therefore confessed to me that Dr. Nielsen was concealing a store of dynamite in her house! So that is how I learned Nielsen's address!"

"So that's it! That's how you learned Nielsen's address? *Merci!* And in return, Father Bonaventura, would you like me to tell you whom I suspect in Beauregard? You! Yes, you yourself!"

Barutanski burst out laughing and in a strange and exalted change of mood once again slapped the palm of his left hand on his right, which he still held behind his back, and poured himself half a large glass of cognac and drank it down in an unbridled wave of momentary merriment, which suddenly swept him out of his melancholic, passive, and head-aching torpor into a state of vital euphoria! And, as though playing with some retarded boy, with both hands he gave Bonaventura a friendly tap on the shoulders and, embracing him just as affectionately, slapped him gently on his belly above his black Dominican belt, as in a mark of exceptional fondness. The friar gaped in amazement. With the cigar still smoking in his left hand, as in a dream, he took the silver crucifix that gleamed on its costly chain around his neck with both hands and, crossing Colonel Barutanski with it, he approached him with ceremony and emotion and once again crossed him with the three fingers of his right hand: Excellency, may God be with you, in the name of the Father, the Son, and the Holy Spirit! Bowing low before Barutanski, in a servile gesture, he kissed his right hand and, cringing like a beaten dog, he backed away to the armchair, where he remained as shocked as an old woman over a spilt jug of milk.

"What's the matter, Doctor? Why are you surprised? Because I suspect you? That's quite natural! I suspect everybody and everything! That's my long-standing rule! One needs to be on the alert. *Homo homini lupus! Blithuanicus blithuanico lupior!*"

"Ah, you see, Excellency, that's exactly what I meant a while ago when I spoke of the gravitational force of sin over spiritual ascendancy," Father Bonaventura commented, as though nothing had happened between them and as though continuing his lecture on the need for the spiritualization of human thought with the help of prayer, feeling automatically that this was an excellent opportunity to return to the agenda of these Beauregard exercises. "One must desire to know God with complete devotion, for if a man is half-hearted or careless, then he always falls back into the satanic miasma, as, for instance, when man becomes a wolf to man! The love a man should feel for his neighbor shines among us like some distant sparkling star, enshrouded in dark, impenetrable storm clouds, and that divine love we need to cherish for one another, like a spark, tireless, like the gleam of distant rays in the darkness, this we need to raise to a cult and not to lose ourselves in low, animal hatred or paranoid suspicion. And here too the heart is the best authority, Excellency! Here neither our reason nor the essence of our experience can help us much. Human reason is no more than an inarticulate blabber and a chattering pedant that clatters around us like a type of Tibetan prayer wheel. The cult of reason is pure fetishism! In the light of the mortal candle of human reason, all earthly things perish as purely valueless concepts, and only through the transmortal pangs of everything physical in us may one pass to the true ecstasy of the spiritual element, and to that higher ecstasy, when the heart feels itself toll like a mysterious, blood-filled bell, that is the path that leads us to the greatest inspiration that is called the triumph of the spirit above all that is dark and satanic within us! And when our spirit attains those triumphal frontiers, then does it feel itself present at the great festival in the city of the Lord. . . . From the balconies hang rich brocades and tapestries. All windows are lit. On all belfries, on all towers, banners fly, torches flare, harps play, and the thunder of blood-pumping hearts shakes one like an incense-filled peal of bells, and all things are bright with the eternity of the stars. At this triumphal frontier of the spiritual and the physical, all of us that was of the flesh, of the will, of the sensual remnants, of earthly obscure passions, all is separated from the body, and the spirit feels nothing but the majestic fullness of silence, peace, and silver tranquillity. To the soul there appears an endless quantity of images, and this bright and sparkling mass is lost in the impossibility of realization and conception. To be consumed in the incomprehensible, the fear before the inconceivable power of that clairvoyance, the dissolving of the imagination, the intelligence and will and the gentle transmortal lassitude, that is the Lord when he is so merciful as to allow us to rise up to him and to the utter, unique, perfectly supernatural, and individual in the enjoyment of unity with the divine. There were not many saints to whom it was given to arise to such a supraphysical flaring of the spirit, where all that is human is melted in the divine fire of sweet unconsciousness and the vanishing of all physical powers, but those who, by the will of Providence, found themselves in this wondrous inebriation, this holy intoxication of the reason and the will, these first pioneers of the Lord have left us written documents of how the Lord may truly be felt essentially, existentially, physically, and that he is indeed present within us, in our bloodstream and in our earthly existence. The Lord, then, appears in the revelation of the unrevealable, in the presentation of the ineffable, in the gentle dissolution of self, in the burning of the heavenly pyre, in the rising above self, where one feels the utter dissolution of every vanity and egoism, in a word, in the full flood of the heavenly light, where is felt utter unburdening, dehumanization, the entering into God, and the sweet oblivion on the edge of the final ascension and supernatural blessedness. In this blessed ascension Saint Teresa, for example, felt herself like a lonely sparrow on a roof, so terrified before death, as if she were already condemned to death and about to be hanged, and felt only that the executioner would kick the chair from under her feet, but that sublime sense of wondrous and final cleansing in the melting pot of the Lord was still, for her, the source of delight, so that she, after this final submerging into God, felt her return to earthly reality as an extremely tiring and exhausting process. For all these unclean, hellish, satanic, evil images of madness exist only in order that we might pass in the ship of God to the other side, to the shore of the divine and starry contrast."

Slumped in his armchair, his feet on the fender, feeling the heat of the fire penetrating his soft boots, in the smoke of his forty-third Maryland-Jaune, Barutanski listened, as though half asleep, to this virtuoso litany, this rhetorically perfect accumulation of adjectives, while his head was full of vague images.

God, what an utter mess this world is. Beauregard, full of false, creeping, masked, suspicious people, a legion, an entire legion of graves set in the mud of Blitva, a stupid comedy, in which this confidant of his preached about Saint Teresa. What the hell did this priest want from him? This fucking friar, after all, was a slimy bugger! A lover who sent his mistress to the gallows. A confessor who sold sacramental secrets. An agent who sniffed around the cafés for the price of petty blood money, a snout who denounced Beauregard to the papal authorities, a bastard with no other idea in his head than thirty pieces of silver. He'd given him the cash for the new seminary through the Ministry of Finance! And according to the report of the rectorate, this well-known Blitvinian scholar and moralist, twice a doctor, had no obstacles or formalities in the way to being elected full professor of Blitva University. . . .

"By the way, Baltrushaitis! Have you done anything about the approval from the Ministry of Works? The minister of finance telephoned me yesterday and said the money for your seminary was allocated. How much did you need?"

"We asked for three hundred thousand lei, Excellency!"

"OK then, Doctor! *Servus!* I've got a headache! I've had enough of your nonsense for one day! Good-bye!"

CHAPTER 2

Where Things Go Full Belt

Barutanski was left alone. One could hear the rain. A strange play of drops on the windowsill. Long metal needles against the window, and from time to time a black squall of dark masses of water against the panes. Wind in the chimney. Sooty. Damp.

Boring! Inexpressibly boring. Bald elderly gentlemen in a Dominican habit taken from some Italian opera, and their occupation was to amass more or less obscure and unclear adjectives that had no relation to living problems. Such a gentleman slept with General Michelson's wife, loved foie gras in aspic, smoked Havanas, drank Hennessy, and preached dematerialization, the spiritualization of the flesh, of salmon, of fish in general. He preached spiritualization as a salvation from hell, but here in the hellish hemisphere of his own life he gave away the secrets of the confession! Stupid! Boring! Anyway: all these friars and churches! Enough to make the angels weep! What did these people want? This illiterate pack of bastards had created themselves a profitable racket out of oppressing the other pack of illiterate bastards! They lie to themselves in the hope that other idiots would believe their lying in the name of some higher being. Everything that came "from above" had the sense of a supernatural mission, even when it ended in denunciation to the police! Truly, unworthy of man!

Under the influence of such misanthropical musings on the failings of humankind, Barutanski stretched himself like a cat in front of the warm fire, sensing the need for some form of physical exertion!

To mount his Penelope and have a gallop through the rain and wind. He got up and walked to the window. Outside, heavy, damp snowflakes began to mix with the rain.

There was no point in tiring Penelope in weather like this!

He returned to the big library table. He took up the literary periodical *Blitvias Lampadefor*. On its front page it bore an excerpt from the first scene of Goethe's *Faust*.

NIGHT—FAUST'S STUDY

In a high-vaulted, narrow, gothic chamber, Faust is discovered restless at his desk.

> FAUST. Philosophy have I digested,
> The whole of Law and Medicine,
> From each its secrets I have wrested,
> Theology, alas, thrown in.
> Poor fool, with all this sweated lore,
> I stand no wiser than I was before.
> Master and Doctor are my titles;
> For ten years now, without repose,
> I've held my erudite recitals
> And led my pupils by the nose.
> And round we go, on crooked ways or straight,
> And well I know that ignorance is our fate,
> And this I hate

Idiocy! These so-called intellectual scribblers sat in the cafés and translated *Faust* and planned uprisings! This intellectual muck needed machine-gunning!

Lying on the large Renaissance table was a mass of various publications, Blitvinian, Blatvian, Hunnish, Ingermanlandish, and English. Turning over this heap of paper, stinking of printer's ink, with his right forefinger, Barutanski drew from this dull and stupid pile of the so-called European press an English journal, an economic gazette with an exclusively propagandistic character. Leafing through the monotonous and repetitious titles, he stopped at an article by an American reporter on the economic state of the world from an international point of view. According to the official statistics of various trade information agencies, the American, an economist by profession, affirmed that in the past year 886,000 wagons of grain and 144,000 wagons of rice had been destroyed in the world. In the USA 6 million pigs and 600,000 cattle had been burned. In the Argentine 500,000 sheep, in Holland 200,000 milk cows and 100,000 wagons of tinned meat. Brazil had sunk 32 million bags of coffee, and Canada had announced that in the present year it would fuel its machines entirely with wheat.

All these bastards needed machine-gunning! Blitva was hungry and Holland was burning 200,000 milk cows to keep up the price of its cheese! And Dr. Bonaventura Baltrushaitis thought that in this satanic chaos all one needed to do was to recite 333 Hail Marys for the recovery of the world!

He pushed aside the economic journal and took up a French edition of the Blitvinian semiofficial *L'Écho de Blithuanie. Edition française, Hebdomadaire du Blitvias Ekos: Rédacteur en chef: Felinis Richard.*

He'd never liked this *Blitvinian Echo.* It had always got on his nerves with its style, its stupid approach, and its Negroid French. Felinis, for instance, and all those other Blitvinian Felinisis, pathetic Parisian students who wasted their years in Parisian cafés, and all they learned there was to perfume themselves instead of using soap, and in those very places where Barutanski in his military regulations for the Blitvinian infantry especially ordered: that they soaped themselves every morning under the armpits, etc. . . . Every such Blitvinian Parisian student polished his nails, smoked Marylands, purchased perfumes, wore spats, stank of sweat and onions, but French he didn't learn. They'd brought symbolism to Blitva thirty years out of date and argued about the sonnet, translated *Faust*, wrote articles about him, and pilfered state funds. Writing about Blitvinian politics, they were quoting *Le Temps*. Bloody idiocy!

Notre politique karabaltique, according to a Richard Felinis, was an old worn-out gramophone record that croaked like a half-dead jay! Such cretins always came late with their slogans by at least two or three political seasons! How often he'd striven to wake these fools, without success! *Notre politique karabaltique* was more than a year out of date!

Déclaration de M. Belinis, ministre des Affaires Étrangères blithuaniennes. M. Belinis, ministre des Affaires Étrangères, a achevé, aux premiers jours d'octobre, la troisième année de son entré en fonctions.

Ce grand diplomate, d'une courtoisie et d'un charme exceptionnel, possède un caractère nature extraordinairement vivant et une intelligence brillante et profonde.

So thank you very much for this profound acknowledgment of the Right Honorable Minister of Foreign Affairs Belinis. You'd never guess what these gentlemen give to be written about. And these toilet-paper publications had an annual cost of 863,000 lei, just so Mr. Felinis could marvel at "the brilliant intelligence" of Mr. Belinis, or Belinis of Felinis: you scratch my back and I'll scratch yours!

Le Pacte blithuo-blathuanien. Quels seront les effets du Pacte? Le Pacte—et son but—est d'assurer une paix permanente, reposante sur une base positive au moyen de garanties réciproques en ce qui concerne les frontières . . .

They were writing about the Blitva-Blatvia Pact and about the mutual respect of frontiers? And who gave them the right to announce the news about a pact and the respect of frontiers? That was interesting. . . . It was a complete madhouse. As if they could have expected me personally to control what was written in the *Blitvinian Echo*! To hell with the *Blitvinian Echo*! Utter nonsense!

He got up with the *Blitvinian Echo* in his hand and went to the phone.

"Hello! This is the Commandant! Give me the Ministry of Foreign Affairs! Hello! This is the Commandant. Yes! Give me Belinis! He's not there? At a tea party at the British Embassy! Marvelous! When he returns, tell him to report to me immediately!"

He went back to his seat and went on fidgeting.

La politique ferroviaire blithuanienne atteint cette année un stade très important de développement: Le rail national avance rapidement vers son but final. La longueur totale de notre réseau ferroviaire est de 978 kilomètres. Lors de la proclamation de la République blithuanienne il y avait en Blithuanie 472 kilomètres de voies ferrées. L'Empire aragono-hounien avait créé ce réseau pendant plus d'un demi-siècle . . .

He turned a page. Engines had never interested him. He'd never wanted to be a signalman. On the next page, an entire octavo of the *Blitvinian Echo,* almost filling the entire page, was a photograph framed in laurel leaves of the equestrian statue that portrayed Colonel Barutanski as the Victor mounted on a mettlesome Arab horse, a picture of the masterly work of the master Roman Rayevski. In large Roman-type characters, covering the whole page, was an excerpt of Colonel Barutanski's famous speech that he gave to the legionnaires on the occasion of the anniversary of the Blitvinian Constitution, which referred back to the Principality of Blitva in the fourteenth century.

Quelque nombreux et puissant que soit l'ennemi qui attaque, notre foi dans la défense tournera la victoire de notre côté. C'est ainsi qu'il en a été et qu'il en sera!

That wasn't bad! The Roman characters suited the monument. And let fussers like Olaf Knutson say what they liked, Rayevski was an undoubtedly gifted man and the monument would be among the best in history. How many good horsemen were there in history? Don't be ridiculous! Was that statue of Marcus Aurelius on the

Capitol good? It was a cow, not a horse! It was a pregnant mare, with all the wrong proportions, and Marcus Aurelius sat this swollen Capitol corpse like a lame grandmother. Roman Rayevski's molding was masterly and the tail flowed out beneath the horse like a stream of bronze lava. Let the little men squeak! Thirty thousand Englishwomen will get hot flashes here in Blitwanen in front of such a stallion and such a horseman! After Padua, Blitwanen would be the only city in Europe to have a bronze worthy of the rider! Well done, Rayevski! We couldn't have thought of anything better for the tourist trade!

Spreading the *Blitvinian Echo* over his knees, Barutanski stretched out in the armchair, so as to gain a general view of events, and, enjoying the entire beauty of a work of art, like a true connoisseur, he even began to appreciate the *Blitvinian Echo*, the Ministry of Foreign Affairs, the chief editor Felinis, and Blitva in general and, in some satisfaction, lit a cigarette and reread the text of his speech, finding that it read well. *C'est ainsi qu'il en a été et qu'il en sera!* Good! Some of it doesn't sound too bad!

On the third page, in the second column, in italics, under the general title of *Monde Diplomatique*, was a load of information concerning the diplomatic world of Blitva which, for some unknown reason, Barutanski held in particular contempt. Those gentlemen in their gold-braided frock coats he had always considered a breed of special chimpanzees, who, by an act of chance, played on the Blitvinian stage the leading roles, without bearing any responsibility whatever. It was OK for those apes to skip from British to Hunnish tea parties! Their pensions were secure! They risked nothing. They couldn't care less what color turned up, red or black. They'd win either way. Yet this evening, still under the impression of his own statue, he was generously disposed even to these gold-braided frock coats.

M. Egon Larsen, nommé ambassadeur de Blithuanie à Calpa-Calpa, capitale de la République cobilienne, a quitté Londres où il représentait notre pays. Il a été salué à la gare par les représentants du gouvernement britannique et le personnel de l'amassade de Blithuanie.

What, Larsen sent to Kobilia? Why? That Belinis was a complete cretin! Larsen was the most capable and most Europeanized Blitvinian diplomat. He was generally a good fellow! Sincere! Without ulterior motive. Wealthy in his own right. A gentleman. A conservative. With all the inborn prejudices against any form of socialism! No careerist. And anyway, Larsen was loyal to the cause of Blitva to the very last. It was clearly time to make a few changes in the Ministry of Foreign Affairs. Belinis had been no damn good for ages. And Larsen? That would be a good idea. At his London embassy the furnishings, receptions, staff, and flowers were all comme il faut. He hated modern furniture. He was no snob like Belinis.

M. Coustodinis, président de la commission des Affaires Étrangères à l'Assemblée nationale "Sabor Blitvinski," a donné mardi soir à l'hôtel Blithuanie un banquet en l'honneur de M. R. Nagel, qui vient d'être nommé ministre de Blithuanie à Halompestis, la capitale hounienne.

Yes, Coustodinis, another good man! And Nagel too! Both good men. There were still people in Blitva with whom one could work. Things weren't utterly hopeless. There were still some gentlemen left, even in Blitva! Chivalrous men, of the old school. There were still men left in Blitva whom one might shake by the hand with an easy conscience. And here they were celebrating Plavystok! Well done! Plavystok was no small thing! It all started in Plavystok! At Plavystok Nielsen was still a man! No! It was Nielsen who took Blitvo–Palatinsk! There was some difficulty there! At Blitvo-Palatinsk! Some unpleasantness! Anyway! *L'anniversaire de la victoire de Plavystok.*

Les remerciements de Son Excellence le président du Conseil de la Guerre . . .

Le Secrétariat général de la présidence du Conseil de la Guerre a communiqué le 27 novembre au soir: Son Excellence le Président a bien

voulu charger l'Agence blithuanique de remercier les nombreuses person-
nes qui lui ont adressé des télégrammes à l'occasion de l'anniversaire de
la victoire de Plavystok. Aha! Even the Immortals glorify Plavystok!

Le cérémonie à l'Academie des Arts et des Sciences.

Une grande réunion a eu lieu lundi le . . . à l'Académie des Arts et des
Sciences à l'occasion de l'anniversaire de la victoire de Plavystok.

M. Burgwaldsen, conseiller légiste de la Maison du Président du
CDLG. . . .

La commémoration de la victoire a été ouverte par un discours de M.
Burgwaldsen. L'éminent juriste a déclaré mot pour mot "La souveraineté,
l'indépendance nationales sont comme la liberté individuelle. De même
que l'individu ne saurait vivre dignement sans liberté, de même il est im-
possible aux peuples privés de l'indépendance de vivre dans la dignité."

That wasn't bad! That was old Burgwaldsen's son! And he was a
good lad! A frank, intelligent, loyal, and excellent chap! Anyway, it
was time to make some changes in Beauregard! It was time to get
new people! A new setup! Blitva was no longer just a provincial
Hunnish garrison! Today we had our own intelligentsia with its
European education. For example, Burgwaldsen! Wasn't he a
Westerner, with European understanding? Or Larsen? Larsen,
even measured by London standards, was class! Or Coustodinis?
They were all European par excellence! They were more European
Europeans than the most European representatives of the highest
European standards. We were printing our own French journals!
We were speaking all European languages. We were translating
Faust, building monuments to European standards that surpassed
all the monuments of the world! We were building! Constructing!
We had built more railways than the imperial muck before us did
for a whole century. Blitwanen, instead of a small Aragon fortress,
had become a European city! Grown threefold! We'd created an
Academy! We had our own Blitvinian scholarship! Wystulanski
would certainly get the Nobel Prize. It was in Blitva's interest!

For some time, behind Barutanski's back, the red light on one of the telephones on his desk had been blinking. Slumped in his armchair by the fire, he could not immediately notice that the deep red light on his desk was flickering excitedly, as though signifying from a distance some news of great importance. Out of the blizzard and fog of Blitva someone was seeking to contact the Commandant, and on the secret telephone at that, which, whenever it was used, always dealt with matters of the utmost importance. That little red lamp on the secret phone went on nervously winking as though, with its dumb persistence, it knew absolutely that the Commandant was in his library and by all the rules of logic had at some time to note the signal of this secret alarm. Indeed! It did not last more than two minutes, before Barutanski felt behind his back, as though someone had tapped his right ear with an invisible hand, and, instinctively glancing at his desk, piled high with books and private correspondence which he had not touched for several days, he noted the red light, sure that it meant bad news.

Who could that be? Kantorowicz, Kerinis, Georgis? The prefect of police, or either of the other two, none of them used the secret telephone without a good reason. And if Barutanski had counted all the good news that bloody secret phone had brought him, it would have been less than 50 percent. Perhaps they'd arrested Nielsen?

"Hello!"

"Hello! Georgis speaking, Commandant!"

"Yes, all right!"

"It's bad news, Commandant!"

"Go on!"

"Rayevski's been killed!"

"Yes, go on!"

"They've killed Roman Rayevski!"

"Yes! I hear you! Roman Rayevski! Who did it?"

"There's a whole lot of them, Commandant! They've all killed him! They've arrested Olaf Knutson."

"You're as pissed as a pig, as usual! What the hell's the matter?"

"It's all right, Commandant! E-very-fing-sh fine! Don't you worry 'bout anything. Georgis is here!"

"Where are you calling from?"

"From Kantorowicz's office!"

"Get your arse over here, you bloody drunk!"

He put the phone down, feeling his hand sticking to the receiver. He knew it wouldn't be good news. That bloody gadget had never brought good news. The old monk was right! All these telephones were an invention of Satan. They'd killed Roman Rayevski! He was just another chimpanzee! He was no loss whatever! No one's indispensable! And he could never stand that slimy neurasthenic Olaf Knutson. Think how he'd always slandered Armstrong. He was the first to start the rumor that Armstrong took his black ape everywhere, because, two years ago, the senile cardinal had had a transplant of his pet's glands done for him in Paris. The sickly, artistic, morbid shit! He needed shooting like a dog! One's first impressions were never wrong! He'd loathed that excuse for a man from the very first.

He rang.

At the door between the books Klement materialized.

"Coffee!"

Klement vanished.

He lit his seventieth, ninetieth, hundred and fifth Maryland-Jaune and, inhaling, felt his throat contract. He'd got nicotine poisoning. Heavy weather again. Sirocco. His heart. Head. Bloody awful! He threw the cigarette into the fire and paced up and down. He rang again. Irritably. Klement appeared.

"Where's the coffee?"

"I've ordered it, Excellency; it's on its way!"

Klement vanished. He lit another Maryland-Jaune, feeling he was about to burst.

So they'd killed Rayevski! That idiot hadn't told him who'd killed him, nor where, nor how. "They've arrested Knutson." Why Knutson particularly? That Georgis was just a mindless, incompetent, alcoholic swine! He was so drunk you could tell he stank of alcohol even over the telephone! He was an absolute idiot! And he needed such a kick in his lazy arse as even 3,333 Hail Marys from that pious, moralistic Dominican wouldn't help him! All these animals around him simply lived to help themselves to state funds. Profiteers, the lot! The moral insanity group! "They've killed Rayevski," but who killed him and where, that he couldn't say! Nielsen had something to do with it! And instead of arresting Nielsen, he was playing cards with Kantorowicz! Swilling rum in the bars! Whoring! And that Kantorowicz, he was a real bastard! He was long due for a bullet. The only one of that lot who was worth anything was Kerinis! And of course, he was the one they neglected. And where was that bloody coffee, Christ all fucking mighty! Did nothing work in this damned Beauregard!

A nervous ringing.

Klement appeared.

"Where's that black coffee, Klement?"

"It's on its way, sir!"

Klement disappeared, but seconds later the door reopened and together with Klement there entered a servant whom Barutanski did not know. In his left hand he held a large silver tray laden with the complete and completely unnecessary accessories for serving black coffee. This consisted of a large silver jug of black coffee and a smaller jug of milk, a bedewed pitcher of water, a sugar bowl, several glasses, several sugar tongs, several napkins, several silver spoons; in short, an entire exhibition of utterly unnecessary stupidities. The new servant's hands shook as he served the coffee on the table beside the fireplace, and Barutanski stared with some curiosity at the white stockings of this unfortunate and at the knees that trembled under his short trousers with their silver buckle, and the fact that this rather older man in short trousers and pumps, decorated with ridiculous ribbons as though taking part in a carnival, shook in his presence like a schoolboy at an examination, pleased him. The man bore several Blitvinian medals, among which one, with a narrow silver and dark blue ribbon, was for services at Plavystok.

"Where does he come from?" he asked Klement, when the new servant had gone.

"He served in the Legion, Your Excellency! He was appointed at Beauregard two years ago, Your Excellency! Before now he was in Her Excellency's service, but he had an affair with a housemaid. He has been transferred with the approval of Major Georgis."

"So! He was in the Legion? Under whom?"

"Under Lieutenant Colonel Nielsen!"

"Was he?"

Barutanski gave a gesture of dismissal and Klement left. All he ever demanded from his personal servants was that they should vanish in a moment, like those small figures at the openings of small barometers which disappear before rain. The fact, for instance, that he never took sugar with coffee, yet they always served a sugar bowl, or that he never in principle took milk with coffee and that that lot hadn't noticed it after nine years, or that he took coffee entirely on his own, yet they served enough glassware for a whole café, or that he never drank water, yet they irritated him with all those stupid pitchers, none of this annoyed him as much as having to ring three times to be served ordinary black coffee, or that his own servants had not yet learned to make themselves as invisible as possible.

A man unable to organize his own household, yet he wished to change Blitva, Europe, even the entire universe, as the friar would say! And this new fellow had served in the Legion under Nielsen?

Interesting! And was transferred to his personal service with Georgis's approval! Even more interesting! And now he was appointed to serve him personally, so that the fellow's hands and knees shook either from fear or bad conscience! And Nielsen was lodging down there on the Promenade and, naturally, Major Georgis hadn't a clue about it! He was looking for him in Blatvia. The idiot!

Draining two black coffees, one after another, two boiling hot coffees, at one gulp, Barutanski felt the scorching liquid rinsing his throat with the bitterness of caffeine and ceased to feel the dryness caused by smoking and therefore lit his 102nd Maryland-Jaune and, once again, began to pace the room from the fireplace to the globe, in endless circling.

People were killing each other, fueling locomotives with coffee, blood flowed everywhere. "Hail Mary, full of Grace, the Lord is with thee. Blessed art thou among women and blessed is the fruit of thy womb, Jesus, who shed his blood for us . . ."

Georgis.

Georgis, deathly pale, without a drop of blood in his cheeks. Major Georgis with his paralyzed left arm, the messenger of death and disaster. Major Georgis, a drunkard and a cretin, who was seeking Nielsen all over Blatvia, while Nielsen was here in Blitwanen, shooting at the president of the Republic as if he were a clay pigeon on the rifle range at a fair. Look at the swine supporting himself on the Regency armchair. The animal could hardly stand up. The pig was about to throw up right there in his presence.

"So what is it? Speak up! Am I reporting to you or you to me?"

"They've killed him! They've killed Roman Rayevski," Georgis stammered, staring absently at the fire and feeling with his right hand in his left pocket, trying to find a packet of cigarettes. He was clearly entirely occupied with the thought of how he was to get at that damned cigarette packet in his left pocket, since how it could have happened that it had migrated to his left pocket was something beyond comprehension. Finally he managed to find a damned, bewitched cigarette and, drawing from the depths of his pocket a crumpled and completely broken tube, he moistened it with his tongue and, having flicked his lighter several times, Georgis finally exhaled his first smoke with visible satisfaction that, despite all the complex obstacles, he had nonetheless succeeded in mastering matter and conquering it in the form of a lit cigarette.

Looking at that drunken idiot, Barutanski felt he was losing control over his nerves and felt a growing and unconquerable urge to take that ape and throw him into the open fireplace. Sooner or later that animal would croak like a mangy dog and one needed to finish him off. The sooner the better. A drunken animal, no better than a stinking burping bowel! Sandersen, Muzhikovski, Kavalierski, Jensen, all those criminal scandals had been thrust upon him by that stinking drunk, that gorilla, who in every such matter had to leave his apish tracks! Just like his last scandal at Dominic's when, with the rest of his gangsters, he smashed a lot of dishes instead of that hysterical burglar, and Nielsen got away. For Nielsen was no porcelain plate at Dominic's. Nielsen knew what he wanted. That sophisticated bastard was sitting on the Promenade near Beauregard and organizing one plot after another while that idiot, together with that nymphomaniac, the Michelson woman, was looking for him in Blatvia. And all he could do was to infiltrate Nielsen's people into his, Barutanski's, service! Yes, to be stupid at any price, that he could do!

"Well, what? Spit it out! For the sake of the bloody Virgin Mary, open your drink-sodden gob!"

"Th–they've k–killed Ro–man Ray–ev–ski!"

"So! They've killed Roman Rayevski? I've heard already three thousand three hundred and thirty-three times that they've killed him, but who 'k–killed h–him'?"

"Knut–son. O–laf Knut–son."

Taking his beloved cigarette out of his mouth, Major Georgis stared at the silvery red glow of the tobacco between his two fingers and, raising the smoking cigarette to the level of his eyes, he examined it between his fingers as though it were some strange, mysterious manifestation of nature. That small pyre, that tiny nicotine volcano, gleamed red between his fingers, smoked warmly like a home chimney, flickered like a night fire in the forest. There'd been heavy firing and there'd be more. The battles continued, but we'd made a good campfire and were roasting Blitvinian potatoes. All we needed was a cognac . . .

Driven by an association of ideas, Georgis staggered toward the table that held bottles of various drinks, with the intention of taking a glass of Jamaica.

Barutanski, seeing that movement toward the rum bottle, halted, galvanized, feeling a strange flame of deep and justified anger bursting from him, sensing something irresistible pulling him toward that drunken idiot, by force of a dark and inscrutable blood instinct that swept all human bodies at such moments, as a whirlwind sweeps rubbish.

In two soft, leopardlike, commandant's strides, with feet apart as horsemen dragged themselves in their boots, when their spurs quietly rang on the carpet, Barutanski came face-to-face with Georgis and, thrusting his face into the drunken mask which, congested in blood, radiated rum, onions, and cheap sausages, with a sudden, lightning movement (with a truly amazing speed, in every way like that with which lion tamers draw their pistols when faced with danger from the lion's jaws) snatched Major Georgis's burning cigarette from the major's mouth and, with a gesture of utter disgust, stubbed out the burning cigarette on the major's left cheek, just beneath the left eye, so that the cigarette scattered over his cheek in a minor fireworks display of hot sparks.

"Major, one does not smoke in the presence of the Commandant! Stand at attention! Do you understand me? *Garde à vous!*"

"For God's sake!" Drunk to his eyeballs, Georgis tried, with his right hand, to wipe off the burn and soot and the crushed tobacco of the cigarette, for the flesh under his left eye was badly burned and he felt the sting of scorched skin.

"Shut up! One more word and I'll have you bound and thrown into the fire! Have you gone mad? You swine! Mind your mouth!"

In that tiny island of remaining consciousness, as yet not inundated by alcohol, like a dog Georgis sensed that all was not well and, with the resignation of a wound-up mechanical doll, he stood at attention, pathetic, blackened by the extinguished cigarette, as though he had come down the chimney.

"Wipe yourself, you drunken swine!" Barutanski screamed at the mask in front of him with utter disgust and, furiously grabbing from the table (where still stood the coffee service on its silver tray) a napkin, began himself, nervously and roughly, to wipe the traces of soot from the face of the drunken man.

Sensing that move of the Commandant as a sign of reconciliation, Georgis bent down toward him and, taking the crumpled napkin, he grabbed the Commandant's hand with it and, pressing it to his drooling, drunken lips, began passionately and desperately to kiss it, while sickly, doglike, maddened tears ran down his face: "Forgive me, for God's sake, forgive me!"

"You're as pissed as a newt. Here's some black coffee—gulp it down!"

Barutanski pulled away from him with disgust and nervously leapt to the table for another napkin to wipe the spittle the drunken cretin had spilt over his hand with his tears and, with a careless movement, knocked over the silver jug with the black coffee and the warm, scented liquid spilt over the whole table and one could hear it dripping down onto the parquet like rainwater from a holed drainpipe.

Barutanski rang.

Klement appeared at the door.

"We've spilt some coffee, Klement! A fresh coffee for the major! And hear this, Klement: If they serve me their damned coffee once more in a jug with sugar and the rest of this stupid clutter round it, when all I ask is one *coffee,* which I drink without sugar, you can tell them, from me, that they'd better not serve me anything else again! And don't let me see that idiot from Lieutenant Colonel Nielsen's squadron again. Throw him out! . . . What're you looking at me like a wooden Madonna for?" Barutanski, in a new onset of fury, turned on Georgis, as Klement vanished silently with the whole unfortunate tray with the spilt coffee.

"This Lieutenant Colonel Nielsen is here organizing plots and assassinations, killing our best people under our noses, and you send his people to be my personal servants! So out with it! Who killed whom?"

"It was Knutson who killed Rayevski." The major gathered himself together with his last remaining strength like a boxer rising to the bell for the last round.

"They've broken our jaw, Georgis, but they haven't counted us out yet!"

"We don't know the details yet. There were no witnesses, but Knutson was arrested on the spot. He threw a bomb into the studio right in front of your statue and survived unhurt. Nothing happened to him. He remained absolutely unhurt. The firemen pulled him out of the rubble. He confessed. It was all his own idea. And I got to the police station while they were interrogating him. That's all I know! Commandant, please, the telephone. It's flashing!"

Since Barutanski had his back turned to his desk, Major Georgis, sobered by fear, drew his attention to the flashing of the red light on the secret phone, with a tone of subdued, quiet servility on the edge of terror. The burn under his left eye stung. It hurt. He felt as if a scab were gathering on his cheek and felt the need to scratch it off. He patted the wound with his handkerchief rather as one powders oneself after shaving.

Barutanski turned wearily to the telephone as though sick at the thought of yet more bad news. Klement appeared with a black coffee for the major and two dishcloths to deal with the tarry pool of spilt coffee. In a small jug, coffee for one without accessories, simply, as in a café, without sugar, without anything, black coffee for one. Quite simply. Puritanically. By High Command. Major Georgis, on the other hand, took his coffee with at least three spoons of sugar.

"Where's the sugar, Klement?"

"Hello, what, ah, yes, that's bloody wonderful, Kantorowicz! Yes! It's just what I'd have expected of you at any time. You're the biggest cunt of all the cunts on earth! I hold you personally responsible! Report to me immediately! Idiot!"

Klement, busy wiping the coffee off the floor, and hearing Barutanski screaming into the phone, indicated his master with a silent movement of the cloth, as if to say Today we're serving only black coffee, and if you want sugar, you'd better ask the Commandant! Politely taking his leave of the major, he just as politely disappeared.

Barutanski began to pace the room and Georgis thirstily sipped the bitter black coffee, dying for some sugar and trying desperately, by an act of will, to sober up.

There was a storm coming! All hands were needed on deck! If only we had some sugar we'd sober up more quickly, but there we were, we were sailing against the wind, the sea was rising, everything was rolling and plunging, the fireplace, the bookshelves, Beauregard, dangerously rolling, everything was going full speed ahead through the night, and the captain was nervously pacing the bridge, up and down. He'd received a message from the boiler room; something was happening belowdecks. Keep your mouth shut, Georgis, not a stupid word! The Commandant immediately regretted his action and, anyway, I really asked for it! He was right! Before the Commandant one stands at attention. For the Commandant, one gives one's life!

Standing by the fireplace, stiff as a broom, Georgis wordlessly watched his Commandant, following his every step with a doglike concentration, in the waxworks stance of attention, as though saying: Commandant, I follow your every move. At a sign from you I'm ready to jump out the window!

Only now it wasn't a matter of Major Georgis's jumping through the window, but of Olaf Knutson, whom, a short while ago, Major Georgis had mutilated and flung through a window, and now, in panic, he dared not admit this to the Commandant, for, driving to Beauregard, he'd realized, through a thick drunken haze, that this act of murder might well hinder the investigation. All the Beauregard logic within him had led him to destroy Olaf Knutson and now, by that very same Beauregard logic, it seemed that this might be unfortunate. Who on earth could get it right? It was Olaf Knutson whom he'd mutilated and flung through a window, certain that that band of people were plotting against the Commandant. Not long ago he'd thrown him through the window of Kantorowicz's office at the police station. And worse still, before Kantorowicz had personally interrogated him, and before Knutson had signed his statement too! And all that was the fault of stupid civilians in the police who had no idea how to form a statement with a man like Olaf Knutson, when caught in the act. They were lawyers, not people!

Hail Mary, full of Grace, the Lord is with thee and blessed is the fruit of thy womb, Rayevski was dead, a bomb had gone off in the studio, and Olaf Knutson had jumped through a window. There was no proof of anything and Nielsen was staying down on the Promenade at old Mrs. Gallen's and was still not arrested.

"Hello, this is the Commandant! Give me the Ministry of the Interior! Hello! This is the Commandant! Yes, yes, I know all about it.

Are you listening, Hansen? Where's Rekyavinis? Is he at tea too? What's the meaning of these damned British tea parties? All Blitva seems to have gone to tea at the British Consulate! OK! Listen, Hansen! If Aage Kohlinis is in the building, tell him to phone me at once! Tell him I've just appointed him prefect of police. Yes! And when Rekyavinis returns, tell him the Commandant has ordered his immediate resignation! The Commandant suggests he gets out of sight for ever and ever, Amen!"

Barutanski, putting down the receiver, picked it up immediately. "Hello! This is the Commandant! Who is that speaking? Ah, it's you, Jensen. And where is Mrs. Michelson? Still on leave? Jensen, is Burgwaldsen there? Tell him to get in touch with me at once! Give me the confidential number of the prime minister's office! Hello! This is the Commandant! Good evening! Listen, Mr. Prime Minister! Rekyavinis has resigned. You have accepted his resignation and nominated Burgwaldsen. I've ordered Rekyavinis (he doesn't know it yet, but he'll be told) to give you his resignation! He's at a tea party at the British Consulate. Appoint Burgwaldsen minister of the interior. Ah? As the president of my cabinet you don't know who Burgwaldsen is? Not surprising! Would I appoint old Burgwaldsen, a man of eighty-three, a minister in this mess? Excellent logic, worthy only of a fool like you! Dr. Burgwaldsen is legal adviser to my household! Yes! That's the young Burgwaldsen! Yes! Yes! The young doctor who plays chess with me! You can sign the decrees at once. The decision is valid from this moment. Good-bye!"

Going back to the desk, Barutanski stopped at the armchair over which lay the *Blitvinian Echo* with an inner page open, dominated by the victorious equestrian figure of Barutanski, mounted on an immense stallion, in the masterly casting of the sculptor Rayevski. Rayevski was dead and there wasn't even the monument left! After a long and painful pause, Barutanski cast an uncertain, troubled glance at Georgis. The major was still standing by the fireplace, motionless, stiff, in the concentrated stance of a disciplined soldier whom his commandant had ordered to stand at attention, and so he'd remain at attention and would do so till death took him, unless his commandant released him from this lifelong attention!

"Well, Major? Have you condescended to return from your trip to Jamaica to our unrelenting Blitvinian reality?"

"Forgive me, Commandant! Look—" Georgis pointed to his paralyzed arm. "Look, I gave my arm for you. If you ordered me to jump out the window, I'd do it, I truly would!"

Barutanski once more flared up. "I don't know what's got into you all this evening. You all want to jump out of windows! You'd have done better not to swill so much Jamaica! Then that other one wouldn't have jumped out the window! You idiotic lot of drunks, you deserve machine-gunning."

A gentle expression of genuine and visible sadness passed over Georgis's face. His eye grew dark, as with a dog when the partridge flew away. Everything had been going well. The Commandant had even wiped his face and treated him to good advice, and now it was all starting again. Playing his false game, as though he knew nothing, Georgis pretended to show concern: "Who's jumped through a window?"

"Who? Knutson. Olaf Knutson! And he made no statement. Yes! That's the situation! And who made Kantorowicz prefect of police? Major Georgis! And who let Nielsen get away? Major Georgis! And who is ignorant of the fact that Mr. Nielsen is staying at Promenade 5A? Major Georgis! And who doesn't know that Mrs. Michelson is a double agent, theirs and ours? Major Georgis! And who appoints Nielsen's agents to my personal service? Major Georgis! And who is personally responsible for the Muzhikovski and Kavalierski affairs? Major Georgis! And who is forever pissed out of his mind, who guzzles Jamaica for days on end and then lets idiots like Knutson jump out of windows . . ."

"Excuse me, Commandant, the telephone!"

The green light was flashing on the desk. It indicated the Commandant's Secretariat.

"Yes! Rekyavinis? I didn't call you! You were a minister, now you're not! Yes! Yes! You've resigned. Make your inquiries from the prime minister's office. Your resignation has been accepted there. Yes! It has nothing to do with me! All right, all right . . ."

Again he picked up the receiver. "Jensen! If anyone else phones me whom I have not ordered, there'll be trouble! Find Major Kerinis and tell him to report to me at once."

He rang the bell for his personal adjutant. Immediately the cavalry captain, Sigurd Flaming-Sandersen, in the red trousers and light blue jerkin of the First Regiment of the Blitvinian Chevaux-Légers, known as Barutanski's own, appeared at the door. He was a blond, slim, very nice boy.

"At your service, Excellency!" Captain Flaming-Sandersen clicked his heels.

Barutanski cast a glance full of dark suspicion. (He's one of those Flaming-Sandersens who have rebellion in their blood.)

"All right, Flaming! Dr. Burgwaldsen, Prefect Kantorowicz, and Dr. Aage Kohlinis are cleared with security! No one else! If the minister Rekyavinis arrives, tell him you are ordered to say that I will not receive him, since I don't want sight or sound of him!"

"Understood, Excellency! Dr. Kantorowicz is waiting outside." Captain Flaming-Sandersen bowed and clicked his heels and left the room. A second later the prefect of police, Dr. Kantorowicz, entered.

"Right, in two words: the situation!"

"The situation, Excellency . . ." Kantorowicz began his monologue so hesitantly that it seemed as if he were about to burst into tears with emotion after only his second word. "The facts are few. The explosion took place at seven forty-three. Rayevski's studio was destroyed with everything it contained, including the statue. When the explosion occurred, there were in the studio Rayevski; one of his plasterers, a man named Wilkins; and, by his own confession, Olaf Knutson. At the head of the firemen, I personally dragged Rayevski out of the ruins, around nine-oh-three. He was scarcely recognizable. In his hand he held a checkbook from the bank of Rogger Brothers and Company. Written out in his own hand was the sum of one thousand dollars, since the explosion, apparently, took place at the very moment when the late master was about to write out the sum in letters. The explosion reduced the maestro to a state of bloody molasses and it appeared that the air pressure threw him directly under the pile of wet clay which was the monument and it crashed down on him with all its, I might say, elemental force and he remained literally crushed beneath the clay torso of the massive horseman. Olaf Knutson, it would seem, survived by equally pure chance. The explosion threw him into the entrance, a kind of glass atrium leading into Rayevski's studio. Except for shock, he was unhurt. He voluntarily surrendered to me, as prefect of police, and volunteered the information that it was he who had thrown the bomb. His motives, according to him, were of an entirely private and personal nature. He offered no further information."

"Good heavens, man, didn't you ask him where he got the explosive?"

"The explosive belonged to Rayevski and the dynamite was his. This was confirmed by the other plasterer, Shaulis, whom naturally I questioned. Shaulis actually stated that this could be confirmed by invoices, since when they accompanied the maestro last year to the Blatvian border near Weider-Hunnen, where Rayevski was exploring the terrain for quarrying, they took with them a considerable quantity of explosives, so much that for three weeks they used it to kill salmon and sturgeon. I searched the lodgings of the dead Wilkins, the other plasterer, but found nothing suspicious.

He was clearly innocent. He was married and leaves three orphaned children. He served in the Legion and had the Blithuania Restituta for his service during the war."

"All right, Kantorowicz, all right, but how could you let that idiot Knutson, as the main witness to this completely obscure affair, jump, like a fish, out of the investigation? Without statement or signature?"

"Believe me, Your Excellency, I had absolutely no reason to be particularly on the alert. The explosion was reported to me five minutes after it occurred and I immediately rushed to the scene, so that I was in Rayevski's park eight or nine minutes after the catastrophe at the latest. Owing to the strength of the explosion, there was a short in Rayevski's villa, so that the firemen and I had to work by the light of their torches. In the middle of that pile of rubble, while none of us as yet had the slightest idea of the cause of the catastrophe, a detective approached me and reported that a gentleman wished to speak to me. This was Knutson. Entirely calm, indeed catastrophically collected, he introduced himself (since I did not know him personally) and almost absentmindedly told me that it was he who had dynamited the workshop, Rayevski, the monument, and himself, but he did not understand how he had managed to survive. I thought the man was in shock and, at first, left him there in the studio under guard and, bareheaded and coatless, he stared blankly at the ground and refused a cigarette and even a glass of water! I returned with him to the police station in my own car, together with four of my agents. During the drive, on the stairway up to my office, during the entire conversation, he was completely collected, logical, and coherent, perhaps slightly distracted but in every way calm. He dictated a statement to Dr. Rondas calmly and collectedly, repeating everything he'd said at the scene of the catastrophe: that he'd thrown the dynamite for personal, subjective reasons, that the act had absolutely no political motives, et cetera, et cetera. And while I got up to amend one of his sentences (it had to do with motive), he insisted keeping to his own style, namely that the intention to kill Rayevski had been with him some ten to fifteen years and that his action had nothing to do with the election of Rayevski as president of the Republic, of which election he had no way approved, neither of the manner in which it was carried out nor of the factual significance of the rank, so that one could perhaps discover a political motive in that, which he did not deny but did not admit. I therefore got up and went to Dr. Rondas, who was sitting at the small desk at the typewriter, thinking to add these extra comments, when, at one and the same moment, the prisoner took a run and with the crashing of glass, vanished through the doubly closed window of my office. He lay on the asphalt in front of the police station, his skull burst like a coconut shell, his brains spilt over the pavement, and his spine broken in three places. He'd leapt headfirst, as swimmers do when they take a run and leap over the barrier."

"A running jump over the barrier, Kantorowicz! And in view of the fact that tomorrow the whole Blatvian, Hunnish, Kobilian, Kurlandish, and the rest of the European press will announce to its readers the latest sensation from Blitva, that I, Colonel Barutanski, have once again thrown an intellectual, an idealist, a champion of humanistic ideals through the window onto the street, that famous running jump of yours won't serve as any proof that it wasn't so! And what you've just been telling me is a lot of sentimental rot for old maids and not for me, Kantorowicz!"

The green light winked on the desk. The Secretariat.

"Yes! Kerinis! I need you! At once! Yes! Yes!"

Barutanski returned from the desk to the prefect of police, Kantorowicz.

"My dear doctor, your evidence before the highly moral European public opinion is merely the voice of a bloodstained Blitvinian paid hound, and it would have been better had you realized that at once! To me it's clear without any doubt that this is the case of a one hundred percent political assassination, based upon the obscure background of an organized plot. What did he mean, a fifteen-year personal hatred as his motive? I knew Olaf Knutson as well as I knew Rayevski! This was a political assassination with all the essential marks of such a megalomaniacal, sick, demonstrative scandal! These gentlemen are just pretentious megalomaniacs like Nielsen, who think they represent the people but who, in fact, are just criminals who represent nobody!"

"All right, Excellency, but then explain to me why that man should have confessed on his own initiative to being the assassin? None of us at the scene had the slightest idea that he was present, for the fact that he was unhurt would have seemed sufficient proof that he was not. And even if we had confirmed that he really had been in the studio at the time of the explosion, he could easily have put the blame on the other plasterer, the worker Wilkins who died together with the maestro Rayevski! With all respect to your views, Excellency, from his very first words I had the impression that this was a case of insane action by a typical psychopath!"

"In my life, Kantorowicz, I've seen a lot of stupid people, but such an idiot as you I've never yet had the honor of meeting! In other words, every assassin who outlives his victim is, for that very reason, beyond suspicion! Too stupid for words!" With a gesture of utter helplessness, Barutanski rang his adjutant's office. Captain Flaming-Sandersen appeared at the door.

"Have the gentlemen arrived, Flaming?"

"Yes, Excellency!"

"Bring them in!"

At the door of the adjutant's office loomed the outlines of the new minister, Dr. Burgwaldsen the younger, and the new prefect of police, Dr. Aage Kohlinis.

"Come in, gentlemen, good evening." Barutanski approached them with the cold politeness of a Chinese mandarin and frowningly extended a hand to them both from some distance, pointing with a tired gesture to Major Georgis and Dr. Kantorowicz, as though to say: Here I am having to deal with these fools and I expect from you new ideas, new suggestions, new plans—in a word, intellectual and moral support. So as to indicate to Kantorowicz that he'd fallen through the stage trapdoor, into the darkness of deep disgrace, perhaps even finally and without hope of return, Barutanski, with a jerk of his chin, presented to the dismissed prefect of police both newcomers in their new roles of civil dignity.

"Dr. Burgwaldsen is the minister of the interior and Dr. Aage Kohlinis will be so kind as to take over your duties as prefect of police, Kantorowicz!"

It all had the tones of the Commandant at an order group. They all stood at attention, fingers tight to the trouser seams, heels together and knees straight and, in the silence, nothing moved except startled eyelashes and the flames in the hearth that leapt utterly carelessly and merrily here and there, with their deep-red silky harlequin cap, above good and evil, like the true exalted divine flame. At that moment, that very moment of sepulchral silence, through the Commandant's private door (that led to his private apartment), Major Kerinis entered the library. With a silent bow, after a discreet glance that told him everything, Major Kerinis remained standing two or three paces in front of the bookshelves, also rigidly at attention like the rest, ready to stand there motionless, like an extra in an opera awaiting a further stroke of the conductor's baton.

As though hypnotizing the assembled gentry with his outspread arms, Commandant Barutanski, with a movement such as poulterers use to collect their scattered turkeys, drew all these his advisers and dignitaries closer to him; that is to say, his closest cooperators in the great task of Blitvinian liberation, and, in his warm, clear baritone, attempted in two or three words to explain to the new-comers wherein lay the argument between him and Kantorowicz.

"So, gentlemen, the question is this! The prefect of police and I disagree as to whether Olaf Knutson's action was politically conscious, an act that carries all the marks of a political assassination, or an act of a crazy neurasthenic, a covert madman, an act that arose from completely subjective incentives—in other words, purely pathological. As you know, gentlemen, I've always been, from the very beginning, a firm and convinced democrat, and my unshakable principle from the very first day has been democracy! Yes, gentlemen, democracy, but not the democracy that settles matters by dynamite, but the democracy that respects freedom of discussion! Democracy is free discussion. That was the old liberal principle, the principle of nobility and aristocratic freedom of conviction! Freedom of conscience! So I suggest we vote according to our democratic conscience! I consider that it was a political assassination, and you, Minister?"

This had to be the debut of the young Dr. Burgwaldsen, till then the private legal adviser to His Excellency, but from that moment on, a leading Blitvinian statesman, who held the most important portfolio, but had not, as yet, been sworn in, and now was called on to take a vote in Council. Aware of the importance of his every word, this three-year-long legal adviser to His Excellency, this accomplished Cambridge doctor, performed his first Beauregard solo with some virtuosity. He already had a picture of the situation. It was clear to him that Barutanski had no idea that Olaf Knutson had been thrown through the window, which the minister of the interior had told Burgwaldsen the moment that it was announced that he had been appointed to that office. He had immediately telephoned the precinct and asked for Dr. Rondas, a person especially trusted by the "P" Section of Beauregard, who instantly informed him of the state of the facts. Major Georgis, as head of the Commandant's

private police, took over the investigation and, since Knutson refused to admit any political motive, the major beat him to such an
extent that when the other officers rushed into the room, there was
nothing left for them to do but to throw Knutson's corpse through
the window. At that time it was a pure formality! Georgis was wild
drunk. Almost unconscious, perhaps mad, delirious?

As he cast a discreet glance at Major Georgis, who was still
standing by the fireplace, motionless in his fateful stance of attention, it was clear to Dr. Burgwaldsen that he would master the situation in this momentary game at Beauregard, without any doubt,
but it seemed to him unwise to turn to the essence of the matter.
Better simply to answer the questions asked of him.

"The matter is completely political, Excellency, and it is a pity
to waste time in further discussion. To dynamite the studio of
such an artist as the late Rayevski, together with that massive
quantity of masterpieces which represented the finest synthesis of
our entire Blitvinian civilization, is no pathological act of a neurasthenic, but an act of assassination, which, as a demonstration, also
bore a symbolic significance in its destruction of your monument,
Excellency! This is a demagogic call to arms that could well echo
from the Karabaltic to the Karapathians. And lastly, that this was
an act of a purely political nature is to be seen from the reaction of
our Blitwanen press. Let Prefect Kantorowicz read what is written
in the *Blitwanen Tigdende,* and he'll see that the reactionary and
hidden political hyenas are forever active and also that his organization is not worth a bent Blitvinian farthing, when I could buy
this rubbish in a free paper stall on my way here a few minutes
ago. And this poison is freely being spilt on the streets of Blitwanen. It is a pamphlet against the late Rayevski, such as the history
of pamphleteering in Blitva has never seen. In this respect, it is
unusually rich and inventive, but, without doubt, between the
lines it attacks the framework of existing order with its more than

transparent allusions to the person represented by the destroyed statue, Excellency!"

With the gesture of a real minister of the interior, Dr. Burgwaldsen drew from his briefcase a copy of a special edition of the *Blitwanen Tigdende* and, holding it between thumb and forefinger, handed it to Barutanski with a deep bow.

Barutanski contemptuously threw this stinking heap onto the library table (behind his back), piled high with similar rubbish, and, without a word, returned to the agenda of the democratic discussion concerning the political situation.

"Good. What do you think, Georgis, my friend?"

The Lord of Blitva addressed his trained watchdog for whom the return to the old comradely, legionary tone of intimacy restored his honor and gave satisfaction for the burn which was on the point of bursting in the form of a fair blister. That hysterical stubbing of the burning cigarette had been brutal, and the red-hot end had burned deeply into the living flesh in two or three places.

"I don't believe that bombs are thrown from so-called personal motives! In the first place, whatever Knutson ever was, he was 'somebody' only because of Rayevski. But this is what I think: Knutson was a Blatvophile. That fragment of metal from the bomb covering undoubtedly comes from a Blatvian arsenal. And then, in any case, Knutson always said he was preparing to go abroad, a type of emigration, so to speak. So that's all, how shall I put it, a matter of politics, in one word, is that not so?"

"And you, Doctor?" Barutanski turned to the newly appointed prefect of the Blitwanen police, Dr. Aage Kohlinis.

"It was a political act in every way, Excellency, both subjectively and objectively. Objectively by the effect it had. One did not have to have a particularly sensitive ear this evening on the town streets to sense whether this assassination was political or not. It only needed a single spark to set off demonstrations! And, in any case, the extent to which this rabble feels at liberty may be seen from the press! What the minister of the interior remarked is absolutely correct, that the evening tabloid press is a symptom of extreme tension! As a consequence, I would suggest counteraction! That all legionary organizations of the LOOLP be activated (and this evening the syndicates of the LOOLP are meeting for their congress in the Redoubt), so this subversive scum may feel some resistance."

"Kerinis?"

"I agree with the last speaker. I suggest political counteraction. Further discussion is pointless."

"So, Doctor, your assessment is in a minority of five to one."

Barutanski turned to Kantorowicz.

"All right, gentlemen," Kantorowicz replied excitedly, "by what logic would a political assassin report himself of his own free will, after a successful political action, when at that time no suspicion fell on him? Explain that to me, gentlemen!"

"So that's a very valuable example of your capabilities, Doctor!" Barutanski shouted nervously at Kantorowicz. "You're not prefect of police in order to think with the logic of political suspects and to their advantage. At the moment of your arrival at the scene of the catastrophe, according to you, no suspicion attached to Knutson. Excellent! Go back to the safety of your civil procedures, my dear chap, for that's where you belong, among obscure lawyers, which is all you were! There could be no suspicion that Knutson might have thrown the dynamite, marvelous, and that because he was the sole survivor! Marvelous! It seems to me you've never suspected anybody in your life! And are you aware that there's an APB out for the arrest of Niels Nielsen? And are you aware that Niels Nielsen was the most intimate friend of this assassin? And perhaps you're also unaware that Olaf Knutson was present at Dominic's in the company of Nielsen when you and your own people shot at them?"

"Bravo, Commandant!" Major Georgis cried hoarsely, delighted by the Commandant's logic. "That's just the direction I wanted to give the investigation! Indeed! But they're all idiots! They all deserve to fly through the window, like Knutson! These apes haven't a clue what they're about! We'll all be shot down like dogs! The Commandant, gentlemen, is on the bridge and we are sailing at full steam into battle, while you, gentlemen, are lawyers, formalists, ministers, you're civilians, not men. You, gentlemen, are wasting time in discussions, but now is no time for discussing. We're not old women. We know our duty, and our duty is the Commandant, and if we need to throw anyone through a window we'll do it, and if we need to jump through a window we'll jump, gentlemen, and . . ."

"Shut up, Major!"

"Yes, but they'll kill us all!"

"All right. Get on with it! How long ago is it since the APB on Nielsen was put out?"

"Five or six days, at least."

"So? Five or six days! A full five or six days since an APB on the moral initiator of this murder and you, as prefect of police, don't suspect the man who's killed the president of the Republic and who was the most intimate friend of the main actor in the plot! Bloody marvelous! And where, according to you, is this Mr. Nielsen to be found?"

"According to the report I received this evening, they're expecting him to arrive in Weider-Hunnen. He's taken refuge somewhere in Blatvia!"

"And I suppose he'll send you a postcard when he gets to Weider-Hunnen! And you'll learn of his arrival in Weider-Hunnen from your secret agents abroad, and these same secret agents in Blitwanen, together with you, haven't a clue that Nielsen is still in Blitwanen, living at the widow Gallen's, 5A, the Promenade, first floor. Kerinis! Regarding this, take a special action group and, please: 5A, the Promenade, first floor right, the widow Gallen's flat. Not a word! I'll be by the phone!"

Kerinis left without a word.

Georgis approached the Commandant like a small boy to his father: "Commandant, please, may I go with them?"

"You, Georgis, may do one thing and one thing only: Go home and put a bullet through your head! And as soon as possible! Good night! Get out!"

Immediately following Georgis's departure, Klement discreetly appeared at the soundproof door. "Excellency, excuse me, Father Bonaventura to see you on an important matter."

"I've no time for his nonsense!"

"Excellency, Father Bonaventura requests you to receive him for just one second!"

Barutanski gestured and the next moment Bonaventura Baltrushaitis was in the room. Pale, nervous, uncomfortable, Father Bonaventura did not know what to say to the Commandant in front of strange people and, therefore, halted at his first word, as though stuttering.

"What is it, Father Bonaventura? Good news?"

"Hardly, Excellency! I've come from the wife of General . . ."

"Good, and how is Mrs. Michelson? Has she come back from her trip to Blatvia?"

"Excellency, Mrs. Michelson hanged herself half an hour ago. She left a letter for you. Here it is!"

Barutanski took the opened letter from Baltrushaitis. In it was a small envelope in the format of a visiting card. He opened it and scanned the text written in violet ink and in a nervous, typically female handwriting, and, as though it contained absolutely nothing of any importance, he thrust both letters into his pocket and returned to the subject of discussion with his advisers, without a single gesture.

"Kohlinis, your suggestion for counteraction by the LOOLP on the streets, if possible this evening, I accept! Most important is to lose no time. Let them know that Barutanski's brigades are ever watchful. That's good! Carry it out immediately! In my opinion we shall learn more with the arrest of Nielsen. I shall be here at the telephone! And you, Burgwaldsen, first put on all the usual formalities for Rayevski's funeral, banners and suchlike, and then in tomorrow's communiqué concerning his death, emphasize that this is a case of explosives provided by the arsenal of a neighboring state. That's the first thing. And then second, announce that Prefect Kantorowicz is under investigation for Knutson's running jump."

"But Excellency, please," uttered the dismissed prefect of police in the voice of a drowning man.

"Don't worry, man, the investigation will be a pure formality! We'll think about your position when it's over. Burgwaldsen will find you an advisory position at the BMV."

"Yes, Excellency. All the funeral formalities are already arranged. Flags are at half-mast. Only one thing isn't clear to me: In what capacity do we bury Rayevski? He was the elected president of the Republic; that is to say, he was nominated as a candidate for the presidency but, since the formality of his election was still incomplete, he counts in fact as a private citizen, that is to say, an artist of fame and reputation, but, formally speaking, still only an individual artist."

"Bury him as if he were the representative of our sovereignty. Give him the full treatment as president, with military honors. What's the name of that painter who's worked for Armstrong? I can't remember his name for the moment!"

"Vanini, Excellency!"

"Ah yes, Vanini. Get him! Give him the job! He has good taste! Give him carte blanche. Lying in state in the Jesuit Cathedral, et cetera. All the way to Chopin. . . . Yes. What's next?"

"As regards the investigation against the prefect," the minister Burgwaldsen announced, like a true beginner in his job, "the thing is, that, that, even if er-er-er the investigation against Kantorowicz is carried out purely formally, it may pose problems!"

"What problems, for heaven's sake? Always problems!" Barutanski exclaimed irritatedly, regarding his new minister of the interior with a look of deepest suspicion, as though his new minister would turn out to be yet another hairsplitter and formalistic fusser, like Rekyavinis, and that this ass would also take the line of greatest resistance and produce unnecessary complications right, left, and center.

"You know, Excellency, I've had the honor to serve you as your private legal adviser and, from my first day, my principle, here at Beauregard, was: The truth above all! The truth at all costs!"

"Well, what of it?"

"Regarding this investigation of Kantorowicz, for instance, I consider it absolutely necessary that you should know the full truth."

"What other new, unknown truth can there be in this matter? In two words!"

"Excellency, Major Georgis killed Knutson in Kantorowicz's office!"

"So! This too? Go on!"

"Georgis took over the interrogation, because he wanted to force Knutson to make a political confession, but he refused to sign anything of the sort. As head of your 'P' Section, Georgis was formally empowered to conduct the interrogation, and so it came about as I've just told you. What was thrown onto the street was thrown, so to speak, for formality's sake. Wasn't that it, Kantorowicz?" The minister of the interior turned to the erstwhile prefect of police, who still stood there in front of his superiors, shattered and with downcast eyes.

"In other words, Kantorowicz, does this mean you lied from beginning to end? All of it lies?"

"Yes, Excellency, I lied, but not about everything. I was defending Major Georgis!"

"Why?"

Kantorowicz was silent, not looking at Barutanski.

"Well, Kantorowicz? Why did you lie?"

"He swore on his mother's grave, Commandant, that he'd shoot me down like a dog if I said a word. And if the minister hadn't disclosed the facts, I wouldn't have said anything!"

"I see! And you're a naive lad who's never seen a game like this before?"

"Not at all! I've got three little kids and the whole of my brother's family to support, eleven people in all, Excellency! And I think, and we've all thought for some time, that Major Georgis is mad. That Major Georgis could shoot somebody down like a dog, if it were a question of his life, is easy to believe, Excellency!"

"And none of you thought of telling me this in time?"

"No, Excellency, because Major Georgis is the one man who enjoys a hundred percent of your confidence!"

Barutanski lowered his eyes. The Commandant's glance fell on the opened page of the *Blitvinian Echo*, where, across an entire page, cast in bronze, in its eternal glory, the glorious rider on his rearing horse, the masterpiece of a dead man who had gone together with his masterpiece, in a more lasting form than bronze, dominated the page.

"So Georgis killed Knutson? And how did it happen?"

"The facts are quite mad, Commandant. It all happened in a second. Georgis grabbed a hunting knife which I used as a paperknife from my desk, and it was all over before we could break into the room. What we found there was pure butchery. It was like a butcher's window . . ."

"All right, but why was he left alone in the room with that bastard?"

"He ordered me out of the room on the basis of his position as head of your 'P' Section. He was certainly in the right! It was the right you gave him yourself, if you remember, during the Kavalierski case! He claimed that he wished to talk to the man alone."

"And Knutson, was he bound?"

"He was!"

"Thank you, gentlemen! Then there's no point in the investigation! We'll keep to the first version: the running jump. And, Kantorowicz, Burgwaldsen will find you a suitable position! Thank you! Good night!"

Naturally! They were a lot of cretins! The only one among all these amateurs who reacted logically was Georgis. He was the only one who saw what it was all about! But it looked as if he was losing his grip! That Knutson, that neurasthenic scum, naturally wouldn't have confessed to the political background of the plot, that was logical! And as for Kantorowicz and others like him, apes like that always lived in cloud-cuckoo-land! Their only worry was the upkeep of "little kids." In any case, the idea of "little kids," that sloppy idea of "little kids"! And it wasn't enough for them to turn children into little, but they had to add the epithet "kids" to them like bells on a jester's cap. They were family men, these Kantorowiczes! Eleven "little kids" and shitting themselves! Georgis was right to throw Knutson through the window. That was logical! But not without his statement and signature! The syphilitic, alcoholic idiot! But all these others had each of them three "little kids" on their backs. Their only worry was "kids," their worry about kids' stomachs. The only one who was a hundred percent with him and who hadn't "little kids" on his mind was Georgis! And that gorilla had gone insane, completely, alas! Yet the only man to act logically in the matter was Georgis! Why question it? To chuck Olaf Knutson through the window was more logical than to be a legal formalist! It wasn't a question of satisfying some so-called idea of justice, utterly senseless, by the way, but it was a matter of life or death! Indeed it was! My head or yours, gentlemen! Such a big mouth as Olaf Knutson who was always finding fault because he didn't wish to be either a sycophant or a servant of the system, to play the part of a Rosencrantz or a Guildenstern! There you are! Everything went according to a deeper law of nature. Such so-called men would never be men, and the fact that they didn't like to play the role of courtier and be Rosencrantz or Guildenstern, that was simply a lie, for where was the human logic in not wishing to be a courtier and therefore to kill a man like Rayevski! And don't forget, Rayevski was very fond of Olaf Knutson, dragged him all over the world like a Pekingese dog. And in return, Knutson gave him dynamite, and that just because he'd modeled a statue of Barutanski. And so while he was writing out yet another check for Knutson (for who else could he have been writing out his last check), Knutson showed his gratitude by killing him. Such was life. A struggle for life—old Darwin put it well. I give you bread and you stab me in the back. But then those were "tragic heroes" as they wrote in the *Blitwanen Tigdende,* and those who shot these "tragic heroes," they were called "usurpers"! And now in all that, to think with the logic of a Witusz Kantorowicz who had three "little kids" was to think as legally and formalistically as possible, with one single idea, that of his three "little kids," and that meant thinking only of his own interests, for he was not just prefect of police but a father of three "little kids"! But when it was a question of our lives, then the question of "little kids" did not come in. We were taken for granted. We were an institution, not people. The lowest dean of the Philosophy Faculty had the right to his civil liberty, only we didn't have it! How logical! And then a hysterical goose like the Michelson woman had the right to spit in his face and call him "the murderer of her husband, General Michelson"! To pose as the widow of General Michelson and to call a Barutanski "General Michelson's murderer," that was utter lies. Who told the idiot to take Muzhikovski's side? And when a senile idiot like General Michelson married a typist, twenty-three years younger than he, then that typist became a "general's wife," and as a general's widow and as his, Barutanski's, close confidante, she expressed moral horror at him and said he should be shot like a dog and that that was her sole desire! And why did she go and hang herself? She'd had two excellent opportunities to kill him! The feebleminded nymphomaniac! At Beauregard she'd got tied up first with the Commandant, then with that onanist Nielsen, and then ended up with Baltrushaitis, and now was he supposed to be responsible for all her contradictions? So to be the confidante of the "P" Section and flirt intellectually with the editor of the *Tribune* and then to piss herself with fear like a bitch at an explosion, and to run not under the bed but to the gallows, that was very good, ha, ha!

Barutanski laughed aloud.

Baltrushaitis was right! Karin Michelson was not to be trusted!

He got up and, without reading any more of Mrs. Michelson's letter (for a moment he'd hesitated whether to read that, her final letter, again), he threw it into the fire, where it burned with a bright, vertical flame which hovered in several agitated fragments and then sent several burning shreds up the sooty chimney.

That whore had had only one idea and that was to kill him, but, as she said in her letter, she lost her nerve! Marvelous! Her farewell note burned well!

Mrs. Michelson's letter, indeed, had vanished in the fire in two or three flaming seconds, and a sooty veil of charred paper fluttered back down the chimney like a small parachute, where it struggled with the flames and, after a desperate struggle, sunk into the embers. A dense heavy rain could be heard beating against the windows. One could hear the barking of Barutanski's guard dogs in the park below.

They were changing the guard. The dogs were barking. That was good, Kristian Barutanski thought, and rang for his servant.

Rafaelo appeared. He was His Excellency's second personal servant.

"Where's Klement?"

"He's been taken ill, Excellency. He passed out in the kitchen."

"What's wrong with him?"

"It's nothing. Influenza! It was his fourth night on duty. He's not very fit. His heart . . ."

"How old is Klement?"

"Fifty-four, Excellency!"

"And you?"

"Thirty-seven, if it please Your Excellency!"

"Are you married? Do you have children?"

"Yes, three, Excellency."

"Little kids?"

"Very little. The oldest is three. I don't know exactly. Three and two months, I think."

"Good! And when they ask you how many children you have, how do you answer? Do you say 'I've three children,' or do you say 'I've three kids'?"

"I beg your pardon, Excellency, I don't understand!"

"What do you mean you don't understand? How do you answer the question 'Do you have any children?' Do you say 'I've three children,' or do you say 'I've three kids'?"

"I say 'children.' 'I've three children.'"

"Bravo, Rafaelo! And now you can give me a glass of rum!"

"Certainly, Excellency!"

"You call it a glass? Klement's more intelligent than you. He distinguishes a glass from a little glass and children from little kids. He had two kids, but they died young. Kids always die young! So give me a glass, man, and not a little glass! That's the way!"

"Sorry, Excellency! I don't know Your Excellency's ways! I so rarely see Your Excellency!"

"Where do you work?"

"I'm an overservant, Excellency! I fall into what they call the lower ranks."

"And where were you in 'twenty-five? Were you in the lower ranks then?"

"I was a sergeant major in the Third Chevaux-Légers. I was wounded here, at Beauregard. I was left lying down there near where the fountain is today. . . . I was shot through the neck. Here, just here, from left to right. I was lucky that the arteries weren't pierced, Excellency!"

"And do you drink rum?"

"From time to time, sir!"

"Here you are, then, Rafaelo. Good health! If the Third Chevaux-Légers goes into action again, where will you be?"

"We're all prepared, Excellency! You are Commandant and we are the Chevaux-Légers!"

Barutanski poured a glass of rum for his ex–Chevaux-Légers overservant and, clinking glasses with him heartily and amicably, with human warmth and completely sincerely, he drained his second full glass of Jamaica and lit a Maryland with total relaxation.

"You say Klement fainted? From four nights on in a row? I've been on duty for four thousand four hundred and forty-four nights and I haven't fainted yet, Rafaelo! Give me another glass! That's it! Thanks! And what are you serving for supper?"

"Chicken soup, Excellency!"

"Go on!"

"Or chicken in white sauce!"

"And?"

"Spinach soufflé! Carrot soufflé! Various salads!"

"Go on!"

"Cheese! Fruit! Stewed fruit! Glacé fruit! Dessert! Dry biscuits!"

"Go on!"

"That's all I know, Excellency!"

"And what did you have for supper?"

"I, Excellency? Potato salad and yogurt!"

"Without onion? Without pepper? Without garlic? Potato salad, with what sausages? The strong garlic ones we call Vengerka?"

"We're not allowed onions, Excellency! Vengerkas are forbidden, and garlic and everything!"

"What, they've put you on a diet too? Well, that I didn't know! That's interesting! Have you got stomach ulcers too?"

"No, Excellency, but we are servants and it is forbidden for servants at Beauregard to indulge in onions. Onions, sausages, and all food and drink that cause, how shall I say, unpleasant smells. That's well known."

"What's your surname?"

"Mazurski, Excellency!"

"Hah, excellent! Rafaelo Mazurski! Listen! I know you're only an overservant, but I think you must know that I live on a very strict diet. So run down to the kitchen and tell that idiot, what's the fool's name, the kitchen manager?"

"Axentowicz!"

"So, Rafaelo Mazurski, tell your much respected chief, Mr. Axentowicz, that the Commandant sends his compliments and requests that he prepare three pairs of Vengerkas, with onions, and plenty of them, and tell him to pepper them, damn him, and forget about Beauregard restrictions, and tell him to roast potatoes with bacon, the good spicy Hungarian bacon, do you understand, Rafaelo Mazurski? And tell him to have it served here in three minutes with plenty of Blitvinian mustard! Eyes front! Quick march! Gallop!"

Kristian Barutanski drained another half glass of Jamaica and went to the telephone. "Hello! Give me the Foreign Ministry!" For some time there was no answer. Then a rather bored, sleepy, undisciplined, and hermaphroditic voice replied, "Hello! Can I help you?"

"Who's this?"

"Dr. Wernis."

"Listen, you, this is the Commandant! I telephoned your minister to report to me more than an hour ago! Oh, really? He's still at a tea party at the British Consulate? All right! But surely somebody could have informed him that the Commandant required his presence? Personally! You're not to blame. You came on night duty only twenty minutes ago, but who was before you? You don't know? Excellent! So, good! I desire to talk with the minister *at once*!"

Irresponsible lot of diplomatic snobs! They grabbed every possible allowance and cost as much as three medical faculties put together and they were incapable of writing a decent official letter. They slept and took tea at foreign consulates, and a man had to do everything himself, on his own!

In the whole of this uproar, Kristian Barutanski felt one hundred percent self-satisfaction. The mother of the Commandant of Blitva had not borne him to voyage in the dead and boring calms and doldrums. He was born for the waves, for the howl of the storm, for driving at 137 kilometers per hour along the Blitvinian highway, for occasions when people were thrown out of windows like raw meat, for hunting down people, for speed, for games of golf with sticks of dynamite, when you never knew at what moment one's opponent would be blown to pieces. He opened the doors onto the balcony and, feeling a profound need for a breath of the dampness that smoked in massive jets, he stepped onto the balcony into a shower of wind and rain that, from time to time, lashed down in dense torrents, only to be followed by intervals of calm, when it appeared as if the rain had completely stopped. Even the weather was confused and alarmed. Way below him gleamed the town of Blitwanen, lit by its street lamps and various colored electric advertisements, among which stood out the pastel blue advertisement for aspirin, a cross framed in a burning circle, on the corner of Jesuit Street and Waldemaras Square, in the very center beneath the bridge. From Blitwanen under Barutanski's feet came the clamor of voices, the sound of sirens and klaxons, the trotting of hooves of cab horses on the macadam, right beneath the rock of the old fortress, and, borne on a gust of wind, came the distant roaring of a crowd.

Ah, that was Aage Kohlinis getting started! It was his first effort, his first performance. That evening he was sitting his first exam for his post, that newly appointed prefect of police!

From somewhere in the town center could be heard the howling of a mob and, together with the surging of voices, one could distinguish a muffled metallic banging, the splintering of glass, a charging, the sounds of a pogrom. The elementally threatening outcry of human voices disturbed the jackdaws in the Beauregard park. From somewhere down under the bridge came the squeal of a locomotive, the echo of the monotonous clatter of metal.

Well done, Kohlinis, Barutanski thought, listening to the distant voices. That was the LOOLP! They were probably demolishing the offices of the *Blitwanen Tigdende*. Excellent! If Jensen's death hadn't knocked some sense into them, nothing would! Rekyavinis was a bloody idiot, but in one thing he was right! He couldn't understand why he, Barutanski, had held so stubbornly to his principle, which he kept to at all costs, which was called the freedom of the press. Let people blather what they like; they'll just get a bloody nose! But Rekyavinis was of the opinion that it was an unnecessary expenditure of nerves and energy. Why? One slept better without a lot of blather! But this way wasn't bad either! Smashing printing presses and thrashing scribblers, that could be amusing too! The masses valued amusement above all else. Anything but boredom! And for that shit, it was a good reminder that we were here! When a man was behind a steering wheel, the most important thing was correct reaction. And what was happening down there in

Blitwanen, apparently to the *Blitwanen Tigdende,* that was correct reaction! You smashed my monument, and I've smashed your *Blitwanen Tigdende*! Well done, LOOLP!

"Excuse me, Excellency, Major Kerinis is on the phone."

"So?"

Barutanski came in from the balcony, wet through, leaving the balcony doors open behind him, since the room was still full of smoke.

"Excellency, nothing to report! He left his room perhaps two minutes before we arrived."

The green light flashed on the private confidential line.

"Hello! Well, at last, Minister! I've been calling you for three whole hours! Yes, tea with the English! I know. But I've no time now. Ring me in five minutes!"

"Go on!"

"I'm sorry, Excellency! We discovered practically nothing. On Nielsen's desk I found the beginning of a rough copy of a proclamation, written in his own hand, to the peoples of Blitva, Blatvia, Hunnia, Kobilia, and Kurlandia. The peoples of the Karabaltic and Aragon!"

"So the man's writing proclamations! He's preparing for battle! And then with a flutter of wings, the bird has flown. What else?"

"Only that he seemed to have been reading the Tauchnitz novels and he'd left a Hotchkiss pistol with two boxes of cartridges in a drawer. I have the impression that he is coming back. I've posted a reception party and blocked off the whole Promenade. Kohlinis has lent me eleven of his men. They're all in position. And what are we to do with the old deaf woman?"

"That's the old Gallen woman! I know all about her. She prays to God for my death! What could you do to her? To hell with her! What you do do is this! Drop by Karin Michelson's place and examine everything to the last detail, that's number one. Number two, just as important: Search Knutson's flat, thoroughly! You can report to me what you find tomorrow. And tonight, if Nielsen returns or if they find him, report to me immediately! If I'm asleep, have me wakened! Good-bye!"

The Commandant went to the other phone, frowning and angry. "The Ministry of Foreign Affairs. Hello! It's I! Listen, Belinis! Who gave permission to print that article on the Blitva-Blatvia Pact in *L'Écho de Blithuanie*? What? You don't know? Is it a case of paranoia? It talks about a pact between Blitva and Blatvia that rests *sur une base positive au moyen de garanties réciproques en ce qui concerne les fronitières*—et cetera, et cetera. And you didn't know about this? You're as naive as the Virgin Mary of Blitva! The official responsible for releasing the article is to be dismissed immediately. It's a provocation. Investigate the matter and report to me at seven tomorrow. When? Seven in the morning! In addition, prepare a report for tomorrow on the matter of the book *The Aspirations of Blitvania* by Blatvanicus, printed by Watson and Viney, London. So? You don't know who Blitvanicus is? So let me enlighten you. According to the reports of my London agents, we have incontrovertible proof that Blatvanicus is the Minister Blatvinis himself. Yes, Blatvinis, your Blatvian opposite number, the minister of foreign affairs of the Republic of Blatvia! This, my dear minister, is just not on! We'll not have an active minister of a country that has its representation here publishing books in London in which he proves to the English that our sea belongs to the Blatvian sphere of interest! Prepare a text for our protest to the government in Weider-Hunnen! And while you're at it, are you aware of the results of the police investigation concerning the assassination of Rayevski? You're not? You don't know this either? You don't know that this was due to explosives whose provenance is confirmed without doubt as being the Blatvian military arsenal? No? You had no idea of this? But perhaps you do know what idiot was on telephone duty in your office before that half-awake nun who's yawning there now? Doctor who? Aha! Then you can kick him out for being totally incompetent. We'll discuss this further tomorrow. By the way, you know what, Belinis? Don't bother to come to me so early; in fact, don't come at all! Tomorrow seek out the prime minister and be so good as to give him your resignation! Yes! By my orders! Good night!"

They were a lot of lazy, dusty sacks that needed dusting day and night! Laziness was in the Blitvinian blood! A man couldn't believe how quickly a fool got lazy in those ministerial armchairs! That Belinis was a good man in the squadron, and now look at him—the devil had got into the man and he was already snoring! They were always crying out for expenses and all they did was to be driven to banquets and tea parties.

Rafaelo Mazurski, the second valet, appeared at the door with a laden table on rubber-tired wheels.

"Well done, Rafaelo Mazurski! No, there is no need to serve anything, I'll take it as we did in the Chevaux-Légers! Do you understand? Do you know how to use the phone? Right, I'm going across to Her Excellency's for just a few minutes! And listen! You'll transfer only the red light calls and no others! Do you understand? The Vengerkas aren't hot enough! The onions are good. The mustard's no bloody good! Pour me a Jamaica! Thanks! The specialists tell me that one such sausage could perforate my bowel! Jamaica, they say, attacks the mucous membranes! To hell with bowels and mucous membranes and diets, Mazurski! Good health! Pour yourself one! To Colonel Barutanski! Cheers!"

"To Your Excellency's health!"

Rafaelo Mazurski clinked glasses with his Commandant, with the stance of a frightened valet, but then clicked his heels like a true cavalry sergeant major.

"And to your health, Mazurski. *Servus!* You're a great chap! God bless you and your three 'little kids'! Cheers!"

CHAPTER 3

"Valse de la Mort"

At Beauregard, which that evening shone in the full glory of its glass candelabra and expensive lamps with their varicolored silk shades, so that their light showered over the carpets and halls, loggias and corridors, like a sparkling silver, greenish, and orange rain, in the central and largest, so-called colonnade, hall, which, for some unknown reason, local tradition had christened the "colonnade," although it did not contain a single column, in that so-called colonnade reception hall at Beauregard, they were holding an evening of Skripnik's music.

The wife of the architect Blithauer-Blitvinski, Mrs. Ariadna Vosnesenskaya, that phenomenal "coloratura Blitvinian nightingale," sang several of Skripnik's songs, and the young Parisian student and famous Blitvinian pianist Kulmoinen, of whom the *Blitwanen Morgenbladet* wrote that he mastered his instrument "divinely," like a Blitvinian Menahem Mehudi, performed to the elite of Beauregard, everything that was the best in Skripnik's oeuvre, for which Skripnik truly deserved to be honored with the attention which that musically highly educated elite dedicated to the posthumous recognition of his beloved and unforgettable memory. Of all Skripnik's compositions played by Kulmoinen, the most successful were the song concerning "the yellow leaves that fall tonight" and his famous "Valse de la Mort," a type of Blitvinian rhapsody, composed in waltz time, based on Blitvinian popular funereal tunes. The musicologist and professor of the Blitvinian conservatory Eric Ericson, who in the *Lexicon Musicae Blithuanicae* had edited a chapter on Blitvinian modern music under the title "Blithuotaya Blithuolainen," this, by his very occupation, without doubt the best expert on Skripnik, after the first intermission gave, formally speaking, a perfect lecture concerning the deceased master, and, after the second part of the concert was over, the elite of Beauregard retired to the side halls on the first floor, where a cold buffet was served for the guests.

Apart from His Eminence Cardinal Armstrong, who, that evening, appeared in the official company of his personal secretary Lupis-Masnov (and without his pet, Giordano Bruno), there were the ladies of Blitvinian trade and industry: Dagmar Baltic (shipping line Ankersgarden-Stockholm-Wyborgen), Karin Peugeot (Chevrolet, Hotchkiss, Peugeot, tires, automobiles, and machine guns), Blitvinian Business Company Charlotte (coal, petroleum, rice, coffee, Blitvinian export-import plc.), the ladies of the cavalry and infantry: the Sandersens, Andersens, Svensens, Jensens, etc., the wives of the establishment, here and there accompanied by their spouses, then the LOOLP—the ladies, in all forty-seven ladies and gentlemen, among whom—that evening—the greatest sensation was evoked by the wife of the soap baron Walterinis, Mrs. Dagmar Walterinis, not so much because the afternoon press of that day had announced that in her husband's soap factory two men had fallen into the vat, where they were cooked like sausages, but because she had appeared in a cape of beaver-furred golden brocade with a diamond necklace and in such Valenciennes lace that Skripnik's memory was simply overshadowed. The other, just as brilliant, surprise of the evening was the appearance of Madame de St-Forçat of the Comédie Française, a waxy beauty with a demonic appearance.

Jules Dupont, the favorite, friend, admirer, and courtier of Ingrid Barutanski, had stopped Madame Thérèse de St-Forçat, the famous tragedienne of the Comédie, on her journey through Blitwanen and she had, following her triumphal tour of Tzigania, Kobilia, and Hunnia, accepted the invitation of Ingrid Barutanski to honor the evening with her presence, and so a new sensational rumor had circulated in Beauregard that Madame Thérèse de St-Forçat would enact some scenes from Racine's *Britannicus,* for the role of Agrippine, apparently, was the crown jewel in her repertoire.

Of all the gathered elite in the colonnade hall of the Beauregard palace, the one who most enjoyed the thought of hearing Racine was the initiator of the whole program, Jules Dupont. Marie-Joseph-Jules Dupont was, in his attitude to life, an experienced, witty, hardened sybarite with no opinion of his own concerning the world around him, yet still he fell into the category of those average Frenchmen who were romantically in love with France, for whom the mere thought that somebody would recite Racine made him tingle with the majestic, sentimental feeling of how fortunate he was to have been born a Frenchman: Marie-Joseph-Jules Dupont from a French father, Marie-Joseph-Camille Dupont, and his mother, Thérèse, born Rochard de la Tour du Pin. He, as a citizen, thought of himself, as did so many of his countrymen, that the Parisian Pantheon, for example, with all its glorious names and graves, was one of the most essential components of his worthy and valued personality, just as were the banners in Les Invalides his personal banners, beneath which he had conquered the barbarians around him throughout the long and dark centuries. In the Jacobin clay Marianne he had never had much faith and preferred, which was more worthy of a Marie-Joseph-Jules Dupont Rochard de la Tour du Pin, the thought of the forty French kings who had built France to the point where he could become a contributor to *Soire,* and feeling that the concept of the Jacobin Marianne to be a coarse humiliation of the Maid of Orléans, he had nonetheless (through his native gift of taste) a constant and certain conception of the fact that 99 percent of non-French European civilization was little

more than utter kitsch and fraud. The country of a Descartes and
of a Jules Dupont seemed to him, at the very least, worthy of Pericles, and when he lay in the trenches around Ypres and in the
Champagne for three whole years, he could scarcely imagine how
such barbarians could exist to pour artillery at the "bravest, most
gifted, most cultured nation in the world," at a people "first among
nations," who were "the only Latin genius among the barbarians,"
who possessed "their forty kings," "their Jacobin mission," and
their Jacobin dividends which the barbarians squandered so short-
sightedly and maliciously.

His *tricoleur,* patriotic dividends—that is, his father's—had been
squandered by a barbarian Swiss chocolate factory in Basle and so
Jules Dupont's father, a man of extravagance and eccentricity, who
possessed more than two hundred different types of cameras, for
example, as well as a poultry farm in Orléans, the largest collection
of Japanese carving, a mansion in Paris in the Avenue de Shanghai,
suffered through well-intentioned and philanthropic cooperation
with the barbarians and Jules Dupont began his career as a soldier
and then, after 1918, became a journalist. As such, having good ref-
erences, he came to the hundred-percent-barbarian Blitva, due to
his professional acquaintanceship with Barutanski, since, in '22, he
had written that Barutanski was "a man above parties" and, apart
from this, that witty and charming colonel was, in the full sense of
the word, "the expression of his Karabaltic nation." Charmed by this
pleasant and polished young man, Barutanski, through Dupont's
agency, launched a number of his politically extremely important
interviews in the French press.

"Tout le monde en avant," for example, was the title of Jules Dupont's famous article, in which he gave his monumental and, in its
apparent sincere simplicity, brilliant sketch of Barutanski's assault
on Wyborgen when, having swum the Blatva one night in a mad
charge, he scattered the Kurlandish troops with naked sabers, took

Wyborgen, and thus, in a single blow, liberated Kurlandia from military terror.

"Have you any particular memories of that fateful morning, Excellency?"

"It was a starlit spring night. Orion was shining over our heads. It was quite dark before the dawn. And I was thinking how orderly was the movement of the stars. What peace reigned among them! What perfect peace and order! The Kurlandish rebels had suffered considerable losses that night and one could hear them throwing their dead into the Blatva. . . . One, two, three, splash. One, two, three, splash. In that same Wyborgen I learned to swim as a child many years ago. The swimming instructor was called Fuchs and the pool was somewhere there just beneath our posts. One, two, three, four, one, two, three, four, our instructor, old Fuchs, chanted over us beginners, and we floundered, hanging on to the pole like fish on a line. One, two, three, I thought to myself, and that was how we took Wyborgen, swimming the Blatva one starry night. The water felt pretty strange, damned wet, yet afterward nobody complained of being cold or catching a chill."

Madame Thérèse de St-Forçat, after the long and theatrical monologue from act 4, scene 2:

Approchez-vous, Néron, et prenez place,

surrounded by a flock of Valenciennes lace, by Chevrolets, Peugeots, Dagmar Baltic, nameless and lower-rank members of the LOOLP, reaped a well-deserved and long-lasting applause from delighted French white kid and Houbigants gloves, and, enchanted by this unexpectedly overwhelming enthusiasm for the beauty of French classical verse in that distant and unknown barbarian country, after some well-simulated deep and serious concentration of memory, passed on to act 5, scene 6:

Poursuis, Néron, avec de tels ministres,
Par des faits glorieux tu vas te signaler;
Poursuis. Tu n'as pas fait ce pas pour reculer:
Ta main a commencé par le sang de ton frère;
Je prévois que tes coups viendront jusqu'à ta mère.
Dans le fond de ton coeur, je sais que iu me hais;
Tu voudras t'affranchir du joug de mes bienfaits.
Mais je veux que ma mort te soit même inutile:
Ne crois pas qu'en mourant je te laisse tranquille.
Rome, ce ciel, ce jour que tu reçus de moi,
Partout, à tout moment, m'offriront devant toi.
Tes remords te suivront comme autant de furies;
Tu croiras les calmer par d'autres barbaries;
Ta fureur, s'irritant soi-même dans son cours,
D'un sang toujours nouveau marquera tous tes jours.
Mais j'espère qu'enfin le ciel, las de tes crimes,
Ajoutera ta perte à tant d'autres victimes;
Qu'après t'être couvert de leur sang et du mien,
Tu te verras forcé de répandre le tien;
Et ton nom paraîtra, dans la race future,
Aux plus cruels tyrans une cruelle injure.
Voilà ce que mon coeur se présage de toi.
Adieu: tu peux sortir.

During this long and boring monologue, Barutanski appeared in the gallery accompanied by his adjutant, Captain Flaming-Sandersen. He had never felt any liking for this Beauregard rabble and, in conversation with these ladies and gentlemen, in his capacity as the boss of Blitva, he constantly kept a stern and watchful guard over his own thoughts, so as not to cause a scandal by some inappropriate question or malicious remark, which would have logically occurred to him, knowing as he did these sycophants and their ways.

And you were still worried by the thought of how it would be if you wrung their necks, Minister? As if I didn't know that you had joined the Legion's Organization of Order, Labor, and Progress simply as camouflage? As if I didn't know that last night at your house there was a plenary meeting of all representatives of the Agrarian Association in the presence of a representative who came directly from Weider-Hunnen, from your chief Kmetynis?

"How are you, Minster? Delighted to see you. I hear you're engaged on a program for the organization of cooperatives for the export of our fish! It's a good idea!"

Your housemaid was an agent of the "P" Section! You idiot!

Or, talking one evening with a Blitvinian baron, the bearer of a historic and glorious Blitvinian name, but in fact the bearer of Blitva's historical shame, when the man congratulated him for his liberation of Blitva, he'd had a deep urge to tell the cretin: Yes, dear baron, I did liberate it, while your ancestors sold it to the Huns during two whole centuries! Your father was a Hunnish agent and we had full proof of it but didn't dare publish the fact, for fear of harming Blitvinian culture! And you, in your club, expressed moral horror that I was a "murderer," your very words, and you, being a gentleman in pure white gloves, considered my efforts beneath the dignity of a man and a true gentleman! I shed blood for Blitva, while you were an officer in the Aragon Imperial Guard who hanged my legionnaires right, left, and center. You shot at Blitva and therefore remained untarnished, while I liberated Blitva and so, in your eyes, I was a murderer!

Or again, there was that dear, charming Gdanyski, that bastard there in the hall with his wife, just behind Ingrid in the second row, listening to that croaking magpie declaiming about Nero and privately horrified at all my Nero-like acts. And the fact that he was minister of the interior in Muzhikovski's government in '22, and that his regime was the bloodthirstiest regime on earth, proved nothing, since His Excellency Mr. Gdanyski fell into the category of pure-white patriotic hands. An idiot like Gdanyski would get away with it! He was off to Chile as our ambassador and he'd play golf and sail, take his expenses, and pray to the dear God for the devil to take me as soon as possible. And in any case, what sense was there in that Racine?

> *Tes remords te suivront comme autant de furies;*
> *Tu croiras les calmer par d'autres barbaries;*
> *Ta fureur, s'irritant soi-même dans son cours,*
> *D'un sang toujours nouveau marquera tous tes jours.*
> *Tes remords te suivront comme autant de furies;*
> *tra–tata, tra–tata, tra–tata, tra–tata . . .*
> *tra–ta–ta, tra–ta–ta, tra–ta–ta, tra–ta–ta . . .*

And that, God knew why, was what they called poetry. When such a plucked and dressed old chicken impudently, unnaturally, and affectedly went tra-ta-ta and moaned and hissed and snorted, that was what they called "classical"! And who the hell brought this old girl here, anyway? I bet it was that stinking "commercial traveler" of a man, Dupont!

"What applause, just to spite me? Just listen to it, Flaming! Be so good as to go down to Her Excellency and request her permission to inform these ladies and gentlemen that the representative of Blitvinian sovereignty is lying dead. It looks as if no one here has a clue as to what's happened! And another thing: I see the academic Vanini down there! I urgently want to talk to him! Send him to me immediately!"

The elite in the colonnade hall, gathered around Madame Thérèse de St-Forçat, sensed the presence of the Grand Master of Beauregard and Blitva high above their heads in the semidarkness of the gallery; as it happens in a church service, when the ecclesiastical dignitaries appear in the church galleries and the service continues apparently peacefully, so did this elite in its gold brocade and Valenciennes lace and white kid gloves grow uneasy in their armchairs, while in their thoughts they began the hasty scattering of small fish faced with a large pike, yet, as regards any outward, conventional expression of such unease, apart from a nervous fit of coughing here and there, not the most skilled eye could have noted any particular change in the hearts of these empty-headed morons. This well-trained Beauregard society sensed that, in all probability, at least something untoward had occurred for Barutanski to appear in the gallery only to vanish silently immediately afterward. Now, through the entire hall, the center of everybody's attention, came Captain Flaming-Sandersen, young, agile, and pleasant looking in his uhlan's uniform with its red trousers and with the gait of a Chevaux-Légers, Flaming-Sandersen, the grandson of the sculptured father and ideologue of Blitva, the national idol, whose statue stood on the square in Blitwanen and in front of the railway station in Ankersgarden and in all the towns of Blitva, as a symbol of Blitvinian thought and significance. Now his grandson, in the full-dress uniform of a free Blitvinian cavalry officer and gentleman, stepped beneath the candelabra and, bowing low before Her Excellency Ingrid Barutanski, whispered to her a message from the Lord of Blitva, and, by all appearances, the message had to be of considerable importance.

What was it? What could have happened? Her Excellency Ingrid Barutanski rose to her feet. Her Excellency grew pale, yellow, like faded parchment, filled with anxiety. Her Excellency, faced with her entire suite of guests and admirers, kept her head, aware of the responsibility she bore before future generations. She held a whispered conversation with Captain Flaming-Sandersen and requested him to announce the catastrophic news to the assembled guests.

Captain Flaming-Sandersen once more gave a low bow to the most noble circle of Blitvinian dignitaries and, freely, without embarrassment, simply and naturally, and still with a certain tone of human warmth, announced to the company what his chief and commandant had ordered him to say.

"Ladies and gentlemen, His Excellency requests your pardon for taking upon himself the unpleasant and difficult duty of being the bearer of the tragic news of a cruel death."

A ripple ran through the mayonnaise, the cream, the brocades, the décolletés, amid the clinking of chains and bracelets, the flashing of diamonds, the creaking of the parquet, an agitation of flesh and shirtfronts, a movement of bowels, nerves, consciences, and digestions—in a word, an uneasy murmur, as a sign of anxiety beneath the shining candelabra of the colonnade hall. It was clear that that first sentence of the Commandant's message had produced a considerable impression on everybody.

"Ladies and gentlemen, His Excellency begs to inform you that the Right Honorable President of the Academy of Arts, the unanimously nominated candidate for the presidency of the Republic of Blitva, our famous sculptor, Roman Rayevski, has fallen victim to a political assassination. He died as the result of a bomb. His Excellency deeply regrets that circumstances beyond his control, due to the exigencies of the situation, compel him to announce this tragic news to you, but, shaken by this atrocious crime committed upon the designated president of Blitvinian Sovereignty, the Commandant requests all of you here to pray in your hearts for the eternal peace of a genius who has given his life for Blitva! May the Lord have mercy upon the soul of Roman Rayevski!"

Barutanski received Maestro Vanini-Schiavone a few minutes later in the outer fortress gallery in Beauregard, filled as it was with armored knights, on whom, the evening before, Father Bonaventura Baltrushaitis had tapped so maliciously.

Maestro Vanini, the cultural historian of Blitva, who had written a monograph on Perugino and on certain Blitvinian engravers of the eighteenth century hitherto unknown. To him belonged the fame of uncovering, to the last detail, the character of Petro Antonio Milanese, the builder of the Blitvas-Holm fortress, whom the Blitvinians affectionately called the Little Italian, the academic who had painted massive ecclesiastical frescoes for His Eminence Cardinal Armstrong, an artist who, from the beginning of his career as sculptor and architect, possessed both versatility and, indeed, universality. This vain and cunning man, already in the colonnade hall, sensed the news of the death of his rival Roman Rayevski, as though Captain Flaming-Sandersen had delivered him a telegram announcing that his lottery ticket had won one of the first prizes. Roman Rayevski, the idol of Blitva, the favorite of the Lord and Chief, the designated president of the Republic, by his gifts, his creative capacity, his social and financial standing, rotated on the merry-go-round of provincial Blitvinian civilization some three horse heads above Vanini, who had declared himself to be another Leonardo, a man of universal talent, who solved aesthetic problems with the exactitude of a scholar and not confusedly and vaguely as was done irresponsibly in the studios of the numberless so-called Blitvinian geniuses. For this reason, to overtake Roman Rayevski on that magical merry-go-round of fortune seemed to him an unattainable dream, and when Captain Flaming-Sandersen, in the choked, tearful voice of a very young man, concluded his report with the Commandant's request that all present should pray for the soul of Roman Rayevski, Maestro Vanini-Schiavone almost clapped his hands and shouted: *Bravo, bravissimo!* And when, a minute or so later, he heard from Captain Flaming-Sandersen that Roman Rayevski had not perished alone, but that, with him, the devil had taken that tasteless equestrian statue of the Commandant and that that madman and malicious hairsplitter, that carping Olaf Knutson, had also been sent to eternal damnation, Maestro Vanini felt a profound and sincere need to cross himself with emotion. In the Name of the Father, the Son, and the Holy Ghost, that divine series of winning tickets steadily grew. Not only were Rayevski and Knutson dead (he'd hated Knutson, yet dreaded his expert eye), not only had that monster of an equestrian statue gone to the devil, but almost Rayevski's entire studio with its mass of competitive, indeed, megalomaniacal stupidities and particularly with the sketches for the fresco in the church of Saint Paul of Blitva. Now Captain Flaming-Sandersen brought a message from the Lord of Blitva, asking him to see him, and immediately at that, because, no doubt, he wished to consult him concerning the aesthetic arrangement of the funeral, for (naturally) there was no one else he could turn to for professional advice. In other words, he, Vanini-Schiavone, had, at that moment, become the artistic adviser to His Excellency the Lord of Blitva, who had not summoned him just regarding the official funeral, but also to consult him regarding the monument, and not just the monument to Roman Rayevski, but also that to the Liberator of Blitva which, apparently, was lost forever, for only a small clay model of the horseman had survived—unluckily—somewhere in the studio, according to Rayevski's widow, the bereaved Silva.

Vanini, one of the most boisterous chatterers in Blitvinian café life, swamped Barutanski with a mass of original but, admittedly, rather expensive plans regarding the state funeral of the maestro and president, Roman Rayevski. Immediately, with the trained hand of a professional artist, in two or three strokes of a pen on the white paper of his sketchbook, he drew out the plan of the funeral. The deceased president's catafalque should be placed in front of the Jesuit Cathedral on Jesuit Square in the center of the town, and torches should flame on tripods around the coffin on a raised red, orange, black pedestal, and the Blitvinian *tricoleur,* in its three colors, red, orange, and black, should fall from the gallery of the Jesuit Tower like a tri-colored canopy, so that it would fall over the rich folds of the fabric, the black fabric on the coffin, as a mark of national mourning, as a symbol of lamentation. All would be black. The entire Jesuit Cathedral, in which the dead president would lie before the main altar until the moment of burial, would be covered in black cloth above the president's silver coffin in its rich drapery and, when the officers bore the coffin of the Symbol of Sovereignty in front of the church, behind them would stand the wide-open church portal with its gleaming Venetian candelabra, and the entire paved square in front of the Jesuit church would be empty, only the president's coffin and a squadron of the Chevaux-Légers, with dipped lances, and, beside the coffin, just one man: the Liberator of Blitva, Barutanski. Above him, to the top of the belfry, in the three colors of Blitva, the monumental canopy of Blitvinian national sovereignty, and, in the dusk, as the army filed past, in the dark red fire of the dying torches, this would be an attractive, simple, yet, in its symbolism, undoubtedly majestic scene.

"OK, Vanini, and where will the nobility, the so-called Parliament, the Estates and Guilds, the officers and the representatives of LOOLP stand?"

"All these will remain in the church while the military procession passes, arranged in order of their rank and position, in the same order as they'll march in the procession."

"And what about the family? Are they to remain in the church? I don't understand! I can't get all the participants into the church! It's impossible!"

"The family, Excellency, good God, yes, the family, you're right. We'll reserve the steps up to the church portal for them, yes, the church portal. I thought they should be in front of the church, because the portal, with its baroque, what's it called, balustrade and steps, at such a moment presents nothing less than a podium for such an occasion! A podium with the clergy, dignitaries, and finally the family. And anyway, if we think of it, what 'family'? The 'family' as such, in this case, is only Silva in her deep mourning as the widow. Except for her, the rest are no family, namely, Dolores de Janeiro and seven or eight other ladies. This funeral, after all, is not a funeral in the usual bourgeois sense of the word, wouldn't you agree, but a type of first-class state occasion, if I may so put it. 'A matter of protocol' . . . As you yourself, Excellency, deigned to suggest, this funeral is indeed the first funeral of a president of the Blitvinian Republic, that is, so to speak, a type of premiere, and, since we've never had a representative of our sovereignty who has died at his post, yes, and so on, something like that, this occasion of the president's funeral in fact serves as a model for protocol itself, don't you agree, and this leaves our hands free, does it not?"

This "yes, something like that" which caused Vanini-Schiavone's stutter was a fleeting and very superficial picture of Professor Sandersen, the former president of the Republic, whom Barutanski had killed in detention and who, as such, represented a dead hero in the position of president, yet who was not buried according to protocol—indeed not—since he was shot while escaping on the Blitvinian frontier and buried where he fell in a small, obscure village cemetery in the Plavystok marshes. This nervous pause of Vanini's lasted no longer than the verbal effort of a man trying to bridge the gap between one sentence and another, and Vanini, one might say, ran over the bridge of "yes, what's it called, and so on" not in fear of the moral and political profundities to his right and left, but rather in the panting enthusiasm of a vain idiot who saw nothing on the far side of his sentence except his own triumph: the solemn spectacle of the president's funeral, when, in front of the Jesuit Cathedral, Rayevski would lie in his silver coffin and Vanini, together with Colonel Barutanski, would bury him at Beauregard, according to his own taste, as the witty and inventive window dresser who alone, at this glorious display, had the right to express his authoritative and expert opinion.

"And where will the public be, Vanini, at this show of yours?"

"The public? At the windows, Excellency!"

"That's not much public, for such an expense, my dear chap! The way you're seeing it, the comedy's going to cost a lot of money. If it's going to be a circus, let the people see the circus!"

Vanini thought for a while. A born improviser, he had ready a complete picture of the drama on paper before him.

There, the cathedral steps. On the steps, three strides apart from the other dignitaries, in a thick widow's veil, a woman, silent, with eyes downcast in her speechless and dignified suffering. The light of the Venetian candelabra through the dark drapery from the interior of the church; here, the coffin with its medieval torches, the *tricoleur* enshrouding everything from the belfry to the coffin, and, beside the coffin, the Commandant of Blitva and the tight ranks of the Blitvinian army in a march-past. Drums, trumpets, gunfire, the empty Jesuit Square, the dusk, the torches—excellent! Yes! Indeed! But where would the public be? The masses? The people? Jesuit Square was so small that the opposite pavement could not hold more than several hundred.

"Why not build a grandstand on the other side of the square?"

"Nonsense, Vanini! We're not an open-air theater! What bloody grandstand? I've no money for your stupidities!"

"Then why don't we lay him in state in the church of Saint Paul of Blitva, Excellency? There's enough room in front of it for the whole population of Blitva."

"That's better."

"But in that way we lose most of the main effects. And that's a pity! Rayevski doesn't deserve that! That is to say, if you see what I mean, Excellency, of course! The outline facade of the Jesuit church and the square, framed in ancient buildings, and the general idea: the *tricoleur* stretching from the tower to the coffin and on the square in front of the church of Saint Paul, the very effect of a coffin with one single man on the square beside it will be lost in the vast space, Excellency! And this should be the main plan of the funeral: Here stands Barutanski, alone, burying his president as if he were a king, for those he has chosen are equal to kings! Saint Paul of Blitva Square and everything on it, its entire aspect, all this gets lost in straight lines. It all looks too common! It would lack our ancient, intimate, Blitvinian atmosphere: the steep Blitvinian roofs, the high baroque windows on Jesuit Square, the heads at the windows and on the balconies, the banners, the bells . . . Saint Paul's Square is made for the noise of trams, for dogs to run in the park, it's a huge playing field framed in fences with advertisements for toothpaste, and there we'd lose the aristocratic sense of the whole occasion! Have you ever heard the bells from Saint Paul's Church? The sound of the bells is lost in the empty space. It's not a square, Excellency, it's a cattle market! It's no stage for the sort of play we want to put on! How can I arrange a decent funeral in front of advertisements for toothpaste and 'Blitva' soap?"

"I don't give a damn whether it's on Paul's square or the devil's, as long as we know where it's to be! Do you understand?"

"Yes, Excellency!"

"All right, then, give it some thought until tomorrow and then report to me what you've decided. Then give some thought to a monument to Roman Rayevski! I want to raise a monument to Roman Rayevski as my personal gift to the people of Blitva!"

"Only not a figure, Excellency! I beg you! Not a figure! Citizens on plinths look ridiculous! Think only of Waldemaras! How stupid he looks in his frock coat! And any other civilian, in a havelock with an umbrella, cast in bronze, dreadful! I have an idea! Do you remember, Excellency, the tombstone to the Burgundian Philippe

Pot in the Louvre: eight mourning priests bear the dead body of an armored knight on a litter and each one represents a district, bearing the crest of a principality: Burgundy, Brabant, Flanders, and so on. If you remember, Excellency, that tombstone is considered to be the work of Le Moiturier, but it's utterly impossible that it could have been his work, since in his tombstone for Philippe le Bon he's more than banal. And, if you recall, Excellency, Philippe Pot, that knight on his marble slab, who lies stiff, with hands clasped in prayer, helmeted, with a rich pillow under his head, rests his feet on his dog. A wonderful idea such as Le Moiturier couldn't have managed. That some fools ascribe it to Le Moiturier, that's stretching it! Yes, Philippe le Bon who allowed himself to be painted by a Rogier van der Weyden, these were sovereigns of good taste! How would Philippe le Bon, for the life of him, have ever agreed to be painted by a Le Moiturier! So, if I may humbly express an opinion, Excellency, the idea of raising a monument to Rayevski as a political victim is excellent, indeed an act of genius, but I dread a civil figure in trousers and jacket and think that the idea of a sarcophagus, for instance, a closed sarcophagus, would be better! The idea of a coffin borne on the shoulders of eight men, no matter who, be they representatives of the Blitvinian estates or peasants or legionnaires does not matter, the main thing is that there should be eight of them and each should have his crest representing the districts of Blitva that have united in the glorious framework of Blitvinian unity which the dead president symbolized: Ankersgarden, Karabaltic, Kurlandia, the Province of Blitvas-Holm, Ilimenga, Wyborgen, and so on! Perfect!"

"Are you suggesting, Vanini, that Roman Rayevski has earned a monument simply as a 'political victim'? Simply as a 'political victim' and not as an artist, as a creator, as a great European name?"

"Excellency, I beg you most humbly and respectfully not to take me wrong when I ask you to allow me to express myself freely! My principle has always been that regarding artists, even when they're deceased, one should say nothing but the pure truth! The late Rayevski was an interesting artist, hardworking, an ambitious man, a relatively inventive sculptor, a craftsman of not greatly refined taste, yes, and in our Blitvinian ambience, head and shoulders above any of his rivals, that is true. He was unusually strong willed, enduring, tough, alive and alert in three directions at once, an eclectic, and, up to a point, a virtuoso, but a great European name, artist, and creator, no! I take the liberty, Excellency, of denying it!"

"Then what do you say to my monument? Is that what you would consider artistically worthless? According to you, as regards my monument, the explosion wasn't such a bad thing? Interesting!"

"Excellency, I've never had the opportunity nor the good fortune to hear your personal opinions on the question, but it was rumored in the town that you made certain masterly objections to Rayevski, since you were the rider in question, concerning both rider and horse, but, with every respect for your taste, Excellency, which I have no reason to doubt as being highly developed, knowing as I do your collections of Renaissance armor and pottery from Pompeii, with all loyal respect for the value of your time, I will nonetheless be so bold as to draw your attention to some, at first sight, secondary matters regarding that monument and, since some higher fate has decided that we touch upon this failed work this evening of all evenings, when it has, so to speak, vanished, inspired in the most noble sense of the word, regarding the solemn significance of the moment, I could not lie, for I would feel it in the depths of my artistic conscience to be a desecration, were I to lie at such an important, indeed, historic moment! No, indeed, Excellency, regarding your monument, its disappearance presents no objective loss."

Weren't people a stinking disgusting anthill, Barutanski thought, puffing smoke and watching that fool waving his arms, growing excited, and sweating with apprehension, selling his cultural historical droppings, wiping the sweat from his petite suburban forehead. The way he dribbled, the way he waggled his tongue, and all for the sake of casting a shadow over a more gifted rival! Such people should be poisoned, Barutanski decided. How would it be if I poisoned the idiot? Gave him a sandwich with strychnine or a drink with cyanide? He'd squirm like a rat, scream and writhe, foam at the mouth, and then he could go on slandering to his heart's content! But, on the other hand, Barutanski was glad to have someone beside him to slander, no matter whom, no matter what, simply to hear a human voice. Let them lie, libel, deny, smear, no matter, just to have somebody so as not to be alone, for the night was long and he was so fresh, collected, as though he'd got out of bed only a couple of minutes before.

"So what's your assessment of the monument, Vanini? Let's hear it!"

"Excellency, take just the problem of casting an equestrian monument as our first point of view! A rampant horse, that is a typical baroque view of sculpture, which after Canova or Fernkorn, only very bad, third-rate creators of kitsch employed in their monuments as a most common, banal, utterly, almost ridiculously, outworn pattern! To take you, Excellency, like Malatesta, in Renaissance armor, that would be, in the sculptural sense, to take the line of least resistance! It would be just as stupid as if some dramatist, intending to glorify your heroic deeds and the rattle of your arms, presented you as the Father and Creator of Blitva in the romantic form of a Schiller. Imagine, Excellency, how absurd and empty the theme of Colonel Barutanski would sound from the stage, clad in the breastplate of a condottiere and that those around you were to speak in hendecasyllabics or dodecasyllabics. It's a matter of style, of a basically erroneous solution of a problem of literary or visual expression! A dumb, lifeless figure sitting on a heavy Blitvinian mare says nothing to anyone! As such, the horseman is a cliché, a very badly modeled cliché, and the mare is spread over the plinth like a lump of marzipan! That awful horse sits on its back legs like a tomcat trying to shit on the lawn and, to tell the truth, gives a pathetic impression, since here Rayevski has completely failed. It's utter impotence! That monument's a proof of his complete creative weakness. What purpose is served by the Renaissance harness on the horse and that brocaded saddle, and the rich ornamentation on the armor, when your entire character is one of dominant, monumental, royal simplicity? You, by all your achievements, truly represent a classical simplicity and not a baroque with periwig and Renaissance cornucopia! And you see, I, for example, prefer the Flemish primitivists or the French illuminists like Jean Fouquet to such disgustingly sentimental careerists as was Canova. To desire to present you to posterity à la Canova, that is a forgery! And forgery in art is deceit, immeasurably greater than in economics or in trade or in private life! I don't know whether you have seen Peter Vischer's King Arthur in the cathedral at Innsbruck? It's costume for an opera rather than a figure of chivalry! And the all-encompassing character of your work is so obviously a matter of simple, logical, straight, upright, and clear lines that I cannot envisage you cast in some artificial style like Petro's, nor on any rampant horse, nor in a baroque gallop (where the horse's tail is more important than the rider). I, Excellency, do not see you mounted on a fat Blitvinian nag. For me, as an artist, you are no Electoral Prince with a sybaritic double chin in the eighteenth-century style, but a cold-blooded, serious, supple, bony rider on an English horse, as bony and supple as he himself. When you take Penelope, for example, for her morning ride, you are more like yourself than like that richly decorative cheap kitsch mounted on a heavy Kurlandish mare with its bulging nostrils like Saint George's dragon on the Kobilian crest. Kitsch peels off art like the scales from a chicken's skin! For an artist, kitsch is the sign of senility! It's lichen!"

From the end of the corridor in whose oval-shaped niches stood armored knights came His Excellency's personal servant Rafaelo Mazurski, as the bearer of a telephone message or announcing some important nocturnal visitor.

"His Excellency, the minister of the interior is asking for you on a matter of urgency . . ."

"Good night, Vanini! Make up your mind by tomorrow! Building a grandstand is out! You can forget that! And, apart from that, it must be a spectacle for the mass of the public!"

Barutanski approached Burgwaldsen, who appeared from the back of the long corridor that led from Barutanski's apartments, slender and graying, making a black silhouette, with his ministerial portfolio under his arm, with extreme politeness, bowing from the waist like a lackey or a well-trained butler pouring a glass of wine for some high-ranking guest.

"Hello, Burgwaldsen, what's new?"

"I received a report from Kohlinis, Excellency, and I went personally to the scene so I could present you with all the facts!"

"Well, let's have it!"

Barutanski left his minister of the interior to explain, setting off down the gallery with its ranks of armored knights.

The newly appointed Minster of the Interior Burgwaldsen accompanied his master on the left, not beside him, but several centimeters behind the Lord of Blitva, on the edge of the carpet, with a discreet alacrity and with an equally servile posture toward the man to whom, in this, only his second audience, he was the bringer of an entire bundle of important news.

Burgwaldsen had been to Rayevski's house, a wing of which had, by pure chance, remained unscathed, but had assured himself (as Kantorowicz had reported to him, anyway) that it was technically impossible to leave the dead president, or rather the mass of flesh and rags that remained of him, in his house overnight. Therefore

he'd ordered him to be taken to the main vestibule of the Thorwaldsen Palace of the Academy of Arts and Sciences, whose first president he had been, so it was natural for him to sleep the first night of
his eternity under the Academy's roof. There'd been demonstrations in the town. The crowd, angered by this new act of bloodshed,
had spontaneously begun to demonstrate against these subversive
and secret elements, with the result that its anger had taken on a
somewhat undesirable form! The crowd had completely destroyed
the premises of the editorial buildings and press of the *Blitwanen
Tigdende* and the *Morgenbladet*. The flat of Kmetynis's brother, the
dentist Kmetynis, had been totally destroyed, as well as the editorial
and administrative office of Nielsen's *Tribune,* and here the mob had
thrown the entire administrative inventory and furniture onto the
street and publicly burned it. Several Blatvian shops had been
smashed and, what was certainly rather more awkward, some of the
demonstrators had managed to creep unnoticed through the police
cordon and had smashed the windows of the Blatvian Embassy. For
the sake of appearances, several demonstrators had been arrested.

"Were they members of the LOOLP?"

"I don't know, Excellency, I haven't yet received a report!"

"No matter! Let them all go home. Why should they spend the
night in the police station? There's no point! They've damaged the
Blatvian Embassy! That's no big deal! All right, go on!"

"On Jarl Knutson Boulevard they burned the Blatvian flag! They
soaked it in petrol and burned it to the accompaniment of the legionnaires' hymn: 'March on, march on, oh you brigade of Blitva!' Here
too we arrested several youngsters!"

"Good! They burned the Blatvian flag! Excellent! Answer provocation with provocation!"

"I've organized a lying-in-state of the president's coffin. People are
already filing past, and this final mark of respect to the dead president
will last almost all night. That's what you suggested, Excellency!"

"Fine! Go on!"

"I've confiscated the whole of the evening press except for the *Gazette* and the *Turulun!*"

"Go on!"

"I've posted the communiqué of the Ministry of the Interior throughout the town! As well as the communiqué issued by the police! Here it is, Excellency! The police announcement says: 'Citizens of the capital! This evening at eight forty-three, on the corner of Ankersgarden Street and Karabaltic Park, a bomb exploded in the house of the master sculptor Roman Rayevski. The bomb was thrown into the studio, which was completely destroyed, together with all the works of art there and the entire inventory. The damage is incalculable. In the explosion the sculptor academician Roman Rayevski and his main caster, Raius Wilkins, lost their lives. The sculptor and academic Roman Rayevski was president of the Blitvinian Academy of Arts and Sciences and, by the unanimous decision of the Plenum of Estates, nominated as candidate for the presidency of the Republic. Investigations by the police, which were carried out only several minutes after the crime and at the scene of the catastrophe, proved that the material used for the explosion stemmed from the arsenal of a neighboring state. At the scene of the catastrophe, the sculptor Olaf Knutson, who was employed by Rayevski as an assistant, reported himself to Dr. Witusz Kantorowicz, prefect of police of the town of Blitwanen, as being the assassin. Olaf Knutson confessed there and then in front of many witnesses from among the citizens present, whose names are registered (some eighteen of them), that he was personally guilty of the crime. Having been taken to police headquarters for interrogation, he flung himself through the window of the prefect's office and was immediately killed. With regard to this assassination, a number of arrests have been made in the town, since a wider plot is suspected. The widow Karin Michelson has been found hanged in her flat. She was the mistress of Dr. Niels Nielsen, editor of the *Tribune,* for whom a general search has been ordered, as an accomplice of the sculptor Olaf Knutson.'"

"OK! And the communiqué of the Ministry of Foreign Affairs?"

"It was in the form of a large poster in the Blitvinian colors calling on citizens to give free expression to their justified anger, but to beware of agents provocateurs!"

"Is there anything else?"

"There is, Excellency!"

"Well, what?"

"Bad news, Excellency!"

"Go on!"

"In the Café Kiosk on Station Road, on the corner leading to Flaming-Sandersen Square, some unknown person has killed Major Georgis."

Barutanski halted in his striding and, looking down, threw away his cigarette as if it had suddenly made him sick.

"How?"

"With a bottle of rum!"

"What rum?"

"Jamaica!"

So! Jamaica rum! And not long before that, he'd put out a cigarette on his cheek and then thrown him out! Why? For he'd have given his life for him! The only man who thought logically, and those bureaucrats around him thought him mad.

He lit another cigarette and, driven by some dark and compelling necessity, stubbed it out on his left palm! This returned him to reality.

"Is Georgis still there?"

"I think he is, Excellency, since just as I was setting out to come to you, Kohlinis phoned me that he was going to the scene."

"Let's go! Where is it?"

"The Café Kiosk on the corner of Flaming-Sandersen Square and Station Road."

The heavy eight-cylinder Packard slid down the curving drive of the Beauregard park, down the slope of the old Jarl Knutson fortress, like some black motorboat making rapid circles with the white fluorescent tentacles of its powerful headlights. That massive lacquered box silently descended down the road of the old city and, a moment afterward, the lights of Jarl Knutson Boulevard gleamed through the bulletproof windows. The treetops of the avenue, the empty parks, distant music coming from the half-open door of a nightclub, the movement and glare of oncoming limousines, the wet granite of the pavement, squares, churches, passersby, and the unpleasant squeal of tires on the damp road. The Café Kiosk, on the corner of Station Road and Flaming-Sandersen Square, was surrounded by a curious mob that pressed around the café entrance, held back by an entire company of police who'd arrived as escort to the new prefect.

The Café Kiosk had two rooms. In the lesser one, at the back, in a corner under a table, lay Major Georgis. What remained of the major, there in the corner beside a spittoon, was truly horrible. The whole room had the sweetish, vanillalike smell of rum which had spilt from the bottle that had shattered Georgis's skull. Georgis lay under the table with his right hand caught in the motion of drawing his Browning from his hip pocket.

Barutanski entered, removing his cap, and thus bareheaded stood for several minutes in silence. All those present removed their headgear in imitation and were silent.

Without a single thought, Barutanski, still without a word, turned and went back to his car. Only when he was seated in the Packard did he realize he was bareheaded. He immediately replaced his cap. Beside the Packard stood Burgwaldsen.

"Ah, yes, it's you, Burgwaldsen? Are you left without a car?"

"Not to worry, Excellency! Kohlinis is here and he has a car, and in any case I am going back to the precinct. Kerinis has called for assistance. It looks as if they're on Nielsen's track."

"To Zheleznyuvka!"

(Zheleznyuvka in a straight line on a relatively good road was some forty-three kilometers distant from the railway station.)

The Packard vanished down the muddy road.

"Zheleznyuvka, Excellency!" the driver announced some minutes later.

"Back!"

The Packard's curtains were drawn. The needle on the speedometer gleamed in a greenish light that reflected with its fluorescence in the complete darkness of the closed and cushioned box. The silhouette of the man behind the wheel, in that greenish glow, had something magical about it, and the lights from right and left crawled over the windows like the flashing of the Morse code. Now long, now short, now long, now short, like the letters on a telegraph. Da-di-di-di, da-da, da-di-di-di-di-di, da-da! It was death calling.

"What lights are those?"

"It's Blitwanen Station, Excellency!"

"Stop here and wait for me!"

In a split second, the man was at the glass doors of the Packard with the door handle in one hand and his cap in the other, bowing from the waist to his master, and, as he bent, one could see that he was almost bald. He had a skinny, tubercular neck that peeped from his fur collar like the neck of a vulture. All that was there were the fences of Blitwanen Station and mud. The real, thick, Blitwanen mud. On the other side of the fence an engine was shunting. An old-fashioned engine, long retired from main service, with a shallow, platelike chimney, and the man who was shoveling coal into the open furnace had a red handkerchief wrapped around his head beneath his sooty cap. In all probability because of a toothache.

He had a toothache but was still working there, shoveling the fire, all bathed in its glow, Barutanski thought, staring over the fence at the wheezing, pitiful engine that moved up and down the rails, leaving in its wake clouds of dense, sooty, and acrid smoke.

> HO–ho, HA–ho, HA–ho,
> HE–ho, HA–ho, HO–ho, HO–ho . . .
> HE–ho, HA–ho, HE–ho, HE–ho,
> HO–ho, HO–ho, HO–ho, HO–ho . . .
> Ksssssssss.

"HO–ho, HO–ho, HO–ho, HO–ho, kssssssss, piha, piha, puffff . . ." Barutanski began to imitate the cranky old engine. It sounded like a pig being killed, that engine on its rails, and everything was being killed and everything went like that. And that fireman had a toothache! And what now? Georgis was gone. And that had its good side! He was the only one left who could have borne witness to the Kavalierski case. It wouldn't have been very likely, since he was the one who did the shooting. But then! That gamekeeper in Luzhovitze, Valent, he'd gone to hell. And now Georgis was gone too!

HO–ho, HO–ho, HO–ho, HO–ho, the little old-fashioned engine coughed and spluttered, whistled, sighed, groaned, grew angry and defiant, and Barutanski, staring over the railway fence into the darkness, comprehended nothing except that the engine was going HO–ho, HO–ho, HO–ho, HO–ho. He felt a burning in the palm of his hand. He felt a pain under his left arm. From somewhere in the distance, from a bar, came the sound of an accordion. Someone was playing "Blitvania is little, but it is its people's pride!"

HO–ho, HO–ho, HO–ho, HO–ho, hissed, whined, and bleated the little engine with its fireman and his toothache, flouncing down the rails and belching hot coals. The richly lit coaches of the Blitwanen Express thundered past. Again the Morse signals in the rails. Again telegrams of death. Da–di–di, dididi. . . .

Who was that waving to Barutanski from the well-lit train? Surely it wasn't Georgis? Barutanski stared after the red lights of the Express that were vanishing in a cloud of smoke and fog, and that tedious little old-fashioned engine came back once more along the same rails: HO–ho, HO–ho, HO–ho, HO–ho. . . . A porter went by pushing a trolley. He worked for the Hotel Blitvania and was dressed in a green jacket with egg-shaped brass buttons no larger than sparrow's eggs. He wore a red cap on which was written in golden letters "Hotel Blitvania." He was wheeling a trolley loaded with luggage, high-quality, gentlemanly stuff with expensive kid covers, and, among the suitcases, a bouquet of faded Makart roses. It was wrapped in white tissue paper, which had come undone and the roses shook, peeping from beneath their white cover. They nodded their limp heads. They showed surprise: Oh, la-la! Oi, oi, oi, just look! said they, looking at Barutanski in surprise and nodding their buds at him. HO–ho, HO–ho, puffed the tired old lady in the fog. The fine rain went on falling and there, on the fence, was a huge placard, an advertisement for shaving soap. A merry, youthful, male face smiled with its healthy teeth out at that miserable night and, boyishly challenging, violently lathered his cheeks and drew his razor through the foam and, over all, in large red letters was written:

> Blitva shaving soap's unique,
> It gives a smooth, well-shaven cheek.

CHAPTER 4

And Melancholy Can Burst from a Man Like Lava from a Volcano

The man who killed Georgis was Niels Nielsen. After the shooting at Dominic's (which ended in spilt borscht, but could well have meant the end of Nielsen), Olaf Knutson, seriously worried about the fate of his friend, hid him in the flat of his relative, the old and deaf Mrs. Gallen, as a last resort, until he could arrange Nielsen's flight to Blatvia.

In the home of this deaf and slightly deranged old lady, Nielsen felt most uncomfortable. The stuffy rooms with their dark brown doors, where all was hung with doubly lined curtains, in the locked and lonely flat of the old lady, there was something fateful, unde-fined, obscure, something that did not lend itself to normal de-scription, but that hovered over the quiet and forgotten area of the first floor like the echo of a passing bell. In the striking of the old-fashioned clocks beneath their glass domes wavered a voice of dark foreboding: that the time for superhuman effort had arrived, that, with every minute, the moment was approaching when Niels Nielsen would dip his hands in warm human blood.

The whole of that first-floor suburban flat at 5A, the Promenade, first right, was really settled and maintained for one reason only: to preserve upon this earth the cult of the memory of Mrs. Gallen's only son, the deceased Sigurd, whom Barutanski's soldiers had shot, only because he had "carried out his patriotic duty as a Blitvinian of-ficer who had sworn an oath to the legal government and had fallen, sword in hand, defending what was, by all positive laws, the legal government!" Everything in those rooms was crowded with Sigurd's photographs, his sabers, rapiers, fencing gloves and helmets, hunting and riding gear, saddles, the photographs of horses and their rid-ers—in a word, the trivia of chivalry which appeared so unimportant and yet, despite this, contained so much vital resistance that they, in their wholeness, their complete and utter objective intactness, ex-isted long, long after the death of their owners, rotting in the grave. The saddle, for instance, was brand new and still had the fresh smell of Russian leather, that lasting, sharp, freshly polished leather. Of the rider who, like a passing shadow, had rocked two or three times in this, his new saddle, there was no longer a trace; two or three snaps on which fanned out the damp spots of time, two or three flowers be-neath the glass of a beloved picture, two or three letters, and such-like: mainly rags and scraps of paper. Or bare cavalry sabers, crossed rapiers, or, in a wardrobe, a uhlan's dress uniform which Mrs. Gallen carefully brushed every second day, as if her Sigurd was about to ring the doorbell, to return home, young and laughing, and begin his elaborate male toilette in preparation to go to a dance. There would be a nervous turmoil throughout the flat, the banging of doors, the shouting for the orderly, and over the velvet tablecloths would be spread a great mass of bottles, jars, wax, scissors, scattered cases. Here would lie razors, soaps, hairnets, polished boots with the wooden trees removed. Spurs would rattle. The orderly would bring hot water. The room, the flat, the whole house at 5A, the Prome-nade, the entire street, everything, the whole of Blitwanen would be filled with laughter, shouting, and whistling, and when all this hustle was lost on the stairs (down which Sigurd, ever boyishly, leapt three steps at a time, at such a speed that he reached the front door like a missile shot from a bow), now, here, remained ever this pile of Sig-urd, like the aftermath of a play. Open bottles, dishes of shaving soap, belts, cast-off underwear, suits, shoes, sabers, revolvers, wal-lets, spilt water over the floor, the parquet, the carpets, over the velvet tablecloth, the smell of eau de cologne, the fresh scent of lavender. Of this elemental whirlwind there remained in the rooms and the whole flat so many waftings, scents, such feelings of health and joy, that the old lady Gallen sensed this youthful energy as her own vital inspiration, which bore her, full sail, toward new possibilities, illusions, the fullness of life. And then, one afternoon, it all stopped and, since that fateful afternoon, everything remained motionless in the same place, like a clock with a broken spring that had stopped, never to move.

The old Mr. Gallen, a relatively wise and farsighted exporter of salt fish, insured his immediate heirs with a small but solid life income from Sweden. It arrived from Stockholm with mathematical regularity every third of the month, by means of a draft on the Blitvinian National Bank, increasing each year, in inverse proportion to the value of the Blitvinian lei, which, year by year, fell with a truly extraordinary and constant mathematical certainty.

The old lady's household was entirely isolated from the real outside Blitvinian life, so that Dr. Nielsen, after two or three days in these rooms, felt like a shipwrecked sailor who had swum out of a stormy, nerve-racking uncertainty into a warm refuge of soft, old-fashioned armchairs, under the warm intimate glow of pearl-shaded lamps, where the silence was absolute, and no sound came even from the Promenade, since there, under the avenue of ancient plane trees, there were usually few passersby. To smoke, to keep awake, to read, to read, to smoke, to keep awake and night after night converse with a deaf old lady concerning things trivial and of no importance became, day by day, less bearable. Olaf Knutson, a man who had lost his nerve and was far more shaken than one could have guessed at first glance, from the first day of this somewhat involved situation had not coped well, and when the driver, a man Nielsen knew and trusted, who worked in a nearby garage and who was to drive Nielsen over the border, was arrested, Knutson was so shaken that he admitted to Nielsen one evening that he was losing control.

From the beginning, Nielsen had felt that there was little sense in wasting days in this dusty, locked flat, but Olaf Knutson, sincerely concerned for Nielsen's fate, so exaggerated every slightest danger that his help slowly became a real and uncomfortable hindrance. Olaf Knutson had put off Nielsen's departure more and more insistently, since he could not understand "how a man could set off into the fog, into the night, into complete uncertainty without a single lei in his pocket," not believing Nielsen that he had all he needed and that for the moment a thousand lei was quite sufficient.

"A thousand dollars, that's the least you need with you," Olaf Knutson repeated day after day, promising Nielsen categorically that he would come the next morning with a thousand dollars, but the next day he would return all the more depressed and miserable, with a brow of thunder, without the thousand dollars, without any money, without anything, saying what swine people were! Everything for Nielsen's departure was ready: identity in the name of a pharmacist from Ankersgarden and a police registration card with Nielsen's latest photograph (without a mustache and wearing dark spectacles), only Olaf Knutson continued to hesitate to set in motion the extremely complex organization of contacts and addresses until he had arranged "the finances." But these "finances" of Knutson's dragged on and on and Nielsen felt, nervously, that it was stupid to lose one's life just because of an imagined thousand dollars, so that gradually he arrived at the decision to go ahead without Knutson's agreement, come what might!

The night before, he hadn't slept a single second, all night, until the ringing of the morning church bells. That morning the police had been at the downstairs flat of the house on the other side of the avenue, opposite Mrs. Gallen's.

Through the open windows one could see into the old German dining room with its sofa in green velvet and, above it, still lifes in flat round frames: peaches, cherries, and apples. The maid had already begun her morning cleaning. She'd opened the windows, placed the old-fashioned German chairs upside down on the table, and so the peasant girl moved up and down mysteriously in the lit room, touching frames and bowing to certain pieces of furniture, mysterious and invisible, concealed behind the walls. In his waking hours, staring at the ceiling of his quiet room, Niels Nielsen knew that it was past six o'clock, due to the lighting up of the yellowish quadrangle of light through the open windows of the opposite flat on the other side of the avenue.

The maid had lit the lamp in the old German dining room; the day had begun!

For reasons he could not tell, Nielsen found the appearance of that empty, well-lit, old-fashioned German dining room somehow appealing. Long ago, while he was serving in the Hunnish-Aragon army, on the outskirts of Blitwanen, he'd fallen in love with a girl who lived at the end of the town in just such an old-fashioned German dining room, with its flat wooden still lifes hung above the sofa. To the right, in the corner, just as in that mysterious room, stood a dark lacquered piano and, beside the sofa, a bookcase with gilt-bound encyclopedia. The love of Nielsen's youth, his ideal, his Laura, had played a Hunnish operatic song ("Hello, Farewell") on the dark-colored piano of a downstairs old-fashioned German dining room. That stupid operatic tune, that popular song about "the falling leaves," around 1911 had captured Eastern Europe from Blitva and Blatvia to Tzigania and Hindustania, and now, so many years later, the same tune stirred like a lyrical memory of a girl who in just such an old-fashioned German dining room painted roses on silk and wrote Nielsen stupid letters. The bells of Saint Bernard's were ringing. Soon dawn would break in the old-fashioned German dining room across the way!

The quadrangle of light fell across the ceiling of Nielsen's room that morning rather earlier. Nielsen got up to see what was happening so early across the street in the old-fashioned German dining room, but that morning the chairs were not on the table, everything in the room was motionless, and why the window was left open, no one could say! A morning police search of the flat. Hurried, agitated movement of people, the slamming of doors, anxiety and disturbance, and on the table of the old-fashioned German dining room a heap of objects: books, bundles of clothes, boxes of photographs. . . . Many detectives. And outside, a police cordon. And then the light went off again and everything mysteriously vanished. A detachment of sentries marched by beneath Nielsen's window with a quiet, rather tired step: left-right, left-right, and the fog was so dense that the detachment of dark figures literally vanished into it. They were swallowed in the Blitvinian fog and, at that, down to their shoulders, so that at one moment it appeared as though the detachment were marching without heads.

That mysterious morning event worried Nielsen not a little. Then there was the fact that Olaf Knutson had not showed up for coffee, as they'd agreed. The whole afternoon passed and still no Olaf Knutson. There was no sign of him and already it was growing quite dark. Waiting every moment for his friend to arrive, Niels Nielsen took up Tacitus, which he had been glancing through for several days, since he'd taken up residence on the sofa in the old lady Gallen's dining room. To pull himself together, to conquer his inner anxiety, he skimmed through Tacitus the whole afternoon.

Dacia, Thrace, Illyria, Scythia, Sarmatia, Mongolia, Hunnia, Blitvania, ever the same picture through all the centuries: filthy waters, thick like overthickened soup; peasants in rough linen trousers, barefoot, hairy, bearded, eerie, hungry, threatening peasants. Huts made of reeds, lathe, of mud. The waters flowed, the Ister, the Blitva, the Ilmenga, the Blatva, all those massive muddy waters flowed and, in their quiet, undisturbed mirror, their flow was imperceptible, yet they flowed constantly, without pause, and there, through that mass of peasantry, today they bore Colonel Kristian Barutanski, just as yesterday they carried the divine Augustus on his golden litter. And what would remain of it all? Bells were ringing in the town.

That was Saint Bernard's and still no Olaf Knutson. Why didn't he come? Somebody rang the doorbell.

That wasn't Olaf! Olaf had his own key. Was it the police? Mrs. Gallen was not at home. . . . She was at church. It was all right for her. She had her father-confessor, Father Bonaventura Baltrushaitis. Someone was still ringing the doorbell! Constantly, persistently!

Nielsen got up, pushed aside the red velvet tablecloth, and from the drawer drew out his pistol and placed it on the red velvet and then quietly, on tiptoe, silently, carefully opening the door so as to make the least possible noise, he crept into the dark corridor, where, on the front door, was a metal-framed peephole. Breathlessly he approached the door and peered through the hole. In front of the door stood Karin Michelson. He hadn't seen her since the day when he'd learned from Major Georgis that his so dear and beloved lady was in the service of the Beauregard "P" Section. At the very beginning of their acquaintance, she'd hinted, more between the lines than directly, that she was doing some work for the "P" Section, but, to judge by what she said, that was only of a technical nature, typing and suchlike, more or less as a means of supplementing her pension, which was so small that she could not live off it. So as to convince Nielsen of her hundred percent sympathy for him, from time to time she had passed copies of certain documents of the "P" Section to him which Kmetynis, as head of the Blitvinian Agrarian Party in exile, employed abundantly in his campaign against Barutanski. Niels Nielsen belonged to that race of naive people who, as males, never suspected their females, yet he had never had any particular faith in that carefree laughing woman. The matter of his "Open Letter" to

Barutanski he had never considered particularly confidential, all the more so since the draft which he'd not only given to Mrs. Michelson for copying, but had also signed, was itself in principle an "Open Letter," hence, by its very nature, public. But when Major Georgis threw his manuscript down on the table as proof that the Michelson was one of their agents, Niels Nielsen, faced with such proof, accepted it and wrote a few words to her, a short letter, logical, succinct, a very dramatic letter, putting an end to their brief love affair. *Major Georgis today has returned my "Open Letter" to me which was in your possession and I think that in this matter, as in all others, words are superfluous between us!*

To which Karin Michelson replied: *The letter you mention was stolen from me and I swear to you by my life that I'm not to blame and beg you to give me the chance of explaining it to you in person,* but they had not met.

Thank you for your letter. I'm glad that it was as you say, but I think that any personal explanations between us are superfluous. I believe you that the letter was stolen, but, unfortunately, I cannot believe that this might not happen a second time.

After that, Karin Michelson came to his flat several times. Twice he found her visiting card and once did not answer the door. Whenever she phoned, he put the phone down. Since then, there'd been the shooting at Dominic's and he'd been nearly two weeks at old Mrs. Gallen's, and now there was that mysterious Karin from the "P" Section ringing his doorbell! Nervously. Insistently. Over and over again. Sighed and rang again.

How could she know that he was staying at Mrs. Gallen's? Knutson? Impossible! Old Mrs. Gallen? The same. . . . They'd found him! They'd be coming to arrest him! Karin would have earned her blood money!

Nielsen stood in the dark hall on the other side of the front door, his eye pressed to the peephole, his heart beating so hard that he felt it in his eyeballs. Goggle-eyed, scarcely breathing, the blood pounding through his veins, he froze there in the dark, waiting for the ringing to stop. Karin Michelson went on ringing, lit by the yellowish lamp that cast a weak light on the staircase, and then turned and, with a deep sigh and bowed head, went off down the stairs. She vanished into the dusk. She disappeared from the glass peephole, as though descending into the grave. Step by step. Nielsen felt relief. He was convinced she was seeking him in the name of Barutanski, Georgis, the police, as provocation, in the name of death.

He tiptoed back into the room, hid his pistol under the velvet tablecloth, closed the drawer, rearranged the tablecloth, and lit a cigarette. Once more he picked up Tacitus.

Ostia and Rome were burned by marauders. The light blue lines of the waters merged with the greenish reflection of the sky, wavering in the sun's rays in the light of a southern morning. Warm spring weather. Boats had arrived from Greece bringing figs, oil, dates, salted fish, and bales of good wool from Asia Minor. And on the narrow Roman streets came the sound of a bloody massacre. Once more an imperial overofficer had led the legions to revolt, promising the mob loot, and his comrade overofficers a general's helmet. . . . Centurions became brigadiers, brigadiers ambassadors, generals became senators with a hope of a pension, and someone stood on the corner and yowled to the stinking mob of slaves that a slave was just as much a man as a patrician! And now? Now just such an imperial gentleman would charge through all of Europe like a wild boar, under the sun, in the shade of the olive trees, through the vineyards and gardens, beneath the clear sky where fountains splashed. Such a centurion would howl like a mad dog. He was howling today through Blitva. He drove peaceful people to have to hide pistols under tablecloths. He bribed whores to spy on their lovers. He broke into the homes of citizens and nothing was to be heard except the march of his brigades. . . . Karin Michelson and her ilk played a role even in Rome. And the Blitvinians migrated from the upper Dnieper, from the Volga. They came from the Ganges together with the Scythian and Tartar hordes, and why do such barbarians today mix with Europe? Where was Blitva going? Rome too lived in an eternal panic. Poisonous snakes poisoned imperial children in their cradles and the entire Palatine was in terror of having such snakes put in their beds. Poisonous snakes crawled around the imperial palaces and it was said that the only guarantee that a man would not fall victim to a snakebite was to wear a cast-off snakeskin. All the courtiers of the Palatine wore bracelets of snakeskin, for none ever knew where snake poison awaited him, to cast him into the underworld.

"Special edition of the *Blitwanen Tigdende!*" A high-pitched child's voice echoed out of the foggy distance, fading away amid the trees of the Promenade toward the Jesuit church. "Special edition of the *Blitwanen Tigdende!* Of the *Turulun Gazette,* of the *Blitva Herald,* special edition. 'Assassination of the President of the Republic'! 'Death of the President of the Republic'!"

Voices from the fog! Voices from the fog and darkness of Blitva! Voices from hell!

What president of the Republic? Blitva had no president! Could it have been Barutanski? Could Karin Michelson have come to tell him about it?

Excited, the tips of his fingers colder than the brass handles on the windows, feeling himself on the brink of unconsciousness like a man choking with asthma, his heart in his throat and in all his joints, Nielsen opened the window in order to hear what was going on outside in the street under the avenue of the park, on the squares, on Jesuit Square from which, out of the fog, came the dread cries of the newsboys proclaiming the death of Roman Rayevski!

"Special edition of the *Blitvinian Gazette*! The assassin Olaf Knutson commits suicide! The death of Roman Rayevski! Bomb attack in the studio of Roman Rayevski!"

All on his own, in old Mrs. Gallen's flat (she still hadn't come back from church), Niels Nielsen did not know what to do.

Had Olaf Knutson killed Roman Rayevski? That day? That evening? That afternoon? Why hadn't he come as they'd agreed, when Nielsen was supposed to depart? What did Karin Michelson want? What a madhouse! One thing was clear: He had to leave that flat immediately! No matter how risky the circumstances. At once!

He found himself outside the front door so quickly that, after he'd slammed the door, which was fitted with a patent lock without a knob, he realized that he'd left his revolver in the drawer in the dining room and that he'd left his draft of his "Letter to the Peoples of Blitva and Blatvia" on the table. No matter! With the revolver or without it! The draft was of no importance! If he managed to get away alive, the peoples of Blitva and Blatvia would have a chance of learning his thoughts, without it! He bought a copy of the *Blitvinian Gazette* from an old woman and, having read a few lines, learned everything he needed in order to get by. Not knowing what was going on until that moment, he'd been in a panic, but now, suddenly, under the pale light of a gas lamp, Niels Nielsen came to his senses. However contradictory it might seem, still in shock as he was, he felt a strange and intelligent, almost an exalted, peace. He needed all his strength of will, for even the slightest error could be fatal. At once, as though he'd planned it, without a second's thought, he took a taxi on the other side of the street under the trees and ordered it to take him to Vilinsk.

Vilinsk, a district of holiday villas about three kilometers from the town center, was the focus of Blitva's affluent suburbia. On an idyllic hill above the Blitvinian marshes were several elegant restaurants with gardens, and there Nielsen planned to gain time. That was the first thing. Second, perhaps, to get in touch with some of his secure addresses in the town? Should he telephone Karin Michelson? What worried him most was that he didn't know what had happened to the driver from the Dynamo Garage. Olaf Knutson had been his only link. Olaf Knutson had killed Rayevski, the Michelson had rung the doorbell at Mrs. Gallen's, it all resembled iron filings around a magnet and presented an ever greater riddle.

"Stop in front of the villa of the minister Dr. Gdanyski!"

The taxi stopped in front of Gdanyski's villa. He paid it and went to the entrance. He opened the gates of the iron railings and vanished into the park. He knew that Gdanyski didn't live there during the winter and that there were only servants present and that the garden gates were open. In any case, he'd find some excuse, if they asked him. However, he didn't have to, since he didn't meet a living person. When he returned, the taxi had gone. There wasn't a soul in sight anywhere in the street. Fog. Distant barking of dogs. He set off to the left, knowing from experience that by going up to the pavilion he'd gain some twenty minutes.

It was ten minutes to ten. The Ankersgarden Express left at 12:05. He'd get on without a ticket and pretend to the ticket collector that he'd lost his ticket a few minutes before. He entered the restaurant. There was a pair of lovers. The radio was on. Live from Berlin. *Ariadne auf Naxos*. Richard Strauss. He was glad not to be alone and to have the radio on. He ordered some food and undertook calmly to play his part. With some effort, he pretended to be hungry. He struggled through a steak, with cheese and black coffee, right up to five till eleven. Then he paid the bill and set off for the town at a swift pace. Three and a half kilometers meant thirty-five minutes, plus ten minutes from the restaurant to Vilinsk, plus seven minutes to the station, which meant he'd be in the vicinity about twelve, and at twelve the Ankersgarden Express would be already entering the station, and he could go straight through the waiting room onto the train. He couldn't get rid of the image of Karin Michelson going down the stairs! Perhaps he'd been wrong not to have opened the door! The closer he got to Blitwanen the more he was aware of the uproar. Beyond the Saint Bernard's monastery, against the misty sky, fires reflected like a huge fan. Over the Blitvinian bridges, from Waldemaras Park, surged a vast black mass of people.

That was the *Blitwanen Tigdende* on fire! His Lordship from Beauregard was cooking his *potage blithuanien*! He was doing a good job of it!

Down the boulevard named for Jarl Knutson, the electoral duke of Blitvania, came a vast procession of demonstrators. They were returning from Waldemaras Park, where, in front of the monument to the bard of Blitvinian freedom, they had burned the Blatvian flag. They came as a huge, restless crowd, with banners, torches, placards, with drums and trumpets, headed by an infantry detachment of the LOOLP in its new dark blue uniforms and accompanied by its band, plus a squadron of its cavalry mounted on well-groomed white mares. The bands banged on their drums and cymbals, the torches smoked, and that mixture of Blitvinian fog and liquor, that skillfully directed rhinoceros stupidity of the mindless mob, that false mixture of the traffic laws, of Blitvinism, balalaikas, of flag-waving romantic enthusiasm, that massive confidence trick made up of conscious deceit and obscure truths, that bloody omelette of hatred and illiterate, shortsighted malice, that aroused element of blind street passions and well-disguised self-interest, all that rolled in front of Niels Nielsen like a hellish flood, dangerously and greedily, and he, standing in the shadow of the trees, felt it passing him like the flow of sulfurous lava that could swallow him at any moment. In face of death, he felt all right! At that moment Nielsen was heading, full steam, toward finding himself.

Behind him, on the lawns of Jarl Knutson Boulevard, stood an entire row of marble busts of the great men of Blitvinian history, mainly foreigners, highly privileged imperial favorites, each of whom had more than forty thousand Blitvinian serfs and now stood in the free capital of the Republic of Blitva as a proof of its ancient greatness and glory! Those marble busts of the Blitvinian great, who died in debauchery, of vascular disease, who fought each other in bouts of drunkenness and lechery, who were shut away in madhouses and monasteries, those Kurlandish grooms, whose one ideal was to be present at some military parade in the imperial Aragon-Hunnish Saint Kristianborg. Those aristocratic gentlemen flogged the flesh off their Blitvinian serfs for centuries, cut their genitals, ears, and tongues, tied them to horses' tails, shot our game and raped our Blitvinian girls, and now people wrote dissertations and delivered lectures about them at Blitva University, all because a letter from Diderot seemed to say that Diderot considered Blitva a cultured nation. "Blitva, even in Diderot's day, was at the height of European civilization," so they wrote today in university essays, and today, in the time of Colonel Barutanski, those same Blitvinian serfs howled beneath their marble lords to a vampire and for his sake burned the Blatvian flags!

"Down with the Blatvian murderers! Down with them! Down with Blatvia! War with Blatvia! Long live our ancient principality of Blitva! Long live the lands of the Blitvinian crown! Long live Barutanski, our dictator! Glory to Roman Rayevski! Down with the murderers! Death to the assassins! Down with the Constitution! Long live the president of the Republic, Kristian Barutanski! Hurrah!"

In general, faced with chaotic events in life, man was helpless! Chaos, from one point of view, which did not have to be very exalted, was truly ridiculous, if that view were only three intellectual millimeters above it. Chaos was ridiculous, indeed disgusting! It needed to be overcome. One had to oppose chaos at the cost of one's own life! What did these cannibals with their banners and their brass bands mean? That mixture of mud, stupidity, wind, and the grimy smoke of their torches, those drunken, lascivious whores who screamed in delirium and every other one of them a Karin Michelson! They'd killed Olaf Knutson, thrown him through a window, and now they were howling like cannibals over his corpse and burning Blatvian flags! Marx had put it rightly when he said that the shame of a people was its anger at itself. And were a people truly to be ashamed of itself, it would be like a lion crouching, gathering itself to spring. But those gentlemen, those democratic members of the LOOLP felt no shame at their Blitvinian debasement, for the spring of a lion was not for them! They were dogs! They were Blitvophiles! And who was not with them according to their ideas and manners, let him settle for being thrown through a window!

> Heh, Blitvinians, our forefathers'
> Spirits still within us dwell . . .

sang the mass of Blitvophiles, and Nielsen removed his hat and remained bareheaded to the very last line.

"Long live Colonel Barutanski, the dictator of Blitva! Long live Barutanski! Death to the assassins! Down with Blatvia!"

On the corner of Skripnik Street, Nielsen caught a taxi and ordered it to take him to the station. The taxi sped down the ill-lit Skripnik Street. He glanced up at Karin Michelson's flat, 27 Skripnik Street, first floor. All the windows were lit. Karin had guests! All her rooms were lit. What had she wanted? The procession had robbed him of more than nine minutes. It was exactly midnight. At 12:03 he entered the old station building, where the counters in the small entrance hall resembled the cashier windows at the totalizators at the race courses in large towns. A mass of squares with numbers. Red numbers. Black numbers. Notices. Windows and faces behind the windows.

There were few people in the entrance hall, yet there was a fair amount of movement. A creaky trolley loaded with chicken coops, women's hat boxes, suitcases, a Dominican friar, and several cavalry officers.

He glanced at the large face of the station clock. It was three minutes past twelve.

There was still two minutes, Nielsen thought; I'd better get a ticket like a normal passenger, it was less conspicuous!

"First class to Ankersgarden, please!"

"Here you are!"

The face behind the glass panel didn't give him a look. The sound of a stamp, the rattle of change on the glass surface. Behind Nielsen were several people with parcels wrapped in newspaper. Everything absolutely normal.

"Has the Ankersgarden Express arrived?"

"No sir! The Ankersgarden Express is running forty-three minutes late. Next, please!"

His plan thus upset, Nielsen stood for a moment and then, head down and at a quick pace, set off for the square in front of the station. The wind was rocking the large street lamps and the shadows of objects and cabs swayed like drunks. Like a lighthouse in the fog, in the center of the square, stood the bronze statue of Flaming-Sandersen amid the mud and horse piss, holding up his right hand constantly and motionlessly, as though intending to halt a cab. Still another forty-four minutes! One thing was beyond doubt, he couldn't go on standing in this empty square in front of the station. Instinctively he set off toward Station Road and there, right on the corner of Flaming-Sandersen Square, in a small garden, was the Café Kiosk.

From the café came the sound of an accordion, to the notes of which sailors were getting drunk and the accordionist, himself drunk, with a sailor's cap on his head, was singing, to the accompaniment of his accordion, rough sailor's couplets.

> As the boat came into land,
> I squeezed the woman by her hand.
> But the woman, like a wise old hen,
> Wanted two, three more jumps then . . .
> Hey, how's that, hey, why's that?

Through the noisy and smoke-filled crush of the café, between the waiters bringing the sailors bottles of rakia, serving the drunken company beer laced with rum, through the uproar of the small and overcrowded space, where behind a marble counter, decorated with silver dishes and teapots (between two brass shelves on which were piled pyramids of sugar cubes, and glass lilies in which were stuck red paper roses), there sat an old red-haired woman. Niels Nielsen pushed his way to the glass telephone booth and closed the door behind him. He'd made up his mind, nonetheless, to phone the Michelson. To ask her what she wanted to tell him. It could have been important!

"Thirty-two-thirty-one, please!"

"Thirty-two-thirty-one," a female voice repeated from the exchange and, a second later, he heard the phone ringing. It went on ringing for some time.

No one was answering! How the hell could that be when only three minutes ago her whole flat was lit?

"Hello," a rough male voice answered.

"Hello, is that Mrs. Michelson's flat?"

"Yes! Who do you want, please?"

"General Michelson's wife, please!"

"She's dead!"

"What?"

"She's hanged herself. We're just taking her to the mortuary!"

"And who are you?"

"We're from the Miserere undertakers!

> When the boat came into land,
> I took the sailor by the hand.
> But he, a right old sexy swine,
> Cared not for manners such as mine.
> Hey, how's that, hey, why's that?

"Bravo, bravissimo, bis, bis, bis," the café shrieked. The accordion echoed. The sailors sang. There was a click of billiard balls on the green baize. Hot punch flamed on silver trays, and the bluish flames played over the glasses of rum that rocked in the waiter's hand like living headstone lamps and Nielsen made his way through the café, pushing through the drunken, noisy crowd without an idea what might happen to him in the next minutes. "The Ankersgarden Express is running forty-three minutes late."

Should I go and sit in the back room? he thought that moment, and, pushing his way through the billiard players who were just chalking their cues with pastel blue chalk, he threw open the dark red curtain which divided the back room from the rest of the café, so as to serve as a sort of private compartment. That light-green-painted room, with gold-framed Alpine scenes on the walls and with round marble tables, was empty. There were two exits. One led to the café corridor, where the yells of drunken sailors came from the urinal, and the other led through the glass doors onto the street. The room was lit by a dark blue lamp wrapped in blue tissue paper, a remnant of some recent party, for neither the garlands nor the various colored paper chains, which decorated the ceiling like a form of canopy, had been removed. To the right, on a round marble table, stood a bottle of Jamaica rum and a burning cigar in the ashtray. Judging by the glasses beside the bottle and the burning cigar and the unfinished black coffee for two, it was apparent that the table was taken by a loving couple who had just stepped out for a moment. Nielsen sat down at the other table, to the left of the red curtain over the door. For some time no waiter appeared and the idiot in the café beyond the curtain was bleating out for the thirty-third time to the accompaniment of his rowdy accordion—

> When the boat came in to land,
> I squeezed the sailor by the hand,
> But the sailor was a randy old boar
> And wanted it thirty-three times more . . .
> Hey, how's that, hey, why's that?

—when, from the door leading to the urinal, Georgis appeared. With a violent, drunken gesture, Georgis slammed the stinking lavatory door behind him and, at that moment, the bloated and swollen hunk of a man appeared to Nielsen like a one-eyed monster. He had made the scar under his left eye bleed by nervous rubbing with his handkerchief. Melancholy-drunk, belching, in the grip of his depression at having, by his own stupidity, made a mess of so many important matters that evening, Major Georgis did indeed resemble a drunken Cyclops, who staggered, one eyed, between the urinal and the sailors' den, like a wild boar, grunting, cursing, and muttering like a mad rhinoceros. Nielsen instantly leapt up with the intention of hiding behind the red curtain, but it was too late. Georgis recognized his prey with the excellent scent of a trained dog.

"Oh, Doctor, Doctor, where are you off to?" Georgis stepped up to Nielsen with a deeply joyous tone in his voice, at the same time reaching with his right hand for the revolver in his hip pocket.

There was no time for thought. At that instant, as though by long premeditated intention, Nielsen struck Georgis on the head with the bottle of Jamaica rum with such force that all he could sense was the green glass of the bottle cutting into the bloody mess that, beneath this animal blow, spread out spontaneously, and Georgis collapsed beneath the table as though, in superhuman fury, someone had hurled a pot of bloody jam, so that that mass of drunken flesh splashed down by the wall near the spittoon like a dead object. The same instant, Niels Nielsen sensed a pause in the café uproar and, in the shocked outcries from the drunken company, to the scraping of chairs, vanished through the glass doors. In two jumps he was out of the garden in front of the café and then proceeded down the pavement with a slow, calm stride, his hands in his pockets, down the avenue toward the station. As he was passing the Flaming-Sandersen monument, he heard from beyond the corner of Station Road cries of "Police, police!" Voices from the mist. The trotting of a cabby's nag on the granite street. The hooting of a car.

"What is it? What's happened?" someone cried, running in the opposite direction from Nielsen toward Station Road.

"There's been a fight among the sailors in the Kiosk," came the answer from a passerby in the fog.

"Those bloody sailors! Wherever they are, there's always trouble! I'd forbid the lot of them getting drunk like that. . . ."

Twelve-seventeen appeared on the lighted circle of the station clock. That meant still thirty-one minutes till the arrival of the Ankersgarden Express, plus at least five minutes' waiting, in all thirty-six minutes. . . .

Calmly and collectedly Nielsen entered the station and proceeded to the first-class waiting room. He was surprised to note that, as he handed his ticket to be punched at the entrance, his hand was completely steady. Beneath the soft kid of his glove, he felt as if his every finger, separated thus in its kid sheath, knew that it must be calm and not tremble, since now the dangerous game was beginning. The game of life and death. The game for the sake of Blitva. In the waiting room were some five or six passengers. Two or three ladies from

Kurlandia. No one he knew. Nielsen sat in one of the upholstered armchairs and remained there until the arrival of the Ankersgarden Express. He was Harold Jacobson, the pharmacist from Ankersgarden, 3 Barutanski Street. There was only one thing he could not recall: When and where had he thrown away the neck of the rum bottle that had remained in his hand? Where had he thrown it? Where? In the café or on the street?

In front of the waiting room, on the station rails, an old-fashioned engine was shunting and appeared to be moving up and down in front of the glass door, with a sarcastic laugh: Ho-ho, Ho-ho, Ho-ho, Ho-ho . . .

Who's that old engine laughing at? Nielsen thought, watching the second hand on the large clock nervously moving around its closed circle. Ten, twenty, thirty, sixty, ten, twenty, thirty . . .

Without further interruptions, Nielsen arrived in Ankersgarden around 3:07 in the morning and, a few minutes later, in the free Kurlandish port area, went aboard the *Möve,* the Swedish-Kurlandish boat that was waiting for connection with the Ankersgarden Express according to its normal sailing schedule on the Wyborgen line. He was free.

CHAPTER 5

In Blatvia

Like a worm-infested dog when it stretches its neck out among the nettles, so had the Blatvian people languished for centuries beneath Tartar, Hunnish, Mongol, and imperial oppression. From those bloodstained days of Hunnish rule survived the old Blatvian folk song:

> All we Blatvians are to born to die,
> All our women born to widowhood.

The wolf had howled over the Blatvian mud and its severed head, bloodstained, in the Blatvian crest still speaks today of the mired, Blatvian wolf life down the dark centuries. Here, by God, one lived like a wolf as one could, as one's skill allowed; the dogs barked, blood flowed and snow covered the roads and approaches. The Blatvian snow, dark, depressing slush, northern, biting gales, and the song of the storm through the windy darkness, through naked ribs and hungry bowels: now live like a wolf, you Blatvian dogs, God have mercy upon you!

The sole morality in such conditions was that of the dog: tail between your legs and lick the feet of foreigners. That method of adaptation for centuries poisoned all principles on which were based theories of European sociability, and so, over the centuries, the Blatvian character developed, unreliable, distrusting, suspicious, and malicious, for it was known by experience that in Blatvia only he succeeded in snoring on the silken cushion of comfort who was born dock tailed and who could lie like a dog. The law of the Mongol and later of the Saint Kristianborg Imperial Aragon plunderer stated: The Blatvian is born for the crumbs, the Mongolian count for the feast. . . . In that mutual hatred and baring of teeth, in that constant devouring and lapping of foreign blood, the Blatvian peasants had so starved for centuries that among them, in the second half of the eighteenth century, there grew up a mad and sick semireligious movement of the Spoon worshipers, who had made an idol of a wooden spoon and worshiped it, for it had become an ideal for them to eat their fill of bean soup out of a spoon once in their lives. The Blatvian Spooners created an entire folk poetry of their own about bread and about spoons, and that rich and extremely original folk poetry was collected by a Blatvian Dominican into an epic collection under the picturesque title *Blatvias Kurtàlà*. *Blatvias Kurtàlà* was really a Tartar title reflecting the main subject of the poetry in which was poetically expressed a situation that, for the sake of a foreigner uninitiated in the elements of Blatvian life, might be expressed by concepts such as: desperate hunger or liberation from bloodstained and mud-caked Blatvianism; that is to say, slavery under foreign invaders. *Kurtàlà* is a purely Mongolian word which may be used reflexively and means roughly "Thank God we are delivered from evil and suffering, namely, from everything Mongolian, aristocratic, Hunnish, and Imperial, that is not autochthonous, local, Blatvian; in a word: 'ours.'"

When, for instance, a poem in *Blatvias Kurtàlà* describes someone's body floating down the Blatvian river Ilmenga (and the waters of Blatvia were flooded with corpses for centuries), then the Blatvian folk song did not describe this sad event with the tremolo of a first violin. The verse reflects the rough humor of Blatvia. Unknown and bloody murder is turned into an ironic and humorous poem to the drowned man:

> The sturgeons dance around him,
> And the perches, hey, hey, hey,
> The deaf old carp plays bagpipes,
> And the pike, he gives a belch, hurray!
> Down the Ilmenga a dead head rolls away.

In other words, it's his fault he let himself be killed and thrown into the water, and now to hell with him! A gun goes off, an empty head falls down! The *Blatvias Kurtàlà* has much to say of dead human heads, of the falling of heads in general, and even the catastrophic fall of Blatvia in the thirteenth century is, for instance, described thus:

> The saber swished, the head of Blatvia fell,
> Blatvia fell headlong into the grass.
> The head, it fell, the head without a pillow,
> A head that's dead will never suffer headache . . .

The Blatvian crown fell in the thirteenth century. Came the Tartar invaders and the Blatvian people beneath these disasters and catastrophes continued to breathe their normal living breath. Believing for centuries in the inexhaustible spring of "living water," the Blatvian people put silver coins or sunflower seeds into a bowl and, soothsaying, humbly and stupidly sought to foretell the future in deadly terror, before the evil eye of a woman or faced with a bite of mad dogs or dread disease. The people mashed swallows' nests with the yolks of eggs and fed them to the sick as a cure for fatal diseases and, sleeping with a dead man's tooth under their pillow, the people secretly revered the Blatvian pagan gods which none of the five churches—the Lutheran, the Kurlandish Adventist, the Roman, the Swedish Protestant, the Moscow Kievan—could ever, over the centuries, eradicate from the Blatvian national soul. The ancient pagan gods of Blatvia concealed themselves in the hearts and minds of the peasants while they apparently were converted and went to the European churches to the sound of bells and the crackle of fireworks. Kneeling before apparitions and secretly praying for centuries to their idols, the Blatvian people cast spells, boiled dogs' bones, and uttered pathetically incomprehensible magic words: *tetragrammaton, adonai-emanuel* (rather as the modern Blatvian intellectual pronounces the word *acetaminophen*), yet believing such mysterious words far more than the completely incomprehensible verses of the prophet Jeremiah.

Over Blatvia, over its poor peasant hovels and huts that rotted in the mud like rotten mushrooms, there ruled the gigantic Tree of the Cross. As above a baroque Blatvian altar, towering over Blatvian reality, in the rich drapery of Latin fantasy, hung in brocade church drapes the exalted symbols of the Lord's agony: and over the bloody wounds, like a golden banner, fluttered Veronica's scarf, and the people, that poor Blatvian people, worshiped the nails of the cross, the bloodstained corpse, the sharp lance and the crown of thorns, the shackles and chains, the sponge and the vinegar, and the saints of the Lord, and the bright angels of heaven, and 144,000 holy martyrs glittered above the kneeling Blatvian people, like 144,000 silver saints in silver armor and golden helmets. The four heavenly musicians struck their harps and cymbals and drums and played celestial organs above Blatvia and they were: Arkot, Marmeoth, Dek, and Amalek, those four heavenly music makers above Blatvia.

The wind howled, the blizzard whined above the Blatvian woodlands. Thunder rattled from the clouds, lightning split the stormy darknesses over Blatvia, and the Blatvian people, deep down at the lowest level of earthly life, crept softly in their peasant sandals, on tiptoe, as though stealing their own existence. So crouched the Blatvian people, like the lad in their own fable. His mother Blatvika baked him a loaf, and the people of Blatvia set off with their nine favorites, nine white Russian hounds, and so set off over the ravines and abysses, across the floods and bridges, and so traveled, by magic cities and lands, and so crept after their national good fortune through European political systems to the Karabaltic, between Blitva and Hunnia and Kobilia, blindly believing in the mystery of their fortunate Blatvian, autochthonous number Nine. Nine hounds, Nine fortresses, Nine clouds, Nine bears, Nine invisible winged horses, Nine golden riders, Nine clocks, and Nine wells, and in the Ninth the enchanted queen, Blatvian democracy, slept away her Ninth year under her glorious Leader and President of the Cabinet Kristofor Blatwitzki, and under the Supreme Protectorate of the wise president of the Blatvian Republic, His Excellency Dr. Aureol Csalloközhmvassiczky.

The well of Blatvian parliamentarianism was deep. Its bottom was not to be seen, except that, deep down in the dark mirror of parliamentary obscurity, one might discern a waxen girl asleep under a spell. Afternoon silence, clouds sailing over the deep blue heaven, and out of the distance, from out of the golden corn, in the shade of a mulberry tree wavered the voice of a Blatvian tamboura:

> All was dying a dog's death of hunger,
> And the Blatvians, like hungry wolves,
> Fed on nettles and on mangel-wurzels.

"Blatvia is starving, because it produces nothing," so they said in the Blatvian cafés around the year '20, after Versailles, when the first groups of the progressive Blatvian intelligentsia began to occupy themselves with (among many other problems) the question of the national economy. And when some foreign visitor appeared doubtful about such original reasoning as "We are hungry because we have nothing to eat," then the Blatvian experts would smile with that strange, so-called "Blatvian diplomatic smile." One could not possibly be sure whether such a doglike baring of teeth meant aggression or simply, doglike, they smiled due to the lack of any real or convincing proof, other than wagging their tails before the Great Powers. "If a Blatvian intellectual smiles at you politely it means, simply, that he is telling you to fuck off," so they said of the Blatvian "diplomatic smile" in Hunnia, where they hated Blatvians, as they hated mad dogs. The Huns and the Blatvians (like all the peoples of this accursed area) created their own political outlook, ideals, and convictions on the basis of mutual negation.

"We are hungry, of course, because our much-loved Hunnish neighbors have robbed and enslaved us," ran the second proof of the experts as to why Blatvia was in such a state, and this any foreign traveler could see at the most superficial glance through a train window.

"For heaven's sake, Kurlandia, Svetonia, Kobilia, are all poorer countries than Blatvia. All these Blatvian neighbors are more overpopulated than you are. They all of them have far fewer national resources, but look at them and you will see that none of these countries is hungry and all have an efficient economy! They build schools, roads, and even railways, yet their standard of living is far higher than that of Blatvia! For instance, take Kobilia! Kobilia imports a hundred and thirty-five thousand accordions a year from Ingermanlandia. In other words, the Kobilians sing, enjoy life. They're not hungry. While your peasant remains with his flute and his tamboura. Your Blatvian peasant has no time for music. He has no ear, he has no bread, he has no sense for song. Hunnish Gypsies in the pubs, that's your only pleasure. Vodka and onion . . . that's Blatvia for you!"

"The Kobilians are pub singers by nature," would be the Blatvian answer, expressed with such aristocratic disdain. "The Kobilians are not a nation in the historic sense of such a European concept. The Kobilians never had their own feudal system. Today they are beggars and spivs. Over the centuries they've labored as Kurlandish serfs without their own national pride or any national awareness. Blatvia struggled for its political sovereignty against Hunnia for seven hundred years, while the Kobilians served the Huns as executioners and musketeers! It's all right for them to play the accordion, a lot of low-class, umbrella-carrying cattle. They produced their own woven goods, their sieves and colanders, their umbrellas, and our people were so good natured as to buy such Kobilian rubbish! We shed blood for Kobilia too so, of course, today they can play the accordion! And Kurlandia," you say, "paves its roads? Kurlandia sells its milk to London and to Danzig. Easy for her to build roads! Indeed, it is!"

"And why shouldn't Blatvia sell its milk? To Berlin, for instance, or to London?"

"A silly question, sir! It's easy for you, a superior and sophisticated foreigner, to split hairs, when you see everything from the perspective of a tourist, between one invited banquet and another! Get this once and for all, my dear friend: We, as a people, as a civilization, for centuries have lost wars with our invaders! While Blatvia suffered and literally bled for the principle of political liberation from its Hunnish masters, while Blatvia groaned beneath Tartar, Hunnish, Swedish, Mongol, and imperial domination, the Blitvinians shot at us in the role of Imperial Aragon musketeers, and today, in this postwar chaos, they've stolen our exit to the sea! Blatvia, my dear sir, lacks its own sea, and all political assumptions that Blatvia could, somehow, organize itself economically without its own sea are utter nonsense! Blatvia will die of hunger as long as it lacks its own exit to the sea! We die in our godforsaken lair, because we cannot get to the sea! At all costs (if not by peaceful means, then by war) we must break through to the sea! That is our Kurlandophile and anti-Blitvinian policy, from the peace in Blato Blitvinsko nineteen seventeen till today, and Blitva will pay, like it or not! And in any case, what's the use of Ankersgarden to an un-cultured, lazy, passive Blitva? Why should Blitva have its sea when we have none? That is why our glorious neoclassical bard Blat-nichki sang:

While the wind of the Karabaltic stirs not your ships, oh Blatva,
Muddy Blatva you'll be, nor from mud will you be resurrected.

"And what do you hope to gain from such a war, given that you win it?"

"What do you mean, given we win it? Our victory is assured! Blitva is so rotten within, it'll fall apart at our first strike! Our anti-Blitvinian policy for us is a matter of life or death! Our people live on oatmeal just to survive the winter, and that's not just a historical joke attributed to Svantenius Blitvanicus, the Weider-Hunnen bishop in the seventeenth century: that he prayed God the snow might melt before Easter so the human cattle of Blatvia might eat grass for Easter! Our Easter meal is not grass anymore, that's true, but we immigrate to America. Two and a half million Blatvians live like slaves in both Americas. Between the years 'eighteen and 'twenty-five alone, around three hundred thousand of our people immigrated to America. Mr. Barutanski, by our modest calcula-tions, earned fabulous amounts with his Blitvinian shipping lines. Work it out yourself: seventy Blatvian dollars per head in the colonel's pocket. That's equal to more than twenty million dollars. Isn't that daylight robbery?"

Immediately, from the first day of his crossing the frontier and ar-riving in Weider-Hunnen, Niels Nielsen fell into the maelstrom of such impassioned conversations. His dramatic flight and arrival in the capital of the neighboring country all became a first-class sensa-tion and even a personal triumph for the man who had had such moral courage as to oppose the Blitvinian tyrant. In the Blatvian press and in the social life of the capital there appeared the highly interesting and legendary figure who had confronted that megalomaniacal madman in Beauregard with the fact that he was a savage animal and a common criminal.

At the banquet arranged in Niels Nielsen's honor by the Municipality of Weider-Hunnen, Nielsen was welcomed by Dr. Gorbo-Dador Jekenö, the mayor of Weider-Hunnen, president of the Parliamentary Club of the progressive opposition, and the chief editor of the leading Blatvian opposition daily, *Flagen Kekor* (which meant roughly *The Banner of Freedom*). Dr. and Mayor Gorbo-Dador Jekenö stated that he raised his glass to the health of a fighter who was a humanist in his ideals but a European in his view that the ideals of the brotherhood of nations should be truly realized. He welcomed Nielsen, who had such culture and intellectual boldness as brilliantly to affirm the right of every nation to an outlet to the sea, speaking of the rights of Blatvia as no one could do better. "The sea does not and cannot belong to anyone, for the sea is an element of life, like the sun, like the air, like the rain, and as individuals have an inalienable right to the sun, to air, to bread, to water, by that same natural law nations have a right to the sea!"

Nielsen, as a well-known opponent of Colonel Barutanski from the time before the coup of '25, Nielsen, as the legionnaire dissident who had published entire volumes of pamphlets concerning Barutanski's adventures, the editor of the independent periodical *Tribune,* and, finally, the author of an "Open Letter" to Colonel Barutanski, Nielsen, the hero of the obscure and unexplained assassination of Rayevski, the friend of the murdered wife of the late General Michelson and friend of the late Olaf Knutson (all of whom Barutanski had crushed like flies), the man who at the last moment had escaped certain death and so became the liquidator of the Blitvinian murderer Major Georgis (who was the terror of the

Blatvian frontier in the year '18), such a monumental and unique figure Blatvia received with open arms as a good and faithful friend and welcome guest. That dramatic night cost the lives of four people, and by the Blatvian accounts, all four were regarded as Nielsen's invaluable political capital.

The Blatvian State Publishing House published Nielsen's "Open Letter" to Colonel Barutanski in 150,000 copies, as a brochure, and, since Nielsen donated his relatively considerable honorarium to the Association of Blatvian Veterans for the aid to veterans' children afflicted with tuberculosis, the Association of Blatvian Veterans named him an honorary founder of the Aid Fund of the veterans' association and the president of the association, General Field Marshal Lieutenant Bellonis-Bellonen, thanked him as a benefactor of the Blatvian people in the name of the orphans of dead veterans (also by an "Open Letter"). The Blatvian edition of Nielsen's book *The Blitvinian Question* achieved record sales of fifteen thousand copies, and his book on Flaming-Sandersen, *The Garibaldian Father of Blitvinian Liberalism,* the Blatvian Cultural Society published in a luxury edition, leather bound with gold lettering, to be placed on the tables of all Blatvian state waiting rooms, and in dentists' and lawyers' waiting rooms throughout Blatvia and, as a mark of respect, paid him in dollars (a thousand dollars at that). In the whirlpool of impressions that swirled around Nielsen, it was as if he were traveling in some lunatic lunar park, by that magic railway of surprises. From a hellish underground full of terror, visions, and apparitions, the little shell of his fate flew to the heights of the shining carousel with the rattle of sleigh bells and rockets. His swing swung on this mad lottery to the jackpot. With four human lives in his baggage, Nielsen disposed of an open account in the National Bank and the sound of gold coins around him tinkled loudly and with demonic insistence. Petras-Doderis, the editor of the most famous Blatvian review, *Blatvias Kalakalis* (*The Blatvian Bell*), which had continuously come out in Weider-Hunnen for eighty-seven years, published an editorial on Nielsen, the Blitvin-ian politician who, for the sake of his just opinion concerning the state of Blatvia's "right to an open sea," had risked his life. The arti-cle was accompanied by a reproduction of Nielsen's portrait by the late Olaf Knutson, of whom Petras-Doderis published, in the same issue, a profound review of his artistic personality, in the form of an obituary, in the style of a ceremonial eulogy. This was written by Patricius Baltic, the most famous and best pen among the younger generation of Blatvian literary talents, of whom there was a great mass, since, in this hungry and backward Blatvia, literature flour-ished, amazingly, so richly that more than thirty recognized poets competed for the honor of being the Blatvian poet laureate.

In the Ritz, the most elegant restaurant in Weider-Hunnen, Niels Nielsen sat in the seat of honor, surrounded by the elite of Blatvia. Next to him, by the white rectangle of the banquet table, in the gleam of candles, silver, and shining glasses (in which sparkled ex-pensive Hungarian wine), gathered a mass of Blatvian minds, pens, political names from various political parties, the whole scale of the Blatvian parliamentary accordion. The elite and the crème de la crème. From the right-wing liberals, through the government agrarians, to Petras-Doderis's group Kalakalis, of which it was said it had close, intimate, that is to say, direct links with the anonymous Blatvian Military League, Toronis. Of Petras-Doderis it was said that, together with General Field Marshal Lieutenant Bellonis-Bellonen, he was preparing a surprise for those agrarian subhuman bipeds under Kristofor Blatwitzki and the president of the Repub-lic, Aureol Csalloközhmvassiczky, of whose stupid and demagogic and corrupt regime all respectable citizens had had enough. "Enough is enough" was the phrase that echoed on all sides, and that that phrase, one morning, would turn itself into a state coup no one doubted.

"There's no sense in bloodshed," objected cowardly hairsplitters to the right and left of the initiators of the League who were, indeed, anonymous, but their enterprise was an open secret.

"What of it?" replied the yellow press, which was under the influence of General Field Marshal Lieutenant Bellonis-Bellonen, and all its publications were marked with a yellow ribbon. Blood had gushed in Blatvia and would do so, by God, today, and in this splattering of human blood that had been pouring over Blatvia since the days of the Mongols the Blatvian conscience had dozed like a rat in bran, and all that was human in the Blatvian people was distorted, and the Blatvians had become like gray bureaucrats and frightened old women. All grew gray in Blatvia. We needed to awake in Blatvia the heroism with which it echoed in the days when the land shook beneath the thunder of Ingermanlandish and Hunnish hooves.

"In today's so-called Blatvian parliamentarianism, according to the model of that cunning old legal fox Kristofor Blatwitzki, the entire state function of the Blatvian nation was reduced to trickery and cunning and crawling on all fours at the clink of gold from the Blatvian state funds or the promise of a state monopoly. Today it meant cunning, screwing one's neighbor, sucking around dogs' behinds. One needs to shoot, Doctor, to shoot as you began over there in Blitva, and not just grow leaves like a dock plant to hide your lowbrow stupidity," said General Field Marshal Lieutenant Bellonis-Bellonen to Niels Nielsen. He was sitting beside Nielsen, and the General Field Marshal's political, military, and legionary policy was quite simple: "Take power, abolish Parliament, declare war on Blitva, and disperse all these Blitvinian subalterns, these little colonels, these inhabitants of Beauregard like the rubbish they are, occupy Ankersgarden, and deal with our own peasants, idiots, and malingerers with two or three bursts of machine-gun fire."

> Blatva River, what then have you brought us?
> I have brought the bodies of three wolves,
> Of three wolves, three fine Blitvinian corpses . . .

The Hunnish Gypsy bandleader, standing in front of his orchestra, began this old Blatvian song, and General Field Marshal Lieutenant Bellonis-Bellonen, moved by the shrill of the violin, bending his head backward (as from a strange nostalgia for the old dead Blatvian heroism), putting his left hand behind his head, began to drown out the bandleader and his poem about wolves:

> The woods are green, and hoots the eagle owl,
> And through Blatvia the brigands lurk.

I first had to kill a man for my friends to indulge me in mayonnaise and white wine as a sign of respect and solidarity, but if that general here isn't the vampire ghost of Georgis, then the belief in vampires is nothing more than a lot of old wives' tales, Nielsen thought, heartily clinking glasses with old Bellonis-Bellonen, who just as kindly bared his teeth in the well-known Blatvian diplomatic smile. I've got four heads in my luggage, was the only thought that hovered in Nielsen's mind, four heads, and that's just the beginning! And what more will come of it?

"And you, Doctor, are surprised at our tempo?" Patricius Baltic, the greatest hope of the young Blatvian literature, asked him ironically (Patricius Baltic who had published that enchanting obituary for Olaf Knutson) when the next day in the Promenade, the most elegant café in Weider-Hunnen, he sat at Nielsen's table.

"I am not the least surprised, my dear young friend," Nielsen replied kindly, warmly, and in friendly tones. "Why should I be surprised? Your tempo is so like our tempo that there's nothing for anybody to be surprised at. Such a tempo is the result of a whole sequence of causes. One needs to change the causes and the tempo will change of itself! That's the problem: how to change it!"

"Yes, but at least you shoot, and that, you see, is where you Blitvinians show manliness. And all we have are lies. Here everyone lies, and I beg you, don't believe anyone! All we have is deceit oiling the wheels, bribery and corruption. All we do is talk all night and do nothing! All people do is lie and deceive themselves and others, slander and gossip, and that's about all. Everybody defames and blackens everybody and our whole Blatvian boiling achieves nothing. Two or three abominations . . . And that's the lot! There you have it, my dear doctor! Peasants, agrarians, they've no political significance! Wherever have peasants ruled a country? Give me one example in history where peasants have ever created anything anywhere or at any time. If we all go on as we are, we'll all go to the devil!"

"It's not like that just in Blatvia, my dear chap! It's exactly the same with us in Blitva and over in Hunnia and Kobilia too, and in all the Hunnias and Kobilias throughout Europe! There, you see, is our problem! None of these questions can be solved on their own. From Kurlandia to Karapathia, it's all the same Blitvinian-Blatvian open question. And we're here to solve it in the face of all difficulties. That's our job! *Vivos voco* should be the motto of all European poets, today more than ever!"

"And on whom should I call? And with whom am I to solve these open questions? I don't know. I've no reason to suppose that you have not seen other such inexplicable phenomena as, for instance, the hatred that our Blatvian people feel one for the other. Each tells lies to the other. Each accuses the other. Plans each other's destruction. They set traps for one another, hiss at one another like poisonous snakes, and nurture only one single idea in their heads: how to destroy each other as quickly and brutally as possible. And what's worst: our Blatvians are cowards! The Blitvinian shoots! All honor to him! That's at least logical! But the Blatvian is all words and lies! Why, I ask you, our boastful, pseudoheroic attitude, the hypocritical cult of *Blatvias Kurtàlà*, when the truth is the opposite? A Frenchman came here, a sociologist. Naturally, he was interested in the ethnographic question of the Eastern European peoples. And he was here, you know. He studied our glorious *Blatvias Kurtàlà*, and he even wrote a book: *Les survivances blathuaniennes*! This foreigner clearly saw what the problem was. We're haunted by the ghosts of the past, my dear doctor. The Mongol times of bloodshed survive within us, and all that exists in Blatvian heads and hearts is simply the echo of centuries of bloodshed. The Blatvian has an organic need to kill, but he doesn't dare because, on the other hand, he's been born a serf, a slave, a lower animal, a clerk! The dream of eighty percent of Blatvians is to become a clerk! Our entire intelligentsia has the mind of a clerk! And what can a man who, by nature, is a brigand do when he's a clerk? He lies! He lies to himself and to others! You don't know that book, Doctor? Read it; it's extremely interesting."

"Who was the author?" Nielsen asked more out of politeness, since inheritances had never interested him.

"Ferdinand Neuilly-Faure: *Les survivances blathuaniennes* in the Jacquemart-Beaulieu edition, Paris, 1927."

"Ah, you gentlemen are discussing the book by that cretin Neuilly-Faure, are you not?" A man sitting at the next table turned to Nielsen. It was obvious he had been listening to Patricius Baltic's conversation with the newly arrived Blitvinian emigrant. Without waiting to be invited, clearly excited by the mention of the author, he got up and, throwing aside the newspaper he'd been reading, came over to their table.

"Dr. Mazurkinis," he announced himself, offering his hand to Nielsen and bowing somewhat conventionally and reservedly to Patricius Baltic, as do people of higher rank and standing to their inferiors. "Delighted."

Nielsen got up, not knowing quite what was about to happen, according to that strange codex by which Blatvians approached the tables of people with whom they were unacquainted.

"Please, please, do sit down, don't disturb yourself." Dr. Mazurkinis tapped Nielsen on the shoulder heartily and warmly, almost obtrusively forcing him to sit down again. Having forced himself on Nielsen, he also imposed on him how he should behave: sit and not stand, and that it was not necessary to be embarrassed as long as he didn't mind it; that is to say, if it was all right with him, if it pleased him, then *s'il vous plaît*!

"Please, I beg you, don't believe a word our Baltic says about reading matter! He's always impressed by the last book he's happened to read! That is to say, he's a poet without any political understanding! Neuilly-Faure's book is just a political pamphlet and no sociological study! If you see what I mean? The man received a pretty fair sum from your Blitvinian state funds to expand against our way of life. For cases like that our people have a good saying: Even a fool knows which side his bread's buttered on!"

"No, Doctor, let's be objective! The book is based on a most detailed study and is full of striking facts. The author worked on it for years," Baltic protested.

"We're only too well aware of such Western gentlemen who come from their decadent, perfumed societies and our native Blatvian sandals stink to them! Scandalmongers and troublemakers, these foreign scribblers who go about our Blatvia, as if our people haven't seen through them, for God's sake! They're just common flatterers, full of false bonhomie, these dear foreigners, just as long as they get paid from state funds! Here a banquet, there an order, a medal, a cross, a diploma, and there a free first-class ticket in soft velvet, in feathers, in a sleeping car, or a sports car, indeed, I ask you, or even a whole luxury limousine for their own use—if you know what I mean—a little present here, *s'il vous plaît*, please have

312

as many Blatvian dollars as you wish, *s'il vous plaît*, and if it doesn't work out, then: Blatvia is the most backward country in northeastern Europe, because Blatvia doesn't let itself be bitten to death by foreign bedbugs! These foreign mercenary flyswatters and parasitic scroungers need throwing out of the country by a single administrative decree! A lot of lying blatherers and lazy good-for-nothings who simply babble and wave their arms, who luxuriate and expatiate, and, feeding on other people's suffering, write such impertinences that should earn them a slap in the face and not free railway tickets and first class, at that! And so we get a lot of layabouts who spend a few summer months here, spreading embroidered lies to all four winds and thinking up ordinary spiteful slanders which *au fond* are nothing but the simplest political deceits and provocations! Am I making myself clear?"

A movement of heads and newspapers at neighboring tables. Interest was clearly growing. Mazurkinis was on the way to causing a scandal.

"Neuilly-Faure, as far as I know, never took part in politics," modestly ventured the leading Blatvian poet Patricius Baltic, who had listened to this rather loud café monologue of Dr. Mazurkinis's with a frown, but still with polite restraint.

"'As far as you know'—ridiculous, as if anything that you 'could know' would be so important, for example, that it could serve as convincing evidence! 'As far as you know'—as far as we know, and you'll allow us the possibility of knowing something, Monsieur Neuilly-Faure engages in nothing but getting as much out of the state funds as he can. There he is today, sitting in Halompestis, writing a new book about Hunnia. Or do you suppose that those anti-Blatvian pamphlets by Monsieur Jules Dupont are not paid for by Colonel Barutanski! Don't be so naive! Ask Dr. Nielsen; he knows better! He knows more about it than you do, 'as far as I know'! As if everything written by Monsieur Jules Dupont isn't the personal view of Colonel Barutanski! We're not a lot of naive schoolgirls! We know very well what's going on, thank you very much. Do you get my point this time? Or, for instance, read the Kobilian Blue Book. The Blue Book quotes your much respected Monsieur Neuilly-Faure at least thirty times. Where he suggests that Blatvia is the Middle Ages, an archaic land of tuberculosis and criminality! The Kobilian Blue Book quotes Monsieur Neuilly-Faure that it is 'scientifically proven that this is the case.' And who has 'scientifically proven' this? Monsieur Neuilly-Faure! And who is Monsieur Neuilly-Faure? The writer of a book which a Blatvian publicist recommends to foreigners who know nothing of our conditions and situation! Kobilia and Hunnia are a nest of scum and spineless decadents. While Blatvia waded in blood not just to the knees but to the throat, all that was heard from Kobilia and Hunnia was the moaning and groaning of layabouts and calumnious fruit bats. A filthy hypocritical game!"

"And what's all that got to do with our guest?" From a table hidden behind a metal screen beside the stove, a frowning, disheveled, and generally massive character rose to his feet.

"Are you addressing me?" Dr. Mazurkinis, angry, superior, pulling down his well-starched cuffs and nervously adjusting his pince-nez, turned toward this disheveled character.

"Who else should I be addressing? Do you think I'm a kitchen hand babbling nonsense? I asked you what has all this got to do with our guest, our much respected Mr. Nielsen?" the unknown giant shouted authoritatively at Mazurkinis.

"What do you mean?"

"I mean the crap you were spouting, my good sir! The man's come to us, having well and truly laid open the mole runs beneath his own roof. And all you can do is blather about spies who are paid to write what they do by Blitva. What nonsense! Typical of your drivel, do I make myself clear?"

"I beg your pardon, but it is not my habit to enter into discussions with people I don't know."

"Pooh, pooh, pooh, my good sir, watch your tongue! My arse is too witty for that blithering mouth of yours! Fuck off! Do I make myself clear? Because if I crack you one, you'll shit yellow muck like a run-over duckling! Fuck off! And save the Gypsies from having to sing 'There Rose the Squeaking of a Little Rabbit'!"

The whole café burst out laughing. There was a pause. For a moment Dr. Mazurkinis was confused, but then, as though nothing had happened, he turned to Nielsen and gave him a deep and sincere bow, together with the obligatory Blatvian diplomatic smile on his lips. "Eh, bless you, Doctor, forgive me for bothering you, but I felt the need to react as any well-meaning Blatvian patriot would have reacted in my place! Please, forgive me, I must fly, good-bye, au revoir, delighted to have met you, *servus!*" In a cascade of words and following more and more excited and troubled gestures, Dr. Mazurkinis took his leave. He had eavesdropped on Nielsen's conversation with Patricius Baltic from the beginning and even noted down some of their sentences from behind his *Times* which was spread on the portable bamboo newspaper stand.

The giant vanished behind the screen without a word and the café resumed its normal tempo.

"An unpleasant type, that Dr. Mazurkinis," Patricius Baltic remarked as though apologizing in his name. "He's a secretary at the Ministry of Foreign Affairs and it's said that he's an agent. He's an Agrarian. A government supporter. A careerist. I'm sorry, but that's how it is! *Vous me comprenez?*"

"Perhaps he's an agent out of political principle, because of his conscience," Nielsen remarked. He'd seen Dr. Mazurkinis for the first time only five minutes before, but he'd known hundreds of such Dr. Mazurkinises. Thousands. "The whole world's crawling

with Mazurkinises," he wanted to say but, at that moment, he recalled that he was carrying four dead people in his luggage.

Puffing sadly at his mild cigarette (which happened to be called
"Blatvia"), Niels Nielsen silently turned his glance inward, into his
profound self, and, for a second, was lost in the dark, hellish con-
volutions of his blood-soaked experience. And after a silent, almost
unnoticeable pause, he plunged back to the surface like a diver
who, fearful of the depths, shoots quickly up. An ironic, scarcely
visible smile hovered on his lips.

"I've known a lot of agents in my life!" he said slowly, almost absentmindedly. "I've known some who justified what they did by
their 'conscience,' their 'convictions,' by their 'Weltanschauung'!
But then, are there any things or acts in the world that one could
not rationalize or justify on the basis of a so-called Weltanschauung
or even on the basis of 'conscience'? For instance, we see how, in the
name of 'conscience,' the Orthodox called for the life of the Redeemer and, in the name of that same 'conscience,' how many heads
have fallen to revenge that of the Redeemer? In that way, everyone's 'conscience' is clear, which is the main thing. . . . 'My conscience is clear,' said an executioner in Blitva three days ago to his
victim and then hanged him. And 'how' he hanged him we read in
the newspaper, a whole description! And the journalist who wrote it
also had a clear conscience. There you see it. A few days ago, I too
killed a man! But does my 'conscience' feel any guilt? No. I think of
the event with a mixture of fear and disgust. As though I'd beaten a
mad dog with a stick. Something like that. In other words, I find
myself in a state where I measure things in a manner that enables
me to think of it all with an easy conscience. Strange! And agents
think of their victims with just the same 'easy conscience.' I knew a
woman once who for two whole years assured me she loved me, but
she was a spy and everything she said was a pack of lies. She slept
with me just in order to rob me, to get to evidence that could have

cost me my life! To cheat someone, to betray him, slap him in the face, sell him, and with the blood money earn a nice trip abroad, perhaps to Taormina. That's human nature! That's the modern European way, the way near ones announce their love for their nearest and dearest!"

Niels Nielsen recalled how Karin Michelson had dreamt of their going together to Taormina. She had dreamt so much of Italy, of Pompeii, of the virginal purity of beauty, of freedom, of that wondrous, harmonious freedom of liberation from that criminal Blitva, of an afternoon in Pompeii, when there was no one among the ruins, when all the streets of the dead town were silent and the two of them would sit somewhere in the atrium of a villa and watch the clouds moving slowly and scarcely visibly. A lizard scampered over a fresco and stopped under the face of a lithe, black-haired girl in a robe that fell in rich folds. The emerald-green lizard flashed its small tongue. Suddenly a white dove flew over the atrium and its shadow fell on the lizard and the small creature leapt with fear and vanished down a crack. There are creatures that are afraid even of the shadow of a dove. . . . The silence of a Pompeiian summer's afternoon. The ancient volcano smokes against the dark blue sky. There the Greeks roast fine lamb, there in the vineyards of Vesuvius, while here the streets are completely empty. Not a soul! They're all gone, yet here on the walls, written in a faded sepia, their words still speak to us. Political placards: "Vote for the noble Marcus Aurelius, an honest man who'll support our cause unselfishly!"

The afternoon breezes play on the curtains of Pompeiian houses and that murmur of fabric is the sole breath of life in this graveyard. Beside him, Karin Michelson, strange, faraway, unknown, mysterious Karin. *Carissima mia Carina!* Yet she had been a traitor! She'd lied! She'd lied from first to last! Perhaps she'd wanted to go to Taormina with somebody else. . . . She'd needed the money. . . . And then, with the blood money, she'd planned to go to Pompeii and there—in all probability—she'd have dreamt of white doves and watched the lizards, while he, Niels Nielsen, could already have been a long decomposed skeleton at the bottom of some Blitvinian canal. And now she was dead! He personally had sent her to that Pompeii from which there was no return! Or perhaps it was all a dream? Perhaps it was only his unjustified and stupid assumptions! Or did she wish to explain it all to him? Or was it like Knutson: a running jump through a window? Mrs. Michelson! Sweet, smiling, dear Karin! What did it all mean? Was life really bereft of any profounder meaning? It was like a heavyweight boxing match! Georgis had given him a hard punch that evening in his room in Blitwanen when he, Georgis, announced Nielsen's death sentence. How victoriously Georgis had thrown the draft of the "Open Letter" to Barutanski in his face! That had meant: You write nonsense, dear man! The woman you sleep with is in our pay. The woman you thought you'd marry and whom you trusted, you fool, that woman was our agent. Like a wasp, Georgis knew exactly where to sting, on which nerve ending! He managed it excellently! But what if they'd really stolen the document from her?

"You seem to be far away, Doctor." The voice of the Blatvian laureate Patricius Baltic brought Nielsen back to earth.

Oh God, yes, he was sitting in the Café Promenade in Weider-Hunnen in the company of a young and pleasant Blatvian poet!

"Yes I was! What were we talking about? Forgive me! Sometimes one gets carried away by silly things! I was thinking of a similar adventure with an agent. . . . But who was that man from behind the screen who interrupted our conversation with that other man, what did you say his name was, I've already forgotten."

"Mazurkinis!"

"Ah yes, Dr. Mazurkinis!"

"That giant, he's a strange chap. There you have it! He's nothing. A character. Blatvia's full of characters!"

"And what in your café jargon do you mean by a character? Does that character fulfill any civic function? Does he have an occupation?"

"I don't think he has! He's been sitting in the Promenade for the last several years!"

"What does he live on, then?"

"Nothing! As he can! He's an agent!"

"I see: He's furious with the other agent because he sees him as a competitor?"

"I don't know. Maybe it's some old grudge! In any case, there's a hell of a lot of turmoil here. There's a feeling that something is going very wrong with Kristofor Blatwitzki. The League is working underground. Mazurkinis is a hundred percent Blatwitzki's man, since with him he either stands or falls. While that one from behind the screen, I think, is changing his allegiance. But these are all matters of ugly everyday life, Doctor, while I would like to ask you a great favor and, if you don't like it, please just tell me sincerely that you're not interested. As far as I'm concerned, if you agree, I shall feel it a great honor, but if you're not interested, I shall be sorry. I simply wouldn't want to impose. So please forgive me for troubling you, and I'd certainly ask you to forgive me if you feel I'm pushing myself."

Showered in a cascade of polite verbiage, Nielsen did not know what all this was referring to. What it was referring to was that Patricius Baltic had written a play and the play was called *The Puppets,* that it was having its premiere that evening in the National Blatvian Theater, and that Patricius Baltic would consider it a great favor if a man of such sophisticated European taste and culture as was Nielsen honored him with his presence in the author's box. Nielsen willingly agreed and, still rather absently, continued to talk with Baltic about his play, still thinking about Karin Michelson. Her image had haunted him increasingly over the last few days. He recalled with affection her voice, its strange rough alto, and her movements and laughter, especially her open silvery girlish laughter, when she got up out of bed, feeling with her feet for her slippers under the bed, and tossing them around the room with the mischief of a child.

"Hello, is that the flat of General Michelson's wife?"

"Yes, but she's hanged herself. We are from the Miserere undertakers!"

There are situations in life when one telephones and from the other end they announce: "Farewell! *Miserere!* We've hanged ourselves! First we sold you, and then we hanged ourselves!"

"Yes! So, judging by all you tell me, your play is symbolic? It's about Yorick. Does that mean it's a sort of puppet, a Blatvian Till Eulenspiegel? That's interesting!"

"Yes, Doctor, but Blatvia isn't Flanders and, while Till Eulenspiegel is above the situation, while he thinks along the lines of his sublime irony, while he is master of the circumstances in which he finds himself because he is intellectually above them, the Blatvian figure of our Yorick is just a fool whom everyone beats! And this is the basis on which I start. My play consists of five acts with an introduction and epilogue. I've called it *The Puppets* because it takes place in a puppet theater, where the main character is a puppet called Yorick who, on the one hand, suffers as a puppet on the strings of a puppet theater, and on the other, suffers as a thinking puppet who is aware of his puppet tragedy! The prologue begins in the wings of the puppet theater where, before the performance, the puppets hang on their strings like dead objects. The atmosphere is obscure and depressed behind the wings of the puppet theater that plays *The Comedy of Yorick,* while Yorick, the main character, hangs there like a puppet among the other actors and thinks how senseless it is for a puppet to be a man or a man to be a puppet! It's a romantic play in verse. *The Comedy of Yorick* which is to be performed, as if in a puppet theater, consists of five acts: the first is 'A Lynching on a Friday Afternoon,' the second 'The Devil and the Youth,' the third 'In Tyrannos,' the fourth 'An Aesopian Fable,' and the fifth

'The Twilight of Sanity.' In this entire play of mine, my hero, or, if you wish, our Blatvian hero, Yorick, plays the main part and in every act gets the worst of it since, being a puppet, he's condemned to get it in the neck! And since the performances in this puppet theater go on forever, so the puppet Yorick eternally plays the same role, hung on his string, against his own will, and since, being on a string, he's compelled to play, the puppet revolts, logically, and so the prologue opens with his revolt in verse. Yorick's view is: Since we're all puppets on a string and since we all enact the same puppet show which lasts forever, our only way to be free is to cut the string and disappear from the stage of this stupid theater that performs such stupid things."

"What is this? Nihilism? Suicide?"

"No. My play is a comedy! Come and see it, Doctor! In the epilogue I've solved the problem of our puppetlike existence by means of a trick! It will be my pleasure to welcome you as my guest. Here is a ticket for box number seven in the first gallery! See you there!"

Patricius Baltic triumphantly moved over to another table set in the oval niche by the window, where a noisy bohemian crowd of both sexes greeted him with a burst of raucous triumphant laughter, with which authors are greeted in cafés before their first night: Bravo, the author!

A pleasant, good-looking, and, I think, talented young man, Nielsen observed, watching Patricius Baltic moving across the café. He'd thought of a trick to solve the problem and so solved the problem of life! Such are poets! All they needed was one little trick! But what about the rest of us who telephone and get an answer from the undertakers? What sort of trick could help us?

In box number seven in the first gallery, Niels Nielsen encountered Panteleimon Kiparis, who was, all the Blatvians had told him, eccentric, mad, unbalanced to a degree, but who was, without doubt, one of the most gifted Blatvian poets. Panteleimon Kiparis had approached Nielsen on the first day of their acquaintance (and this was immediately after Nielsen's arrival in Weider-Hunnen) with the greatest sincerity and with the warm frankness with which one approached a man deeply respected and in whom people had complete trust, and everything that Nielsen had been able to confirm regarding Blatvia and its situation with his own experience, all that agreed, as by a stroke of fate, with the views of Panteleimon Kiparis. Panteleimon Kiparis, the poet toward whom in Weider-Hunnen people behaved as one behaves to mentally disturbed patients greeted Niels Nielsen like a drowning man who, in his last moments, glimpses a boat on the horizon in the form of vertical black smoke coming steadily nearer. . . .

"My dear doctor, I am absolutely on my own here. I have no one I can open my heart to. What we call intellect in this country is either cretinism or mere cheap fraud. With us, poetry is not drowned in ink but in barbaric, illiterate, backward stupidity. Good! OK! There's poetry and poetry: that of the academy, of the pub, of verses written on gravestones, occasional poetry, celebratory poems, but allow me, Doctor, to quote you one of our Blatvian academicians! Judge it for yourself!

> To arms, to arms, oh dearest brethren,
> To fight for nation and for home!
> For in war there lies our strength and greatness
> That with its power drives us on!
>
> Ankersgarden, to our homeland
> We deliver as a gift!
> Let our love unite forever
> Our first Blatvian ship!

And so on and so forth. . . . What can I do against our bellicose and glorious academician, who publishes his works on the front page of

the monumental irredentist publications, financed by our glorious
Blatvian Academy in support of pro-Ankersgarden propaganda: a
seaport for Blatvia! Can I sit beside him in such a glorious Academy
as ours is? I won't! It's beneath my intellectual dignity! And because
I won't, they call me mad. In all our periodicals they write about 're-
alism,' 'utilitarianism,' 'nationalism,' 'socialism,' 'idealism,' 'materialism,' about 'tendentious writing,' about 'the ethical aim of literary
creation in general.' In Blatvia, everywhere, an immense amount is
being written and published, while I think that, about Blatvia and
Weider-Hunnen, about us as a people, there's a need to write such a
pamphlet (about our conditions, relations, people), that such a poet
as this would be lynched. But to be lynched, as an ideal, is madness!
I began several times to write that final, sincere, and utterly negative
pamphlet, and I've already collected quite a lot of material, but then
. . . what for? Better get drunk out of one's mind and kick the bucket
somewhere, run over by some stupid local train, like a Blatvian hog
on the line, than to tell the truth to these cretins of ours and get a bullet in the head for one's pains. For instance, the other night I got as
drunk as a pig at a friend's and, while they were swilling and yelling,
I retired into a back room, a sort of drawing room with a couch covered in red velvet (you've seen those 'gilded drawing rooms' of ours),
and so I lay down on that gilded couch, feeling the velvet knots and
fringes of the cover, listening to those stinking swine from the other
room and thinking of them, one by one, from the host (my friend) to
some young officers at the far end of the table. I thought of them all
puking and grunting in the other room, that that was what they really
were! At the head of the table sat a banker (who finances our main
publishing house in Blatvia), one of our Blatvian pillars of society,
describing to the sodden scum around him the 'sociology' of the female body, the sociology of the feminine center. I'm quoting him:
'milieu and ambience'! The meaning of milieu and ambience. In detail! Crudely! Those swine sneered at everything: at art, at chess, at

politics, at the feminine body! Those drunken animals sing our Blatvian *Marseillaise,* 'Throughout our Blatvia blood is shed' with pornographic rhymes, kill one another, denounce one another, travel to Constantinople in their private Packards (with their servants in a separate Buick), sell Blatvia wholesale and retail, and the result of all this? That a drunken cretin like me arrogantly and idealistically belches in a gilded drawing room and thinks of describing it all in his capital work of which (indeed) not a line is written except for the title: 'The Banners of Filth'! Am I really such a swine, such a bastard? Am I really a malicious scoundrel of the lowest order? Am I really a sick and disturbed character who thinks of others as being totally rogues and swine, scoundrels and cheats, and that not one of them is worthy of respect? For if my ideas are right, if my belief about these scoundrels is not mere fantasy, then it would be better for Blatvia for the devil to take it now, immediately, this very moment and forever! And if I'm wrong, and if I'm 'mad and eccentric' and can't distinguish idiots from wise men and scoundrels from honest men, then it would be more logical to cut me down here and now, on this very spot! One way or the other, no matter how you look at it, it all ends in nothing, my dear teacher, if I may call you such! Look, I ask you, at that pathetic Blatvian intelligentsia beneath your feet!" Panteleimon Kiparis was sitting in the author's box number seven, hidden behind Nielsen's back by a damask curtain, in the half darkness, and pointed his guest toward the elite of the Blatvian intellectuals down in the stalls. "Look at that arrogant scum that comes to our premieres, and remember that in all the orchestra seats there isn't a single honest or normal person and, moreover, remember that this is supposed to be our 'progressive' lot! All those people down there are supporters of Bellonis-Bellonen's League. Those gentlemen are preparing to liquidate 'the peasants and their satraps.' Those people are the opposite number of your LOOLP General Field Marshal Lieutenant is our future Barutanski! The whole Kalakalis group is here tonight! Patri-

cius Baltic is one of their favorites! Look, I ask you, at Petras-
Doderis, who wrote of your 'Open Letter' to Colonel Barutanski that
it was 'a masterpiece worthy of a modern Junius,' and remember my
words, Nielsen, when that same Petras-Doderis becomes the Blatvian minister of the interior! One could write whole books, thick
tomes, about that lot in the orchestra seats, but then for whom?
Why? Who, in three hundred years' time, could be bothered by the
stupidity and lack of character of some Blatvian giant such as Petras-
Doderis? There you have it! If the whole of our Blatvia together with
its National Theater and our elite were to vanish, swallowed up by
the earth here and now, what loss would that be to European civilization? Those gentlemen write books, dramas, poems, novels, stories,
and our literary mill grinds out these books, this mass of printed paper, and all for what? Verism? No! Description according to living
models? No! Propagation of certain so-called ideological principles?
No! Technique? No! Skill? No, yet again! They act politically. They
prepare obscure ambushes, in whose name? Their own! Politically
they represent absolutely nobody. In the name of their principles or
convictions? They have no convictions! In the name of trade?
They're utterly incapable as merchants or organizers, since if they do
engage in trade, they supply lubricants to our state railway or hay to
our cavalry. Have they ever done anything on their own initiative?
No! Do they think they're fighting for the victory of some, no matter
what, human aims? No! Do they move on any line of development,
of progress, ethics, humanism, aesthetics, thought, or anything else
that might be regarded as positive, honest, intelligent, or good? No!
Look, Doctor, they've seen you. Look, Petras-Doderis, chief editor
of *Kalakalis,* our standard Blatvian review, he was the first to notice
you and start applause in your honor. The League's cheerleader (the
League's here to assure the success of our laureate, Baltic), the cheerleader has taken up the applause. The whole theater is standing.
There's a scraping of chairs. They've all turned toward you, shout-

ing to you. They're all greeting you. The entire intellectual elite of Blatvia are stamping their feet and clapping their hands, and you, Doctor, you express your gratitude to those people who deserve from you simply another open letter, for it's quite incompatible, my dear doctor, for you to be triumphantly greeted by the scum of the scum of Blatvia!"

A gong. The curtain of the Blatvian National Theater, which portrayed the Triumph and Victory of the Blatvian People through the centuries, rose, with its thirty depicted kings and princes and crowned poets, steeply and remarkably quickly, and from the boards of the stage, Patricius Baltic began to speak, introducing the first performance of his romantic comedy *The Puppets.*

The stage represented a large puppet theater in the wings, where actors on strings were thrown onto the stage, dressed like dolls in various costumes. There were convicts, prostitutes, sick people in hospital gowns, soldiers in full equipment with tin hats, and this whole motley of kings in their ceremonial dress, ladies in ball gowns, clowns, workers, cardinals, bishops, gentlemen in frock coats, and middle-aged executioners was both picturesque and impressive. The stage was European. On the so-called European level! An entire humanity in miniature was to be seen in the wings of a puppet theater suspended on the strings of the Invisible Director, and among them lurked the Blatvian Till Eulenspiegel, Fortunato Yorick, who was in revolt against the establishment of puppet theaters as such and who, in his revolutionary verses, had but one idea: to turn this mute world of puppets against blind submission to the Imperative of That String on which they moved and played out their life's role in that stupid theater, against their own will and against their own interests.

Fortunato Yorick, dressed like a Blatvian jester, recited, as a Prologue, to this small humanity of wooden puppets his ballad with its tirade concerning how stupid it was of them to submit to the Imperative of the Invisible Entrepreneur and to act out a stupid play, which had only five subjects and which had been performed daily in its several variants for the last five thousand years, always feeblemindedly the same and always just as fatally tedious! On Friday afternoon (in the first act) they hanged the Innocent Man from a lamppost. The devil tempted the Innocent Lad (in the second act). In Baden–Baden plots were afoot in the court of Count Contemonteconte, plots which ended in bloodshed, in train crashes, wars, and unhappy love affairs. Everything was Chaos, in which Fortunato Yorick was fated to be the only sane one, and, for this very reason, being the only one among these stupid puppets who thought reasonably and logically, just as logically, he got the worst of it and became the stupid Fortunato Yorick whom every ass could beat, slap, and mock.

"Gentlemen," Fortunato Yorick declaimed to his wooden companions, "I plead for a New Role in this cosmic drama. I appear ridiculous in this comedy of ours simply because I'm an intelligent puppet! But to whom am I ridiculous? To a mob of stupid puppets! And why? Because I foresee the development of events and because I foretell that which logically (in the world of puppets) must come about! And why do we all act this puppet nonsense? Because we're hung on the String and because, through it, we are directed by the Invisible Fingers! Let us cut this String that controls our movements, and so free ourselves from the Imperative and cease to be mute puppets and cease to act out stupidities."

From its wooden puppet's sleep, an angel awoke. It had angelic wings and bore a silver trumpet. He hung from paper clouds: "Shush, I beg you, sir, calm yourself! This world in which we play our wooden roles is one of the wisest worlds in the Cosmos! I'm satisfied with my role: *Gloria in excelsis Deo.*"

Dr. Faust, who was present in the crush of bishops, executioners, and madmen: "You, my dear sir, have got yourself the easiest part.

You trumpet with your silver fanfare the same phrase about the glory and the heights, while you don't have to bother your head about other matters."

The devil, sleepily: "Gentlemen, our program is eight hours sleep, eight hours acting, eight hours rehearsal! We haven't time for Faust's problems during our sleeping period!"

Dr. Faust: "I didn't ask you, you infernally class-conscious gentleman! I'm Dr. Faust, and you don't expect me to talk a lot of demagogic nonsense, do you? Fortunato Yorick is right! Our performances go on being repeated forever and our humanity as puppets on a string plays the same performance from the very beginning of its civic existence."

So Fortunato Yorick's idea spread among the wondrous humanity of puppets, and the awareness of the passive, wooden, helpless role of puppets who had no other function in life than to submit to the Imperative of the Invisible Power, that puppet-consciousness of resistance, grew in the puppets from word to word, and Fortunato Yorick prepared a revolt of that wooden company, and, at that very moment when the excited world of the puppets rose to move to its Master somewhere in the unknown heights, a gong rang out and a Divine Voice announced: *Incipit comoedia . . .*

The curtain rose on the puppet theater, where the puppets—who in the Prologue had spoken like thinking beings in revolt against their parts—now, on the stage, acted like puppets the roles assigned to them, against their better intellectual and moral conviction.

The scene opened on the street of a modern city. It was a winter evening, when the first streetlights were being lighted, and in the silken grayness of twilight the outlines of various buildings with their lighted windows and shop fronts were scarcely distinguishable. The

staging was excellent and one might never have supposed that, behind God's back, in remote and isolated Blatvia, one could stage such
a first-class European scene.

A mob of convicts, gentlemen in frock coats, women and children, generals and horsemen led the Innocent Man to his execution, to the music of a military band, to the squeaking of fifes and
flutes and the beating of drums. The Man, condemned to death,
was carrying his own coffin on his back and, under its weight, fell at
his first appearance. The crowd shrieked, beat him, spat on him,
ready to lynch him, but the Man fell under the weight of his own
coffin, lost consciousness, and lay still. A doctor arrived and, by
means of an injection, returned the Man, whom they'd condemned
to death, to consciousness, and Fortunato Yorick, who was there in
the crowd of passersby, stood with his harp and sang how things
and events in life have their own direction and that it was no good
interfering with the direction of things and events. Thank God
Fortunato Yorick was so wise that this puppet circus had no effect
on him. At that moment the condemned Man, whom the representative of science, the learned man of universal medicine, had returned to consciousness, condemned to death as he was, again attempted to raise his coffin, but fell right at the feet of Fortunato
Yorick.

"I can't do it, brother; help me!"

"What's your trouble to me, fool? It's up to you," Fortunato Yorick answered the condemned Man who, with his coffin, had fallen in
front of his feet. "People are animals and require no Ideas and you've
preached Ideas to them, so carry on; take what you've asked for!"

"Help me, brother; I can't manage." The Man passed out at
Fortunato Yorick's feet.

"Help me, brother; I can't manage"—these quite common
words struck Nielsen with a magical power and something gripped

him in the diaphragm. Karin couldn't manage either and she rang his doorbell and he was a wooden puppet and didn't answer. She'd turned away and gone to her death! Oh how bloody silly the whole thing had been! And he had felt her going away like a relief.

Executioners, butchers, doctors, lawyers, women in evening dresses, the populace of puppets threw themselves at the Man to beat him into completing his final journey, but a doctor in a white coat confirmed his premature death. A condemned Man had deserted before completing his final social duty. The mob, led by various puppets, representing various worthy and reputable social callings, in a state of mad delirium, hanged the Man on a gas lamp and danced around him in a state of drunkenness and debauchery. Wine was poured, spirits flowed, music played, pyres were lit, and the moon appeared above the rooftops.

Fortunato Yorick watched this lynching and sang to his harp: "See, once more the Innocent Man, shamed and spat upon, and that same moon, for a few days, will look on him as a Prophet! Behold a tribune of the people, who's suffered for his Idea, but who will see his Apotheosis."

While Fortunato Yorick was singing, the stage turned into a basilica. And in its center, on a golden throne, the Innocent Man, who had been condemned to death by the mob, sat in imperial purple, crowned with a laurel wreath, enthroned beneath a canopy, and all the puppets who had lynched him sang to him an imperial hymn. The sound of organs. Bells.

Fortunato Yorick: "They've hung him on a lamppost just so that they can clothe him in purple and crown him with laurel, so tomorrow they can hang him on a lamppost all over again! You puppets! Your heads are stuffed with straw!"

Outcry of the authorities; the puppets fling themselves at Fortunato Yorick and the scene ends with the fool Yorick being beaten. Curtain.

There was a tremendous applause and the actors took several curtain calls, but, despite all this, there was no great enthusiasm. As regards the play's success, it was all rather halfhearted.

"What do you think of it?" Panteleimon Kiparis asked Niels Nielsen, who was rather distracted, plunged more in his own thoughts than in the play.

"What shall I say? The thing seems to me overloaded with ideas so that quantity overrides quality. It's bold, I'll give it that! But as regards verses, as far as I can judge, his technique is excellent!"

"His technique's nothing, and in Blatvia generally nobody's ever mastered any technique and no one ever will, for what our people write, Doctor, is utter nonsense. In a word, that's how it is! It's mere craftsmanship! This whining and scribbling idiot is just what he is: a muddler. You see, the League unanimously approves his hundred percent stupidity. What are these obscure symbolic phrases to do with the League's policy? The man writes feeble introductions in party organs so as to make himself a career! Otherwise he is just a nihilist! In the future cabinet of Petras-Doderis, Patricius Baltic will become the envoy to Portugal. That's all there is to it! The poetic gentleman feels like a bit of traveling! That's the whole story!"

Two or three boxes to the left, on the edge of the gilded, red-velvet-upholstered balustrade, Niels Nielsen noticed some white, chalky white, powdered, slender, spiderlike fingers trembling in the restlessness of living female hands, playing with the red velvet of the balustrade. That nervousness of the fingers, that subtle bend of the knuckles, that curve of the powdered tissue up to the rich décolleté draped in its black silk, that luminous aquamarine glance which, even during the first scene, had reflected in the irises of Nielsen's eyes. It all acted like a warm magnet on the flustered man, who, apart from his own troubles, carried with him the dark and heavy question, which would have given him fear the moment he recognized its existence: the question of Karin Michelson. To unburden himself of his moral panic, Nielsen was ready to forget everything and just this auto-suggestive plunging into a bosom, no matter whose, in moments of greatest personal danger, belonged to the typically self-defensive qualities of a man in the grip of such questions which love, God knows why, turns so maliciously into madness and hellish monstrosity.

There was the sound of a gong and the lights were dimmed. The stage presented a town street, shaded by houses, and a gas lamp flamed. In the lamp's greenish light one could see snow falling. Under the gas lamp stood a youthful puppet who spoke a long monologue about the fact that he was hungry and that his hunger was due to his having Ideals. A car sped up and came to a halt. The inside of the car was lit and in it could be seen an elegant lady in evening dress. Beside her sat a gentleman. That gentleman was the devil. The devil is one of those gentlemen who do not give away their age. Probably because they're eternal. In fur coat and top hat. When he removed his expensive glove, lined in rabbit fur, many rings glittered on his soft, well-kept hand. They shone in the rays of the stage floodlights like a powerful symbol of affluence. With an ivory-headed cane in his hand, the devil emerged from the luxurious limousine which was driven by a liveried black, in the full dignity of his satanic seductiveness. From that moment till the end of the scene, Niels Nielsen no longer paid attention to what was happening on the stage, occupied by the shining aquamarine in the eyes of the unknown woman in the third box left. Karin! She could be Karin!

I am sitting in a box. This is Blatvia. I'm flirting with an unknown woman. The performance goes on. It's all paranoia, Niels Nielsen thought, looking at the attractive young woman in the box beside him, feeling rather abstracted and tired, as though he were dreaming and everything that moved around him was at a distance that made it somewhat hard to grasp. Karin Michelson sold me and this one, in all probability, will either infect, deceive, rob, shame, or sell me! And this operetta on the stage, these puppets that aren't puppets, so that one can no longer tell who is a puppet and who a devil and why the devil's a puppet or why the young man doesn't want to go away with the devil and with that demonic woman in the red wig, this is all the premiere of a Blatvian drama, the work of a respected poet, and it all goes on eternally and so are new civilizations born in the northeast of Europe. Yet in reality it's just the glitter of magnets, the glitter of animality, the beating of hearts, flesh, blind, warm human flesh . . .

Between the second and third acts the lights did not come up and the third act was immeasurably better than the second, vital and full of theatrical élan. The scene depicted the main lounge of the Golden Crown Hotel in Baden-Baden in the year 1864. His Excellency Count Contemonteconte, pretender to some imaginary Kobilian crown, in his sixties, dressed in a gray jacket, with light-colored spats and with a large chrysanthemum in his buttonhole, with the natural nonchalance of a gentleman who pretends to thrones, was conversing with three Kobilian generals. It presented, apparently, some episode from the history of Kobilia-Blatvia which was totally unknown to Nielsen. A general was holding forth to Contemonteconte, constantly addressing him as "Sire," concerning a certain Colonel Laurean who had destroyed Kobilia and its monopolies: cinnamon, pigs, and tobacco!

"The people of Kobilia, Sire, expect that you will fulfill your duty!"

"Yes, yes, my dear, that's all very fine and charming, but I'm old, at the end of my career, so to speak, and, anyway, don't you know, I'm busy collecting porcelain and writing treatises on butterflies. I, so to speak, live in my own world, and now you're asking me to turn myself, so to speak, into a bronze horseman."

"Sire, everything for Kobilia! To us, Sire, you are worth seven Trafalgars!"

"Of course, I haven't the slightest idea about all that; that's the first precondition, is it not?"

"Naturally, Sire! But just one other detail of a technical nature. We need a hundred and seventy thousand francs . . ."

Just at that moment when, from the stage, came the words "a hundred and seventy thousand francs," from one of the boxes came a burst of automatic fire: *tac-tac-tac!*

Voices. Panic. People running in all directions in the auditorium.

"Police! Help!"

Voices from the theater corridor. The echo of firing from the street: *tac-tac-tac!*

"What is it? What's happened?"

"Nothing! A small matter of settling accounts! They've killed Mazurkinis! Two ladies are wounded! By accident!"

"And what about the performance?"

"It's stopped! It's had it, anyway! In any case, it's the custom in Blatvia! Whenever there's a shooting in a public place and somebody's killed, shows are automatically stopped. People get their money back. That has become a lucrative Blatvian tradition. It's not even certain that the author didn't organize the whole thing himself, to publicize his play! He has no talent, so he takes part in politics. The government press will make mincemeat of him, but the League will sing his praises!"

The Banquet in Blitva is not, perhaps, a book for the reader seeking an "easy read." Miroslav Krleža combined the satire of a Jonathan Swift with the style and tone of the Austrian Recession and the extravagant technique of expressionism.

The novel takes place in a number of imaginary Baltic states that form an allegorical expression of the history of the Balkan states that once comprised Yugoslavia.

The plot follows two main characters, Kristian Barutanski, the dictator, and Niels Nielsen, an undecided liberal, connected from childhood, almost brothers, yet representing two opposing forces.

What might so easily have been mere caricatures are portrayed as complex beings. Even Georgis suggests a real man behind the superficial "hit man." This is due to Krleža's power as a dramatist, and drama forms a considerable element in the novel.

The second noteworthy element is invective—a torrent of verbiage that requires the reader to enter into its tone and rhythm. The third is nature description that combines both color and sound. Added to this are the interior descriptions of furnishings and so forth, which, in their detail, evoke the nature of the society portrayed. People are their fashion and taste.

An essential leitmotif is the artificiality and hypocrisy dominant in that society. These are forces that can vulgarize and thus kill all human expression, and this is nowhere so clear as in the field of art. Larsen's suicide is an act of despair on the part of a true artist.

Knutson's killing of Rayevski is almost accidental; his real act is the assassination of Barutanski's statue: a protest against the supremacy of kitsch. Barutanski despises those beneath him as the hypocrites and sycophants they are. Despite the statue, he is utterly alone. The dictator is helpless against the vulgarization and hypocrisy which make up society.

Society in Blitva consists of the "mute" masses and those who act with the sole aim of owning luxurious houses and foreign capital.

Nielsen's "Open Letter" is a protest. Yet, as Barutanski immediately recognizes, this is a protest on the same "ideological" and abstract level of all politics. Barutanski's aim was Blitva and his means were force and terror. He knew what he wanted. As yet, Nielsen does not.

There is, however, a more real and forceful element than any political ideals, the existential moral force. Krleža presents this in two ways. First, he satirizes the false morality of vulgarized religion in the person of Baltrushaitis, not to mention the lurking figure of Cardinal Armstrong. Second, Nielsen is beset by the very real doubt whether he betrayed Karin Michelson when he refused to answer the door. Was she really a betrayer, or had he, out of fear and anger, betrayed her? By killing Georgis to save himself, had he not descended to Georgis's level? The theme offers a new and individual dimension to the entire novel.

Out of this riot of expressionism emerges Balkan reality and also the sad facts of human social and political behavior. The truth lies in true art and in the individual moral sense (always a question), and both are vulgarized and suppressed. The novel, then, is all too relevant to today's events, and also to the philosophy of existence generally.

As regards the translation, an effort has been made to preserve the general impact of Krleža's style, although some long sentences have been broken into shorter ones. Many foreign words and phrases have been retained as being essential to the atmosphere and style of the original and have been explained only when not obvious to the average reader.

Krleža wrote these two volumes prior to the Second World War and published them in 1939, when they fell victim to the political situation. Only in 1962 did he republish them, together with the third volume. Here we offer only the first two volumes of 1939 since, despite their ending which leaves Nielsen up in the air (fleeing from Blitva to Blatvia, he has found only the same thing), these two volumes form a unity and may be offered as such.

Edward Dennis Goy

»»» NOTES «««

4   *the "Peace Mire"*   *Blato* means "mud" or "mire." As the text suggests, the peace was signed in the place called Blato Blitvinsko ("Blitvinian Mire"), hence Peace Mire, or the Peace of Mire.

5   *The Law of Blitva*   Dr. Nielsen's book was published immediately after the coup by Colonel Barutanski, that is to say, in 1926.—AUTHOR

6   *Flaming-Sandersen*   Flaming-Sandersen (1818–85), the great ideologue of Blitva and follower of Garibaldi.—AUTHOR

8   *Pantocrator*   Greek: ruler of the universe. In Christian art, a representation of Christ as the almighty, combining in one person the Creator and the Savior.

8   *All the histories . . . mayor of Blitvas-Holm*   Nielsen is alluding to the suicide of a well-known Blitvinian politician of the 1890s, Petersen.—AUTHOR

12   *Ister*   During the seventh century B.C., Greek sailors reached the lower Danube and sailed upstream, conducting a brisk trade. They were familiar with the whole of the river's lower course and named it the Ister.

12   *zemstvo*   A democratic political body. The Russian word refers to a local assembly that functioned as a body of provincial self-government in Russia from 1864 to 1917.

12 *pörkölt* A spicy Hungarian stew.

54 *néfaste* Unlucky.

75 *Petronius* Petronius Arbiter (d. probably A.D. 66), reputed author of the Satyricon, a portrait of society of the first century considered to be the first Western European novel.

75 *Stirner* Pseudonym of Johann Kaspar Schmidt (b. October 25, 1806, Bayreuth, Bavaria [Germany], d. June 26, 1856, Berlin, Prussia), German antistatist philosopher in whose writings many anarchists of the late nineteenth and the twentieth centuries found ideological inspiration. His thought is sometimes regarded as a source of twentieth-century existentialism.

100 *Feldwebel* German: segeant.

100 *Stimmung* German: mood.

112 *a certain Giovanni Gualtieri, and a Cimabue . . . il Perugino* Giovanni Gualtieri Cimabue, whose original name was Bencivieni di Pepo (c. 1240–c. 1302), was a painter and mosaicist, the last great Italian artist in the Byzantine style, which had dominated early medieval painting in Italy. "Ceni di Pepo" in the next paragraph also refers to this artist. Pietro di Cristoforo Vannucci ("il Perugino," born c. 1450 in Città della Pieve, near Perugia, Romagna; died 1523) was an Italian early Renaissance painter of the Umbria school.

113 *jour de vernissage* French: the day of homage.

113 *Sâr Péladan or Landru* Reference to the type of beard. Joséphin (Sâr) Péladan (1858–1918), interested in the occult, founded the Kabbalistic Order of the Rose-Croix; he had a big black beard. Henri Landru, France's infamous "Bluebeard," family man, philanderer, and murderer of ten women and a boy. Apprehended by the police in 1919 following a description of him as a bearded man visiting widows.

118   *nostromo*   Italian: Boatswain, bo's'un.

120   *unmöglich*   German: impossible.

123   *Akhasverian*   Ahaseurus, in Christian legend the Wandering Jew.

136   *So then that is interesting . . . a kind of milk separator*   Passage in ital-
      ics is in English in the original text.

140   *Stanislau Augustus*   In 1795, Stanislaus Augustus Poniatowski, the
      last king of Poland, was forced to abdicate.

151   *Sigismondo Malatesta*   Feudal ruler, condottiere, and patron of the
      arts, member of a prominent family of Rimini (1417–68). He is of-
      ten regarded as the prototype of the Italian Renaissance prince.

167   *Nous sommes plaisants . . . comme si on était seul!*   "We like to rely on
      the society of our equals, as miserable and impotent as we ourselves;
      they will not aid us; one dies alone. One should act as if one were
      alone!"

170   *hic non videri potest . . . quantus est notus*   "He cannot be seen, for he
      is too clear to see; nor can he be grasped, for he is too pure to touch;
      nor can we value his worth, for he is beyond all of our judgments—
      boundless, immeasurable, and he alone understands the extent of
      his greatness." The quotation is from the dialogue *Octavius* by Mar-
      cus Minucius Felix, a Roman lawyer of the third century B.C. It is
      the earliest known work of Christian literature in Latin.

170   *Chef de toutes les personnes . . . cité ou république*   "Lord of all per-
      sons or intellectual substances, the absolute monarch of the most
      perfect city or republic."

172   *Ara Coeli*   The church of Santa Maria on the hill of Aracoeli (or al-
      tar of the heavens) in Rome. Santa Maria in Aracoeli, built on the
      site of the ancient Roman capital, rises precisely above the ruins of a

temple to Juno Moneta. From the ninth to the thirteenth centuries the church and monastery belonged to the Benedictines, and in 1249 a papal bull ceded the complex to the Franciscan order. Santa Maria in Aracoeli is still designated as the Church of the Senate and the Roman people.

182   *Ex nihilo nihil fit, et in nihilum potest reverti*   Nothing comes from nothing, and to nothing it may revert.

183   *Saint Teresa*   The lyrical inspiration of Dr. Bonaventura Baltrushaitis derives from Saint Teresa of Jesus, since the learned spiritual guardian has adapted to the feudal, snobbish taste of his patient.—AUTHOR

202   *excerpt from the first scene of Goethe's Faust*   Johann Wolfgang von Goethe, *Faust* (1808–32), translated by Philip Wayne (Penguin, 1949).

204   *Déclaration de M. Belinis . . . brillante et profonde*   Declaration by M. Belinis, Blitvinian minister of foreign affairs. M. Belinis, in the first days of October, has marked the third anniversary of his taking up that position. This great diplomat, of exceptional courtesy and charm, possesses an extremely lively personality and a profound and brilliant mind.

204   *Le Pacte blithuo-blathuanien . . . les frontières*   The Blitva–Blatva Pact. What will be its results? The pact—and its purpose—is to assure a permanent peace resting upon a positive basis by means of reciprocal guarantees regarding frontiers . . .

205   *La politique ferroviaire blithuanienne . . . d'un demi-siècle*   The Blitvinian railway policy this year reaches an extremely important stage of its development. The national railway is rapidly approaching its final aim. The total length of our rail network is 978 kilometers. Before the proclamation of the Blitvinian Republic there were 472 kilometers of railway lines in Blitva. The Aragon-Hunnish Empire created this network over more than half a century.

205   *Quelque nombreux . . . qu'il en sera!*   However numerous and powerful the enemy may be, our faith in national defense will turn the victory our way. So it was and so it ever will be!

206   *M. Egon Larsen . . . l'amassade de Blithuanie*   M. Egon Larsen, appointed Blitvinian ambassador to Calpa-Calpa, the capital of the Kobilian Republic, has left London, where he represented our country. He was seen off at the station by representatives of the British government and the personnel of the Blitvinian embassy.

207   *M. Coustodinis . . . la capitale hounienne*   M. Custodinis, president of the Commission for Foreign Affairs at the National Assembly of Blitva, "Sabor Blitvinski," on Tuesday evening at the Hotel Blitvania gave a banquet in honor of M. R. Nagel, who has just been appointed Blitvinian minister at Halompestis, the Hunnish capital.

207   *Les remerciements de Son Excellence . . . dans la dignité*   His Excellency the President of the War Council expresses his gratitude . . .

The secretary general of the presidency of the War Council announced on the evening of November 27: His Excellency the president has instructed the Blitvinian agency to thank the many people who have sent him telegrams on the occasion of the anniversary of the victory at Plavystok.

Ceremony at the Academy of Arts and Sciences

A grand meeting took place Monday . . . at the Academy of Arts and Sciences on the occasion of the anniversary of the victory at Plavystok.

M. Burgwaldsen, legal adviser to the House of the President of the Blitvinian War Council . . .

The commemoration of the victory was opened by a speech from M. Burgwaldsen. The eminent lawyer stated, and we quote, "National sovereignty, national independence are like individual liberty. Just as the individual cannot exist with dignity if deprived of liberty, in the same way it is impossible for nations deprived of liberty to exist with dignity."

231   *LOOLP*   The Legion's Organization of Order, Labor, and Progress. —AUTHOR

245   *Tauchnitz*   The nineteenth-century German publisher of *A Collection of British and American Authors.*

248   *Skripnik's music*   Skripnik, the leading light of modern Blitvinian music (1887–1925).—AUTHOR

252   *Approchez-vous, Néron, et prenez place*   Come, Nero, take your place.

253   *Poursuis, Néron, avec de tels ministres, /. . . Adieu: tu peux sortir*   Oh Nero, follow you such councillors. / You will gain fame by your glorious deeds. / Follow them. You've not set out only to withdraw. / You have begun by shedding your brother's blood; / And I foresee your blows won't spare your mother. / I know that deep within your heart you hate me; / You wish for freedom from my favors' yoke, / Yet I see my death shall not avail you, / Think not that, dead, I shall leave you in peace. / Rome, these heavens, the life you got from me, / At every time and place you shall remember. / Your conscience will pursue you like the Furies, / And, by further crimes, you'll seek to assuage them. / Your fury, in its course, shall increase of itself / And all your days will be marked by a bloody deed. / Yet I hope, at last, heaven, tired of your crimes / Shall add your death to the list of your many victims. / Having covered yourself in their blood and mine, / You'll see yourself enforced to shed your own; / And your name will go down to future peoples / As an insult to even the cruelest of tyrants. / See then what my heart does tell me of your fate. / Now fare you well and let you now depart.

263   *Philippe Pot*   In 1403, Régnier Pot, chamberlain to the Duke of Burgundy, Philip the Bold, bought the castle, then called La Roche Nolay. The Château de La Rochepot owes both its name and its entire architecture to two lords: Régnier Pot and his grandson Philippe Pot, two powerful vassals of the Dukes of Burgundy and Knights of the Golden Fleece.

Born within the castle's walls Philippe Pot was said to be "the most accomplished knight of his time." A private adviser to the Dukes of Burgundy, Philip the Good and Charles the Fearless, he became their head chamberlain and ambassador to London. When Burgundy was finally annexed to the French crown in 1477, Philippe Pot rallied to the French kings Louis XI and Charles VII. He became the Grand Seneshal of Burgundy and was entrusted with the role of representing the king in his own province. Involved in all major political matters of his time, he distinguished himself as a skilled diplomat, a fine negotiator, and a brilliant speaker.

264   *Le Moiturier*   Philippe the Good entrusted the task of the completion of the tomb of Philippe the Bold (Philippe de Commynes), the son of a knight of the Order of the Golden Fleece and the godson of Philip the Good, duke of Burgundy, to Antoine Moiturier, the nephew of Jacques Morel, the author of the tomb of Charles of Bourbon and Agnès of Burgundy with Souvigny. In 1470, the tomb took seat in the chorus of the fathers of the church of Chartreuse de Champmol, in front of that of Philippe the Bold.

264   *Philippe le Bon*   Philippe III the Good (1396–1467), duke of Burgundy; creator of one of the most powerful states of Europe of the fifteenth century. Philippe extended the Burgundian authority to the Netherlands, acquiring the duchy of the Brabant-Limbourg in 1430; Hainaut, including the counties of Plank, Holland, and Zealand, in 1433; and Luxembourg in 1443.

In 1460, it reigned on what is nowadays Belgium and Luxembourg, most of the Netherlands, and of the significant portions of the north and the east of France.

The court of Burgundy was one of the most brilliant of its time. As a patron, it supported the work of painters such as Jan Van Eyck and musicians like Johannes Ockeghem; attached to the *chevaleresques* traditions, it created in 1429 the Order of the Golden Fleece, most prestigious of the brotherhoods of knights in Europe.

264   *Rogier van der Weyden*   Influential Flemish painter (1399?–1464) who was Brussels's official painter; also known as Roger de la Pasture.

266   *Canova . . . Fernkorn . . . Jean Fouquet . . . Peter Vischer*   Antonio
Canova (1757–1822), Italian sculptor, one of the greatest exponents
of Neoclassicism. Anton Dominik Fernkorn (1813–78), Austrian
sculptor whose most famous works are his knight statues of the
duke Carl and the prince Eugen at the Helden Platz in Vienna. Jean
Fouquet (c. 1420–c. 1481), French painter and illuminator who
worked in Rome, where he made a portrait of Pope Eugenius IV.
Peter Vischer the Elder (c. 1460–1529), member of a family of
Nürnberg sculptors. The King Arthur sculpture is part of the tomb
of Emperor Maximilian.

275   *Makart roses*   Hans Makart (1840–84), fashionable Austrian
painter of historic scenes executed in a rich style; a devotee of
pageantry and exuberance. "Still Life with Roses" (1870), oil on
canvas. Salzburg, Austria, Residenzgalerie.

310   *Vivos voco*   *Vivos voco mortuos plango, fulgara frango* ("I summon
the living, the dead I mourn, I break into thunder"). The usual
inscription on church bells. A motto of the famous poem "Das Lied
von der Glocke" by Schiller ("The Song of the Bell").

311   *Les survivances blathuaniennes*   *The Blatvian Inheritances.*

Miroslav Krleža (1893–1981) is one of the most important Central European authors of the twentieth century. His many works include *The Return of Philip Latinowicz,* published by Northwestern University Press, and *On the Edge of Reason.*